Elizabeth Hay

HIS WHOLE LIFE

MACLEHOSE PRESS

QUERCUS · LONDON

First published in Canada by McClelland & Stewart in 2015
First published in Great Britain in 2016 by MacLehose Press
This paperback edition published in 2017 by

MacLehose Press
An imprint of Quercus Editions Limited
Carmelite House
50 Victoria Embankment
London EC4Y 0DZ

An Hachette UK company

A CIP catalogue record for this book is available
from the British Library.

ISBN (MMP) 978 0 85705 544 6
ISBN (Ebook) 978 0 85705 543 9

10 9 8 7 6 5 4 3 2 1

Designed and typeset in Cycles by Libanus Press, Marlborough
Printed and bound in Great Britain by Clays Ltd, St Ives plc

For my son and daughter, reluctant Canadians,
with love and gratitude

. . . It was cold
Was the point of the dream
And the snow was falling

Which must be an old dream of families
Dispersing into adulthood

George Oppen

AUTHOR'S NOTE

This novel has close to its heart the 1995 referendum on Quebec independence that came within a hair of succeeding. It wasn't the first of its kind in Canada. In 1980 René Lévesque and his sovereigntist provincial government asked Quebecers if they wanted to leave the Canadian federation. The campaign was dramatic and corrosive, and to Lévesque and his followers heartbreaking, for they lost by a wide margin to the federalist forces whose main champion was the Canadian Prime Minister, and another Quebecer, Pierre Trudeau.

What followed was a long series of political and constitutional manoeuvrings that in the end only increased the level of alienation in Quebec. And so in 1995, finding themselves once again in power in Quebec City, the sovereigntists launched a second referendum. This time the two sides battled to a photo finish.

The Quebec question – all the arguments for leaving, all the arguments for staying – has permeated Canadian life for decades. How these arguments work on the level of the imagination, how they shape our thoughts about ourselves, was much on my mind as I watched my characters contemplate separations of all kinds.

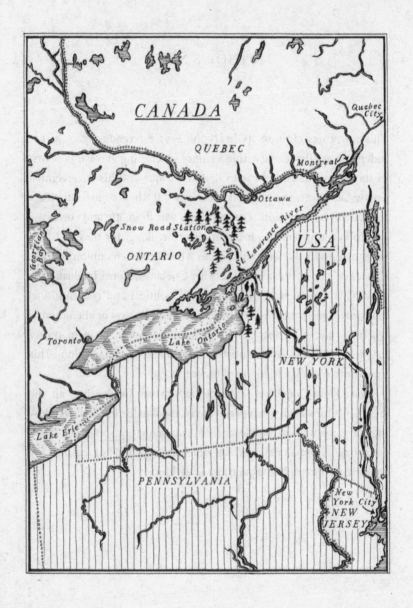

THE FIRST SUMMER
AND WINTER

1

FROM THE BACK SEAT OF THE OLD CHEVETTE, HEADING north, the boy asked his question into the restless air. He had on a T-shirt big enough for a big man and he was being cooked by the late-August sun streaming in on his side.

He asked, "What's the worst thing you've ever done?"

There was a moment's pause, during which his father kept silent behind the wheel and his mother turned to face him in the back. "Well," she said, "there was that murder I committed last year."

He smiled for a fraction of a second, then waited.

How small and by himself he looked to her, wedged there between the hot window and a pile of pillows. He needed a haircut, that crazy thatch of coppery hair. And a towel draped across the window to block out the sun. And a mother whose mind was not so far away. A different mother, she thought, shifting her gaze to whatever answer she might find beyond the windows.

They were moving through beautiful country. The landscape opened up and closed in, opened up into valleys then closed in with mountains, but she was somewhere else now, on the back roads of the heart. Into view (dimming the green hills and valleys and turning them grey) came that article she had edited to make someone rich and successful look vain, poor slob; occasions when she had shaken her children and squeezed their young arms as hard as she could; abusive, scalding things she had said to her husbands, including the one beside her; and friends she had hurt. And then there was the secret she had kept. But whether that was a good thing or a bad thing, a best thing or a worst, she had never been able to fathom.

"I'll have to think about it, Jim," she said, turning to look at him again. She was a small woman, sinewy, strong, at times indolent, who tanned easily except for the shiny scar in the middle of her forehead. Anyone could have told her something else she didn't know: her steady eyes were exactly like his.

Leaving the highway, they took a less travelled road into farmland and woods. The trusty white Chevette had a bullet hole in the back passenger door, easily one of the best things in Jim's life. It came from having parked the car on Amsterdam Avenue a few months ago only to discover in the morning bits of metal and flakes of white paint on the floor inside: a source of puzzlement until his parents thought to examine the door and there, not far below the window, was the deadly puncture. The bullet itself they found in a very strange place. Occupying the back seat at the time were twenty-three *Encyclopaedia Britannica*s sitting in boxes, a complete set from his grandmother's. The bullet had drilled a hole through eight volumes and partway through the ninth, stopping on *Fencing*, "'the art of defence or offence with a sword'," his mother had read out in an awestruck voice, "'when life or death may be decided by'" – and here parts of words were torn and so she had to guess – "'may be decided by'," she said, "'the movements of a blade'."

She had saved the bullet in a wooden cigar box of old coins, baby teeth, paper clips. It looked like the dented tip of a tiny circumcised penis, the miniature lead penis of someone who lived under a toadstool.

His father broke the silence. He had no trouble choosing the worst thing he had ever done. It happened when he went to camp one summer. "I don't know what came over me," he said, his eyes on the road and not a trace of doubt in his voice. "Maybe I'd been picked on so long by my brother that when I saw a chance I couldn't resist."

Jim knew which brother he was talking about: the pushy uncle who had hated everybody's jokes except his own. Kevin, not Martin. He waited for his father to go on. From here, directly behind him, he could see the plastic-tipped arms of his father's glasses curving behind his ears and the pink plug of his hearing aid poking out a little.

"I was eight," his father said. "I couldn't stop tormenting a certain kid. All week long I was mean to this kid, who just kept asking me to leave him alone. Then, on the last day, I punched him in the mouth and his lip bled."

"I hope he punched you back," his mother said. She directed her voice at his father's ear and spoke clearly so as not to have to repeat herself. "Or did you get away with it?" Everything she said, even the funny things, sounded as if she meant them.

"I got away with it." Shaking his head in disbelief. He was back in that mosquitoey cabin, back with his famous temper, which had vanished somewhere along the way, along with much else.

They were passing fields now and a few grazing cows. Jim asked his mother, "So have you thought about it?"

She turned to look at him again. He was her interesting, persistent ten-year-old son, a book-loving boy without many friends and she wondered why. "It seems to me the worst things are my thoughts, not things I've done."

Then she said, "What's the worst thing *you've* done?"

"I don't know." And he looked down at his hands.

They have been making this trip every year since he was born. They go north in late August and stay for a week with the Canadian side of his family, at his mother's brother's place on the lake of many bays. Last year the dark woods were suddenly brighter because the hemlock loopers had arrived in force. By late August the trees were covered with tea-stain moths, little ones, dainty, hatched from thousands of caterpillars guilty of feeding on the needles and causing them to dry out, turn the colour of rust, and shed.

This time Jim was picturing a bandaged forest. His uncle had told them about painting strips of butcher paper with something called Tanglefoot paste and wrapping them around the trunks, hoping to keep the caterpillars, which hatched in the ground, from climbing up into the foliage. Tomorrow they would see exactly how many caterpillars the sticky rings of paper had trapped.

A bullet hole in the side and on they went, travelling through New York State. "Are you alright?" Jim said to his yawning father. "You're not sleepy?" His mother had switched places with him, taking a turn in the hot sun, and he was beside his father now. "I'd slow down on those curves if I was you. You should slow down on those curves."

He was a boy who kept a weather-eye open for disaster.

Soon they found themselves behind a red pickup truck that his father kept trying to pass and it reminded her of her childhood, his mother said from the back, when you pulled out to overtake a car only to duck back into your lane to avoid the vehicle looming up, and when you were forever rolling your windows shut against the clouds of rolling dust. Her voice had that reminiscing quality Jim liked so much. He had waited forever to turn ten years old. Now he could say that ten years ago he had done such and such, and gone here or there, the way his parents were always saying that ten years ago or twenty they had done this or that.

While he was thinking these thoughts, the pickup ahead of them drifted left, like a red leaf, into the next lane and met a yellow car head on with a sickening crunch of metal. Jim saw it all. The car spun around and rolled over twice, the pickup sailed into the ditch and flipped. They slowed down in the Chevette. Nothing but hot wind came through his window.

His father pulled the car over to the side of the road and swivelled his head around. "Did you see that? Did you see it? Now what are we going to do?"

They were all looking back, gaping, horrified.

14

His mother got out of the car and so did Jim, coming around to stand beside her on the gravel shoulder. She made a fist of her hand and pressed it against the scar on her forehead, then started to grind the side of her fist around and around in the same spot as she stood there, looking back. Jim knew she wasn't aware of it. He leaned against her and she put her arm around him. Inside the car his father was talking to himself in that distressed, scattered, nervous way he had. "Should we drive to the next town and call the police? We should get hold of the police. What's the next town anyway? How far is it?" He had pulled maps from the pocket-sleeve on his door and was flipping through them, dropping and spilling them. "The old guy had white hair. In the truck. Did you see?"

It was like a ghost, that accident. As fleeting as a deer appearing out of nowhere. Around them the fields were dazed.

Other cars were pulling over. Then a truck. Two men got out of their cars and walked across the road to where all was still. Before long they heard a police siren in the distance and knew the truck driver had radioed for help.

Those men knew what to do, thought Jim, they weren't fiddling with maps. They were walking around the vehicles, peering inside, speaking to each other. Meanwhile, his mother stroked his head, pushing her fingers through his thick, resistant hair the way he liked. He felt a tug in his chest, an urge to cross the road, but leaned his head into her hand instead.

"The gods sweep down and change things, Jim."

He turned and looked into her face, into the thoughtful eyes that did not need glasses, and felt instantly one hundred per cent better. They were a very small family on the side of the road staring at disaster in a helpless way. But other things were going on, he knew, and she knew, invisible things that had been going on for a long, long time.

They got back into the smelly old Chevette and pulled out onto the road and drove on. His father was saying the poor guy behind the wheel had probably dozed off, like his father. This was the old story of the car crash that had taken his father's life and smashed his mother's legs, and injured his young nephew Paul so badly, when his head hit the dashboard and split the windshield, that he died in the hospital two nights later.

From the back seat his mother said, "Accidents of death and birth. They change everything."

Jim only half listened. Mostly he was seeing the red truck drift across the road and the yellow car spinning like another leaf. And for a moment he felt that back-to-school, September panic in the pit of his stomach. Yet here they were, without a scratch. Unreal, he thought. Like a dream.

And suddenly he was dying of hunger. All the sandwiches were gone and no, she was sorry, there wasn't any chocolate, there weren't even cookies. "You didn't bring anything sweet? Nothing sweet? I can't believe it." He stared out the front passenger window in a mounting rage. "I can't believe you didn't bring anything sweet. No dessert. That sucks." And under his breath, "Idiots, jerks, stupid, stupid, stupid." He kept it up until his mother leaned forward and said, "I'm getting angry."

"Well, too bad. I'm already angry. I beat you to it."

She laughed and soon she leaned forward again. "George, pull into that place."

His father turned off the road and parked in front of a diner that looked like a silver mobile home with a big blue-and-white awning. Inside, Jim slid into a booth and happily studied the menu until his mother showed him the children's section, which offered either a hamburger or spaghetti, and suggested the hamburger might be good.

"I'm sick of hamburgers."

"Then spaghetti."

"I don't want spaghetti. I don't like spaghetti. I want chicken."

"So," she said, "we're here because you're hungry, you're in agony you're so hungry. But you won't order from the children's menu, you have to have more expensive food. Why is every meal so unpleasant? Why is it so hard? Why don't you just take a gun and shoot me?"

That's the sort of mother she was. "Why don't you take a knife and cut out my liver," she said. "And mince it up and serve it raw to the gulls. To *that* gull." She pointed out the window. "Hughie over there."

They came to these wrathful impasses and then they were laughing. They didn't have enough money, she said. And then she relented. They ordered one meal of chicken to share and that was actually cheaper than the other way.

She unfolded her smile at the waitress. "I would *love* a glass of water. And so would the young gentleman."

That evening they camped outside Boonville, upstate. They built a fire in the firepit and sat around it and grew calm. Jim saw the stiffness go out of his father's neck and the irritability leave his mother's face. She, far more than his father, loved the simplicity and rough luxury of camping. To have everything you need at hand, to be always outside in the soft air. Broken now by the sound of mowing, the smell of hay.

"Mosquitoes!" he suddenly railed.

"They're not bothering me," his mother said.

"That's because your blood is bitter and cold, and mine is hot and joyous."

How she loved this surprising and amusing boy, whose long bare arms, wrapped around his knees, were offering themselves up to the mosquitoes. Would he wear a sweatshirt if she got him one? Probably. She went to the car and got a sweatshirt and he put it on. What a moody stripling he was. Christopher Robin as Job, she thought, combining in one temperament her own father's mournfulness and flash-anger with her mother's loving spirit and attachment to family – to her and his father and his half-brother, Blake – her son from before and a source of continuing heartbreak. Into her mind came the memory that was never far away of Blake climbing onto that Greyhound bus with his suitcase full of religious books, heavy ones, as he set off for the evangelical school in Philadelphia, while she stood behind the filthy plate-glass window in the bus terminal, beset by so much emotion that she didn't know whether to laugh or cry.

It was nearly dark when they walked down the dirt road to the small public toilets. Moths were batting against the screen door and against the light bulbs inside and out. Jim and his father brushed their teeth on the men's side; she brushed hers on the women's. Through the thin wall Jim heard the faucet, her brushing, her spitting, the faucet. Then together they walked back to their grassy campsite. In the tent she stretched out beside him on top of her sleeping bag while his father tended the fire outside, and in the light of her flashlight she found the illustrated page where they had left off and picked up the story: after twenty years Odysseus returning home, where nobody knows him except his ancient dog. She stopped reading and said, "That's one of the worst things I've ever done."

"What?"

"I gave my dog away."

"Stan?"

"Yes."

"What happened to him?" He wanted to hear it again, this story of misfortune.

"He was hit by a car." And because she knew he liked her to repeat stories from her past, she carried on and told him the rest of it. How when her first marriage ended they gave Stan away to friends who wanted him – they had asked if they might have him – and he was having a good life with these kind people out west, who already had a dog named Buddy, and so Stan had company. Then several years later, as he was running beside the road, he was hit by a car and killed. Afterwards Buddy missed him a lot.

"Why did you give him away?"

"I wanted to travel, Jim. I went away for a long time."

Her son was asleep beside her now. George had stretched out on her other side and was grumbling about how bumpy the ground was. "Nancy, I'm on a rock heap."

She closed her eyes. This marriage was nothing to write home about either, that was a fact, and she couldn't help blaming George for not generating the love she wanted to feel. She knew the blaming was unjust. Indeed, this might be the worst thing. The words had lodged in her head and she wanted an answer as badly as Jim. In the dark warmth of the tent, the day swam up, the endless road and fields and hills. She wondered if Kevin used to pick on Martin too. Her husband's brothers were of enduring interest to her, especially Martin, the tall, slender, younger brother with the swan neck who years ago had moved to South America and never come back. She imagined meeting him, at George's funeral, say. "Here I am. I've been waiting all this time."

"George," she said aloud, "did Kevin pick on Martin too?"

"Both of us picked on Martin. It's what happens when you're the youngest."

"And the nicest?"

"That's your fantasy," George said.

So she was that transparent. Behind her lids everything flickered with light and movement. Pine boughs, expanses of water, the chrome of passing cars, the accident, the contours of her son's face – they all unspooled in their silent-movie way. Long car rides draw things out of us that hang in the mind for hours, like a ball slowly turning, a snowball gathering to itself new snow, old snow, grass, gravel, dirt as it builds its rolling life on slopes and sidewalks and backyards until it comes to rest in a cool woods, hidden away from sunlight and summer and self, biding its time.

Tomorrow she would be back in Canada and her eagerness was offset by regret at how long she had lived away.

She had become an expatriate without meaning to. Canada beckoned to her, such a stable and reasonable country. Yet always on the verge of coming apart, it had to be said, because Quebec was so unhappy.

As unhappy as I am in *my* marriage, she thought, startled by the turn her mind had taken. That she was like Quebec in her unhappiness.

The next morning was hot and still. The smell of cut grass and sweet white clover, the sun beating down on the lemon-yellow tent. They slept late, locked in uneven dreams on uneven ground, their heads close together, their faces relaxed. When Jim woke up he didn't hear pigeon wings in the airshaft sounding like the beating of chopsticks, or the clicking of false teeth, or a commotion of ballpoint pens. He heard his parents building a fire and soon afterwards came the swoosh of coffee inside their little espresso-maker and their murmurs of joy.

"Jim," his mother said through the tent door, "are you hungry?"

That morning they crossed the wide river into Canada and all of his worries fell away.

2

THERE WAS EVEN MORE LIGHT. THE RINGS OF STICKY PAPER
had not trapped much at all. A motorboat went by, leaving waves
that lapped the shore, while the reflections of the waves lapped the
underboughs of the trees. Some of the hemlocks were like smoke,
most of their needles down. You looked into the distance more easily
now. You looked from the picnic table, placed on a level outside the
log house, down the slope through the open shaded air and beneath
the cedars to the water, the sun on the water, the watery sun flicking,
flicking, flicking the undersides of the trees, and out to the first island
and the island beyond. Or you looked to the left through the smoki-
ness of nearly dead hemlocks, very soft now, like an old woman's
wispy hair, into more trees and more, so that all you could see were
a few peepholes of sky. The air was sweet, the woods were quiet.

Jim felt that he had been here all his life. A path took him from
the front lane to the log house and from the house down to the shore
and along the shore. He loved paths, any sign of them through the
grass or through the woods.

His tall uncle put a hand on his shoulder. "Look around you," he
said, his voice full of feeling for the place. "Do you think about
the lake when you're in New York?"

His uncle had a calm face and his mother's clear eyes.

"I do," Jim said. He thought about it a lot.

He asked his uncle why he liked it so much, eager for a full
accounting of any attachment. He wanted to make certain of it and
to feel such certainty.

"The quiet, first of all," came the satisfying reply. "The quiet, the size of the trees, the animals, the canoes."

Close to the water were a few mighty trees, one of them more than two hundred years old.

"The trees are dying."

"They're in distress. Not all of them are going to die. Infestations like this aren't new, Jim. Forests recover."

If you looked straight up you could see how sparse the needles were. His aunt loved the woods, yet how many times had he heard her say she wished they would cut down a few trees, just a few, to let in some light. She was getting her wish now, though in the worst way. The best trees, the tallest and oldest ones, were dying on their feet.

It was so hot they took the old dog for a swim in the early evening. His uncle held the canoe steady against the little platform made of four planed logs staked against the grassy shore as his aunt helped Duke lift his back legs up over the side of the canoe. He had rheumatism, she said, among other things. Everybody was patient, even though the horseflies were bad and they were entering the second week of a heatwave.

The dog's breathing was laboured and his bones were weary. But he would like the swim. He would like getting cool.

In the canoe his aunt sat in the bow with her fishing rod at her feet. Duke stood in the middle just ahead of the middle thwart. Jim knelt on the floor close to his uncle in the stern. Once they were underway, sliding across the water under the big sky, Jim began talking about light years. He knew the sun was 93 million miles away, he knew it took the light from the sun eight minutes to reach the earth. Other stars were light years away, some of them thousands of light years away, or millions. The moon was rising orange above the dying hemlocks and he felt the universe enter his skull as an infinite number of things never arriving, but being there, all around him. "Say a star blows up. We won't know for a million years."

"That's right," his uncle said.

"The star isn't there anymore, but the starlight keeps coming."

"Yes," his aunt said, turning her head to join in. "I can't quite figure it. Dog years, on the other hand," she said.

"Do you know what a dog year is, Jim?" his uncle said.

"Is it longer or shorter than a year for us?"

"A dog year is seven human years."

"How old is Duke?"

"Thirteen. Thirteen times seven."

"Ninety-one," said his aunt.

"You should have let him figure it for himself." His uncle sounded put out but not angry. He was a mild-tempered man.

"Does he look ninety-one to you?" his aunt asked him.

"No!" Jim's voice was eager, waving a flag for the old dog. "He looks young and spry." A moment passed. "What happened to his breathing? He breathes in rasps."

"I like the words you use," his aunt said, her head half turned towards him. She was paddling slowly. "Those are good words. Something's the matter with his lungs."

"Do you think *you'll* live to be ninety-one?" he asked her.

"That depends how well you look after me."

His grandmother was the oldest person he knew, his father's mother in New York, Grandma Bobak, so old she had put her name down for a nursing home in Nyack a few months ago. She was eighty-five. They had taken her for a swim earlier in the summer, driving to the shore at Far Rockaway. His grandmother got out of the car, cane first, and walked with her right hand on the cane and her left on his father's arm. His mother followed along with the folding lawn chair. On the beach his grandmother hung her cane over the back of the chair and proceeded into the water, his father holding her on one side and his mother on the other. She didn't care how cold the water was. It was way colder than the lake. That didn't stop her. They held onto her until she was up to her waist, then she let go of them and floated. She was the best floater. She lay on her back with her legs straight out as if the salt water underneath her were a floor. Like a dumpling in chicken stew, his mother said. Grandma Bobak was very plump. He loved her soft flesh, loved the way it hung full and loose on her arms and under her chin, the way it had so much give. She let him lean into her at the kitchen table and touch and stroke her pillowy parts. His mother's flesh was only soft in a few places, her upper arms if she relaxed them, and then he liked to knead and flap the flesh with his fingers and tell her he liked her fluff. Once, years ago, when his father was helping him spread sunscreen over his cheeks and forehead, he said, "Jim, your skin is soft, like your mother's," and though it drew the three of them together, it also made him uncomfortable. He remembered not really wanting to know what his father knew about his mother.

The dog shifted and the canoe lurched. Jim, who was on his knees, grabbed the gunwales. "Better sit right on the bottom," his uncle said. They had almost turned over and Jim couldn't help his wild laughter.

They called the sturdy old fibreglass canoe "the barge" because it weighed a ton. Where they were heading to was the uninhabited island that had a small sandy-gravel beach. Duke would be able to walk into the water and cool down. Yesterday his uncle had dropped him off the end of the dock, intending for him to swim to shore and get cool that way. But the dog panicked. That was an awful sight. His uncle laughing he was so horrified, his aunt mad at his uncle for laughing, and the dog thrashing about as if he had forgotten how to swim, rearing up like the pair of horses pawing the air when Zeus sent a lightning bolt down among the Greek troops. After half a minute or so, Duke recovered his wits and swam to shore.

The lake bottom was leafy, oozy muck. That's why they had the dock to dive from and the raft. Nobody, not even a dog, wanted to wade into that muck. The shore itself, in choice places, was grassy and mossy and nearly comfortable. His mother had a small folding

24

chair low to the ground that she liked to sit on and beside it she stacked her books and old *New Yorkers*, which she read one after the other. He was getting ready to be a *New Yorker* fan too, trying his best to appreciate the cartoons. You had to be proud of coming from a place with a great magazine named after itself. He certainly was.

Yesterday, looking up from her reading, his mother had said to him, "That's another one of the worst things I've done."

"What?"

"I made my mother cry."

And she had shaken her head and fallen silent, lost in her memory of that moment seven or eight years ago when she and her mother were sitting side by side right here and her mother was weeping like a girl, sobbing, "I want to go home. I thought we were all getting along so well. I just want to get back to my own life." And she had taken her mother in her arms and held her as she wept. And over what? Over some disagreement in the kitchen. Some snapped retort of hers – she couldn't even remember – in response to something disapproving her mother had said. What was it? That she threw out the good chicken juices after roasting a chicken. I DO NOT. Then her mother tried to shoulder her aside to do the dishes and leave her free from chores, and she had shouldered her back. "I'll do them. Leave me be." Later, she found her down by the water, forlorn, hugging her knees on the dock, and she sat down to talk to her, to make up, and her mother had wept.

Fragility itself, the construction of camaraderie between a parent and child after the child leaves home. Blown down by the least rebuff.

Afterwards, after her parents had driven away, heading back to their home in the southwestern corner of the province, she had placed a hand on the bed where her mother had slept, still so disturbed by their words that it was like touching a hot iron, the rumpled foam mattress thinned flat by shoulders, buttocks. A fight that blossomed out of nowhere, if a shared past is nowhere, and Nan still felt transformed by it all these years later. So that when she splashed her hands in the lake, leaning over the dock, her hands brown and weathered and worn-looking like her mother's, it gave her a feeling of pain. To be so reminded of her.

She noticed tiny moths moving across the ground like roaches.

"I made my mother cry," she said again. "It happened here. The same place the mink came at us like an arrow. Do you remember? You burst into tears and climbed into my lap."

He remembered the mink. It came at them like a rat. His mother had screamed, the mink had reversed course in a flash, disappearing under tree roots, glossy black. They saw it later in the water.

She said, "And over there I uprooted maple seedlings, and out on the road I ran like a mad woman away from the black flies. Right here your uncle taught me the names of ferns. Up there, at the picnic table, I really lost my temper with Blake. You remember."

He did. They had been roasting marshmallows and Blake wouldn't let him have one until he first thanked the Lord. His brother was weird that way.

Nan let him keep his worst thing to himself, respecting his privacy. At the same time she was fishing, using her worst things as bait to catch his worst thing.

"Things don't seem so terrible once you talk about them," she said.

"I don't want to talk about them."

"I know. But some day you might give it a whirl. Telling someone about the terrible thing really does make it less terrible."

The question hovered. The worst thing, the worst thing. As if she and Jim would know what they needed to know if they knew the worst thing.

At the island, level with the water, was the little landing dock overgrown and grown through with weeds. You had to step carefully to avoid nails and holes. Jim got out first, then his aunt, then Duke, helped out by his aunt. Duke lost his balance, regained it. "Good fellow," his aunt said.

Duke stepped off the dock into the water. He walked out a few feet. The sandy-gravel part was not much wider than a bathtub. The old dog stood in the water. He was still handsome, although one ear flopped permanently and some spots on his legs were bare and some awful red lumps grew here and there. His head wasn't grey, he was golden-brown everywhere, except for his white belly. He still hated to be rubbed behind the ears. Everybody, except his uncle, avoided his ears. The dog put up with anything from his uncle.

Now Duke stood in the water and sounded like a car without a muffler.

"Hand me that stick," his uncle said.

There was a fairly long stick lying on pine needles on the bank. Jim gave it to his uncle, who threw it out a ways, not far, and told Duke to fetch it. Duke turned his head and slowly he swam out to get the stick, wetting his belly and sides. He turned and swam back in, dropping the stick in the shallow water. His uncle did not throw it again.

"You should climb up there," his uncle said, indicating the path up the side of the hill. Duke was shaking himself, spattering water far and wide. "Go have a look and see what they've done."

Jim scrambled up over cedar roots and pine needles to the top. Even though it was getting dark he could see that somebody had made an outdoor camp of benches in a circle around a campfire and waist-high counters out of wood to put things on. There was a long wooden bow hanging from a nail in the tree, but no arrows. A clothesline. Even a light switch and Christmas lights. But the switch didn't work.

"They must bring over a car battery," his uncle said behind him.

His aunt said, "It reminds me of Huck Finn. An outdoor hideaway. Remember Huck and Tom Sawyer on the island?"

But this wasn't like a book. This was different. Jim walked around the site, trying out the benches, leaning on the counters, pushing his toe in among the pine cones, the ashes and half-burnt sticks of the campfire. It was pretty amazing that nobody lived here or on any of the islands in the lake when you considered that the island of Manhattan had space for one and a half million people. And it came back and filled his head, the torn blue-and-yellow shirt, himself on the ground being kicked and jeered at; the desire to run away.

Duke did not come up the bank, so they went back down. He was standing in the water waiting for them.

Jim sprinkled water on the old dog's back.

He could not forgive himself for what he had done, that was his trouble. And he would not say what it was, so that no-one else could forgive him either.

His uncle picked up a smooth stone at the edge of the water. "Twenty thousand years ago this stone was under a mile or two of ice," he said, passing it to Jim, who examined it. Jim knew about the ice ages, when snow and ice never melted and there was no summer at all. He let the stone warm up in his hand before slipping it into his pocket.

In the canoe he sat on the bottom again. His aunt was back in the bow, his uncle in the stern. Duke stood where he always stood, just ahead of the middle thwart. He must like feeling cooler, Jim thought, but he breathes just the same.

They moved across the water. Some stars were out now. Clouds were covering the moon. His aunt tucked her paddle beside her and picked up her fishing rod. She made a nice long cast and waited, then slowly reeled in, then cast again.

"The flies are biting, but the fish aren't," she said, whacking at a deer fly. "They're biting because it's going to rain."

"They always bite," his uncle said.

"But it's worse now because it's going to rain. Milfoil," she said and reeled in her line in time.

Jim looked over the side of the canoe. He could just make out the milfoil waving below the surface of the water like an evil forest. Small bits, like green feathers, floated by. Motorboats broke it up, spread it around, took it from lake to lake on their propellers. It was wrecking the lakes, clogging the water, shading out all the water plants that fed and protected the birds and fish, ruining the swimming. The water had to be less than eight feet deep for it to grow, as he knew from his uncle, who had laid a ladder flat on the floor of the lake next to their shore and then stood on it, trying to pull the weeds up by their roots without himself sinking into the mud. But it was too much, he had said, shaking his head. The roots were the size of basketballs.

It pained his uncle and therefore it doubly pained Jim to see a noxious weed spreading underwater unchecked while on land the precious old shade was going bald.

He tilted his head back. "I see that starlight coming," he said.

"Yes," his uncle said, "it's coming towards us like a headlight without a car."

And with those words the sky turned into a night highway and stars were headlights bearing down upon them. They were old, old light, his uncle said. They were the light that left those faraway stars untold years ago. "We're seeing the past. We're seeing things as they were, not as they are, as they were when man was climbing down from the trees."

Light years, thought Jim. Ice ages. Dog years. So many different speeds of time. Summertime, he thought. Recess time.

Back at their put-in, he got out of the canoe first, then his aunt, then Duke, then his uncle. His uncle tied the canoe's painter to a small cedar while Jim went up the short, steep rise to the lit-up house.

"Why don't you let me get a dog?"

He faced his mother. She was reading on the screened-in verandah at the side of the house. She put down her book and looked at him.

"I want a dog," he said.

29

"I know you do."

"So why won't you let me have one? I'll feed him. I'll take him for walks. I'll do everything. You won't have to do anything."

"Will you clean up his poop?"

"I'll clean it up. You won't have to do a thing. Just because you gave your dog away, you won't let me have one. That's not fair."

He was very serious.

She said, "Dogs always want to come along. Do you know what it's like to leave a dog behind?"

He didn't say anything.

"Dogs break your heart," she said. "Or you break theirs. They get hit by a car, or they get left behind." She paused. "New York is no place for a dog."

"Duke didn't get hit by a car. Duke doesn't get left behind. Lots of people have dogs in New York."

"Life is easier without a dog. Life is much easier without a dog."

"A boy should have a dog." He stood there, stubborn, angry.

"Who have you been talking to?" But her voice was soft and bemused because she knew he was right.

Then his aunt came into the verandah and he appealed to her. "Don't you think she's mean? She won't let me have a dog. I'll do everything, I'll feed him, I'll walk him, I'll clean up after him, but she won't let me have a dog."

His aunt put the fishing rod in the corner, then turned around and without looking at either of them said, "Life with a dog is complicated." She shrugged her shoulders. She went into the kitchen.

A boy should have a dog, he said to himself.

That night he was lying in the upper bunk in the room off the kitchen when he heard his aunt say to his mother, "I think this will be his last summer." The old dog had been breathing heavily, then he was quieter and in the quiet his aunt spoke. Jim looked out the window at the stars. It was the first summer he could see them from here, that's how thin the trees were from the hemlock looper. It was

30

beautiful. Millions of stars in the dark sky. He didn't know anywhere else where the darkness was so complete. How many stars did he ever see from the playground at Amsterdam and 104th? Practically none.

His aunt had been wrong about the rain. The sky was clear again.

If he had a dog he would be able to stay on the island in that camp with the Christmas lights. He would build a fire. He knew how. His dog would keep him company.

He heard his aunt talking again, but too low to make out the words. Then he heard her weeping. She was given to weeping, his mother had said to him once, because her life was full of past hurts that she could not stop thinking about.

He heard his mother say, "I don't think I can last another winter either."

He lay perfectly still and she went on in her clear voice. "George is a magnet for bad luck. Accidents love him."

His father was asleep upstairs. She must think I'm asleep too, he thought.

His aunt asked a question. All he heard was his own name and his mother's sad, clear voice saying, "I don't know."

* * *

A week later they were on the dock, saying goodbye to the lake. "Today," Jim announced with a flourish, "is the champagne of August."

Nan gave him an admiring, quizzical look. "That's a wonderful phrase. How did you come up with it?"

And immediately he was less sure of himself. "They call Canada Dry the champagne of ginger ales," he said, checking to see her reaction. "I thought I could call today the champagne of days. Can I do that?"

"You can," she said.

His father came down to the water to squint and say it was time to go. George had spent most of every day in the screened-in verandah, his briefcase open beside him, his reading glasses on – unhappy in his work, yet always working. "Nancy," he repeated, "it's time." And it was easy to see how much he wanted to be on his way.

They climbed the slope to the house and all too soon, in Jim's opinion, they were gathered in the lane beside the car. He patted Duke one last time and hugged his uncle and aunt, then got into the back seat of the over-packed Chevette. His father got behind the wheel. His mother kept talking to her brother. Then finally she got in too, and they were driving down the laneway to the road, where his father beeped the horn twice in farewell and his mother waved like mad through the rolled-down windows, and so did Jim. They waved kisses towards his uncle and aunt, who waved their kisses back. Jim loved this more than anything, these open expressions of heartfelt love. Though open loathing appealed to him too, so long as it wasn't directed at him. Half an hour later, approaching the town of Lanark, his mother pointed out in passing the house where Janet Hepburn used to live. Janet, who had dropped her cold when she was eleven. Janet, the first-class jerk.

"She still lives around here," his mother said. "We passed her farm about ten minutes ago."

Ancient history, Nan thought. The feeling wasn't unlike the blankness on your tongue hours after it's been scalded by tea: a rough and almost dusty absence of feeling, and such a sense of loss and pity for those dead little taste buds.

"I imagine there were less than exciting things about me," she said, half-turned towards Jim in the back. "I'm not saying I don't blame her. I blame her with all my heart. I blame her to pieces. But I don't suppose I was the most exciting eleven-year-old to be around." She was watching the trees go by, her mind on the past. "Then Lulu Blake came along and my life stood back up again."

"Lulu." Jim repeated the name with relish. "Lulu."

"She was wild and brave. My Lulu. What a long time it's been. The last I heard she was living in Mexico."

Lulu's mother and brother lived at the far end of their lake of bays on land that stretched way back and supported a farm and a big sugar bush, but neither mother nor brother ever had news of her.

Soon the road was taking them into Lanark itself, the lovely, old, preserved part of town, all stone, that had escaped the great fire of 1959. Nestled in the curve of the road was the chip wagon, where they always stopped in an end-of-summer ritual. George, who wasn't hungry and didn't like French fries at the best of times, stretched his legs by walking to the bridge over the river, while Jim and Nan got their fries and carried them to a picnic table and sat blowing on them.

She said, "It was the first and biggest shock of my life, being dumped when I was eleven. Has anything like that happened to you?" She was still trying to discover what might be troubling him.

Jim pretended not to hear the question. He didn't want to think about friends.

"Jim?"

"No," he said and concentrated on his fries. He held one up that was black at the tip. "Is this diseased?"

His frowning seriousness amused her no end. At his age it never would have occurred to her to use so dramatic a word. "Just break it off," she told him. "The rest is fine."

Only later was she touched to realize that he was probably seeing everything in the light of the diseased and dying trees.

After they finished their fries, they drove on. Soon enough they crossed the border and then, in the way of these long, long drives, the old argument started up about Canada versus New York: her home-sickness versus George's love of his hometown. It was something they would never resolve and so she changed the subject by slipping an audio book into the car's cassette player, boosting the volume so George could hear. And then they were caught up in Kurt Vonnegut's brave jokes and brave questions about terrible things done by supposedly good people. It was an anti-war book, she said to Jim in the back, and the voice was the hero, the voice telling the story.

The atmosphere in the car grew easier. They were under the spell of the gifted actor, not at all famous, who was reading *Slaughterhouse-five* with real finesse. Jim could feel the crease in his forehead smooth out.

Lunch came when they got to Boonville. In Slim's Restaurant he studied the five big clocks on the wall giving the times in Tokyo, Los Angeles, Moscow, London and Boonville. It was twenty-one minutes to one in Boonville. At Slim's everyone knew one another by name; he and his parents were the strangers in town, who did not want ice in their water or ketchup on their eggs.

Seven hours and two brief stops later they were closing in on the city, coming down the New York Thruway, picking up the Major Deegan, then the Cross Bronx Expressway (everybody going like crazy), then the Henry Hudson Parkway (everybody still whipping along), until they reached the 95th Street exit, where things calmed down. His mother unclenched her hands. His father rolled his window all the way down.

They turned up West End Avenue, stately and beautiful, and passed his grandmother's building. Then turned right on 104th and made their way to Amsterdam, busy and poor-looking, where they double-parked and unloaded the car. His mother stood guard, as always, while he and his father, in three trips, lugged everything up to their apartment on the second floor. Then, while his father took the car to the parking garage, he and his mother went inside and opened wide all the windows that would open and in came the noise and smell of New York: voices speaking Spanish, car alarms, slamming doors, fans and air conditioners and snatches of music, the smells of car exhaust, garbage, coffee and pizza.

The blast of energy beat back the silence of the lake. Jim leaned out the window and took it in. This is where I'm from, he said to himself. I'm a New Yorker.

In his own bed again, he fell asleep within seconds and dreamt long, detailed dreams about classrooms he could not find, and in the morning he woke up knowing it was all over, the long weeks of summer. Nothing but worry lay ahead. He had a bedroom to himself now that his brother was in Philadelphia, but he didn't want a room to himself. In two weeks he would turn eleven and he wouldn't want a birthday party either. "I'm too old for that," he would say.

And so the months passed, autumn into winter, and he would get through them by not looking at one boy and not talking to another, not looking at the boy who used to be his best friend and not talking to the boy who was so popular. And by reading all the time. He read the children's versions of the *Iliad* and the *Odyssey* twice, and *The Story of Canada* three times. His favourites were Hector, the Trojan prince, and René Lévesque, the Quebec politician who was "rarely seen without a cigarette". Noble strivers and losers, that's who he liked (also interesting bad guys, like Long John Silver).

He said to his mother, "I like Levesske's face and cigarette."

She looked up smiling. "Lévesque," she said, giving it the right pronunciation. "It's French." And she repeated the name.

It was obvious that it mattered to her that he get it right. "Do you like him?" he asked her.

She weighed her answer. "I could always see his charm, but I was on Trudeau's side in that battle." She went over to him and looked down at the open page. "How does Trudeau come across?" And he told her the book said he would invite reporters to watch him dive off a springboard into a swimming pool. In his opinion, that was nowhere near as appealing as never being seen without a cigarette.

He watched her chew on one of her fingernails. His father was a Yankees fan, but the first game they had ever gone to was a Mets game and he'd come out a diehard, a loyalist. "You didn't tell me I had to be a Yankees fan *and now it's too late!*"

She shook her head a little. "They're giving you Trudeau's physical vanity and Lévesque's romance. It's not quite fair. Trudeau was actually more appealing than any Canadian politician had ever been."

Jim then asked her what sovereignty-association meant, proud of himself for getting the pronunciation right and for being interested in these things. He knew nobody else in his class would be. And she told him it was what Lévesque wanted for Quebec. He wanted them to be a separate nation that still had certain ties to the rest of Canada. Independence, but not quite. He hedged his bets. Trudeau, on the other hand, wanted Quebec to be fully at home in Canada itself. "Don't tell me you're on Lévesque's side?" she said.

He nodded slowly. He liked his look. He liked the glamour of the cigarette. He could see himself in the same role one day, a politician devoted to a dream, written about in books.

"He's dead, you know," his mother said. "But his cause is stronger than ever." She was rubbing the scar in the middle of her forehead. "There's going to be another referendum in Quebec very soon. Another vote on independence. Likely next fall, they say."

That was seven months away. "What's going to happen?"

"Who knows?" she sighed. "All I know is that it tears me apart."

* * *

On the last Friday of April, bent under his knapsack like a weary pilgrim in a woodcut, Jim walked home from school as usual. The day was warm and cloudy, perfect for the Mets home opener.

At first he thought his mother wasn't home. The apartment was silent and dark. But then he found her in the living room, on the sofa, her face in her hands, rocking herself back and forth.

When she looked up, her eyes were red and puffy. She had been weeping. He could not remember ever seeing her cry, except over a book. She wasn't reading.

"I'm sorry, Jim."

"What's wrong?"

She extended her hand towards him. "Come sit beside me."

He went over to her and she helped him slide out of his knapsack. Then she said, "Something terrible has happened."

He had time to wonder if his grandmother was dead. But it was far worse.

Early that morning, she told him, his uncle and aunt had been on their way to an appointment with an eye doctor in Ottawa, a double appointment, when a snow squall arrived out of nowhere, and in the whiteout, Jim heard her say, their car slid into the path of an oncoming truck, killing them both.

His little splat of laughter happened before he even had a chance to think.

"What about Duke?" he said, shocked and ashamed and trying to recover.

They had left Duke at home.

"They died instantly, Jim. No pain. That's what the police told me on the telephone."

He felt more bewildered than he had ever felt in his life. His uncle and aunt were gone in the blink of an eye, and with them all that was safe and unchanging.

A big trailer truck, she said, not a pickup.

THE LAKE

3

THIS IS HOW JIM CAME TO BE LIVING IN CANADA AS CANADA
and his parents were breaking up. Nan inherited the property at
the lake and would not leave it until the old dog had died.

Two months after the crash, while George stayed on in New York,
Jim and his mother remained ensconced in the big log cottage, which
seemed a strange shell of itself now. They spent most of their time
outside or on the screened-in verandah. As with everything else in
and around the house, the verandah had been rebuilt and improved
upon by his uncle and aunt: windowsills were as wide as you wanted
them, hooks were where you needed them, every chair and table
was steady as a rock. Feeling this presence, Jim could not forget
their terrible absence. He and his mother talked about it. She saw
her brother everywhere, she said. In the porch untangling a tangle of
string with infinite patience; at the stove using tongs to place each
bacon slice perfectly flat in the fry pan; outside splitting wood, then
inside laying a fire and never needing more than one match. She had
photographs of her brother and sister-in-law just about everywhere,
even on the refrigerator.

"I sense them all around me," she said to him. "Do you?"

He was getting used to her being different, calmer, less perturbed
by things. She was more like her brother now. He knew she didn't
mean his uncle and aunt were ghosts haunting the lake. She meant
they lived on in some mysterious way. "Like the gods in Homer?" he
said, though that seemed a stretch.

"A bit like that. They're looking out for us."

He felt his throat tighten and fixed his eyes on the floor.

She didn't have clear words for it. It had nothing to do with religion as Blake practised it.

"It's a feeling I have. Maybe as time goes on I'll lose it. I hope not."

*   *   *

On a hot evening in the middle of June, one of many that long, dry summer, Jim was on the verandah brushing Duke, who was splayed out on the floor, all cooperation. He was avoiding the ugly lumps and thinking about death when a character out of *Treasure Island* came up the steps.

She had a black eye and a bloody ankle and reminded him of Blind Pew approaching the other Jim. There was a peacock feather in her leather hat, a well-worn knapsack over her shoulder. She was older than his mother and carried herself with a certain swagger, an obvious enjoyment in the impression she made.

Duke raised his head as she set down her pack to the slosh of bottles rolling about. "Old scout," she said, kneeling beside him, "you're down on your luck, aren't you?" She ran her freckled hands through his fur until Duke laid his head back on the floorboards and grinned.

"Tell your mother a peddler's at the door," she said to Jim. "Tell her a dusty old peddler's got some comic books for sale."

He could hear his mother coming from the far side of the house. He didn't move.

"Honey, don't tell her it's me. Don't ruin my surprise."

He had never seen her before. "My name's not honey," he said.

She smiled a worn-out smile. "I stand corrected, Jim. But it's no fun to be so literal."

The porch door opened and never before had he seen such a look: the sun and the moon rose as one in his mother's face.

"Lulu!" She stepped forward into Lulu's embrace and stayed there. After a while she leaned back and said, "It's been so long.

Twenty-five years? But I'd never mistake you for anybody else. Lulu, how *are* you?"

"Well, I'm sort of. I'm in the middle of." Lulu paused. "How do I *look*?" And the two of them laughed and laughed.

The verandah was wide enough for a sleep-inducing sofa and a hammock, the old family hammock from India, a great-uncle's gift, perhaps great-great, when hammocks in that faraway time were made to last. Wavy light coming off the lake through the screens turned it into a watery room that rippled with reflections.

"Let me see your ankle," his mother said.

Lulu sat on the sofa and let herself be tended to. She knew she was in bad shape, having tangled with barbed wire, trespassing, she said, but she wanted to see the river. Nobody owned the river. As for the black eye, she said, touching it gingerly, she had given it to herself, putting out the eyebrow she had set on fire trying to light her cigarette. "Strong winds play havoc with your looks," she said. "They're vicious."

It turned out she was staying in the campground on the far side of the lake, where buying ice one evening at the camp store she had overheard people discussing the fine old log cottage that Tom Waterman had taken such pains to winterize in the year before his tragic death. "Darling," she said to his mother, "I can't tell you how sorry I am." And then she turned to him, "I am so sorry about your uncle and aunt, Jim."

His mother sank down beside her on the sofa and rested her head against her shoulder. "Stay with us," she said, and she shook off her sadness. "Forget your tent. Stay here." And she got up and went into the kitchen and came back with their dented dishpan half-filled with warm water. She set it on the floor, removed Lulu's dusty leather sandal, and lowered her bloody foot into the pan.

"The gods always put on supple sandals when they travel," his mother said, glancing up at him. "In Homer."

He looked at Lulu's eyes to see if they were grey like Athena's. More green than grey; greyish-green.

He watched her rest her hand for a moment on his mother's head. It was easy to see she was one of those women like his aunt who has had a hard life. An emotional seafarer, his mother had always said of his aunt, who took things to heart and from whom tears spurted and flowed. "My sister-in-law was an open house," she had said after her death, "a summerhouse of feeling."

They were on the verandah long enough for his mother to bathe and bandage Lulu's foot before she told them she was travelling with a companion. She would introduce him if they didn't mind. Off she went to the car, on one good foot and one bandaged foot, and came back with a black-and-white border collie. "Ninety per cent," she said. The dog waited on the steps while she consulted Duke, speaking to him in a voice anyone would have welcomed, telling him he was still the boss, asking his permission to let another dog enter his domain. Until six months ago, they would learn, her dog had belonged to now-late Aunt Roberta, as had the rusty Buick she was driving. His name was Pog.

A boy who had wanted nothing so much as a dog now had two.

Pog let himself be patted. Silky coat, longer and softer than Duke's. He sat perfectly still, not as old as Duke, though grey in the face and rather stiff. Once the women went into the kitchen and the screen door closed behind them, Pog stood and followed, pushing open the door and joining them.

Then Jim witnessed an exchange that charmed him to the core. Lulu said to Pog in mild reproof, "Were you born in a barn?" And the dog turned and pushed the door closed with his nose.

Next to Lulu, his mother seemed frail, pale, small, fit, loosening, boyish, alive, half-drunk. She and Lulu were drinking Martinis and she had given him her Martini-soaked olive to chew. Gin and dry vermouth were the bottles in Lulu's pack. She travelled with her vermouth stone too, a narrow, porous stone with a hole in the middle through which a string was tied. Her technique was a simple matter of lowering the stone into the bottle of vermouth, then into the pitcher of gin, in the firm belief that however much vermouth clung to the stone was as much vermouth as a Martini should have.

Jim watched his mother and Lulu in the golden light, their faces touched and transfigured by the magic wand of the evening sun, and he couldn't wait to be old enough himself for the bottles and glasses, the ritual, the hour, the gurgling liquids, the jokes. "Drinks sure do evaporate fast in this climate," said Lulu, eyeing her empty glass, while his mother, amused, offered the opinion that one Martini was never enough, as they say, and two were too many. Lulu, reaching for the pitcher, said what she liked best in Albee's "A Delicate Balance" were the repeated moments when the characters said, "Wow, what a good Martini." Not the first sip, but after the first sip took effect.

And his mother said to him with a smile, "That's a play."

In Lulu's company she relaxed and had more thoughts and deeper questions. She was what she must have been like twenty years ago, thirty years ago, before he was ever born. "Lulu, do you ever go home in your dreams?" she asked, eager and intent upon getting an answer. "Do you wake up thinking you're in your childhood bed?"

"*All the time*," Lulu said. "Do you want me to tell you a dream?"

Maybe this was where it began in earnest, Jim's deep susceptibility to the past. This summer-filled evening when Lulu arrived out of the blue. She was like a figure from an old story with her strange, sad looks and her openhearted revelations.

"My life is something out of a Russian play," she said, mournful and proud, "and so are my dreams."

Only the night before she had dreamt she was losing her childhood home on the Klondike River. "Up north, where we lived before moving to Ontario," she said to him. In her dream water rose so high it lapped against the walls, and huge waves, full of snowballs, crashed against the door. "I was inside holding pillows against the windows to keep them from breaking. I was the only one left. I felt like the old servant at the end of 'The Cherry Orchard'."

She was a vivid dreamer and an embittered one, since the men in her life refused to take her dreams seriously. She didn't mind saying it either. Her dreams, she said, were violent, meaningful, surprising, poetic, unparalleled, while the reactions she got from lovers, brother, father were sceptical, teasing, quiet, and cruel; smiles of disbelief played around their mouths, driving her to fury. They were not a good match, she and these men in her past. "Me so dramatic," she said, "and them so stingy with applause."

Here, on the other hand, on this perfect June evening, they all knew she had an appreciative audience of two in a mother and son ready to listen for hours.

"My life is out of Chekhov," she said, and Jim could tell it was something she liked to say and said often.

"Chekhov," his mother said to him, "was a great Russian writer."

"The greatest," Lulu said.

"I'm not sure he was the greatest."

It didn't matter. Lulu was in the grip of her own story. And out it came: her father's will, her mother's will, her mistreatment at their hands. But not like that: "My father left me out of his will and so did my mother." She said, "You remember my father?"

"Red Blake," his mother said. "I always liked him."

"I know," said Lulu. "That's the best thing about him – that you liked him and he liked you."

Ten years ago, she went on, elaborating and going back to the beginning, she had made one of her rare, grudging visits to the family farmhouse at the end of this lake, the farm that had been in her family for more than a hundred years, belonging to her great-grandfather, then her great-uncle, then passed to her father when he was sixty years old. Her visit extended itself when she saw the shape he was in. Over the course of his final months – the terminal illness of old age and self-disgust – she and her mother shared the burden of looking after him. She was the prodigal daughter looking after the father she had run away from. "Your mother knows that story," she said to Jim. "She knows everything about me."

Nan smiled. "Well, up to a point."

"Everything that matters. Your mother rescued me. She saved my life."

"Lulu's talking about school in Lanark. Where the great chip wagon is." Then to Lulu, "Go on about your father."

They had opened his will a few days after his death, she said, and discovered that he had left everything to her brother, Guy, and nothing at all to her mother or to her. Guy was thrilled, of course. She paused to convey how thrilled he was. Her arms spread wide, her face lit up. He was thrilled to be his father's chosen one. Out of fairness to their mother, however, he was persuaded to renounce the will, and then their mother, also in fairness, drew up a will leaving everything jointly to him and Lulu.

Then a year ago her mother had written to her saying she had been unwell for a while and the trouble was cancer of the lung and it had spread. Again, she came back to help, though by now Guy was living on the farm, having built a house for himself and his second wife, while their mother remained in the old farmhouse. "The three of us shared the work of caring for her," she said. After her mother died, she gathered wild flowers for the funeral. She went out into the fields and along the road and came back with baskets of black-eyed Susans and yarrow and wild phlox. She filled the church with flowers. Then the day after the funeral, they opened the will. She read the first page about the division of property and it was what she had expected, so she folded it back up. "Wait," Guy said. "Read the whole thing." And she opened it again and read the whole thing, all the way to the codicil at the end.

Her mother had warned her. There had been a change, she said, but she didn't want to talk about it.

47

The codicil, added without her knowledge in the last weeks of her mother's life, gave the farm and the sugar bush and the river and the lakefront to Guy, and left her with nothing except a sum of money. A generous enough sum, she admitted, but that was hardly the point. He had gone behind her back to take all the land for himself.

Even her mother. Even her mother bowed to the wishes of a son who put no value on a sister.

She had been planning to turn her corner of land into a summer theatre – as Stratford was to Toronto, or the Berkshires to Boston. All those years of scraping together a life as an actor, all those years of dusty Shakespeare in out-of-the-way places, and what she wanted now was to settle down and be the one to hire and fire and encourage and humiliate. Her brother had stolen it from her. Her mother had sided with him. They had been partners in her disinheritance.

"The rupture is complete," she said.

Lulu had a habit of spreading her fingers wide, Jim noticed, then bringing them into soft fists. She did that now with her small expressive hands, nearly fifty years old and out of work, as she would tell them quite freely. She wasn't pretty, he didn't think she was pretty, but he would always find her beautifully alive. She said, "I'm going to get even with my brother."

"I see him from time to time," his mother said. "Guy Blake," she explained to him.

"He gave us a venison roast," Jim said to Lulu.

"Did he?" Lulu paused and considered. "He always had a soft spot for your mother."

You could hear the lake then. The evening. A boat passing.

His mother said, "I don't understand. Unless he wasn't aware of what you wanted or had some other—"

Lulu's voice came down, a sharp hoe on a weed, cutting her off. "He's not interested in what I want. I'm just a sister."

There was silence. They had turned down a darker road. Lulu was in the lead and they were following.

His mother said, "Was it his barbed wire you tangled with?"

"Down by the river. He and his second, no, *third* wife fenced off the old communal path."

"Lots of parties down there," his mother said, a yielding expression on her face. "Broken glass."

"Nan, don't you dare let him off the hook. He's not a good brother. He doesn't look out for me the way Tom looked out for you."

The light was beginning to fade along with the wow of the Martinis. Cooler air. You could smell the water. Jim saw his mother draw herself up a little, her face full of what she was about to say. Leaning forward, she delivered the line, "'Forgiveness in families is a mystery to me, how it comes or how it lasts.'"

The borrowed words hovered in the air, in their completeness, and Lulu asked where they came from.

"A story by Alice Munro. It's about a sister who's furious with her brother."

"I don't know it." Lulu sat still and thoughtful, her eyes on his mother. "Darling Nan, what are you telling me?"

"That if you don't treat him as an enemy, it will become harder and harder for him to keep that up. Otherwise, he will be able to hold on to his stubbornness for a long time." Nan was thinking as she spoke of her first husband, thinking of her other son. Reminding herself to remember things she had learned the hard way: offer anger and anger comes back; offer love and there's a chance of love coming back.

A moment passed. Then she cocked her head. "*Third* wife? I thought she was his second."

Lulu shrugged and the mood was broken. "She's from around here. I guess she caught his eye after Linda took off. Julie Gemmill. Well, now she's Julie Blake."

"So she's attractive?"

"She is. And she's a hard worker. He got lucky. Though I don't suppose he knows it." Her mouth tightened. "I drove by the farm the other day and he's got a Canadian flag the size of Texas out front. But he's always been like that: unnecessarily and never-endingly aggressive." His front door and his car were plastered with stickers, too, she said. MY CANADA INCLUDES QUEBEC.

And now the subject of Quebec filled the verandah: a breeze, a temperature all its own. On this June evening, the referendum was four months away.

His mother said, "All we're saying is that we don't want them to go. It's an appeal, an embrace. Unlike the people who say good riddance."

"No, Nan, you're laying claim. You're trying to enclose them. Nobody in Quebec feels that way."

"Except the Anglos." His mother was rubbing her forehead. "Not just the Anglos either. All the federalists. Anybody who feels an attachment to Canada."

Lulu shook her head. She couldn't disagree more. Well, her mother came from Quebec, that's why she felt as she did. It had always been a big joke in the family, she said, a sick joke, that her father had rescued her mother from the priest-ridden backwoods of New France. Personally, she wanted to see Quebec finally break away and then watch complacent Canada shatter into pieces. Enjoy the fight over who got what. Here was a will-in-the-making, she believed, that might come right.

"I can't bear it," Nan said, and Jim felt sorry for her. It seemed to him she was on the losing and, what's more, the less exciting side.

"It will be something new," Lulu said, "something *different*."

"It will be the end of my country."

"It's a dull country, darling. Admit it. It has no depth. Nothing important happens here. Nothing interesting. Canada is the centre of nothing."

"But you've come back," his mother said, scoring a point.

50

Lulu didn't speak.

"You don't have to have a reason," his mother said, since she really wasn't looking for a fight.

"I have a reason. I'm going to raise a little Cain."

His mother smiled. "You're not serious."

"Did you know," and Lulu was speaking directly to Jim now, "that I have my advanced certificate in dramatic combat? Using single sword, small sword, broadsword, rapier and dagger, and unarmed combat."

By this time it was nearly dark and Lulu said she was working up an appetite. "You can help me, Jim." She took him outside with her and from the trunk of the old Buick she heaved out a cooler. He took one handle and she the other, and they carried it to the house, pausing when she stopped to look at the sky. "What a comfort to see the stars," she said, breathing deep. "They're always there. They never change."

He looked up too. He didn't have the heart to tell her that all of those stars were leaving themselves behind at a terrific rate.

It was so quiet. Only a few night sounds. His eyes shifted from the vast sky to her wide, upturned face, and she said, "Their light will be there tomorrow night and the night after."

She met his eyes and smiled, and he was newly won over.

In the kitchen they hoisted the cooler onto the counter and while he and his mother looked on, she proceeded to take out carrots, meat, potatoes, onions. "I'm going to make sonofabitch stew," she said.

He wanted to know if it had to have onions, being no fan of onions.

"Without them, it wouldn't be sonofabitch stew," she said. "That is a fact."

Nan was happy to leave them to it. She went out onto the verandah with her book, soothed by Lulu's attentions to her son, and for a while she leaned her head against the sofa and closed her eyes, content just to catch the inflections and energy in her old friend's voice.

51

Growing up on the Klondike River, Lulu was telling Jim, had acquainted her with basic grub. Rivers in the Yukon rolled along smooth as Jell-O, she said, until they tumbled into sets of rapids, the smooth and the rough, like her two brothers in the run-down house that got flooded every spring. Guy was the smooth one, the smooth talker, and Bernie was the fisherman out in every weather, turning ruddy, getting hacking coughs, a river boy. Their mother had boiled up onions, she said, and slathered them hot on a piece of cloth, then folded the cloth in two and pinned it to the chest of his pyjamas, afterwards scraping the cold onions into her stew pot on the back of the stove. Bernie was not to be saved, however. He drowned in a set of rapids the spring he turned eighteen. They found him upside down, his heel caught between two rocks.

"Dear Bernie," she said. "Guy, on the other hand. Guy sneaks around. He even fools your mother."

"He's got a new Ford Ranger."

"A pickup?"

He nodded. "With a white cap on the back."

"Venison makes excellent sonofabitch stew," she said, "if he happens to give you more venison. He's never given any to me." And she took a step back from the counter and folded her upper body forward. Her hands formed fists on the countertop.

Jim asked if she was alright. Did she want to sit down? He dragged over a chair and she sat, her hands spread out on the counter and her head bent down.

"Sometimes I cook standing," she said, "sometimes I cook sitting, and sometimes I lean. It depends how many Martinis I've had. You're a gallant lad, Jim, and I love you for it."

She stood up and straightened herself. She was an actor. She knew about carriage. Stamina. Aplomb. Defeat.

For a while she took a rest from talking and showed him how to peel a potato, then when he appeared to have the hang of it, she went back to the subject of her brother Bernie, how he liked to eat until he hurt and Duke Ellington was the same and so was Byron. "Byron was a poet," she said, "as you probably know. Duke Ellington was a composer. They were so brilliant they forgot to eat and then made up for it by eating too much. Me, I never forget."

Following his progress with the peeler: "See if you can take less flesh – go for a thinner peel. That's the way."

A moment passed and she said, "Sometimes I have the feeling Bernie's here in the room with me. Or in the car. Watching out for me."

Jim concentrated hard on the potato. Just like his mother. She had the same feeling.

"I wouldn't rule it out," Lulu said.

He had to blink back his tears. Taking his time, making a long, careful peel, he said, "My brother believes in God. But I don't. Do you?"

"Not really, darling. To tell you the truth."

"He thinks people go to heaven when they die."

"It's a nice thought. It gives people a lot of comfort. You're a dab hand at that, Jim."

"When you're dead, you're dead," he said.

"A lot of people believe that."

"Don't you?"

"Well, there's more to life than we know about. I expect there's more to death."

He could see how that might be so.

Once they had the stew simmering on the stove, Lulu went to the piano in the living room and began to play from memory what she called old standards. "How Deep is the Ocean", "Blame it on My Youth", "There Will Never Be Another You", "Moonglow". Nan left her book and joined them at the piano, sometimes humming, sometimes singing along, and Jim had never seen her so entirely happy. The music had a strong effect on him too. It lifted him, as if in an elevator going up, eight feet off the ground, from which height he looked down at his mother and Lulu and Pog, whose ears twitched and quivered, and Duke, who barely stirred he was so deaf. He saw the furniture, the piano, the old wooden floor, the hooked rug – all of them in silvered detail – and he saw himself playing the same songs one day, effortless at the piano, applauded and talked about. Jim Bobak at the Blue Note. In that moment, it seemed all of life was calling out to him and all he had to do was grow up.

4

AND SO IT BEGAN, THE OUTSTANDING SUMMER OF HIS childhood when he had two dogs and two happy women who wanted his company. He didn't miss his father as much as he thought he should, but he talked to him regularly on the telephone and pitied his pale, unrugged days.

Pog would lean against his knee, panting in the heat, his long tongue hanging out unbelievably far, its undersides bluish. Jim was never sure when to stop patting him. Even when he tired of it, he didn't want to hurt the dog's feelings and so he kept on. When finally he stopped, Pog lay down, not having wanted to hurt the boy's feelings either.

You see more than you bargain for in the summer. Jim saw all of Lulu. She was like those illustrations in books where the front of the house is removed and all the rooms and stairways are visible. *Father Christmas*, which he would pore over without fail come December, paging through every weather and every hour to get to the ultimate cosiness of warm kitchen, hot bath, cognac, cigar, cocoa, bed. One afternoon he and Lulu bicycled to her brother's farm at the end of the lake. They followed the dirt road that rose and fell and curved and dipped, Pog running beside them. Jim always felt relaxed and competent on a bicycle. His mind was clearer and more open, noticing things. Wild turkeys in a nearby field. Dappled sunlight on a mossy log.

In the shade of Guy's old sugar maples, whose upper branches reached across the road, they propped their bicycles against the cedar-rail fence, grey and whittled down with age and secured at the ends with rusty wire. They took a moment to drink from the Thermos of water Lulu had brought along, while Pog lapped from a metal bowl, and in the breeze the mosquitoes were not too bad. Lulu also stole a few swigs from the flask in her front pocket and Jim knew without asking that it was gin. Then, "Let's investigate," she said, slinging the daypack over her shoulders.

She went first and he followed, climbing up the rails and dropping to the other side, after which they were walking in a grassy, hummocky sort of parkland through trees spaced wide to allow for easy passage in the spring. Blue tubing ran between the trees, and Lulu passed her fingers over a length of it, saying musingly, "The sap gets sucked into gathering tanks and then pumped through to the sugar shack. A few cuts with a razor blade would do a lot of damage." And she raised her eyebrows. "Wouldn't you say?" She knew an old Portuguese gentleman, she said, who had grown the most glorious grapes in his backyard, year after year, until the summer every one of his vines got severed in the middle of the night before the fruit had a chance to ripen. "Henrique had enemies. They knew how to break his heart."

She led the way through the trees to a rough and sloping pasture, where she plumped herself down on a wide rock and Jim sat beside her and Pog stretched out in the grass. "When my brother drowned," she said, "when Bernie died, everybody around me was crying. I didn't cry. Oh, some feelings are there right away. I got hit by a bicycle last year and I was so angry I wanted to kill myself. I burn my hand and I'm ready to tear the house down. But some feelings take a long time, they sort of grow behind your back. You turn around thirty years later and there they are." She threw her hands high and wide. "I love it here, Jim. I love this pasture. I love these trees. I had the idea the actors would come and go, and the trees would form a screen, a back stage, and the audience would sit in this pasture."

Opening her pack, she took out an orange and began to peel it, gazing around her and remarking on how healthy the trees were, how well cared for.

Jim told her that his uncle knew a lot about trees.

She looked at him for a long moment. "Was it a big funeral, Jim?"

It was. They had driven up the day after his mother got the telephone call, and stayed. That is, he and his mother stayed on. His father had gone back after a few days. They had driven him to the Ottawa airport and he had flown home. People from all over came to the funeral, bringing trays and containers of food, but he wasn't hungry at all. Afterwards, there was laughter and chatter in the church hall as people talked to one another about any number of things. They were happy to be alive, his mother said to him later. It was natural. It didn't mean they weren't sad.

"Your aunt and uncle were well loved," said Lulu. She was handing him half the orange. He took it, not minding her sticky fingers, and ate it, one section at a time. "Let me tell you something, Jim. You're going to live to be an old, old man and I'm going to live to be an old woman. I'm too tough for my own good and so are you." Pouring a little water on her hands, she got rid of the stickiness, and then she took his right hand in hers and spread it open. "Where's your lifeline?" Her fingertip tickled him and she had to take a stronger grip, squinting as she studied his palm in the bright sunshine. She didn't speak for a while.

He remembered asking his mother once if a watch left the time on your skin. She had been explaining why he had creases on his legs – from your jeans, she said, like the mark your watch leaves on your wrist. Does it leave the time on your skin too? And she had given him a surprised smile and said she liked the way his mind worked. Lulu turned his palm to view it from a different angle. If she had read his uncle's palm, he wondered, would she have seen the car crash?

Lulu refolded his hand. "You won't be alone, darling. Sometimes you'll worry about that. But you're going to have friendships and love affairs worth mentioning."

"Which one is the lifeline?" He was curious.

"Darling, listen to me. It's all bullshit." Her voice had tensed up and he was taken aback. "I'm sorry, Jim. That was a dumb idea. I should stop pretending I'm some kind of gypsy."

She was lying on her back in the grass. She had fallen asleep. Her body gave a little tremble every half a minute or so. Pog's did the same. Like waves coming in. Jim began to count her breaths. Sometimes the tremble came on the fourth breath, sometimes the tenth. She was a calm sea producing waves. Then something made him look to the right and he saw about fifty feet away a man standing amid the trees, regarding them.

Everything went prickly and quiet.

Pog rose, taut with anticipation, his arthritis magically gone.

Lulu, raising her head mere inches, told him *go*, and he coursed towards the man in the trees and proceeded to herd him back towards them. Pog worked intently and without barking.

Lulu and Jim stood up and waited. The dog came to her side.

"We're in your woods," she said.

It was easy to see they were brother and sister. The same stocky build, the same hands, small, practical, freckled. Guy had bloodied the middle knuckle of his right hand.

"You are," he replied.

It was the coldest voice Jim had ever heard. The coldest set of eyes.

"Oh, come on, Guy," Lulu said. "You're not going to fuss yourself just because we're passing through." Her voice sounded sure of itself until it cracked on the last word and she had to clear her throat.

Jim could see that all of her invincibility crumbled at a touch from this brother behind whose back she made bitter jokes. "We'll feed this to my brother," she had said of the grease in the fry pan, the well-picked bones, the potato peelings. "We'll make my brother take out the garbage next time. We'll make him scrub out the pail with a toothbrush. *His* toothbrush."

"What are you up to, Lu?"

"What does it look like?" She licked her lower lip.

Jim felt her tension move into him and set up house. Usually, he felt this way on his own behalf. Or when a story began to move in a book.

Guy's iron regard bore down on her and Lulu was no match for him. She had no comeback. She cared too much. She would always lose. Jim knew this in an instant. He had seen it all in the schoolyard. It had happened to him, both the shunning and the being shunned. What it meant, he realized, was that this stuff never ended. It kept on until you were dead.

"Jim," Guy said, shifting his glance to him and losing the iciness in his voice, "you're welcome to tramp through my woods any time. Feel free."

Then he turned on his heel and headed back into the sugar bush.

They sat down again and Lulu said, "Just because somebody asks a question, you don't have to answer it. It took me a long time to figure that out. Hold your counsel, hold your counsel."

"Maybe we should go home."

She looked at her watch. "We'll leave soon."

Jim would remember her talking on and on, telling him not about Guy but about growing up, what a fall from grace it was, shifting from a remote river in the far north to a big school in Ottawa and no friends, to being backward and from the sticks. She was thirteen and they put her back two years. She took it for several months, she said, until on her fourteenth birthday she ran away to her grandmother's in Lanark and went to school there and discovered his mother: Nan Waterman.

"We were going to be poets," she said to him. "We read our poems to each other. We sat at the table at my grandmother's and stapled together our little books. It killed me when your mother moved away. There I was in grade eleven and all alone."

59

"She still writes poems."

"Your mother was good. She has the talent and I have the ambition. Does she read them to you?"

"No."

He had seen several lying on her desk and read a few lines, only to stop in dismay and walk quickly out of the room. How unhappy she was in her poems.

"When I ran away, all I packed was my brush and my comb."

"Was your grandmother glad to see you?" He looked into her face, hoping hard.

"What do you think? The only other person to welcome me like that was your mother."

Lulu found the scythe in the shed that housed the bicycles. Taking it over to the meadowy field behind the house, she proceeded to mow a pathway in the shape of a *J* through the long grass. She gave Jim a rake and he worked behind her until they reached the split-rail fence kept in good repair over the years by his uncle. Sinking down then, she rested her back against a post and Pog stretched out beside her. Pog had been keeping track of them, attentive and off to the side. It was early July and there had been unbroken warmth and almost no rain for weeks.

They climbed an old apple tree and looked down at their work. "That's a beautiful *J*," she said. "*J* for Jim."

"*J* for jerk," he replied, and she nearly fell out of the tree laughing. He had to grab her by the shirt and haul her back.

Over the next few days they scythed the whole small field. Lulu said it would cut down on mosquitoes for one thing; they loved to hide in long grass. For another, she needed the exercise. Sometimes she worked alone, sometimes she and Jim held the scythe together and swung, or she let him do a few strokes by himself after which they compared their flayed hands. At the end of one bout of teamwork, dripping sweat, he pulled off his T-shirt and she followed suit. She peeled off her shirt and he was face to face with breasts nearly half a century old.

The sight knocked words out of his head. To have the veil lifted like that. To see how her full breasts were of a piece with her creamy flesh. To see the nipples brownish-pink and spreading wide and poking out. And then the tracery of bluish-green veins hovering at the very surface of her skin. To have it all there right under his nose. Except for the first time in his life his penis was pushing up against his pants and all he could do was shove his hand into his pocket and try to force it down. "Jesus," he thought. "So that's what erection means."

Lulu used her shirt to towel away the sweat as the wind cooled them off. "Look your fill, Jim. I don't mind."

Her chest was magnificently more than his mother's and utterly different from his sagging-in-folds-and-pleats-and-wrinkles grand-mother in her swimsuit.

Lulu gave herself a look. "I'm starting to sag, but you have to treat gravity with levity." And she smiled such a broad, roguish smile that he laughed hard and helplessly. Now all he had to do was recover from his hysterics. He felt like a capsizing boat that rights itself and sails boldly on.

She slipped back into her shirt and they went down to the kitchen and from there to the lake, his mother joining them, even Duke. On the dock they compared war wounds: the impressive jagged scar on Lulu's thigh from a long, slow slide into a tall mirror in a dance studio in Mexico City; his, the length of his right thumb, from being too wild and happy next to a single-paned window on Fire Island. His mother was silent about the scar on her forehead until Lulu pressed the point, and then she made her usual joke – a sabre-cut on the high seas. It always got a laugh, even if people didn't clue in to *Treasure Island*'s old seaman with the sabre-cut across one cheek, "a dirty, livid white".

*

61

That night the telephone rang. Nan went into the kitchen and stayed talking and listening for a long time. Jim could tell she was speaking to his father about his grandmother's move into the nursing home in Nyack. "And Martin did all that," he heard her say, sounding surprised, impressed. Later, she would explain that George's brother Martin had come from Peru to handle the move for his mother (meaning that she had missed her chance to meet this younger brother who so intrigued her). But for now she simply said, "Your dad is on the telephone, Jim. He's tuckered out from moving all our stuff into your grandmother's apartment."

"Dad," he said, picking up the telephone. "When are you coming?"

"You miss me."

He heard his father's sigh of satisfaction.

"Lulu's showing me how to scythe the long grass."

"Is the scythe sharp?"

"She sharpened it."

"It has to be sharp. Blades are more dangerous when they're dull. A dull blade won't cut the grass, it will cut you. I learned that the hard way."

It was sharp. "When are you coming?"

"In a week or so. Sooner if I can. What day is today? July 8th? I'll be there on the 15th."

"O.K."

"You miss me," his father said again, not hiding his delight.

"Do you want me to get Mommy?"

"Jim. Be careful with the scythe."

*   *   *

They thought he was asleep.

"Last summer he hounded me for a dog," his mother said. "Something was troubling him."

"He's a lovely boy, Nan. He reminds me of Bernie. Take good care of him."

62

He was in the hammock under a quilt as old as the cottage. His head on a pillow and his eyes closed. His mother said, "He wanted to know the worst thing I'd ever done."

Lulu's voice was huskier than Nan's. "I would have known the answer when I was ten. There are too many things to pick from now."

"He wouldn't tell me *his* worst thing."

So he had given her the worry, passing it on as an unfinished story, and now she was thinking about it more than he was.

"Something happened at school, I think." Her voice was so low he missed the rest, aware instead of a gentle breeze off the lake and the sound of rain, which was really the air moving in the leaves. He thought how the air touching his face made no sound while touching the leaves it did. He began to drift off, their voices receded, until his mother said clearly, "How does a marriage that's stopped working start working again?"

He opened his eyes. Candlelight played across their arms, the glasses in their hands.

He heard his mother say, "In my first marriage I had to remove us from John's anger. Things were better for a while and then they got worse and we left for good."

"We?" Lulu said.

"My first son and me."

"Jim mentioned his brother."

"He's twenty now and barely speaks to me."

At the foot of the hammock Pog gave a sigh, a quiver from his dreams, and Lulu said, "Darling, what do you mean? Barely speaks to you?"

"I mean, Blake doesn't want to be around me. I embarrass him."

"Blake," Lulu repeated, and there was surprise and an unspoken question in her voice.

Nan took long enough to answer that Jim became aware of the night again, the dark trees, the moving air. "If I'd had a daughter," she said at last, "I would have named her Lulu. I had a son."

63

"Darling, I'm touched."

They were quiet again.

Lulu Blake, Jim thought. He knew who *he* was named for.

As if reading his mind, his mother said, "Blake for Lulu Blake, burning bright. And Jim for *Treasure Island*."

That's right, he said to himself.

He closed his eyes. The air felt as soft as his penis, maybe softer. They were talking about his grandmother now, his mother saying how generous she was, taking pity on them in their cramped rooms and transferring her great apartment on West End Avenue to George. "Even so, I'd rather stay here." Their voices receded again. He was almost asleep when Lulu startled him awake. She was asking his mother if she had a razor blade by any chance and his mother thought she might. There was a loose blade somewhere, maybe in the tool drawer in the kitchen.

"They're great for cutting fishing line," Lulu said.

But Jim knew what she wanted it for. He saw blue tubing lying in a mess all over the sugar bush, and Guy rampaging and calling in the police. He should warn his mother, take her aside in the morning and tell her. But telling on people had been a big mistake in the past, leading to other things, worse things that he wanted to forget but couldn't.

He closed his eyes. He heard Lulu go into the kitchen. Soon he would hear the fridge door, the ice cubes, the glass being filled, but for now his mother was laying an extra something across him: her sweater, light and warm.

Nan had once told Jim how restful it was to be immersed in a past that was over. She knew the history of nearly everything in the house, every patched and faded tea towel, every stray dish and worn rug and dusty blanket whose shared afterlife was the heaven of this old cottage. Her brother had bought the place as a young man and it became a repository for parts of their childhood: the light blue bowls and plates, the tall blue plastic glasses, the mismatched forks and knives. Here was the clock from home, the empty Mason jars on high shelves, the carved wooden bowl full of elastic bands, shoelaces, fishing line (even a razor blade in a paper sheath). In the closets were garments she had worn as a girl and outgrown, only to see them reappear on her mother: the light-grey jacket that was hers when she was twelve, the summer dress that fitted perfectly when she was fourteen, the dark-green trench coat she had worn at sixteen. In her old age her mother would put on the trench coat and go fishing in the rain. She would wear the summer dress on hot days and know that it was getting one more use. For a time the two of them had been as crosshatched as a window screen: Nan was going forward, her mother was going backward, and they overlapped in their clothing. A black-and-white Sunday-best dress, worn to church when she was eight or nine, had been turned into a pillowcase. And so pieces of her past went fishing in the rain, or dried the plates and bowls, or supported her head as she fell asleep.

Out on the screened verandah, on sills ample enough for field glasses and hardback books, were natural abodes and beings collected by her brother and sister-in-law, including a warbler's nest made of twigs and birch bark and lined with the soft dark hair of some secretive creature; the skull of a small rodent, perhaps a mink; a dead Viceroy butterfly knocked about and tattered by the wind; variously shaped rocks loaded with quartz; a dried Chanterelle mushroom as orange as an apricot; a chunk of tree fungus, bone yellow, as the moon is sometimes. And there was Jim himself, who loved the idea of sleeping in the hammock but in truth slept little when he was in it. He wandered back into the kitchen, dazed, and she took his hand and led him to his bed.

*   *   *

One night after dark, when Lulu was asleep upstairs and Jim was in his room off the kitchen, Guy put in an appearance. His voice, intent and persuasive, woke Jim in his bunk bed. "All winter. I took out the trash. I saw the bottles."

"I know she drinks . . ." His mother's voice was guarded.

"She's a lush. She alienates everybody she knows."

"Not me. I don't remember a single fight. And she's wonderful with Jim."

A chair scraped the floor. Then they were right outside his partly open door, standing there, and his mother was asking why he'd cut Lulu out of the will, and Guy said because she ruins everything she touches, she's irresponsible. And anyway he hadn't cut her out, she'd inherited a tidy sum of money, which she needed a lot more than she needed land. His mother argued back in a low, urgent voice, saying he should give her more credit, he should appreciate her, her life had not been easy. And Jim heard them breathing close together. And then he heard his mother whisper, "Don't."

5

IT WOULD BE REMEMBERED AS A SUMMER OF MARAUDING bears – bold, effortless, swaggering black bears. A summer so uncommonly hot, long, and dry there were no wild berries to speak of, and so the marauders took over northern towns, turned them into traplines, stopped at certain apple trees, entered houses, cars, sheds. They hung out in the parking lot at Grey's Bar & Grill in Kenora. In Beausejour, Manitoba, a boy went down into the basement to watch television and a bear was eating potato chips by the fireplace. Near the Gatineau River in Quebec, another hungry bear, emerging from the bush, got hit by a car with such force that it ricocheted across the road and slammed into an oncoming car, taking off the roof and decapitating the driver, a woman in her twenties, whose boyfriend was sleeping it off in the back. The boyfriend lived on.

Down by the water Jim and his mother and Lulu ate their meals in the relaxed manner they fell into when his father wasn't there. They put their food on trays and carried the trays down to the folding table on the dock, where they benefited from every passing breeze and could trail their feet in the water if they felt like it.

As was usual with northern summers, the month of July gave the impression it would never end.

"You know what to do if you meet a bear," his mother said to him. "Don't run. Stand your ground. Make yourself as big as you can by holding up your arms and making lots of noise."

"Then what?" he said.

"Close your mouth."

He closed it.

"Walk backwards slowly, looking the bear in the eye."

"Darling, are you sure? Aren't you supposed to *avoid* looking the bear in the eye as you walk backwards saying soft words?"

"Lord," his mother said. Which was it?

Jim said it must depend on whether the bear was charging you or not, and his mother looked at him with respect. "That's it. If you come upon a bear, back away without making a sound. And if the bear charges, make a racket."

Lulu said if the bear charged, she'd be having a heart attack.

Jim learned more that summer than he had in his previous life – how to dive off high rocks, how to pick out a song on the piano, how to wield a dagger and a broadsword. Lulu (beside him in the passenger seat) let him drive her Buick to the foot of the long lane, her left hand poised to steady the wheel if need be. It was something he never could have done in New York, he knew. Another time they spent an hour on the raft, after which he cut the water like a knife. The trick, Lulu said, kneeling beside him, was to go deep. Keep your head tucked down between your outstretched arms, aim for the bottom of the lake, and keep your feet together as you kick up. Lesson mastered, they then paddled to a small island with a steep rock from which they dove repeatedly, until they were sunburned and so waterlogged Lulu said her bones felt loose and drunken inside her.

She used to swim with Guy, she told him later, growing up. She used to bathe with him too, when she was little. Her mother put them in the tub together. She was three, he was five. Older Bernie had the tub to himself after they were done; another kettle of hot water and in he went. She used to reach out and pull Guy's peter, that little floaty, rubbery, irresistible thing, and how he would giggle. From such friendly, sportive proximity grew half the pains in the world, so it seemed to her.

"You haven't got even with him yet," Jim said.

"I'm still cogitating. He always beats me, that's the trouble. It doesn't take much, to tell the truth, because I always rise to the bait. I go out on a limb and fall off." She gave him a ruminating smile. "Have you got advice for me? You strike me as the kind of person who would give good advice."

Jim smiled with pleasure and shoved his hands into his pockets. This was the summer he added a tan and calluses to his old daydream of getting up at dawn to grab a coffee-to-go and a bagel with cream cheese, full of confidence and no destination in mind beyond walking the streets of Manhattan and admiring how the buildings filled the air above his head. He could see himself taking his nut-brown face back to the pale city and having people stop in their tracks with envy. One thing was sure: he was not going to be like his father, who worked all the time at his office, fighting for the rights of tenants but getting no satisfaction from it. Or his mother, who had retreated from any number of things, former this and former that, former traveller, former teacher, former librarian, and now made do with short-term writing contracts, mostly from museums, cobbling together a sort of income, and worrying, worrying.

During the second week of July, on the hottest day so far, he and his mother were in the Chevette, windows rolled down, and she became very quiet. They were in downtown Ottawa looking for the narrow bridge that would take them across the river to Quebec and the Canadian Museum of Civilization on the riverbank. Jim was conscious of the bullet hole in the back passenger door. No other car had a bullet hole, certainly not in Ottawa, which was hardly a city at all. What must it be like to say you came from here instead of New York? People would scratch their heads.

Nan found her way onto the bridge, and halfway across she took deep breaths and muttered to herself. They were in the other country, she said. They were in Quebec.

But for Jim it was another country inside another country. He was an American in Canada, and Quebec was not a problem. It was where Lévesque came from. Trudeau too. "What are you afraid of?" he said.

She winced and shot him a look. "You're right. What am I afraid of?"

Well, it went deep, she told him as they came off the bridge, this English-Canadian insecurity about Quebec. There was such a long history of feeling bad about not learning French, feeling ashamed, resentful, unforgiven. Of course, lots of people didn't feel bad, they didn't much care. But any way you cut it, there was a lot of mutual distrust that went way back, and this imminent referendum was bound to make things worse. "You can be sure the separatists are working hard, preparing a campaign that will vilify Canada. Now keep your eyes peeled for a parking spot." And chewing on her lower lip, she added, "And of course English Canada will return the favour and vilify Quebec."

They were scanning the street for a place to park when she took him aback by saying thoughtfully, "You're the right age to learn French. If you were in an immersion programme at school, you'd pick it up fast. Would you like that? Would you like to live at the lake year-round and go to school in Lanark and learn French?"

He was too surprised to know what to say. "You mean never go back to New York?"

"I guess I thought you liked it better here."

"I do like it here."

"Let's try this street," she said.

On a side street of poor-looking houses, they found the parking spot easily, and she was backing into it when Jim asked her what the motto on all the Quebec licence plates meant. "*Je me souviens*," she said. "It means 'I remember.'" She sat on behind the wheel, saying what a great motto it was, and Jim said he liked New Hampshire's more, "'Live free or die'," and she chuckled and agreed it was good too. "One looks forward and the other looks backward." Then she shook her head. "No, Quebec's is better. It conveys such a sense of history, of what could have been as well as what was."

On the sidewalk she put her hand on his shoulder for a moment. "Have I worried you? Even if we lived here, we wouldn't lose our ties to New York. We would go back and forth."

He didn't want to lose either place, that's all he was certain of.

They set off walking through the heat to the museum and in no time they were in a place much older than either New York or Quebec.

Inside, leaning over the railing, they gazed to the far end of a vast totem pole room utterly different from the dark, enclosed, mysterious hall lined with totem poles that they knew and loved in the Museum of Natural History on 79th Street. This hall, three storeys high, extended nearly the full length of the museum and conveyed the feeling of a hushed and infinite forest – more valley than room, the floor far below, the backdrop misty and remote, the house fronts and totems in a row along the shore, the sound of ravens and the sea. They leaned and looked. The solitude, the strangeness, the beauty: it was an enchantment.

For Jim it was like finding himself in the opening pages of *The Story of Canada* with the early peoples, the long houses, the forest. He wouldn't mind working here, he thought. Maybe if his mother got a job here, she would find him a job too.

There were other worlds besides. They went down a hallway and turned right through glass doors into a wide opening of ghostly light, ghostly music. It led into a circular area of fine wooden cabinets with glass facing, glass backing, glass shelves on which were arranged arrowheads, amulets, needles, and hooks as tiny as buds made by an ancient people who had worked without metal in the coldest part of the world. They had vanished, these Palaeo-Eskimos, hundreds of years ago.

His mother picked up the telephone beside a television screen showing a white wolf wandering over snowy wastes and heard the words: *From this life of endurance, insecurity and dreams came a*

71

remarkable artistic tradition. She put the telephone to his ear. "Listen. It's the best phone call I've had in a long time."

Only a few nights before, in a Sherlock Holmes story, they had come upon the sentence "Genius is the capacity for taking infinite pains." Not a very good definition, Holmes admitted, but it did apply to detective work. And it seemed to apply here, she suggested, to archeological detection and to the things detected. A tiny ivory mask, tiny floating spirit-bear, tiny ivory falcon; arrowheads of chipped stone; quartz micro-blades as sharp as any razor – all unearthed and identified, or guessed at.

They moved from telephone to telephone, exhibit to exhibit, snooping on the past, overhearing on the party line all the sad gossip about troubles, deaths, disappearance, meagre food, inexplicable loss. Sometimes they stopped in their tracks and looked around the way they stopped sometimes in the woods, forgetting the rest of the world, absorbed in the movement of the leaves, or the deep blue of the sky, or the clouds moving overhead.

A people had disappeared. Why? What had become of them? The museum posed the haunting questions and they expected answers, continuing on through the small, winding exhibit in a state of suspense, as if through a good detective story. Certain sudden changes the Palaeo-Eskimos adapted to, so they learned by reading the texts on the walls. The climate got colder and what was known to archeologists as the Dorset way of life developed, with oil lamps rather than open fires, stone and turf dwellings rather than skin tents. The Dorset became efficient hunters of sea mammals. They carved more, their art flourished. But then the climate became warmer, animal patterns changed, newcomers arrived and took over, bringing more sophisticated tools and weapons, and the Dorset were required to accommodate, entertain, even teach. They taught the newcomers everything they knew and the newcomers became envious and cruel. One day they took a Dorset man, tied him up, and drilled a hole through his forehead. Jim and Nan heard this over one of the telephones from an Inuit elder remembering what his ancestors had said about the earlier vanished people, known to him by the Inuktitut word, *Tunit*. The victim closed his eyes while they drilled. Then he opened them to see the world one last time before he died.

Jim felt the drill enter his forehead. He heard his persecutors murmuring among themselves, impressed by his courage. He closed his eyes, then opened them wide.

"They survived the weather," his mother said dryly, "but they did not survive the people. I can understand that."

So could he.

They made the circle once, then twice, drawn forward by the strange, low, hypnotic music and the atmosphere of subdued and mysterious twilight.

Many of the tiny carvings were birds – the ones, that is, brought by the newcomers, the Thule people, and displayed at the end of the exhibit to show the displacement that occurred. But the riddle was never solved, it turned out, the mystery of what happened to the Dorset, the puzzle of where they had gone. Scientists speculated, but they did not know. Jim's disappointment at the lack of a definitive answer cut into him. His mother did not hide her disappointment either. "The curators set us up, Jim. They set us up. Well, the truth is most of the time there are no clear answers. But it's a letdown, there's no denying it." All the experts knew for certain was that the Thule had arrived from the west with more advanced materials and techniques, amber, for instance, and objects more elaborately carved, and that the Dorset had disappeared, rendered extinct by 1500. Everything they possessed, that is each of the things that survived, fit easily into a child's pocket.

"Scientists try to answer the unanswerable," his mother said. "You're like that too. You want serious answers to unanswerable questions."

"Don't you?" Didn't everybody?

"I guess I do. I just don't think I'm going to get them." She gazed around her. It was a fine exhibit even so. It was like a poem full of nuggets of meaning. "The Dorset had nothing permanent in the way of settlements. No Troy. They were nomadic, like birds of passage."

Birds of passage, he thought, turning the phrase over in his mind. He was still imagining opening his eyes one last time.

"Your Uncle Martin's an anthropologist," she said, "Your father's brother. An anthropologist and filmmaker." She pictured bringing him here, walking with him through the exhibit, pausing, discussing. Dreamy thoughts. She had them a lot. "He would be interested in this," she said.

She opened the exhibit guide that she'd been carrying under her arm and thumbed through it now as she stood there, soon caught up in what she was reading. "Listen to this." She read two quotations out to him. "'The Tunit were strong people, but timid and easily put to flight.'" And a longer one: "'The Tunit were a strong people, and yet they were driven from their villages by others who were more numerous, by many people of great ancestors; but so greatly did they love their country, that when they were leaving Uglit, there was a man who, out of desperate love for his village, harpooned the rocks and made the stones fly about like bits of ice.'

"I don't know how to pronounce the speaker's name." She showed him with her finger. *Ivaluardjuk. Igloolik.* 1922. "So greatly did they love their country," she repeated, "that one man harpooned the rocks. That's wonderful."

A small child drew their attention by repeatedly darting away from a plump woman they took to be his indulgent grandmother. The third or fourth time the woman went to collect him, she caught Nan's eye and they shared an amused smile. The child continued to wander and meddle and be collected.

"Excuse me." The woman had come up to them and was smiling. "Are you Nancy Waterman?"

74

"Yes." Very surprised. "I am."

"Do you recognize me?"

The sweet-faced, round-faced, grey-haired woman's smile was confidently expectant.

"No." His mother shook her head. "I'm sorry."

The woman's face fell. "I'm Janet Hepburn."

"Good Lord." And his mother did not pretend to be pleased. "Janet Hepburn."

"I kept looking at you for a long time and from different angles. I was pretty sure it was you."

"Janet," his mother said again, in disbelief, and Jim could see that she had no idea what to say next. Here she was, face to face with her old enemy, Janet the first-class jerk. Who was asking, "Is this your grandson?"

Jim moved closer to his mother and she put her hand on his shoulder. "My son. My younger son Jim."

Janet was all smiles as she pulled the small delinquent to her side. "This is my grandson. He is so attached to me."

It was the same smile, Nan said later. The same mouth, the same teeth, the same voice. Nothing else was the same. She had put on so much weight. She used to be skinny, tall, arrogant. The girl who had ruined her life when she was eleven.

"It's been a long, long time," she said, trying to get her bearings, searching for something to say. "My mother told me about seeing you in the grocery store in Lanark. A dozen years ago maybe?"

Janet nodded and her lips trembled. Her eyes filled with tears. "Yes, and I could tell by her reaction to me that nothing had been forgotten. I want to say," she said, "please forgive me."

Rivetted, Jim watched his mother put her hands on Janet's shoulders and reply with warmth and without hesitation, "Of course I forgive you."

His mother's face was smooth and open. She was smiling too. So it was easy, he thought. All you had to do was ask.

The grandson had curled into a ball on the floor and was humming to himself. Jim kept his eyes on the women, fascinated, as Janet wiped away her tears with her fingers and said, "The last time we saw each other was in Toronto, at the corner of College and Yonge, in 1966. You invited me for dinner and I meant to come."

"I don't remember that." His mother's voice changed. She sounded cautious, sceptical. "I remember seeing you in the library." Remembered that in her surprise she had been too friendly, too ingratiating. The old story.

"Yes, but I was going to come for dinner." Janet was smiling again. "Then Eric, the man I married, showed up at my door, determined to take me back to Montreal with him. He couldn't stand being away from me. He couldn't live without me." Her expression faltered and she looked down, evidently moved by the depth of his love for her. "And so I drove back with him to Montreal." Then she looked up again, beaming once more, smiling to beat the band. "And there you were," she said, "out searching for me. Knocking on my door again!"

All Nan could hear was pity and triumph mingling in her old enemy's voice and she felt their childhood history gasp and sway in the air between them. *There you were knocking on my door again, but I was somewhere else with somebody important to me.* She had no memory of Janet not showing up for dinner, or why she would have invited her in the first place. Most certainly she had never gone searching for her, not then.

For Jim it was like watching a goal go into an undefended net. His mother could only say that she didn't remember that at all while Janet smiled and smiled and kept repeating that she felt so bad. "But I want you to know that I wasn't there for an important reason."

The small delinquent was on his feet again, yanking on his grandmother's arm, so Nan indicated with a turn of her head and a lift of the hand her intention of going back to the exhibit. "Jim and I haven't finished taking it in," she said, unable to hide her awkwardness.

Perhaps they could meet for tea some time, Janet offered. "If you do that. Do you ever do that?"

Nan said no, she never did.

They stayed on for a while after Janet's wide back disappeared through the door. They sat on a bench and Jim watched his mother search in her handbag for chocolate. Her troubled face was a million miles away.

Janet's pity for her, she was thinking. Janet exerting her version of events. Janet painting herself as the beloved, sought-after one while she, poor Nan, had to knock on doors begging for scraps of attention.

She raised her eyes and looked around at the bits of ivory, the bone remnants hanging in the air. Janet, a name with a twig of hurt inside it.

Well, people had been ditching each other since time immemorial, shouldering each other aside, seizing their land, writing them out of their wills. So what? Get over it, she said to herself. But my God, the pain was shocking.

"Imagine," she said to Jim. "They never had the sensation of leaves over their heads." She pointed. "Those tiny arrowheads look like the tips of beech leaves." In her mind she saw unbroken light extending over fur-clad heads and not a leaf of shade. How tough they were, how resilient, admirable, and doomed.

She gave herself a shake and resumed her search for the chocolate. Jim could tell how upset she was by the way she treated her handbag.

"You forgave her," he said.

"Yes." She found the chocolate and unwrapped it and gave him a good-sized chunk. "I said I forgave her. It's easily said."

"But you don't want to see her again."

"No." She looked away, and he knew there wasn't going to be a miracle of reconciliation after all. "I don't have the heart for it, Jim."

They left the museum soon after that, exchanging the air-conditioning for the dog days of summer. On the treeless street the

Chevette sat boiling in the sun. They rolled down all the windows and waited on the sidewalk for the car to become less stifling. She had been eleven years old, nearly twelve, when Janet dumped her and took up with Mary Fitzpatrick. There was that long September of realization as she tagged along and the two of them whispered, giggled, had their jokes and secrets and laughs at her expense. Then followed months of being on the far edge – a long, bitter course in loneliness – until Lulu arrived, a girl even stranger and more scorned than herself.

With a sigh she wasn't aware of, Nan got into the car and so did Jim. The steering wheel burned her fingers and her head ached.

"An encounter like that takes you right back," she said, staring ahead of her, car keys in her lap. She turned to her son. "And yet so much time has passed that I didn't recognize her. That was a shock, Jim."

It had stirred up her entire life, the past knocking into the present like that.

"It's alright," he said to her. "You've got Lulu."

She smiled and reached across and pushed the hair off his sweaty forehead, then raised her gaze to the rear-view mirror and for a moment couldn't recollect where they were. They were on a street of small cinderblock and stucco houses, far less prosperous than the Ontario side of the river, here at least. If Quebec separated they would get the museum and the thought tore her apart.

"The Dorset weren't good at defending themselves, Jim. That's always the question. How to defend yourself without being nasty."

Once they were out of the city and driving again on back roads, she slowed down and took in the scruffy fields that increased in number after Almonte. Scruffiness presided over by cedar trees that had secured a place for themselves in the middle of fields and along their sides. All tilled at one time, at least attempts were made in that direction, or more fully occupied by cows than they were now. Almonte, Middleville, Hopetown, Watson's Corners, Dalhousie Lake, McDonalds Corners, Elphin. She loved these scruffy fields, she told her scruffy son.

At Snow Road Station they dropped deeper into a world that was even quieter and more alive. The familiar gravel road, narrow and leafy, extended about a mile, then turned left and ascended a little, going past more woods, until the old cedar-rail fences began with the stands of sugar bush on either side. Soon, twisting up and down and up again, their view opened to fields lying lower than the road – not flat and tilled but rough and uneven and full of character. Like a boy, she thought, going slow so Jim wouldn't get carsick. Trees grew out of the fields here and there, and stones of considerable size were everywhere, some flush with the field, some protruding, the ground all aflow with hilliness and undulation.

"What music makes me feel this way?" she said, gesturing at the land. And Jim waited for the answer to come.

With every turn the winding, hilly road offered a new angle of vision into an older, secret world of effort and beautiful, private places. Wilderness had given way to pioneers whose clearings were now drifting back to bush. The land revealed itself and concealed itself, soothing her eyes, soothing her heart; a glimpse of bare rock in an old field touched her as deeply as a friend confessing some troubled part of her life. Maybe she was Janet's worst thing, she thought, the old question flaring up again in her mind. If not the worst, then one of them. *I want to say, please forgive me.* And she wished now that she had taken her time and said, Forgive you for what? What am I forgiving you for? Instead of assuming that she knew and thereby missing her chance to find out. Forgiveness, she was thinking, was in some terrible, overeager way a lack of curiosity. It was a big, powerful hose that washed everything away. She had, in effect, turned the hose on herself. "Of course, I forgive you." As eager to reconcile as she had been in the schoolyard and in her first marriage too. Only to think now that she should not have been so hasty. Forgiveness was the premature end to the story. She had skipped to the last page instead of reading the book through.

Jim said, "Is it a song?"

"You know it," she nodded. "Johnny Cash's 'Wayfaring Stranger'." And she looked over at his receptive face. "There are lots of versions, it's an old folk song," she said, "but I love the way he sings it." And she sang the words, finding and losing the tune as she went along, "'I'm just a poor wayfaring stranger, I'm travelling through this land of woe, yet there's no sickness, toil nor danger, in that bright land to which I go.'"

They were passing a field in which a dozen cows in a line were following a narrow path, their big, big bottoms swaying above their dainty feet.

"Or the theme from *High Noon*," she added, which was a song he had by heart he liked it so much. "It makes me feel this way too." She hummed it. They both knew the words.

They drove on and the opening widened further with more pioneer fences dividing fields and woods, until they passed the farm that went with the sugar bush, Guy's farm with some cows and a few horses, Guy being the one who took such prodigious care of the fences and trees. He'd once told her that he had two thousand taps among his trees.

Jim said, "You should honk before going up that hill."

His mother honked the horn. You never knew when a vehicle might come barrelling over the top and take you out.

They worked their way to their side of the lake, nearing the spot, she said, where she had once seen something so marvellous she had stopped the car and gazed in wonder. A scarlet tanager had been investigating the damp dirt in the middle of the road, the small puddles, the old wet leaves. As red as the red of a Japanese kimono, the colour set off by the black of its wings and tail and eyes, and by its grey twig-legs.

And now she stopped the car and pointed to the spot, transported once again to another level of existence.

"I'd never seen one before and I've never seen one since, yet I knew exactly what it was."

She took her foot off the brake and drove slowly on. "I was so excited I phoned my mother." She gave Jim a look that was mostly amused. "Your grandmother was a peace-loving woman, but startling things came out of her mouth. I told her I had seen a scarlet tanager in the middle of the road and there was a long pause, and then she said, 'Nan, have you been drinking?'"

He smiled.

"Jim." She was still driving very slowly. "You asked me once what was the worst thing I'd ever done. Remember?"

He remembered. She was so close to him it was like looking at her through binoculars.

"I'd forgotten all about knocking on Janet Hepburn's door when I was eleven." She tapped her fingers hard against her forehead. "I mean, completely forgotten." And she imitated a mother's pitying voice. "'Oh, poor Nancy. You're looking for Janet again. She isn't here.' I can see the poor-you look on her face. I even remember the apron she was wearing. It had clusters of cherries across the front. She was shorter than Janet. A nice woman." She saw herself trudging back down the steps to the stone walk that took her out to the street, a figure of desolation going home under the trees. And she gave a shrug. "It's not knocking on the door that's the worst thing. I mean, so what? I was eleven years old. The worst thing is having no self-respect. I had no self-respect."

6

THEY WERE DOWN BY THE WATER, DRYING OFF AFTER THE evening swim. It was cooler by the lake, though not by much on this hottest of July nights. "She probably needed to hear that," Lulu remarked when his mother described Janet Hepburn asking to be forgiven, and forgiving her.

"She's a stout, round grandmother," his mother said. "All I recognised was her teeth. Like the wolf in 'Little Red Riding Hood'."

Duke had been leaning against her side and now his old bones slid down and stretched out on the dock and he closed his eyes and slept. Pog lay between him and Lulu, that is to say, as Nan liked to say, between a soft place and a soft place.

"Did you have it out with her?" Lulu wanted to know.

Nan shook her head.

"These chances don't come along very often," Lulu said.

"There wasn't any point. There's no way I could win. Not *win*. Emerge intact. I felt her drawing me onto her ground, getting the upper hand again, and it was only a few minutes."

"What does she do?"

"I think her whole life is her family. I don't know."

"She must have married young," Lulu said.

"Nineteen. She was young. Blake's age."

"Blake is twenty," Jim said.

"Twenty. I forget sometimes."

Lulu had had her own bruising encounter that afternoon. "My

brother tells me I'm an alcoholic. I said to him, 'Darling, I prefer to think of myself as an old inebriate.'"

"A lush," Jim said.

"A lush." Lulu savoured the word. "You've been reading again."

"I can't wait to get plastered," he said.

"You don't want to get plastered. You don't want to be a sot. Or a souse. Or a guzzler." A blue damselfly landed on the back of her hand and she said, "Honey, I love you too."

She had got a little of her own back, she then confessed, by dropping into the public library in Lanark and going through their stock of well-thumbed bodice-rippers, titles like *Tenderloin* and *Riptide of Desire*, and writing her brother's name large and clear on the flyleaf of each one. "I'm a shit," she declared with energy, "and my proudest moments are when I've done something nasty."

Nan's laugh was merry even as she shook her head.

"So you didn't mean it," Jim said to her, "when you said you forgave her."

"Who?"

He waited.

"I meant it as far as it went." She studied his serious face and he averted his eyes. "It didn't go very far," she said. From across the bay came splashing and laughter. Kids jumping off a raft. And in that moment she understood something. "You want me to forgive her, don't you, Jim?"

He kept his eyes on the distant raft and didn't speak.

She understood that it had nothing to do with Janet in particular. He needed to know she could forgive. "Then I will," she said.

He checked her expression to see if she meant it. She had that thoughtful-amused look that meant a dozen things. She said, "I'm not going to have tea with her, though. You're not expecting me to have tea with her?"

"No."

Soon after that gunshots rang out across the lake. The shots were followed by cries and shouts and a chainsaw starting up. They saw a couple of boats heading towards the source of the commotion – it appeared to be the new cottage in the next bay – and curious, they got into a canoe and followed. From a distance they made out about a dozen cottagers gathered on shore and others besides themselves were arriving. Loud curses came over the water, but nothing else was understandable until they drew up to the dock. Then a fleshy woman in a baseball cap told them about the large female bear.

"Nobody's hurt, thank the Lord. So far."

They remained in the canoe, holding onto the edge of the dock, while the woman told them that her neighbour Dave had been laying out his burgers on his outdoor grill when he went inside to answer the phone. Then all hell broke loose. From the window he saw his barbecue over on its side and the bear large as life. "So he got his rifle and brought her down. Now her two cubs are up that tree." The woman pointed to a sizable maple. "That's their third perch. They went up that one first," indicating a felled spruce, "and then that one." She gestured to another felled spruce.

The chainsaw started up again.

"This is nuts," Nan said, raising her voice. "What are they going to do if they get hold of them?"

"A zoo, I guess."

"A zoo?"

"They'll die on their own," the woman said.

Jim could see that his mother was ready to push away from the dock and paddle home, away from the craziness, but Lulu had handed up the painter and the woman knelt and tied it to a cleat. He got out first, then Lulu, then Nan. Once they were on shore, the chainsaw cut out.

In the sudden stillness, amidst the jumble of people, they saw Guy. He was talking to the chainsaw operator, who was listening and nodding and wiping the sweat off his face.

Jim couldn't help but be impressed by people who knew what to do. He was the son of an indecisive father and an over-decisive mother, the former sliding off the riverbank of his life and the latter riddled with second thoughts about her moments of rashness. So he watched Guy with considerable admiration as he directed what followed. First, he had a couple of men go with him to his truck and remove a large empty dog cage from the back. Then he judged where to place it in relation to how the tree would fall. Next he conscripted several men to arm themselves with shovels and rakes and form a gauntlet as backup and aid for his border collie, who was younger than Pog, Jim saw; he heard Guy speak to the dog and learned his name was Coal.

And so the tree got felled, the small cubs tumbled to the ground, and Coal was right there to work and cajole them into the cage.

After that, a few children announced they were going in search of acorns for the bears.

A boy came over to Jim and offered to show him the dead bear. He said his father was going to make a rug out of its hide and put it in front of their fireplace. They went up the slope, the two boys, skirting the tree stumps and rocks, to the flat and grassy space next to the cottage where the bear lay on its side. It looked to Jim like a small fat man in a fur coat. The skin around the head was tight, the snout was long, the one eye he could see was small and ugly. The lips hung loose and purply. He thought of homeless men asleep in doorways dressed in baggy coats and newspaper. *She*, he reminded himself. The mother bear.

The other boy had stopped talking and Jim couldn't think of anything to say either. They turned together and went back to the water and there Jim saw another sad sight. Lulu, trying to win over her brother, while his mother stood by. Guy wore a checked shirt and tan shorts with many pockets. He wasn't smiling, but he had been, and the smile hadn't gone cold. Lulu's voice was way too loud. She was telling him he had saved the day, his sanity, his expertise, she was thanking him, and everything she said he received with a tolerant, distant expression on his face, gazing at some vague point above her head.

Jim watched with a sinking heart. For all her harsh talk, he could see that Lulu wanted her brother to like her. But she embarrassed the man, she got on his nerves, and he wished she would go away, and the more he wished it the more she did whatever made him wish it. Jim knew he had the same effect on people sometimes, trying too hard and not knowing how to quit. He watched Guy turn away abruptly and address his mother. "Nan, you made it back O.K. The city must be an oven." Lulu was left there, like somebody waving at nobody. Until his mother, in speaking to Guy, spoke to them both and brought her back into the fold.

Guy had no time for Lulu and a lot of time for his mother. Jim felt pained for one and gratified for the other.

It was dusk when they paddled home. The moon was rising, a pale glow in the east. They could see the dark forms of the two dogs waiting for them on the dock, and the pale forms of the other canoes, overturned, on shore. Stars were out. You had to be pretty smart to know the constellations. He needed his uncle to find Orion's belt and the Seven Sisters. But there was the Big Dipper, whose stars were the brightest in Ursa Major, meaning Greater Bear, he knew, thanks to his uncle telling him the story of Zeus lusting after Callisto and jealous Hera turning her into a bear, in which form she encountered her hunter-son who was about to shoot her with an arrow when Zeus turned him into a bear too and put them both in the sky. The Greeks put these terrible things where they belonged, up in the heavens, where you wouldn't forget them. Although people did.

Later, he and his mother took a bedtime dip, the air still so warm, then they stretched out on the dock beside Lulu, who was lying on her back, staring at the sky. The moon was higher and brighter, and the stars had faded. The bears were safe up there, Jim thought. Down here one of them was going to be a rug and the other two would end up in a zoo, if what that woman had said was right.

Lulu murmured a line. "'My nativity was under Ursa Major, so that it follows I am rough and lecherous.'"

"That must be Shakespeare," his mother said.

It was *King Lear*. Edmund.

"The bad brother," his mother said to him.

"I've been waiting for a reaction from him all my life," Lulu said. "But why would he come to a play of mine? He wouldn't like it and then what would he say? So he spares himself and he spares me." She paused. "If *he* were in a play, I would move heaven and earth to see him."

A breeze came up and Jim shifted closer to his mother's warm side. She felt his cool after-swimming arms, his eleven-year-old arms. And for a moment she saw her brother's eyes, the blue glint of kindness before they faded away.

From Lulu came a soft snore.

Jim felt his mother smile in the darkness. She said into his ear, "I'm remembering the first time I met her. Those are bats – look – skimming over the water."

He watched the bats and waited, more patient now than when he was small and used to lie in bed in his pyjamas, head tilted back, hands stretched wide, and demand, "Tell me the *whole* story."

"I saw her from behind," she went on, "and fell in love with her auburn hair. It came all the way down her back in the longest ponytail I'd ever seen. I went over to tell her my name and we never looked back." The bats were gliding in and out of view, incredibly fast and free in the dark. "She had these great stories about the Yukon. How every spring the ice jammed up in the Klondike River and there were floods in a matter of minutes. One year their station wagon floated away."

Jim pictured this. "Did they get it back?"

"They must have, because the next spring Lulu's mother told

87

her and her brothers she was going to drive the car to the road and park it there, out of danger. If the river flooded while she was gone, they were to stay in the house and she'd be back to get them in the canoe. So she came back on foot and found them in the living room, side by side on the sofa, with paddles in their hands and their life jackets strapped on tight." Nan laughed a little. She was picturing Lulu about five years old and Guy about seven, very serious, very prepared, sitting next to the older brother who later on would drown in that very river and cast a long, sad shadow over their lives.

"Why did she ask you for a razor blade?" Jim whispered.

Nan drew her head back in order to see his face. "I don't know." She was trying to remember when the razor blade had come up. "Didn't she say she needed it to cut her fishing line?" And then she placed the late-night conversation when Jim was asleep in the hammock. Except he hadn't been asleep. "Why?" She was whispering too.

He was silent, thinking he shouldn't have brought it up.

"Something is worrying you," she said.

It was that picture in his mind of blue tubing lying in a tangled mess all over the forest floor.

"Jim, that razor blade is so dull it doesn't even cut string."

"It could cut something soft, though."

"Like what?"

"I don't know."

"Are you worried she's going to hurt herself? She's not the type to hurt anything, not even herself."

"She's mad at Guy."

"Oh, that. She'd give her life for Guy. She would, you know. You have to understand she adored him when she was a girl. She loves him too much to ever hurt him."

And so it is beside the water. You say things you would never say otherwise. You say them because you realize what you've been thinking.

The next morning, warm and overcast, gave way to a long afternoon of near-rain and rain, the first in a long time.

"Jim?"

He looked up from the hammock to see his mother's questioning face and the shirt he had been partial to once upon a time. She had found it, a blue-and-yellow ball, in the back of his closet.

"I wondered where it went," she said.

It was torn across the back, as he knew before she shook it out, this shirt he had inherited from his brother, Blake.

She sat on the far end of the hammock, and he and the hammock bounced a little, then settled. It wouldn't be hard to mend, she told him. He shouldn't fret about that. Then resting her hand on his lower leg, "Were you in a fight at school?"

"I wasn't in a fight."

"I wish you would tell me what happened."

"I'll tell you later."

"Tell me now."

He went back to his book. "I won't tell you later either."

He was reading his uncle's collection of Pogo comic books.

"Was Pog named after Pogo?" he said.

"You'll have to ask Lulu about that."

His favourites in these tales of Okefenokee Swamp were melancholy porcupine and the trio of bats in their raggedy overalls and top hats, and Albert the Alligator, of course, and Pogo himself, who always brought the lunch. He shouldn't have thrown the shirt into the back of the closet, that was dumb. He had hidden it first, folded up carefully, at the bottom of his other shirts in a drawer, then forgotten about it, more or less, until discovering it, still folded, in the pile of clothes she had packed into his suitcase and brought here. But he wasn't going to be drawn out about it. He turned another page. He loved this strange and knowable world into which frightening intruders sometimes came, though at the end there was always the sweet Christmas message, when peace reigned over the swamp at night.

Rain showers were all around them, darkening the horizon in every direction, and then they were upon them. Wind and rain: the two sounds were one. In the middle of the afternoon he had to pull the chain on the reading lamp at the head of his bunk bed, by which time, stretched out behind his barricade of books, he was drifting in and out, too, like the rain. Suddenly it pounded down hard for about fifteen minutes. After that, the sky was a light that came on and he turned off the one behind him.

He heard Lulu and his mother in the kitchen. From the smells reaching him he gathered they were cooking up delicious things. He heard his mother say, "Lulu, what do you want to be?" And he frowned. Didn't they know it was too late for such questions, they were too *old*. But here came the answer and it was a good one. "A hero out of a myth who bides his time and then strikes," Lulu said. "I want the male parts. I get the secondary women." With sudden vehemence, "I need a new agent. Stanley is useless. Oh, not entirely. He told me to give the self-denigrating voice in my head a name. 'Lulu, give it a name.' I gave it a name. Gertrude. Gertrude Bumfuck."

He left his books and joined them at the kitchen table.

"You didn't hear that," Lulu said, ruffling his mop of hair, which he liked her to do, since it made him feel as beloved as a beloved dog. He asked her if Pog was named after Pogo.

"No, after a lake in northern Ontario my aunt used to go to. But that would have been even better."

His mother said that supper wouldn't be ready for another hour, so he went down to the dock and fished for a while, and when he came back he heard her too-eager voice on the telephone. "Well, you should go eat then, you're starving. But may I call you again tomorrow?" Hanging up – the telephone rested on its own small table in the kitchen – she turned in her chair, sadness and disappointment playing across her face. "I asked Blake to come for a visit," she said. "'We haven't seen you since Christmas,' I told him, 'we miss you.' So he's going to think about it."

A minute into the call, her firstborn had pleaded hunger, forcing her to hold onto the shirt tail of their conversation for all she was worth.

"When you're Blake's age, you'll be busy too," she said. "But your dad will be here tomorrow. He'll leave this evening and drive through the night."

That evening the air was soft after the rain. Nan felt a breeze come through the kitchen windows and thought of George packing his bags into the trunk of the rental car and getting underway after dark. Her free and easy days would end with his arrival. George took up a lot of room, it had to be said.

These peaceful moments before everything changes. She knew them. In the middle of a Sunday afternoon, you might turn around to see the first snow of the year falling on everything in sight and whatever you were doing gives way to the old yearning for a deeper life. Or it might be a beautiful evening, as it is now, she thought, and you look up from slicing the coffee cake and see the ghost of your brother serving food with never a wasted motion, his fingers longer than yours and more precise, dancing a little above and around the cake, taking its measure before cutting the first of several evenly proportioned pieces. Summer light spreads low through the woods and July won't last forever.

A vehicle was coming down the lane. Nan, alert to the sound of something bigger than a car, paused as she passed out plates of cake to Lulu and Jim at the kitchen table. And soon a tread she recognized came up the steps.

Lulu raised her eyes and watched her brother open the screen door and come through the verandah into the kitchen, nodding at her and Jim, and fastening his smile on Nan. Pog got to his feet and rested his muzzle on Lulu's knee. She stroked his head. Dogs know

91

everything, she thought, watching Nan smile her welcome and root around in the drawer for another fork.

Settling himself at the table beside his sister, Guy fell upon his piece of coffee cake like a lost love. Lulu put hers aside, half-eaten.

It was hard to watch the two of them together if you cared about either of them. Jim, across the table, had to put down his fork too.

Guy had come to make a report on the bear cubs and what Jim noticed most was how he looked at his mother, and nobody else, as he talked. The cubs were drinking water and eating the berries from Julie's garden plus the last of last summer's berries from her freezer. On Monday morning he would take them to the wildlife officer in Perth. Guy talked with his hands, square working hands, weathered, scraped on the knuckles. He framed his remarks by spreading his hands as if conveying the size of a hefty fish he had caught.

Lulu asked a question then, which Guy answered by saying to Nan that he thought either the zoo in Winnipeg or the one in Toronto. It was weird, Jim thought, the way he never looked at Lulu. It reminded him of the way Blake could be sometimes – talking over their mother's head as if she wasn't there.

So it was no surprise when the quarrel began. Guy remarked that the cubs were lucky to be on Canadian soil rather than in the gun-happy United States, where they would be dead by now. And Lulu scoffed. "Come on," she said. "Your gun-happy Canadian neighbour just shot their mother." He ignored her. And she said, "Canadians have no modesty."

Guy looked at her then. "We're *all* modesty."

"You're smug." She was running her hand down Pog's back, combing her fingers through his silky coat. "A more complacent country it would be hard to find. English Canada I'm talking about. It's no wonder Quebec wants out."

Jim could see it was always like this between them. They always took each other too seriously. They were always fighting leftover fights. They always had to be right.

Lulu held her brother's baleful gaze and went on. "They're convinced that in their *quiet* way they're superior to Americans. English Canadians, I'm speaking of. Quebecers have their own hang-ups."

"They love Americans," his mother said.

"Yes."

"Because they're not Canadians." His mother could be bitter.

But Lulu's eyes were on her brother. "Canadians think dull and polite is so much better than loud and brash. Dad believed that." She raised her left hand a few inches and let it fall on the table with a thud. "It's just boring."

Jim recognized on Guy's face the same icy look he had fastened on Lulu when they'd trespassed on his property that day. And when he spoke his voice was wintry too. "Dad hated being quiet. Canadians hate their quietness."

Jim saw his mother look over at Guy. "That's true," she said, sounding thoughtful.

"And if I'm right, you're wrong," he said to Lulu, leaning in and resting his arms on the table.

Jim caught his mother's eye. He knew she would try to rein in the ill feeling, but didn't expect to have much luck.

"I'm not wrong. Canadians have no modesty and they have no pride. Forever casting about for crumbs of international recognition."

"Ah, Lulu, you're harsh," his mother said with a smile. What she really wanted to say was that they were like children at dusk, crazy and competitive. Grow up, both of you.

"I'm not wrong. Dad hated having nothing to say, but he hated easy talkers even more. I mean, maybe he didn't like himself very much, but he *really* disliked anyone different."

"Lu," said Guy, "you don't know the first thing about him."

It was like a play, Jim thought, or a movie. The animosity between them. And he remembered that Hera and Zeus were brother and sister as well as husband and wife, which was why they really could not stand each other, not for one minute.

"I know the first thing," she said, "and the second and the third."

"You don't know *anything*," Guy said.

Lulu smiled, as though she had heard this insult a million times. She bent sideways and sank her teeth into her brother's wrist.

The yelp and look of utter disbelief made Jim laugh in a strangled sort of way. He couldn't help it. It was hilarious. Guy was staring at the teeth marks and spit, and he would have punched his sister in the arm – he raised his fist – had she not been ready. She had her fists up first.

Nan leant forward. "For God's sake, stop it, you two! Grow up!" And they lowered their fists but not the hate in their faces.

"I'm sorry, Nan," Guy said. He was rubbing his wrist and he was furious.

Jim watched his mother get up from the table and go over to the sink. "The two of you rip me apart," she said, and she was kneading her chest with one hand.

She turned on the tap and filled a glass and raised it to her lips, taking a few swallows before setting the glass on the counter.

In the silence they heard a loon call from the far side of the bay and another loon answer. The calls went on and on, the two loons outdoing each other. It was a sound they all loved and they stayed quiet until it was over.

Lulu got up and went to the window that overlooked the lake. "I'd love to see a loon's nest. I've never seen one."

"I can show you," Jim said, coming to her side.

"Can you, darling?"

He knew two places on an island at the wilderness end of the lake. His uncle had taken him and he would take Lulu.

Her glass sat on the wide sill in the verandah: never empty, never full. Birds had birdbaths, horses had water troughs, Lulu had her glass. She nursed herself through the days and nights, Jim noticed, sipping, refilling partway, sipping.

That evening, after Guy left, she turned to his mother and said, "My brother likes you, Nan. He wanted to see you. That's why he came."

Nan blushed and said nothing. They were on the verandah and the air was still twisted and awkward from Guy's visit.

Lulu said, "He has always demolished me. That's his style. He learned it from my father, who practised on my mother."

She was drinking wine, not gin, but steadily. She went into the kitchen to refill her glass to the two-thirds mark, came back out and resettled herself in the corner of the sofa. Staring into her glass, she began talking about the past.

Her reminiscing voice was different from his mother's. His mother's came from a place where she wanted to be, while Lulu's seemed to rise out of sharp rocks jumbled all about. She was talking about the little grocery store her grandparents used to own on the Quebec side of the river, on the corner of Notre-Dame-de-l'Île and rue Saint-Etienne in Hull. "My mother's parents," she said. "I worked behind the cash the last two summers in high school. You'd moved away by then."

"That was when we moved to Toronto," his mother explained to him, "the summer after I finished grade ten."

She had lit two oil lamps and they cast a yellow glow, peaceful, both dogs asleep, though Lulu was not at peace: she was brooding and drinking her wine. "What a different world it was over there. The other side of the river. My father had a job in Hull for a while. That's how they met." She was remembering family car rides across the iron bridge, looking down and seeing on the far shore the mountains of pulpwood being sprayed, a constant wetting to avoid fire. She was recalling how the Ontario side of the bridge was paved and the Quebec side wasn't. How halfway across your wheels dropped a bit and hit wooden boards that rumbled, and you knew you were somewhere poorer, more backward, and you felt both excited and a little ashamed. She had met a boy the second summer. He walked into the store one day. Jean-Guy. Dark hair, pale skin, dark eyes. He said his name the way it should be said, the French way, not the English. He began to seek her out, arriving as she was finishing up her afternoon shift, speaking to her in French, and they would go for walks along the river and over to the chip stand at the baseball diamond and eventually wend their way back to the wooden swing with two facing benches under the big maple behind the store. Holding hands, kissing. A summer love, and it worked on two levels since she loved speaking French as well. Her mother's language, not that her mother had the chance to use it except with her own parents. It ended late in August when her father came to collect her and proceeded to interrogate Jean-Guy about who he was and what he was doing with his life. Jean-Guy's English wasn't even bad, but his gracefulness and fluency vanished, his personality disappeared, and suddenly he sounded awkward and uneducated. Worse than that, she didn't have the courage to speak up for him in French. "Jean-Guy," she said aloud to herself, giving it the French pronunciation, "not *Guy*." She was lost in her thoughts, talking to herself and to people who weren't there. Night poured into the verandah and the past poured into her head. That anti-French shit. Her brother got it from their father. Anti-French, anti-their mother. She raised her head and looked towards the kitchen, seeing Guy as he had appeared earlier that evening, so sure of himself and refusing to look at her, like a bull fattened on disdain. And she burst out, "Yet six months ago he told me he wanted to be close!" Throwing her head back, she stared up at the ceiling, locked in tortured thoughts.

"Lulu," his mother said, her voice gentle and reaching across to her, "*talk* to him."

Lulu's smile was bitter. "You mean, have it out with him?" And Jim caught the echo of their earlier conversation about Janet Hepburn. "There's no point."

"He feels guilty," his mother said. "It's obvious. He can't even look at you." She was speaking in a low voice because sound carries farther than you think over water. They could hear music and talk from a cottage across the bay.

96

Lulu turned to set her glass on the windowsill, then swung back, the glass still in her hand, her face tormented. "Guy was the apple of my father's eye. But then, he *admired* my father. You know what I can't figure out?"

"What would that be?" Nan's voice was sad.

"Was it because I didn't admire my father that he didn't love me? Or because he didn't love me that I didn't admire him?"

Nan said, "You're loved."

It was late, but it was summer. The lateness didn't matter.

Some time after that, after his mother was in bed and so was he, Jim heard the click of the porch door and Lulu's step on the path. She passed by his window, then turned and spoke to Pog as if to a person. "I'll be back," she said.

She got into her car and the minutes passed. Maybe she was looking in the glove compartment for a map, maybe a bottle. After a while the old Buick started up and pulled away – tyres on gravelly dirt – a pure summer sound that took Jim to the end of the lane and out onto the road, and then lost itself in the quiet reaches of the night.

In bed he thought back to something that had happened earlier in the day, during one of the intervals when it wasn't raining. Lulu had gone down to the water with a book, only to be driven back by a couple of deer flies that would not leave her alone. She left the book on the kitchen table and he picked it up and leafed through it. It was a collection of plays.

"Lulu is wonderful on stage," his mother said to him, noticing the book in his hands and speaking with utter conviction. Lulu made a wry, pleased face. The compliment soothed her. Water the parched lawn; see it turn green.

His mother recalled seeing her as Hedda Gabler at university, finding her in her dressing room before the show. "Your hands were ice cold."

97

"Your mother held my icy hands in her warm ones. That's what gave me the courage to go on stage. Darling, have I ever told you that?"

He fell asleep, reliving this moment in an old and abiding friendship.

She came back very late. Jim heard tyres on gravel and opened his eyes. It was pitch-black, the middle of the night. Briefly, car beams scooped out his room before Lulu's Buick swung in beside the Chevette. Then, almost in the same motion, she backed up and the world split open with a high, narrow scream of pain.

He saw it all without seeing it. Pog approaching with his stiff welcome, Pog run over by the back wheel.

He lifted his head off the pillow and saw his mother fly past his door in her nightgown. The outside light went on and he pictured what his mother saw: Lulu and her dog, who licked her hand, licked her hand, and could not get up.

Jim dropped his head back on the pillow and stared at the ceiling. He heard Lulu's sobs, her blurry voice, her broken-hearted noise, and after a while his mother came into his room. "Stay in bed, Jim," she said to his open eyes. She reached into the cupboard and pulled out blankets.

"Is he dead?"

"Just stay here. I won't be long."

"Where are you going?"

"Nowhere. Just outside."

She left with the blankets. He pulled his sweatshirt on over his pyjamas and followed her in bare feet through the porch and down the steps. He stood uncertainly on the bottom step. Lulu was a heap of sorriness on the ground. Pog lay next to her. A blanket lay across his body, a blanket covered her shoulders. Headlights punched out a hole in the woods.

He went inside and got a glass of water. His grandmother, at a low ebb, always revived with water. Duke was awake on the porch, his head raised, his old old eyes trained on the screen door.

Lulu looked up when he gave her the water. Her eyes were naked and in a million pieces. "Thank you, Jimmy."

What shame, he thought, what guilt. Running over your own dog. At least he had never done that. She took a swallow and began to choke and the water spilled.

His mother took the glass and said to him, "Go back to bed now. I'll be in soon."

He knelt down instead. Under the blanket Pog twitched and shuddered. His back legs paddled. Blood came from his mouth and nose.

"What do I do?" Lulu said.

"What if I call Guy." And his mother stood up and went inside.

He was alone with Lulu and for the first time wished he wasn't. He could feel the distance inside him, as if he were edging away with his eyes down. Certain smells found his stomach, however. Cigarettes, booze, dog, warm blood. His stomach heaved and settled. Tears came into his eyes.

His mother was back. She knelt beside them and put her arm around Lulu. She said that Guy was coming right away.

"What did you tell him?" Lulu's voice was thick. "I ran over my dog, that's what you told him."

"He knows it was an accident. It was an accident."

"It's the worst thing I've ever done."

Jim became aware of a stone digging into his knee and shifted a little. Lulu's hands holding Pog's head were clumsy, useless.

"What's Guy going to do?" he asked his mother.

She put her hand on his arm and didn't answer.

He remembered seeing a flopping pigeon on the way to school. Hit by a car, flopping about next to the kerb. Another pigeon gazed at it from only a foot away. Nobody stopped. Everybody just kept going. What should he have done? It was something you should know. It was something everybody should know.

Jim was still huddled next to Lulu when Guy bent down and with surprising gentleness kissed the top of his sister's head. "Lu," he said, "go inside. I'll take care of things." He helped her stand up. She was unsteady, looking down at her dog, her face blotched and wet, her arms hanging loose. Guy put his hand on her shoulder and she reached up and held it, held his hand in place with her own, pressed and held it.

Jim didn't want to like Lulu less and Guy more. He stood up too. But he couldn't help wondering if he would ever be grown up enough to behave the way Guy was behaving right now.

His mother took Lulu by the arm and the three of them went inside, into the kitchen, where she pulled out a chair for her and asked him to put on the kettle.

Then, "That's enough," she said sharply to him at the sink. "You don't have to fill it to the top." As if he were stupid.

"Then why don't *you* do it," he yelled at her.

He watched her face go angry, then shift to sorry. She came over to him and took the kettle out of his hands. "It doesn't matter," she said. "I'm sorry." And she led him from the kitchen to his lower bunk, helped him get in, and sat with him, stroking his cold hands and wrists.

"You said she wouldn't hurt anything," he whispered.

"She didn't mean to."

"Why did she back up like that?"

"I don't know."

"She was drunk."

His mother continued to stroke his hands. After a long moment she made as if to get up but sat down again. "Oh, Jim," she said.

She turned and looked into the kitchen.

"We have to help her." And her voice was heavy and shocked. "You run over a part of yourself when you run over something that has such a place in your heart."

7

JIM WOKE UP SLOWLY TO A DIFFERENT WORLD. IT WAS
late in the morning and quiet. A page of a newspaper turned in
the kitchen.

He slipped out of bed and there was his father at the table. He
flung himself at him and his father held him tight. "You're glad to
see me," George said with emotion, and they were both overwhelmed
by their mutual affection.

He hadn't seen his father for many weeks and had forgotten
how old he looked. Everything about him was smaller and older
and more tired, except his eyebrows, which were even bushier and
springier. "We can have breakfast together," his father said, obviously so cheered by the prospect that Jim realized he had been
sitting there for some time, all alone.

It turned out he had timed his arrival to coincide with them
getting up, meaning to astonish them with his bag of fresh bagels.
But everybody on this pleasant Saturday morning, halfway through
July, was sleeping late. George had thought at first they were out
on the water, fishing.

"I would have crawled into bed too, but somebody was already
there."

His father had an unreadable look on his face when he said
that. Pushing back his chair, he went over to the fridge and began
to rummage around for eggs and milk. "I guess that's your mother's
friend. Lulu."

It was silent upstairs. They were still asleep.

"Why don't you go up and tell them breakfast is ready," his father said.

"O.K."

Jim went up the creaky stairs and down the short hall and stood in the open doorway. His mother was asleep beside Lulu, close, with an arm around her, exactly the way she slept with his father.

Nan opened her eyes and saw him and smiled, reaching out her hand as she had to George a couple of hours ago when she woke to see him in the corner chair, looking at her from the depths of his bleakness. George had turned his back on her and gone downstairs, where she knew he was waiting for her to join him, but she had stayed with Lulu.

Jim took his mother's hand. She squeezed his and whispered, "She finally fell asleep a few hours ago. Tell your father I'm coming down."

Nan came down alone, hair combed, eyes exhausted. She saw Jim setting the table and smiled, "You're helping your dad," as her glance went to the serving bowl of scrambled eggs, the fresh bagels sliced in half. "George, you've made breakfast! Thank you." Only then did she turn and look directly at her husband. "Thank you," she repeated and went over to him standing next to the toaster and put her arms around him.

George kept on making toast; he wouldn't give up his mood.

And so Jim stepped in, as he often did, and gathered both of them into a hug, crushing them together until they were laughing in protest.

His father said, "Alright, son. That's enough."

"George, we've had quite a night," his mother said, and she launched into the story, directing her voice at his good ear.

Later, Jim would find Lulu by the water, gazing out at the lake. She wiped her nose with the back of her hand, wiped her eyes, her nose again; dug around in her pockets; found them empty. "Shit."

In a fairy tale she would have shrivelled up and blown away. But there was actually more of her rather than less: more suffering flesh.

He offered to take her to see the loons' nests.

She turned and said, "What a prince you are."

That afternoon they would bury Pog wrapped in a clean blanket in the hole Lulu dug at the far edge of the scythed field. Then she took their hands, his mother's hand and his (George didn't join them), and hummed and sang "St James Infirmary Blues," hitting the bull's-eye of his grief with such accuracy that tears gushed into his eyes.

He wished his father liked her. But George kept his distance, never looking at her except in a strange and fishy-eyed way.

* * *

To get to the loons' nests they paddled out of their bay, keeping to the left and crossing another small bay and skirting more shore. Then they turned west into the long narrowness they called the dog's leg, at the foot of which were two small islands, one much smaller than the other.

On the grassy point of the smaller island, a point not much bigger than a single bed, there was a subtle indentation the size of a large round platter directly below a sheared-off rock. His aunt and uncle the summer before had spotted the loon backed by the rock and just above the water, her long neck lowered like a dancer resting her torso on the floor. Through binoculars they'd observed the red eyes, open, watchful. She was hiding herself from them; early July and still on her egg. And here it was, July 15, and the empty nest was nothing but a breast-made depression and the depression a matter of soft earth and the pine needles that happened to be there, and that's all.

The second nest, as inconspicuous, was at the foot of the same tiny, grassy point, with a small cedar to the left and a small alder to the right and low bushes of sweet gale at the water's edge.

"I would have my nest here too," Lulu said.

They let the breezes carry them, drifting, from the island to the shore, where they poked the canoe into a channel made by beavers. They paddled and pushed forward into deep foliage until they were marooned among ferns and tiny frogs hopping like fleas. Hidden animal places were off to the side, where no motorboats could go. Pond weeds. Burr weed.

He couldn't explain. How your heart corresponds to a place and leaps with recognition and joy.

Lulu said, "Maybe I won't kill myself after all." She was in the bow of the canoe, turned towards him, and he was in the stern, his arms aching a little from all the paddling. "Thank you, Jim." She meant something besides their little journey. "I thought you might write me off. I'm not sure what I would have done if I were you." She reached out her hand and touched the ferns.

He looked around him. Back in the city, fresh from the lake, his mind before going to sleep would swim with leaves, twigs, branches, greenery. Cars would pass below, garbage cans would rattle. There were rats in the garbage and one summer their neighbour César had driven a stick right through one, killing it on the spot. Yet upon closing his eyes the green forms swam up.

"Lulu?"

"Jim."

But he couldn't bring out the questions pressing on his mind.

"Fire away," she said. "I don't mind." He wanted to give her the third degree, she suspected, and who could blame him.

And so Jim would learn that she had forgotten her wallet, that was why she had backed up as she had: she had left it sitting on a table in the bar. He would learn that her brother kept a tyre iron in his truck. It was clean and quick if it was done right. A blow to the head.

He tried to imagine doing it himself and asked if she ever had. The flopping pigeon was at the front of his mind again. Putting something out of its misery.

"I killed a dying squirrel once," she said. "It was near the kerb, run over. You need something hard – a rock, or a big stick. I used a rock." She looked to see the effect of her words and he seemed stoic and interested. "What else are you wanting to know?"

He considered. "Why aren't you famous?"

She laughed a little. "Goodness," she said. "What a question." She dug her paddle into the mucky bottom and pushed them back so they were floating in more open water. "Maybe it's just as well."

It was such a private, secluded spot. All the reflections in the water from the trees. The canoe as simple as a pencil.

"I told on someone once," he heard himself say. "He cheated and I told the teacher."

She nodded slowly. She knew he was telling her something he hadn't told anyone else. "And then what happened?"

He couldn't talk about it. "Nothing," he said.

She nodded again. "I'm dealing with nothing too. It goes on and on."

He wanted to keep talking about everything that was hard to talk about, without talking about himself. "You said it was the worst thing you'd ever done."

"There are lots of those, Jim."

She met his expectant, churned-up eyes, and said, "Right now, I can't think of anything worse."

The simple way she acknowledged the enormity of what she had done had the desired effect. His face cleared. He looked less burdened. And so she took up the paddle and he picked up his, and they applied themselves to getting home.

That evening, over supper, Lulu told them she would be poking along, heading back to Toronto in the morning. They had been eating in silence.

George said, "That's a long drive. You'll want to leave early."

"I don't think so," Nan said. She put down her knife and fork.

The awkwardness caught Jim in the throat. It was hard to swallow and hard to breathe.

Lulu had a sad and wonderful smile on her face. "We go back," she said to his father.

George cleared his throat. His mother opened her mouth to speak and Lulu stopped her by saying, "Nan."

His father then made an effort to converse, though it pained him. He said, "You're the first Lulu I've met."

"Louise."

"Oh."

"My grandmother's name. On my father's side. Louise Irene. Nan knew her." She looked across at his mother and smiled again.

His mother filled their cups. Even though his father shook his head, she filled his cup to the brim with tea he didn't want. She was going to have her way. "Lulu, stay till the end of summer," she said, for she was thinking how much happier she had been living with Lulu than with George, how much she was going to miss her. Why should a husband displace a friend?

"There *is* something I'd like to do," Lulu said.

She wanted to take her tent to the island in the far bay, not the one with the loons' nests but the larger island alongside, and stay there for a week. No booze, no food; water and fresh air. She wanted to clean herself out, body and soul. It was time for a radical self-assessment, she said, with a shame-faced laugh, and shame rounded her shoulders and spread across her face.

His father offered her the use of the yellow canoe.

"Thank you, George. I appreciate that."

At the end of the meal George tried again to bring his influence to bear. Wasn't it time to take the old dog to the vet and have him put down? It would be a kindness.

Nan gave him a hard look. "Not yet."

Despite the strained silence, George blundered on. "I'll take him for you," he said.

106

"You don't care about him," Nan said, stating a fact. "Why should you decide?"

"*Dad*."

"What?"

And finally his father woke up to the effect he was having on a household in mourning for a dog, and he ducked his head in angry embarrassment.

The next afternoon Jim and his mother, carrying the paddles, followed Lulu down to the water. Everything she needed she had squeezed into the knapsack on her back. They helped her arrange the pack in the canoe, situating it forward to balance her weight, and as she paddled out of their bay they heard her singing the song they both loved, the one about only knowing you must be brave: "'Or lie a coward, a craven coward, or lie a coward in my grave'."

*　*　*

George hung on the edges, ill-defined, less important. He was "the rest of the family" the way English Canada was "the rest of Canada". R.O.C. for short. That summer Quebec seemed serene in its power, secure, as if all packed up and ready to leave.

George liked to have a daily newspaper. Every day he drove twenty minutes to the nearest store to pick up the *Ottawa Citizen*. He, too, became familiar with the man his wife liked to call the dark prince.

"I wish to God he'd died," Nan said, staring at the picture in the paper of Lucien Bouchard, leader of the separatist Bloc Québécois – his pain-etched face, his black suit, the cane – and thinking back to his miraculous recovery the year before from the near-fatal disease that took his leg. He had the bluish-white skin that sometimes goes with dark hair. Moonlight without the beauty of moonlight, she thought to herself, of this skin that refuses to tan. "The separatists might just win," she said, "because a peg-legged man of sorrow is leading them to their destiny."

Intrigued, Jim studied the photograph for traces of the seafaring man with one leg and saw a big-faced, moody man in a business suit, devoid of any of the good cheer that Long John Silver had deployed to fool the other Jim. But maybe this man was also "too deep and too ready and too clever".

"Nancy," his father said, "you can't wish a man dead just because you don't like his politics."

She could. She could also admire him and sometimes she did. Sometimes she caught herself thinking that separation might be the best thing for everybody. There was a certain intoxication in watching things come apart, even a country you loved. She pondered her marriages, the reasons for having left, the reasons for leaving. But then there was everything that held her back and that everything was Jim.

George was more reasonable on the subject of Quebec and less so on everything else. Jim heard his accusations one night when he was in the hammock and his parents were doing the dishes.

"Nancy, you love that dog more than you love me."

To which his mother did not reply. And then, even more provocatively, "You left my bed and climbed into hers."

"*Your* bed?"

"You snuggled up to her."

"I took her a cup of coffee!"

"She snuggled up to you."

"George, do not antagonize me or I'll crack this cup over your miserable skull."

In her fury that he wanted to deprive her of the pleasure of her oldest friend, Nan swung the cup into the dish rack, bringing it down with such force that it chipped her favourite bowl. Then she swore and it was a word Jim had never heard before. She used it twice.

"Pisswilly," he whispered into his pillow and grinned.

*

He went fishing with his father. They stayed out in the rain, sun, rain, sun, getting wet and drying out and catching trout. There he was with his three: big, medium, and small. And his father, who had not caught a single one.

"Did I catch that one?" Pointing to the one in the middle.

Jim half smiled. He was wearing his uncle's fedora, though it was a little too big for him, despite his unruly hair.

"No?" George said, his eyes pleading. "You caught them all?"

The final burst of sunshine had dried them out, all but the damp seats of their pants. Only when Jim was bringing the canoe alongside the dock did he notice the audience on shore, half-hidden by cedars. Guy was holding a little girl by the hand. On the other side of her was someone in a blue dress. Guy's wife, it must be. But no, the someone else was Nan, who never wore dresses at the lake. Stepping forward, she wanted to know if they had had any luck.

Jim didn't answer. He was scrambling out of the canoe and steadying it so his father could get out without falling flat. George stood up and promptly lost his balance, flinging out a hand and bracing himself on Jim's shoulder before executing an ungainly stumble onto the dock in full view of the Canadians on shore. "Daddy caught one and I caught two," Jim called out. He had not intended to say Daddy. It came off his lips in the same surge of loyalty that made a fisherman of his father.

"But we'll eat Jim's beauty first," George said.

To have a father you could not admire. To be fond of him all the same and sorry for him. To wonder why your mother had married him, instead of a man like Guy.

This was the summer when Jim began to call his father George. It had the same effect as putting on his uncle's fedora: he felt grown-up and apart.

The little girl, Guy's four-year-old daughter, Irene, didn't say a word. She was the child of his second marriage and spending a month with him and Julie at the farm. Irene studied her sneakers.

She was the kind of child of whom a parent says apologetically, "She is very shy". But Guy did not apologize. He talked to her, kneeling down to show her the lures Jim had used. "Jim's lures," he said, and Jim knew he knew who had caught the fish, and felt a wave of gratitude.

Guy had dropped by to see how his sister was. He didn't stay long.

"I thought you said they couldn't stand each other," George said afterwards. He spoke out of a spirit of contradiction. It was an old and jealous habit.

"He came by because he knows she's shattered," Nan said, impatient with him for being so literal, so wide of the mark. "He didn't know she'd gone to the island."

"I thought he came to see *you*," George said evenly.

And to that she had no reply, since he wasn't so wide of the mark, after all.

"I'm at odds with myself, Jim," his father confided the next time they were on the water. "Your mother and Lulu are such pals. I don't have any friends like that."

Jim didn't know what to say. His father's wistfulness depressed and troubled him, even if he understood it well enough.

"I'm too old for your mother. Twelve years. That's a big gap."

"It's not so much." It was, though. It was more than his own lifetime.

"She has her enthusiasms. She gets carried away. I'm not like that. I'm not passionate."

"You're passionate." He was in the bow, trolling, while his father paddled slowly and awkwardly in the stern. They were facing each other.

"Am I, Jim? What am I passionate about?"

"The Yankees. The *Times*."

His father shifted his baseball cap farther back on his head. "I was thinking you might come home with me."

This he had not expected. He darted a swift glance at his father.

"Think about it," his father said, promising in the next breath that they would go to Yankee stadium for a couple of games, they would eat takeout every night.

"I don't know. I like it here." Then he had to repeat himself, raising his voice. "I like it *here*."

He saw his father's hurt gaze reach across to the wilderness side of the lake and linger on the islands, the trees, the shorelines, the rock; and not a park bench in sight. "I'm a city boy, Jim. This is your mother's world, not mine. The more she blossoms, the more I retreat." He pulled his handkerchief out of his back pocket and wiped his forehead. "I haven't told her that."

But he would, Jim knew. He would tell her one of these days just as he had told her that she loved that dog more than she loved him.

"Think about it. You don't have to decide right now."

"What about Mommy?"

"She has Duke. She has Lulu. I don't have anybody. Think it over," his father said again. "I won't be going back until late next week. We'd have the month of August together."

A boy ashamed of his father and protective, and with secret shames of his own. He thought of his mother's old enemy, Janet Hepburn, and could see it happening to him. He could see himself making an apology and having it met with the same deeply unsatisfying response: forgiveness up to a point. He forgave his father up to a point for diluting his fishing triumph, since George didn't know what his uncle had taught him, namely, the best spots, the best lures, the necessary patience. Guy never would have done that to a fellow fisherman, though, let alone to his son.

That week Jim took to spending more time alone, either on the water or upstairs in his uncle's study. He retreated in order to escape the tension between his parents, who used to be happier together, he was sure of it. He remembered how they would hold hands when they walked down the street. They didn't do that anymore. His uncle's study had a narrow couch, wooden desk, an Underwood typewriter, and shelves full of old books and magazines. He hunkered down among the old *New Yorkers*. If you like different points of view, and Jim did, then you like old magazines. They open doors into other worlds and you slip in so easily. He used the typewriter too. Typing with two fingers THE SKY IS BLUE, he discovered he had made it so, even though it was raining outside and was supposed to rain all day.

HIS PARENTS STAYED TOGETHER. And there was the happy end of the story.

"I heard you typing," Nan said when he came down one morning and found her at the kitchen table reading the paper about the latest polls in Quebec. They showed the federalists firmly in the lead, but that could change overnight, she told him. In politics anything could happen. She was wearing the black cardigan she favoured for its two deep pockets. He leaned against her and she adjusted herself and put her arm around him.

He asked her what she thought of people who cheated.

"Do you mean, is it all right to cheat? It's not." And looking into his face, "Jim, who are we talking about? You?"

He shook his head. He was trying to get her to say something he wanted to hear but didn't want to say. That it wasn't the worst thing in the world to tell on someone who cheated. It was one of the worst things to cheat.

"Your father?"

His eyes went to the floor. Then he surprised himself by expressing a thought he hadn't even formed. "He feels left out."

She was giving him her full attention.

"It's like what happened to you," he said.

"To me?"

"You do everything with Lulu."

"When she's here. She's not here now."

Dry crumbs dug into the bare skin of her right wrist. She hardly felt them. Sometimes you wake up to the history beside you. The man lying beside you in bed. The province adjoining yours. The country. She sat quite still, her face wide open.

In her case it had been summer too. Away with her family, swimming every day, immersed in the glory of a northern lake. At the end of August, home again and knocking on Janet's door, she discovered that everything had changed. For some reason she didn't understand, she had become unwanted.

George came down in his pyjamas and they fell silent. Every morning he made himself a big bowl of oatmeal porridge. He busied himself at the stove now with a saucepan and measuring cup. "Son," he said, "your mother says it's *not* a fine line, but it seems like a fine line to me. She won't eat porridge because it's slippery. But I say it's creamy. What is the difference between creamy and slippery?"

"It's not a fine line," his mother said. "It's a Berlin wall."

"What would you say is creamy?" his father said.

"Chocolate mousse is creamy," his mother answered. "Whipped cream is creamy. Have you seen the bottom of a porridge pot that needs to be scrubbed out? That's slippery."

She wasn't alone in her views either, she said. Lulu loathed porridge. They were both refugees from porridge-wracked childhoods. Her voice was emphatic but more entertained than it usually was around his father.

"Jim, we got off track." She was ruminating still. "You asked me about cheating."

Morning light was slanting across the table and his mother was going to tell him what she thought.

"Remember Jacob and Esau?" she said.

He did. In his opinion it was one of the best stories, full of tricks and double-dealing. Under the fleece, behind the veil, lay the sneaky truth.

"Jacob was the biggest cheater of all time," she said, "yet the world is full of Jacobs and there aren't any Esaus." It was hardly fair. Did he know anybody named Esau? Neither did she.

"Ditto for me," George said.

"I love Esau," she declared with a burst of feeling. "And one of the reasons I love him is that he forgave his lousy cheat of a brother."

"Here, here," his father said. "Let's hear it for forgiving lying cheats."

"Even cheating fishermen," his mother said, and Jim smiled.

"*Especially* fishermen," his father said.

The next morning Jim was up at dawn. He had his fishing rod and his fedora and the Thermos of cocoa his mother had made ready the night before. He had his life jacket. He had his thoughts. He wondered if Lulu was up, had the feeling she was, and pictured her coming out of her tent and down to the water's edge, splashing water on her face, contemplating the view. He missed her, but paddled in the other direction as she would have wished him to do.

Soon the sun was warming his sunrise bones. It was while he was in the calm lee of one of the islands, facing the last of the sunrise, that he became aware of the otters, three of them, then four, their heads rising like periscopes to inspect him. He kept still, not moving his paddle until the first small breeze gradually took him far enough away that he had to begin a stealthy pursuit. They were swimming over to the biggest island and along its shore, snorting, snuffling through their whiskers, and the younger two squeaking, and then all of them disappearing, their home apparently that rock face full of cracks and crevices and holes in which to hide. From deep within the rocks came their tough-guy talk, loud, a big squeak, and a deeper grrrr. The grrr made Jim grin with happiness.

Another family of four. Their address: under the dying birch to the left of the dead hemlocks. In the place of the hemlocks more maples would grow, his uncle had told him, and the outbreak of loopers would subside as rapidly as it arose, you'll see. He had been proven right, since this summer there weren't many loopers at all. And so catastrophes get softened, Jim learned, and you persuade yourself that you can live without certain things and so can the world.

His father wasn't tough. He didn't growl or yell or strut or preen. He hid behind his hand. Spoke from behind his hand. Came out with nervous, restless little laughs. Had a way of saying "very good, very good" to fill a silence. It wore you out after a while, the soft speaking, the hard hearing. He had to wonder if his father hadn't been quite different once upon a time, when his mother first met him, say, on that hiking trail in Vermont. Hiking wasn't something his father ever did now. Yet he had been adventurous enough for that, and adventurous enough to have three wives. There was his dead wife, his ex-wife, and his current wife. There were two grown-up daughters in California who almost never visited. Jim never thought of them as sisters; they were strangers. They were what happened when families didn't work out.

He understood his mother's impatience with his father, knew its every aspect, for he had grown up watching her like a hawk, gauging the degrees of her disappointment. Once, she had turned to him thoughtfully and said, "Jim? Why do you care if I'm disappointed or not?" As if inviting him to care less. He remembered his small involuntary smile. She had seen through him.

He couldn't recall a time when he hadn't intervened to smooth things over. And they had always submitted, amused and rankled, to the bony embrace. A sort of tent they formed, all poles and no canvas. He remembered his mother muttering darkly that group hugs were only one step removed from group sex, and his father wasn't crazy about them either. They only gave in to them because it was him. He didn't care. The important thing was to remind them they were a family. And to save them pain and regret.

*

115

The walls were thin in the house and when he heard his name he listened.

"Jim might come home with me. He's considering it."

"But he's happy here."

He heard the alarm in his mother's voice, heard his father counter it by saying there was a good August day-camp at the Y: he would make friends, he would learn useful things.

And with those words, despite more than a week in July remaining to them, Jim felt the beginning of the end-of-summer countdown.

"I thought he might go to school here, in Lanark," his mother said. "I know we haven't talked about it." She hesitated. "Where we'll be, I mean."

"You can't deny the teachers are better in New York."

"Maybe. Maybe not. He had that trouble there ..."

"What trouble?"

"Some trouble," she said. "He doesn't talk about it."

"Why don't I know about it?"

He rolled over and lay on his back and stared at the ceiling. He heard his mother admit that the teachers had said not a thing to her. It was all her own surmising.

There was no such thing as quiet speech with his father. You had to raise your voice. He heard his mother shepherding George out the door, taking him down to the water where they wouldn't be overheard. And he left his old *New Yorker* and went back to crafty Odysseus, Athena's favourite, because the two of them were so much alike. They knew how to work things, how to get their own way. Everybody has weapons, he was learning, some sneakier than others.

*   *   *

Duke had stopped eating. Nan put ice cream in her palm and knelt beside his big head and spoke to him tenderly. Then his long pink tongue curled out and slowly licked her palm clean. At night she took to sleeping beside him on the verandah, putting her hand on

116

his back or on his head whenever she woke up, to make sure he was still alive.

One evening, when Jim was patting the old dog and George was asleep on the sofa, she said, "Jim, would you like to go back with Daddy?"

She never called him Daddy. *Your father*. *Your dad*. She was giving him every opportunity to say yes. She was opening the gates to the vast fields of loyalty.

He stroked the dog. He didn't speak.

"What are you thinking?" she said after a bit. "What's going through that head of yours?"

He was thinking about everything he cared about: his mother, Duke, his lonely dad, the canoe and the lake, and Lulu, who would be coming back any day. "I don't know," he said.

"Give me a clue. Say one thing."

He couldn't, though. "What do *you* think?"

She was wearing the mended blue-and-yellow shirt that used to be Blake's and then was his, having done the mending so that he could wear it again. But he didn't want to wear it, and so she did. In slipping it on, Nan had felt like her old mother donning the outgrown sundress, the outgrown trench coat, finding a use for an old garment, yes, but also finding an unexpected way to be close to the distant, grown-up child. "Well, I would miss you terribly. You know that," she said. "But I guess it would be O.K. either way. Whatever you decide is going to be fine."

And a feeling of farewell went through him – she was giving him up – passing him along.

Later, when they went down to the dock, they stood side by side, craning their necks to see the stars. After a few minutes her neck rebelled and so she looked at the starlit lake instead, at the dark shadows of the islands reaching across to her. Then she turned to watch her son. His long flexible neck, his swan neck, was perfect for stargazing.

"Wow," he murmured.

"Shooting stars?" But she had missed them. Well, shooting stars were a dime a dozen, but there was only one Jim.

Some time in the night the old dog died. Nan was aware of his warmth about two in the morning and went back to sleep, falling into dreams so vivid one of them woke her at dawn. Her mother had been pulling hot currant scones from the oven, setting them on the speckled-grey Formica table of her childhood, the kitchen table with the unmistakable scorch mark at one end. She lay on her side, eyes open, smelling the scones. Then brought her wristwatch close: about half past five. She reached over and rested her hand on Duke.

Jim woke up to her sitting on the edge of his bed. "He's gone," she said. "In the night some time. I was asleep."

He sat up. "We have to tell Lulu. She'll want to know."

"There's no hurry. I'll bake something first. She'll be ravenous."

* * *

Lulu had been on her island for seven days, doing penance and thinking with obsessive futility about everything she had done wrong in her life. What kind of pathetic person runs over her own dog?

For the first three days her mind had been screamingly, painfully, sorrowfully full of the endless critical noise from her brother, her father, her ex-lovers and directors and agents, and from herself. Gertrude Bumfuck. "I don't care," she said to herself. But it was surprising how much she did care. She had been caring in the same raw way for a long time.

All her failings were leaf litter. A deep leaf litter of bad things, worse things, that had deepened over time, each one covering up the next. Now her foot kicked up the leaves, and kept kicking. Guy's recent kindness was large in her mind. It moved her, but that did not mean she trusted it.

On the fourth day she couldn't say that she wasn't hungry anymore, but the blinding headaches were gone and she felt an energy coming from nowhere familiar. Its source seemed external. Some purer source of fuel, like a thin note of music, carried her along.

There was a loon circling her island, coming close, drifting off. It seemed to be fasting too, never dipping its head in search of fish, never diving or taking flight or calling its famous call. A mute and silent loon, like the poor wretch in Shakespeare whose tongue was cut out and whose hands were cut off. Either something was wrong with a natural bird, or a supernatural bird was guarding her island.

You have such thoughts when you don't eat.

On the fifth day Lulu felt the fight go out of her.

She wanted a family. A child, but she was too old for a child. A husband who liked to talk, but only about interesting things, in a house with a bay window and wallpaper and a drop-leaf table.

On the sixth day it rained non-stop and she slept.

Then came the seventh day, when just before waking she dreamt about a batch of currant scones so mouthwatering they woke her out of a deep sleep. Reaching around, she unzipped the tent door and stuck her head out into a view of the sky and the lake flushed an engorged orange-red. Lavinia. That was the poor wretch's name. And the play was *Titus Andronicus*, that lamentable tragedy. She had been dreaming about her grandmother's kitchen with its old gas range, and she was so hungry she could have eaten a chair.

She was swimming as the sun came up over the hill. The gold! Everything was dripping in honey.

Then a few hours later two beautiful souls came paddling towards her across the water.

The coincidence of their dreams clinched Lulu's pleasure and resolve. This was her new-found family. Nan was her sister, Jim was the son she had never had.

Sipping the orange juice Nan had thought to bring along as a

119

way for her to break her fast, and eating a few nibbles, only a few, of a sweet currant scone (still warm from the oven, this old-fashioned funeral food, in honour of Duke), she wanted to hear again the details of his passing and the details of Nan's dream, and then she shared her own.

It seemed to Jim that her eyes were bigger and the rest of her was smaller. She was like a plant that's had too much shade, yet she was browner. He had never known anyone to go a week without food.

She caught him sizing her up. "Darling, I've never felt better in my life, especially now that you're here."

"We missed you," his mother said.

"And I missed you more. Not that I've been alone." And she pointed out the solitary loon. "There's my guardian angel."

But Nan had better eyes and so did Jim.

They got into one canoe, Lulu in the middle, and paddled towards the bird gliding like a ghost into the sheltered foot of the dog's leg. Soon they were close enough to understand that the loon was entangled head to foot in nylon fishing line.

They paddled closer. A handsome bird the size of a small goose, its soot-black head and slender neck and pointed bill, its red eyes, its necklace of vertical white stripes and its long body checkered black-and-white – every part of it was trussed up in somebody's jettisoned fishing line. The loon had been starving to death all this time.

They agreed they should rescue it. So they manoeuvred the canoe alongside. By now they were in shallow water close to shore. Nan and Jim dug their paddles into the lake bottom to steady the canoe, while Lulu, on her knees, reached for the bird. In its panic, it tried to dive. Her hands went around its back and she lifted and dragged it, dripping, over the side. And then the canoe was full of dying loon.

It wasn't as sad as the death of Pog but nearly. Lulu felt the heavy body go limp in her hands and she let it slide to the floor of the canoe.

"Is it dead," Jim said, "or just hurt?"

But he knew.

"Fishermen are careless," his mother said. Anger made it hard for her to speak. They should report it to the wildlife officer. If that's what he was called. If there even was one.

"Guy will know," said Lulu. She was staring down at the wild corpse at her knees, absorbing its terror, about which she had been absolutely ignorant every single day she was on her island, all those days of being caught up in a stupid mesh of her own making.

That a wild bird of the water and air – intimate with lakes and oceans and every manner of sky – should have come to such a helpless end.

A breeze came up and they began to slide across the water. They never would be able to describe it adequately, the feeling it gave them to have a wild bird right *with* them as they moved like a wild bird over the water. They were gliding in a featherless craft with the feathered source of its gliding shape. Nan and Jim took up their paddles. They swung the canoe around and headed to Lulu's island, where she struck her tent and stowed her rucksack towards the bow of the yellow canoe. Then she followed close behind them as they headed east, turning into the narrows and following the shoreline into the next bay and the next.

Canoes really were magical, thought Lulu, the way they allowed you to skim across the water using wooden wands.

And then they were alongside the dock and there was George.

He said of the bird, "That's quite a fish you have there."

But he helped them empty the canoes and he fetched the camera for Nan, who wanted to document the travesty.

This time it was Lulu, not Nan, who phoned Guy for advice. She took her courage in her hands and called her moody brother, telling him the story, and saying she wanted to have the loon donated to a museum or school, preserved by a taxidermist, in other words, and studied. At his suggestion, they put it in the meantime into the freezer in Nan's back kitchen, wrapping it in clear plastic and discovering in the process how sharp its long-dagger beak was, how good at stabbing, and how its toes were equipped with significant claws.

Guy came over the next day with Irene. The little girl sat on the sofa in the verandah and looked away. She did not respond to overtures. She did not speak at all.

Nan went to her and offered her a glass of chocolate milk, then lemonade. "Jim is going to have lemonade."

George said, "We have the best lemonade. I grow the lemons myself."

The child would not be coaxed. Nan thought her eyes were the blankest she had ever seen, big and blue and strangely pale in the small white face scabby from being picked at. Around her Guy was buoyant, amiable, teasing, making up for his withdrawn daughter by exerting his own charm and acting as if nothing were wrong. His manner, Nan thought, wasn't unlike a bird's attempt to distract all eyes from the vulnerable egg in its nest. He was his daughter's protective colouring, and she did not let him out of her sight, this knowledgeable man who was saying that loons were a very old species with a primitive nervous system, and no doubt this one had been so weakened by lack of food that when they pulled it out of the water it died of shock. Loons, he added, were a protected species and there were regulations to follow.

Nan led the way to the back kitchen and raised the lid of the long freezer. Beside her, Guy reached in and touched the long black beak under the plastic with evident appreciation. In the winter the red eyes went brown, he said. A taxidermist would replace the eyes with red glass.

Irene stood in the doorway and watched by looking away.

"Do you want to see?" His tone of voice was tailored for her alone. She joined him and he lifted her up to look. "It's about the same size and weight as last year's Christmas turkey," he said. And she gave a nod and kept gazing down.

Over supper, George was all gloomy bluntness. "Having that child is awful," he declared. "She is nothing."

Seeing the pained surprise on Jim's face, Nan spoke more gently. "I think your father means she doesn't have much personality yet. She sits and says nothing. And looks away."

George ploughed on. "Her father pretends there's nothing wrong with her. Something is dead wrong."

"My brother is wonderful with her," Lulu said, stating a fact and brooking no argument.

Jim saw his mother give her a grateful look. "He is," she said.

"Oh, Guy is charming all right," George said.

Nan smiled. "You sound jealous. There's no need to be."

"You'd be the last to know."

"The last to know what?"

"Nancy, you're over your head before you know it."

She laughed and winced. "When have I been over my head?"

George didn't answer.

"George? When have I been over my head?"

Then Lulu said, "It's touching to see a child trust and admire her father so much." She paused. "It's not at all typical."

And George said, "But why doesn't she trust anybody else?"

That night it rained a little and in the morning Jim went to the window and saw Lulu under the trees. She was wearing Hef'r sandals and a short-sleeved dress, standing outside in the damp and the flies as comfortably as if she were in her living room.

It was nine days since she had taken her last drink. To reinforce her new self she had washed her hair and put on a summer dress.

Guy returned with Irene after breakfast. The child went to her solitary place on the sofa in the verandah, while Guy, seated at the kitchen table with a mug of fresh coffee, told them about his conversation with the game warden. The loon would have to be delivered to the ministry office in Kingston to verify the cause of death, after which permits for taxidermy were required, and not just anyone could apply.

Leaning against the counter, Lulu let out a snort of exasperation and her brother said, "They have rules. Do you want to know what they are or not?"

"Well, that depends on how uptight and stupid they are."

Guy shoved aside the newspaper in front of him with his square, nicked hands. He addressed the table. "You always have the answer, Lu. I hate that." And she felt pouring off him the kind of infernal coldness that pours off a Christmas tree carried from an outdoor lot into a warm house, to be set up in its metal stand. The dead of winter comes out of the trunk and off every needle, biting your hands and freezing your eyeballs. "I always know?" she replied. "I *never* know." No less aggressive, but shocked, she always was, by the antagonism she aroused in him.

The room fell silent. George began to whistle under his breath.

It was Nan who attempted to smooth things over, asking Guy if the game warden had said anything about educating fishermen, and the strained atmosphere eased a little as he answered her question and she asked another.

Lulu, still at the counter, turned her head away from her brother's fortress shoulders and not unhandsome face and saw in memory the extravagant colour his face used to turn when he was a boy in a rage: a dark shade of orange. A scary boy. The colour used to form a belt of fuelled tangerine around his cheeks and eyes and ears that went beyond apoplectic into finer fury, into the lividness of some tropical fruit. He was in another country. Sometimes they were in the same country. She remembered the queasy-metallic smell of porridge rising into her nostrils, heard the sound of him gagging across the table, remembered raising her eyes in sympathy. She was nine, he was eleven; they were dressed for school. He gagged and so did she, a redoubled retching that turned his face a desperate, eye-watering crimson. They sat on, she remembered, marooned and suffering in unison over their cold and lumpy porridge.

He was talking so easily to Nan. They had always liked each other, those two. There had always been something between them.

Lulu straightened her shoulders and looked around the kitchen and out at the verandah, feeling the old family loneliness – that immeasurable desolation – and looking for some way *in*.

A breeze, coming through the screens, worked on the sections of the newspaper and ruffled the child's hair.

Her small, troubled niece.

She went out to the sofa and sat down beside her.

"I'm Lulu," she said.

"I'm a duck," the child said, speaking to her shoes. She sounded like a little old man.

"Why didn't you tell me?" Lulu said. "I'm a duck too."

She took her niece's hand and to her everlasting pleasure felt Irene clasp hers in return. Hand in hand, the two of them proceeded to quack around the porch, unembarrassed and lost in the pleasure of being ducks. They opened the screen door and quacked their way down to the water and along the water's edge, where the sun found them, Lulu in her summer dress and supple sandals, Irene in her shorts and T-shirt and sneakers.

Jim wasn't the only one to notice the change in Guy, who went over to the window to watch his daughter take to his sister as she had to no-one else. His body relaxed and the altered expression on his face was something to behold.

8

THAT EVENING GREAT GUSTS OF WIND SHOT ACROSS THE lake like jets of black dye, drawing even George onto the verandah to watch. "Look!" Nan cried, pointing to waterspouts like geysers three or four storeys high, whipped up by the wind. Then came torrential rain so dense it reminded her of being in a store on Broadway and looking up to see a long grey delivery truck parked directly in front of the window. But it was the rain.

Lulu was in her element, her hair stirred and loosened by the spray coming through the screens, her face fully alive. She shared a look of joy with Nan and Jim while George stepped back, disinclined to get wet.

Less than an hour later, it was over. They could see the near trees, the shoreline, the first island, the far shore, and in that moment the biggest tree of all came crashing down less than thirty feet away. It fell with what Nan would later call a biblical thud, as if Samson had tripped over his feet and measured his length on the forest floor. There was a walloping splash and the ground shook, after which the silence was complete, except for spatters of rain shaken off leaves.

They stood amazed and spared. The power was out. No lights glimmered around the lake.

Nan found the flashlights in the kitchen and they trekked down the soppy path in the gathering gloom and trained them on the endless length of tree. Under its bulk, smashed to smithereens, were the dock and the canoe they called the barge and even the outlying raft, so far did its branches reach. The shoreline wasn't shoreline anymore, it was fallen tree. No walking along the beaten path, no walking on the dock, no setting out easily in a canoe.

They were dumbfounded. Pillars, roof, and temple walls had all come down.

George broke the silence. "Nancy, you'll need a chainsaw."

"I'll need a lumberjack," she said.

In the quiet they became aware of the first stars peering down.

"You'll need Jim," he conceded in a change of heart inspired by the destruction all around them. Not that Jim could operate a power saw, but that Nancy depended on him for peace of mind.

She touched his arm. "Thank you."

The next morning, shaving at the kitchen sink, he turned to her, aggrieved, his right cheek half shaved. "Nancy, what's this?"

She went to him and felt on his cheek the tiny, determined bump below the skin that his razor and some sixth sense had detected. "You should get that checked," she said, taking its measure with her fingertip. It was hard and rooted, on a level with his ear. "As soon as you get home, go see Dr Michaels."

George tilted his head to the side and examined himself in the shaving mirror beside the sink. He pushed out his cheek with his tongue.

"Call after breakfast," she said. "See when you can get an appointment."

He finished shaving. The bump was minute, infinitesimal. Nevertheless, when Jim joined them at the breakfast table, he said to his son, "There wouldn't have been time for baseball games, anyway. Who knows what tests they're going to put me through."

They heard the swelling of self-pity in his voice. George himself heard it and ran his hand back and forth across his mouth, ashamed, and wishing he could think of something lighthearted to say. He could not and he was ashamed of that too.

Two days later, his packed bags were by the door, one suitcase, a gym bag. They were at the breakfast table again, all but Lulu, who had climbed over the fallen tree and taken one of the undamaged canoes out for an early paddle. She had said goodbye to George earlier, down by the water, out of hearing of Jim and Nan. "I hope everything goes well for you, George."

He had thanked her and she had turned, about to get into the canoe.

"Lulu?"

She looked back.

"They're *my* family," he said, "not yours."

The great mess of fallen tree framed him, having come down like a patriarch, it seemed to her, like the death of her father. In its wake rose spindly, twisty George Bobak, one of those lesser characters it is easy to overlook.

"Darling, they're my family too. And there is nothing you can do about it."

Now at the breakfast table Nan was saying how much it pained her to have the trees come down around them. Why was it happening now, all the diseases weakening the oldest and most beautiful trees? She was glad her parents weren't alive to see it.

And then they were standing beside the rental car, making their goodbyes. George gave his son one last hug, then put his hand on Nan's shoulder and kissed her. It was July 27. She took his hand and held it, and asked him what he was going to do that evening when he got back to New York. He sighed and looked away. He would organize himself for work, he said. He had to catch up on certain files, including the one about the pregnant Canadian whose landlord was evicting her for being too noisy. "If you can imagine a noisy Canadian," he said. "I can't."

"And maybe call someone? To let them know you're back?" A gentle prod. "Call Bridget." The old friend who had lived down the hall from them until she had moved to Brooklyn a few years ago to be an artist.

128

George got into the car and rolled down his window. Jim, who was standing where his uncle and aunt were standing the last time he had seen them alive, told his father not to drive too fast and George promised he would not.

And then he was gone and peace descended in all its fullness. The place became their own again.

They turned back to the house and Nan wondered aloud why men don't have more friends. "Some men do," she said to Jim, "but your father doesn't."

He didn't try to answer, unsettled by the remark and reminded of his own shortcomings, his own failures.

She looked at him, her eyes sad and knowing. "He hasn't had and that makes it harder to have. The longer you go without, the harder it is to have. He's shy. And no one seeks him out."

That evening Nan stood at the kitchen window, lost in thought. She had a bad feeling about the bump on George's cheek. Perhaps it was nothing, but if so that would fly in the face of his usual luck. And in her mind she went back to their wedding day in Vermont when one of his elderly aunts had told her more than she wanted to know about his family. "The Bobaks never had soft words. They always needled each other. Except for young Martin."

"Tell me about Martin," she'd said.

"He was a lovely man. He impressed me."

"And George?"

The aunt smiled. "I was impressed by Martin."

By then, the day of her wedding, Nan had known George less than six months and become so fondly protective of his restful, recessive manner that she had chosen not to think about how many hard peas might lie under the mattress. He was, she knew, a fragile, hurting, pliable man – one word from her and he had given up his beloved cigars – and she was taking a risk in becoming his third wife. What she found attractive was how different his manners were from John's bullying ways, asking shyly if he might kiss her the first time they went out.

His brother Kevin was at the wedding, already suffering from the cancer that would kill him a year later. Kevin lent her a hand when she set up the wedding cake on a card table, a pound cake made by her new mother-in-law and the older brother eager to tell all about George as a boy. "My brother was an obese, rough-tempered kid who said very little besides, 'Are you going to eat that?'"

Well, that was funny. She didn't pretend it wasn't.

She had known about the series of losses – part of his hearing to boyhood mumps, a teenage toe to a lawn mower, his teenage fat to a crash diet, his first wife to breast cancer, his second wife to a lesbian named Doreen. Now, on her wedding day, she was learning that all of those losses were subsequent to the first major loss – of anger, of personality – so that he had become, in people's minds, a passive figure, virtually silent, with a kicked-upon look. That is, they kept telling her, until you came into his life. He's changed dramatically and it must be you, they said. Finally, after years of silence, George was talking.

During the wedding it rained fitfully, threatened to rain more. Despite the weather, half the guests huddled afterwards on the verandah, since the house was so very small. She escaped too and found an old woman in a deckchair smoking one cigarette after another. This was the elderly aunt, Rena, who wanted to know if the family was making her welcome.

They were. George's mother, especially. "What a good person she is."

The old aunt said, "She's a jerk."

And Nan sat down.

The aunt lit up another cigarette and told her that she, too, was a Bobak by marriage. She and her husband had travelled a lot in Europe, reading a great deal and accumulating many books, so that when they returned to Pennsylvania most of their luggage was that: books. She was a sharp-tongued wisp of a thing, her weathered skin the same colour as her thinning hair, itself not far off the brownish-grey of her coat. Her bright eyes shifted back and forth and up at you, good-humoured but implacably free of any desire to please. She said, "You've married an unlucky man."

Nan's heart, already low, sank out of sight. She knew with sudden despair that this was George's self-image too: a sorrowful man beset by misfortune. What had seemed like gentle intelligence now came across, in the context of his family, as a kind of mental vacancy. He had given up on anger and nothing but bad luck had filled the vacuum.

There was a swirl around the verandah of wind, children, noise, and it lifted her up like a leaf and from that height she looked down at the tiny old woman lost in an oversized deckchair, and beside her, in her pretty flowered dress, a bride, just married, named Nan. At the foot of the driveway were three white balloons tied to the mailbox. She had blown them up herself.

She said to the aunt, harking back to the impressive brother, "I thought Martin might come to the wedding. I'd like to meet him."

"Don't hold your breath," the old woman said.

After which Nan excused herself and went inside. George was in the kitchen, wrestling lobsters into a pot of boiling water. She saw his glasses fogged up and his face smoothed free of everything but the nervous notion that nothing he did was going to work. She went over to him. Together they held down the lid.

She said, "Your Aunt Rena is quite the character."

George pushed his steamy glasses up on his forehead. "She's demented."

It used to be that you left the brightness of the water and entered the darkness of the woods. It was like opening a door. Now so many trees were sick or dying or fallen that the remaining woods were full of an agonized light.

Nan sought Guy's advice on removing the toppled hemlock. He recommended Ronnie Hepburn, a sandy-haired cousin of Janet who ran a tree removal service; he was the best.

Ronnie arrived one afternoon when they were standing outside pondering the Herculean task that lay ahead. A man of medium height, his baseball cap pushed back off his forehead, a massive orange chainsaw in one hand. Nan stepped forward and introduced herself and then Lulu and Jim.

"Hello, Ronnie," Lulu said.

"Lulu. It's been a while."

"You know each other," Nan said. "Were we in the same class?"

"No such luck," said Ronnie.

Ronnie had an easygoing face and the relaxed-alert eyes of someone who made a decent living from coming to the rescue. In his hand the chainsaw appeared to weigh nothing. His sidekicks were a man in his forties named Marcel and a boy of seventeen they called Junior; they, too, had massive orange chainsaws. In the next couple of hours, whipping them around like rapiers, they carved up the mammoth tree and reopened the shoreline, all the while smoking and cracking jokes, apparently heedless of the risk to fingers and toes.

Nan stood watching. In her stillness and her white canvas hat, hands shoved into her pockets, position staked out on a knoll next to the wrecked tree, she reminded Lulu of a lighthouse on a cape. Lulu herself stood with Jim, farther back, out of the way. To Lulu's way of thinking, Nan was a beacon of steadfastness and always had been, even when it was against her interests, even when she should have moved on to better things.

The three lumberjacks sent up golden spumes of sawdust and afterwards they would walk on a sawdust-softened forest floor. Spumes of yellow, although the wood was reddish and the exposed bark singular in its tones of red. Slicing through the bottommost part of the trunk, they separated it from its upended stump, then lopped off the side branches, turning the tree into a giant log, three feet wide at its widest, after which they sliced it into discs, one disc after another, each about eighteen inches thick. In short order, they were down to what remained: an amputated torso, most of it submerged in the lake. The hardest part for last. Wrapping the base of it with wire cable, they ran the cable to their tractor (on higher ground beside the house) and tried to haul it out of the water. Too heavy; the tractor stalled. More amputation, more discs rolled to the side. They tried again, laying down a rolling floor of smaller logs to ease the way, and this time they succeeded in dragging the monster-remains up on shore, all but its fifteen-foot farthest-most tip, which had broken off and buried its pointy parts in the bottom of the lake. That was a problem for later (when Guy would come and, working from his aluminum motorboat, handsaw the branches free and tow the hacked-off treetop out into the middle of the lake, where he let it go, and it sank out of sight. Lulu would spend the whole of that time with Irene. "My darling, tell me, what bit you?" And Irene explained: gnats, mosquitoes, raspberry thorns. They played on the verandah, dressing up in all the long-ago clothes and boots, pretending to be firemen putting out Jim, who let himself be doused with a dust-buster).

Unlike cedar, hemlock smelled acrid, a little foul, though Nan got used to it and came to like it. The red in the wood was like the distinctive reddish beard of a man with brown hair, a nearly red-headed man. Menelaus, she thought, thinking of the running metaphor in the *Iliad* of warriors falling like trees. In Homer's time there must have been forests in all directions, she thought, covering the hills and valleys down to the wine-dark sea.

The three men were nonchalant, cavalier, and fast, playing to their impressed audience. Ronnie at one point drove the chainsaw's spinning blade straight down into the huge disc closest to Nan, then turned off the power, and the blade sat, still and upright, like a knife in cold butter. A big smile spread like an ovation across her face.

One hundred feet high became fifty-one discs by four in the afternoon, ready to be chopped into firewood. They would count the rings at the widest part and arrive at two hundred and forty-three.

Jim had his first small glass of beer that afternoon and it lent a lustre to everything he heard. Marcel was a playwright, working for Ronnie on the side. His wife came from Snow Road Station. He liked to write at night, he said, drinking coffee laced with rum. He had written three plays this way, only one of which had been performed, once, in a school gym to a crowd of three dozen people. "I'm getting known," he said with a trace of a smile.

"Lulu's an actor," his mother said. "You should write a play for her."

"Why stop at one?" said Lulu. She was sipping lemonade. "So tell me, do you write in French or English?"

"In French. I've translated two of them into English."

Only then did Jim hear his slight accent for what it was.

Ronnie scratched his head under his baseball cap and confessed he had been to only one play in his life and then he had gone three times. *Saint Joan* at Lanark High School. "Lulu, you were great."

A remark so sincere and well-meant that Lulu smiled and looked down, only to raise her eyes when she heard Jim say, "What made Lulu great?" In his voice there was the same ardent over-eagerness that once had declared Duke to be young and spry.

"Lulu *was* Joan of Arc. You were Joan," Ronnie said. "You were like a bolt of lightning."

A bolt of lightning. And everyone, including Jim, was content.

The warm sun beat down. The bottles of beer and jug of lemonade were empty. No-one stirred. Ronnie said his memory was hit and miss: "But you were born in the States, if I recall."

"Seattle," Lulu said. Nearly half a century ago.

"And you're still acting?"

"Not much, Ronnie. I'm old. I'm old and ambition has ruined my life. I don't even go to plays anymore."

"Well, why not?"

"Oh, I can't bear seeing actors in roles I should have." She laughed a short, sharp, self-mocking laugh. "Thwarted ambition is never pretty."

"I wouldn't know," Ronnie said. "I'm a happy man."

His smile was infectious. Jim could see that everyone liked him as much as he did, especially Lulu. If only his father were the same, he thought. If only he could be easy and open and make everyone around him relaxed.

"I was four years old," Lulu was saying, "when we moved from Seattle to the Yukon. I loved Canada. Then nine years later we moved to Ontario and Canadians hated me and I hated them back."

"I didn't hate you," Ronnie said.

Lulu ran her hand across the ground, picking up twigs, snapping them between her fingers. "I see Canadians travelling all the time with those self-satisfied maple-leaf flags sewn to their bags. They think they're liked. They really do." She shrugged. "I'm not talking about Quebec," she said, turning to Marcel, "when I'm talking about Canada. *Tu sais. Le Québec est un pays.*"

"Or it will be soon," said Marcel with conviction. "*Une nation comme les autres.*"

"Let them go," Ronnie said. "We don't need them."

"Oh, but we do," his mother said.

Jim had noticed her eyes open a little wider when they exchanged those words in French. A certain look came over her face of surprise and envy.

"You're never going to please them," Ronnie said. "Let them please themselves for a change."

It might have ended there, with Ronnie's philosophical wave of the hand, had Marcel not revealed that he was writing a play about Trudeau. Was he for him or against him, Lulu wanted to know. Oh, as against as against could be.

Jim enjoyed watching people take sides. It increased the drama and he loved the drama. Yet it worried him too, since he wanted

135

people to like each other and he wanted to be on the right side, the brave and exciting side.

Marcel said, "Everything goes back to Trudeau and his hatred of Quebec. He's the reason things have reached this point."

"God, you oversimplify," his mother said, wrapping her arms around her knees and leaning forward. "Trudeau wanted to do things *for* Quebec. That's why he went into politics."

The argument accelerated and Jim had to look away, though he didn't stop listening. "No," his mother was saying. "He wanted to reshape his country and give Quebec its equal place. Equal. Not better than. Not special. *Equal*."

And Marcel threw counterarguments in her face, reminding her of everything Trudeau had done to thwart Quebec's ambition, and Lulu was nodding, clearly with him, while his mother sputtered and kept saying it was more complicated than that. What he was fighting was separatism, not Quebec.

Junior, long and lanky and with nothing whatever to say for himself, picked at the scabs on his hands, and Marcel shook his head and spat off to the side. "The trouble with you Trudeau federalists is that you think you know more than anybody else. I come from a humble people. Lévesque – you can see it in his face – was a humble man. All that mattered to Trudeau was getting his own way."

Jim agreed with him about Lévesque's face. There was something he did with his mouth, turning it down while he looked up with his eyes. It made him look modest.

"Canada mattered to Trudeau." His mother leaned forward again. "And it matters to me."

"But *why*?" Lulu said. And Jim detected a new note in her voice, an impatience with his mother that he hadn't heard before. "*Why* do you care? You moved away years ago."

His mother rubbed her forehead and took a moment to answer. In the silence Jim heard the crickets he hadn't been aware of till then. Fall was coming. He felt drawn to Marcel and Lulu's side of the argument, yet protective of his mother, whose hand moved to her chest and massaged the area over her heart, and to his embarrassment her mouth began to work and her eyes filled with tears. She had to shake her head hard to stop them from streaming down her face. "It's visceral, Lulu. Either you feel it or you don't." She wiped her eyes and gave her head another hard shake, as if getting dust out of a mop. And Jim fixed his eyes on the ground. "Quebec occupies the middle of the country," he heard her say. "If it separates, nothing will ever be the same."

Then she said, "Canada is the country of my heart. Laugh at me if you like."

Everyone was quiet.

"I understand," Marcel said. "Quebec is the country of *my* heart."

And Jim saw that the problem had no remedy. Marcel's heart was going to destroy hers; her heart was standing in the way of his.

"Darling, I can see you on the bridge to Quebec, wielding your broadsword, hacking off heads left and right."

His mother laughed then. "It's true. I get worked up." She felt alone, her feelings faintly ridiculous, except to her. "Jim, you're very patient, listening to this stuff. I know it makes you uncomfortable. I just want to have a country to come home to." And looking around her, she gestured towards the lopped-up tree. "There's our magnificent hemlock. Why are the beautiful old trees dying? Tell me, Ronnie. A tree lasts two hundred years. Maybe more. And then a breath of wind knocks it flat."

"Trees topple when they're old and sick," Ronnie said simply. "Or just old. A tree falls, another grows up behind. It's natural."

"I guess it is."

"Look at those roots," he said. All around them was the root-gnarled ground, uneven and thinly soiled. Roots extended like long fingers in split-open gloves. They grabbed on to rocks, worked their way around them and through them, splitting them apart. Some roots were the size of wrists, some the size of arms. "Trees finally get too tall and heavy," Ronnie said. "Their shallow root systems can't hold them up anymore."

"It used to be dark in there with the most beautiful shade," his mother said.

"And now there's more light!" countered Lulu with energy. "You see more clearly. Other trees have a chance to grow. Clear away Canada and watch Quebec take off!"

"Well, that's a hefty price to pay to get more light." His mother's voice was so mournful that Ronnie smiled and said, "My cousin Janet says the two of you were great friends."

That shut her up. Mention of Janet Hepburn and Nan was twelve years old again, knee socks sliding down her skinny white shins.

The sun was gone from their side of the bay. It was nearly five o'clock. Lulu went up the slope and returned with several cold beers, declining to have one herself. She asked Marcel what angle he was taking in his play. "*Si ça ne t'ennuie pas.*"

"I don't mind at all," he said. "Trudeau's a tired-out, old man. He's looking back on his life, seeing all his mistakes. Like Lear. A Canadian Lear finally seeing how he abused his power and betrayed his own people and ruined everything."

"'King Lear'," Nan said, turning to Jim, "is a great play. It's about an old king making terrible mistakes and then realizing just how terrible they were. How blind he was. That doesn't usually happen, people can't figure it out. They can't figure out the worst things they've done."

I can, Jim thought. The worst things were cowardly acts of betrayal. Betraying a friend and in the process betraying yourself. He knew all about that.

The old question had a way of bumping up against them, like a big carp coming around at irregular intervals to their end of the bay.

Lulu said, "I take it there's not going to be a happy ending." And

138

Marcel returned her smile with a look of amusement. He was waiting, he admitted, to see how things turned out.

"Marcel," his mother said with feeling, "you could write a great tragedy. I mean it. Here we are, about to have a second referendum, and where is the hero of the first one? Nobody cares about him. He's shoved out of sight, blamed for everything." She paused. "It must be the bitterest moment of his life."

Jim saw that her face was stretched tight from feeling too much and saying too much, and he realized he was holding his breath. It was like when Blake was in that school play and he was in the audience, worried sick he would blow his lines. Blake, who couldn't be bothered with them anymore. And in his constricted chest he admired her for sticking up for somebody no-one else had any time for. "He must think," she was saying now as a motorboat roared into the bay, destroying the quiet, "that everything he did only made things worse." Nan hated motorboats, but she didn't react to this one. She waited. Waves thumped against the raft, the dock, the shore. She wasn't finished yet. "It's like a Greek tragedy," she went on when the noise had subsided, "a classic Greek tragedy, where unbeknownst to you your actions undermine everything you lived for. He went into politics to do things for Quebec, to bring the French fact to Ottawa, to make this country bilingual and independent and just. His vision and his loyalty were one. Then in getting what he dreamed of – a constitutional deal and a charter of rights and freedoms – he undermined his whole purpose. Because," she said, with sad finality, "Quebec got left out."

Jim felt himself swing to her side. He felt a surge of sympathy for Trudeau, the tough guy who turned into a loser. The popular guy who became unpopular. And he felt a certain triumph at seeing his mother hold her own.

But Marcel wasn't buying it. "We've dreamed about this for so long." And he patted his heart. "We need our own country. It's a simple question of self-respect."

And his mother had no comeback, none at all.

Marcel went on, "I can't wait to see the look on Trudeau's face when Quebec votes Yes."

"You want to see his heart break," she said.

"I want to see the look on his face. I want to project his face in defeat this fall and Lévesque's face in defeat in 1980, side by side, onto a screen at the back of the stage. Lévesque saying *à la prochaine fois*. Remember how he had tears in his eyes? Everybody in the Paul Sauvé Arena was weeping. And beside it I'll project Trudeau's face when he loses his country."

His mother looked suddenly tired and beaten. But then she raised her head and said, "He wouldn't give you the satisfaction of tears. He'll never lose his pride. And anyway, you're forgetting. You're forgetting that what broke Lear's heart wasn't losing his kingdom, it was losing his favourite daughter. Lear had daughters. Trudeau has sons."

And everybody knew how much he loved the three sons he had done so much to raise after Margaret left him.

That evening it was perfectly still as they sat on the only bit of unsmashed dock and breathed in the hemlock-scented air. The men were gone and an early August moon was coming up. Its gold lip came first and drew the rest of itself quickly up, a golden molten coin, dented on the left. Nothing but moonlit water lay between them and the far, dark hills.

Lulu seemed different to Jim, more preoccupied. They sat for a while without talking. Then she shook herself and apologised for being bad company. She told them she was remembering being in Peru years ago and riding on the back of a policeman's motorcycle through eleven shallow rivers and half as many clouds of butterflies, each cloud consisting of hundreds upon hundreds of one type of butterfly, intricately patterned, astonishing. "I was brave in those days," she said, mystified by herself, and full of all-too-sober disappointment.

"Martin lives in Peru," his mother said. "George's brother. I've never met him.

"That's the second time you've mentioned him," Lulu said.

"Is it?"

"Darling, if you want to meet him, get on a plane and go."

That note of impatience again.

"I do want to meet him," his mother said, and to Jim's relief her voice was firm but not offended. "However, I'm not going to get on a plane and go find him."

Lulu smiled. "O.K."

"Lulu," and her voice lowered a notch, "why don't you look for work in Ottawa? It has a theatre scene, low-key, but that's the way Ottawa is."

"It's not, darling. Ottawa's not low-key."

"But it is."

"It's not relaxed. It's organized. There's structure. It's a kind of organized quietness."

Jim loved to watch his mother absorb the truth. She became still and her shoulders dropped a little.

Lulu went on. She compared Ottawa to Montreal, where everybody was busy disagreeing with each other all the time, working long hours into the night, talking about many things, and she didn't mean fashion. Quebec was a real country with a real culture. "Canadian identity. What is it? It's so fragile it's meaningless."

"There are cultures and there are cultures," Nan said slowly, thinking what a shame it would be if their friendship broke up over politics. "Some are obvious and some are – subtle." She weighed the word. "O.K., subtle. Implicit. Some are explicit and some are implicit."

Jim was surprised by the evenness in her voice. She didn't have it with anyone else, not reliably anyway. Then she put her hands on her chest and pressed hard and she was no longer calm. "The separatists despise us, Lulu. They don't care about destroying what we love. What will become of us?"

Lulu looked at her with baffled affection. "It could be a very civilized break-up and rearrangement. It doesn't have to be ugly."

"It will be ugly. Things degenerate. They always do."

"Not always."

"*Always*. It's naive to think otherwise."

"It's like a bad marriage, Nan. Admit it. Call it quits."

His mother had been looking down and now she turned her eyes on Lulu. "What's wrong with trying to make things work?"

The moon behind her was midway up the sky now, and the colour of ivory.

"I hate seeing you—" Lulu said, then stopped. She looked from Nan to Jim. She drummed her fingers on the dock and shrugged.

His mother said, "I don't want to do the wrong thing." And having said it she guessed it must be true, or she would have left her marriage by now.

"I know you don't, darling."

"And identity *is* fragile," his mother said. "You're an actor. You know that." Her face looked pale and thin with utter conviction, and Jim was torn between embarrassment and love.

"They don't despise you," Lulu said.

"They're indifferent. It's like a brother's studied indifference to his sister. They can take us or leave us."

Lulu smiled. "*Touché*."

"Or," and his mother tilted her head, "like two siblings incapable of appreciating each other."

"No." Lulu looked Nan in the eyes. "Your comparison doesn't hold. It's not like two siblings because there is no fraternity. They are strangers to each other, with nothing in common."

* * *

Jim read the air around people, the calm or seasick air. He noticed that Lulu was talking more easily to Guy now, tentative conversations about their father, fragments of revelation that happened whenever Guy brought Irene to visit. Or Ducky, as they called her.

"Ducky likes you, Jim," Lulu said after one visit.

He knew she did. He had taken to reading to her, his Pogo comics mainly, and she curled up beside him on the sofa and leaned into him, transfixed by being read to. It was like having a sister.

One afternoon the two of them were on the floor of the screened-in verandah playing checkers. Guy sat in one of the wicker chairs and every so often reached down to help his daughter figure out her next move. From the sofa Lulu watched.

"Dad terrified me as a child," Jim heard her say to her brother, as if picking up an earlier conversation, though it must have been an ongoing conversation in her head.

"He terrified me too. That one." Guy pointed to the next checker to move.

"But you lost your fear. You admired him so. How did that happen?"

Guy paused for a long, thoughtful moment before saying, "It had something to do with getting a dog."

Lulu leaned back and nodded. She understood. Even before he went on to recount that long-ago Saturday morning when Scooter was chasing him and Bernie the length of the living room floor, biting playfully at their heels, and they were laughing like crazy, "And then I slid into the coffee table and smashed the glass top," Guy said. "I thought I was dead."

Her eyes were glued to her brother's face. They were the only two people left in the world who had been there and remembered. He had expected to be grabbed and belted and tossed about like a football. It had happened before.

Not this time, though. "Dad laughed it off and said it didn't matter."

"I remember."

Boy–dog–man, thought Lulu. It was a combination that contained its own solution to anything that went wrong. It was its own

143

particular breezeway of flowing affection. In having a dog again, their father was reconnecting with *his* dog, Jock, the boyhood dog whom nobody else could handle. And so while a roughhousing boy had to be punished, a boy roughhousing with a dog had to be indulged. It was written in the laws of the boy–man heart.

Guy was remembering something else. "That time he dragged you by your hair," he said. And on his face there was nothing but pure fellow feeling. "He went over the top."

"I'd forgotten that."

Not being dragged across the kitchen floor and peeing herself, twelve years old and peeing her pants: she had never forgotten the shame. She had forgotten the assault on her head of hair. It came back. She felt the roots of her hair all but yanked out of her scalp, saw the swirly-grey linoleum, felt the hot pee making its involuntary escape.

Guy said, "I think he hated himself for it."

And the tone of his voice would stay with her to the end of her days. It was the tone of someone who knew what it was to hate himself too.

* * *

George telephoned them every evening about seven. He had undergone scans and other tests and was waiting for the results. Then one afternoon he telephoned out of the blue and after that it was two or three times a day. Nan asked questions and sometimes she argued. "If you don't believe me, talk to someone else. Talk to Bridget. She used to be a nurse. She always has good advice and you like her."

Then she went down to the water to be by herself.

She tried to get the order straight in her mind: the storm, the fallen giant, the small bump on his cheek. That was the order. The oldest and tallest tree had toppled like a giant and the next morning George's plaintive voice had said, "Nancy, what's this?" The storm, the tree, the itty-bitty tumour.

She explained everything to Jim over breakfast one morning. "Your father is stubborn. I won't say unreasonable. Alright, I will. He's afraid, naturally enough. And that makes him unreasonable."

George refused to let a surgeon come near him. He had found a Chinese wonder-worker instead, a woman who was seventy-three yet looked thirty, or so he claimed. Huan. Huan believed a macrobiotic diet would starve the malignancy, and therefore he was giving up bacon and eggs in favour of brown rice and steamed vegetables.

A macrobiotic diet, his mother explained dryly, was what cows ate, minus the salt. "I exaggerate. It's mostly brown rice, certain vegetables, a bit of fish from time to time. No cheese, no eggs, no meat or chicken or chocolate or bread or pasta or sugar or coffee or tea or milk. A lot of seaweed," she said.

With every call, George's fear came down the line. *Nancy, when are you coming?*

She told Jim they had to go back sooner than they'd planned. "Your father needs us." A chipmunk started to scold in a nearby tree. It was so little and so loud. "Is he going to die?" Jim said.

Worry spilled off his serious, eleven-year-old face, and Nan felt shaken by the dark leap his mind had taken. She herself hadn't been fearing George's death so much as a long, demanding illness. "You know," she said, putting conviction into her voice, "cancer isn't the death sentence it used to be."

And Jim wanted to believe her. But in his mind the bump on his father's cheek was like the black spot. He saw the old seaman backing away in horror from Blind Pew, who told him to stay put and hold out his hand for the little round of paper with the black spot on it, the summons, the death knell.

"People recover all the time now," she said. "Most people recover."

"Like forests." Jim was remembering what his uncle had told him.

She felt her heart turn over on his behalf. "Yes," she managed, "like forests."

"What about Lulu?"

"She's thinking of staying on here. For the winter, anyway."

"And then what?"

Nan took her son's chin in her hand and held it. Children were so unsentimental and tough, except when they weren't. It worried her that he cared so deeply that people be entirely devoted to each other.

"You have to give people room, Jim. They change, they travel, they do many things and go many places. Then they come back together again."

He waited.

"Lulu is our dearest friend," she said, telling him what he longed to hear. He had never understood how his mother and Lulu had managed to fall out of touch for so long. He knew how they had met, how they reconnected in Toronto when they went to university (though not a lot since they went to different universities some miles apart), how Lulu was living in a commune in those days, and that was the style, headbands, embroidered shirts, bare feet, drugs. "It was never my thing," his mother had told him. Until by chance they had come together again here at the lake.

"We're not going to lose her either," she said. "O.K.?"

"O.K."

It was cooler now, though the midday air was still run through with warmth and scented with summer. On August 20th there was a crescent moon when Nan got up at 4.00 a.m. A strong breeze filled the verandah. She spread an extra blanket over Jim, asleep in his room off the kitchen, and began to pack.

NEW YORK

9

AND SO GEORGE HAD HIS WIFE AND SON ALL TO HIMSELF
in the third-floor apartment on West End Avenue, the spacious
rooms he had inherited from his mother after her move into the
nursing home. Nan and Jim turned in circles, taking in the chaos of
boxes piled against every wall, and then Nan began her exasperated
sorting and organizing, knowing full well that she had been pulled
deeper into the marriage she had been on the brink of leaving.

A cool September brought New York's hot, dry summer to an end.
In Central Park, where they measure the rainfall, the charts verified
how dry – over the course of August only sixteen-hundredths of an
inch had fallen, making it the driest August since 1938 and producing
the sort of breathtakingly fractional result that she would see again
at the end of October on the night of the referendum. In Ontario,
water levels were so low, she learned from Lulu, that beside the
Ottawa River thousands of tiny rare plants – quillwort fern, umbrella
sedge, narrow-leafed water plantain – underwater for decades, were
having the chance to flower, while across the border in Quebec
the referendum question finally unfurled itself in long, ambiguous,
tendril-like legalese. "*Do you agree that Quebec should become sovereign
after having made a formal offer to Canada for a new economic and
political partnership within the scope of the bill respecting the future
of Quebec and of the agreement signed on June 12, 1995?*"

The question harked forward to a groundless future and back to
an agreement no-one remembered. It was designed to make voting
Yes seem the safest thing in the world.

Nan studied the wording in one of the newspaper clippings Lulu had mailed to her (it carried a photograph of the two main leaders of the Yes forces conferring with each other, Quebec premier Jacques Parizeau and Lucien Bouchard of the separatist Bloc) and then she lost sleep over it and more sleep over George's cancer. Her wakeful mind ran itself ragged in the middle of the night repeating endlessly the same few thoughts. There is a price to be paid for everything, she heard herself say. You refuse medical treatment; you pay a price. You separate; there will be consequences. It is dishonest and cowardly to imply otherwise. "I am speaking to you, Premier Parizeau and to you, Monsieur Bouchard. I am speaking to you, George Bobak." Then she would say it again.

Sometimes George was awake beside her and then his brand of anger mingled with hers. "They can put a man on the moon," he muttered from his pillow, "but they can't figure out what causes cancer. Billions they've spent and what do they know? Less than they know about canned dog food."

She had lived with him for a long time. She knew he believed the world was a corrupt and polluted place and eventually cancer would hunt everybody down. She understood that it was a point of intellectual and moral pride with him to be sceptical of established opinion, medical and otherwise. But she hadn't been prepared for the extent of his reckless obstinacy.

"And you know the reason?" he went on, working himself up. "Because there's more money in treatment than prevention. In fact, there's a lot of money to be *lost* in prevention. You think the big corporations want to stop poisoning the air and water? Like hell they do. That would cut into their," and now he was sputtering, unable to come up with a trenchant enough word, "their *revolting* profits."

"George," she said, resting her hand on his pyjama-clad shoulder and not keeping the weary strain out of her voice, "if you had an embedded sliver, you would dig it out. Let them cut out the lump. Don't be afraid."

"I'm not afraid. I'm *resistant*. Put me down as a conscientious objector. I am not handing my fate over to those greedy bastards."

The window was open a few inches and in came the low thrum of night-time, the steady noise of cabs, trucks, rooftop ventilation units, and every so often the wail of an ambulance.

"What does your mother think?" she said.

"The last thing my mother needs to hear is that another of her sons has cancer."

"So you're not going to tell her?"

"I am not."

"Well," Nan sighed, "you know what I think. At this stage it would be a pretty simple operation. The longer you wait, the more dangerous it becomes." She knew she was stating the obvious, but apparently it needed stating and she would continue to state it. What she could not say was something equally true, that if he refused treatment and died, then they would be spared the longer drama of a divorce.

"The world is so screwed up." George was muttering again. "We used to be smarter. We used to know more."

She slid her hand from his shoulder to his chest. Listening to him made it hard to breathe.

"Television makes everybody stupid," he said darkly. "Who'd have dreamt that T.V. would peak with Milton Berle? I'm sticking with Huan."

She had heard the crack about Milton Berle before. "Why do you have to be so headstrong?"

And she felt his chest expand under her hand. He had taken her criticism as a compliment. "I saw what happened to Kevin," he said. "I saw what happened to Shelley." His older brother dead from lymphoma, his first wife dead from breast cancer. "Big medicine is a racket. I am not going down that road."

"And suppose you're wrong? Suppose Jim ends up without a father?"

"I have no plans to die," he said.

Well, nobody does, she felt like saying. Nobody ever thinks they're going to die.

*　*　*

Lulu remained at the lake. Most of the leaves were down by now and the skies were full of colour and movement, blues and greys and big clouds hanging low. Lulu had drummed up a certain amount of work for herself as a voice and combat coach in Ottawa and was paying Nan more rent than she had asked for or wanted.

They spoke on the telephone every few days, Nan relying on her for updates about the referendum since it was barely mentioned in the *Times*. At the end of September the No side, the federalists, were ahead in the polls, as had been the case all along, and it looked as if they would beat the separatists easily on October 30th.

But then something happened that changed everything. With only three weeks left in the campaign, Jacques Parizeau, the premier nobody trusted, stepped back and handed the reins to Lucien Bouchard.

The separatists were smart, Lulu enthused to Nan. They knew they had to make enough Quebecers understand there was nothing to lose before they would take a leap into the unknown. In Bouchard they had a first-class persuader. "He comes into a hall," she said, relaying what she had seen on television, "he makes his way to the front and you know he's tired, he's in pain, you can see it in his face. He's using his cane, he's limping. And the effect on people is incredible and so is the effect on *him*. They want to touch him, they reach out to touch his coat. And for him, well, darling, it's the role of a lifetime." There was awe in her voice and it was partly appreciation for a fellow actor who got better and better with every performance. "He feels things so deeply," she said. "He can say, 'I used to be a federalist. I went to Ottawa and got slapped in the face. We Québécois all share this humiliating past. And voting Yes will be a magic wand. Everything becomes possible. It is the key that opens the door.'"

"Lulu, he lies." Nan felt her hands shaking. "Quebec can't turn its back on Canada and keep the Canadian passport and the Canadian currency. It *can't*. That's ludicrous." She became even more heated. "I hate what he's doing. Telling people they can keep the best parts of Canada and reject the rest, everything's to be gained and nothing lost, it's all easy, no sacrifice, just wave a fucking wand." She realized she was hyperventilating. Jim was listening and she caught a glimpse of his stricken face and made a gesture to indicate she was alright, everything was O.K., and she closed her eyes and took a long, slow breath.

Lulu said, "He's inspired, darling. His speeches are hypnotic. You know what I realised the other night? The campaign has released in him the kind of energy that independence will release in Quebec."

"God."

"How can you deny them that? How can you stand in their way?"

"Because," Nan said, "it will all turn to shit."

Lulu laughed. "Well, we'll see which side has the best negotiators." And when Nan groaned in reply, she said, "O.K., I'll change the subject. How is George? More important, how are you?"

"Oh," Nan said and stared up at the ceiling. It was almost too complicated to talk about. These things were supposed to stabilize you – country, marriage; but it was all a bad joke. Only later, when Jim was out of earshot, could she speak freely and tell Lulu that George was too frightened to admit he was frightened. "Yet he's very proud. Salivary gland cancer is rare. He likes having a rare cancer. And he thinks he can cure it with healthy eating. He's going to show them all."

"I can understand that. I'd probably do the same and let nature take its course."

"If you had a young son?"

Lulu went silent. "That's a good question. How's my Jim?"

Jim was wonderful. "He lights up our lives. He's got a rummy tournament going with his dad and the aces won't leave him alone. He wears his uncle's fedora for luck."

"Take good care of him, darling."

Jim had shot up several inches over the summer. He was going to be tall. Nan loved to watch him at the kitchen table, head bent in concentration, taking no prisoners, keeping his father company. "Nancy, our son is killing me," George liked to say, counting up his cards. Seeing them together, Nan understood why she had come back and why she wouldn't be able to leave. And all the separatists who thought leaving was easy were out to lunch.

Nan paced the kitchen. In her mind her country was crumbling into fractious bits, like poor Yugoslavia: everybody hating one another with a vicious passion and grabbing whatever they could.

She felt George put his hand on her shoulder and turned to face him.

"Don't talk to her," he said, and her shoulder dropped under his hand. "Next time she calls, give me the phone. I'll tell her where to get off."

Nan leaned into him for a moment, her cheek against his clean-smelling shirt, then stood back and went over to the sink. "She keeps me informed. I need to know." And staring into the sink, "It's looking very close. I think the separatists are going to win."

"Good."

She turned her haunted face towards his. "Don't say that."

"It's exciting," he said. "It's exciting to see people stand up for what they want. They want an end to the old system. They want to remake their world."

"You're such a New Yorker," she said, and she spoke with despair and admiration. She realized that he had changed in recent weeks. His illness had brought out qualities in him that she had either

154

failed to notice or never seen because he had repressed them. He enjoyed a fight. He wasn't going to break stride for anything. He was still a rough-tempered boy.

For the next two weeks, the last days in the campaign, all of the momentum was with the Yes. This sudden turning of the tide – the separatists surging in the polls, Lulu's mounting joy, the passive helplessness of the No forces, her own helpless absence from the scene – ate into her and in her anxiety she thought often of Trudeau, who was as much on the sidelines as she was. Lulu told her about Prime Minister Chrétien going on television in the hope that a last-minute appeal from his humbler self would avert disaster. All he managed, Lulu said, was to look haggard and desperate, with nothing to offer. But the most desperate thing of all, according to Lulu, was the spectacle of thousands upon thousands of English Canadians flying, busing, taking the train to Montreal in order to stage a last-ditch rally to profess their love for Quebec, all the while draping themselves in red-and-white Canadian flags. Afterwards they roamed the streets, talking English, hitting the bars. She said, "They don't know the first thing about Quebec. They've never bothered to find out. They don't give it a thought from one day to the next. And yet they *love* it. Do they think Quebecers are complete fools?"

"Lulu, I would have gone."

There was silence at the end of the line.

"I would have gone," Nan repeated. "You can't lump everybody together like that. So some people hit the bars. So what? People are trying to say their country matters to them. How often does it happen that you realize how deeply you care about something?" She stopped. Her heart felt as if it were being squeezed.

"Well," Lulu said, "your guy watched the rally from his office window in that law firm he still walks to every day. No-one on the federalist side would let him speak."

And Nan pictured him, a small figure at the window, isolated from the crowds and flags and speakers below. Old. Unneeded.

On the Saturday the clock fell back and the temperature dropped. At the lake Lulu smelled winter in the air and on Sunday she witnessed every kind of weather: black cloud, sunlight, hail, rain, wind, snow.

She telephoned Nan. "Guess what? It began to snow fifteen minutes ago."

"Good." Nan heard herself sounding like George. Surely, she thought, people would think of winter when they voted tomorrow and retreat into safety.

Monday, the day of the vote, was bitterly cold. Lulu called her in the morning and they found it in their hearts to wish each other well. Lulu promised to call that night from Guy's, where she would watch the results.

That night Jim was struggling with his math homework at the kitchen table and so he was more than happy to look up whenever the telephone rang and listen to his mother's end of the conversation, and then ask her what Lulu had said. He felt tugged in two directions, excited about the idea of a new Quebec but afraid for the old Canada. His father was in his favourite armchair, seemingly oblivious, his lap full of documents detailing the case of yet another tenant being harassed by yet another landlord. Their television was tuned to C.N.N., which was giving updates every fifteen minutes, something unheard of for Canadian news. It was obvious they expected the Yes side to win and Canada, as everybody knew it, to break into bits.

George turned in his chair, "Nancy? It won't be the end of the world."

"It will be the end of *my* world," she said with such feeling that Jim left his homework and went to her. She put her arms around him.

This was the night, in one of the lulls, when the two of them had their conversation about which one Homer would have liked more, Trudeau or Lévesque. Nan would never forget how consoling it was to take such a long view and to have her son as interested as she was, even if they disagreed. Jim was convinced that Homer would have preferred Lévesque as he so obviously preferred Hector to the rich and spoiled Achilles. And she went along with that, but then maintained that Trudeau was really a combination of Achilles and Odysseus, for he had no end of cunning and was never less than interesting. The comparison between the two foes embraced not just the *Iliad*, she said, impressing her son, but the whole Homeric story: war and unquiet peace.

"And don't forget," she said. "Trudeau was defending Canada as Hector defended Troy."

"But Hector lost," Jim said.

"He did. Hector lost."

To occupy and calm herself she hemmed the frayed edges of a big Indian bedspread she had been given years ago, using needle and thread, one stitch after another. She knew her method belonged to the Dark Ages, but so did she. So did she, with her horror of change.

The handwork helped when the Yes side took an early lead and held it for a long time. Lulu couldn't keep the exultation out of her voice when she telephoned, and all Nan could say was, "You'll phone me if it changes?"

She continued to sew, making inroads on her fingertips, jabbing and puncturing them to a fare-thee-well.

When the No side began creeping up, Lulu called again. And again when the Yes and No camps were in a dead heat. And then she left off calling because it remained unbearably close. At ten o'clock, when Nan sent Jim to brush his teeth and get into his pyjamas, there was still no outcome. Twenty more minutes had to go by before the newsflash on C.N.N.: if the trend in Montreal held, then the Yes side did not have enough to win.

"Jim!" Nan cried out, "the No squeaked out a victory!" And a moment later the telephone rang. She grabbed it and heard Lulu say into her ear, "Darling, you still have a country of the heart to come home to."

Nan couldn't speak.

"I'm glad for you. It matters more to you than it does to me. Guy is happy too. In fact, he's insufferable. I'm seriously considering smashing a plate over his head."

Jim was at her side and Nan handed him the telephone, smiling a tired smile, "I am so relieved. Here. Talk to Lulu."

"What a shame," George said, passing by on his way to bed.

"George," she called after him, "I want a divorce from you."

"I'm deaf," he called over his shoulder.

In the final tally a little more than 1 per cent divided the two sides: 50.58 per cent for the No and 49.42 per cent for the Yes. A No as small and fragile as an Arctic flower had given Canada one more chance.

The next day Nan felt utterly depressed. Her sense of relief was gone and she felt worse than ever. She knew no-one was happy with the way things were. Lulu added to her dejection, for she and Guy, having had a blazing row, were no longer speaking to each other.

The sourness was countrywide, Lulu told her. In Quebec and across Canada people were either dispirited or mad as hell. They had wanted more conclusiveness, a clearer outcome, rather than another near-departure that was only more of the same: an almost-end to an almost-country, a near miss, a close call, and another referendum in the wings, and soon. No-one doubted that for a moment. A neverendum, it was being called by the weary and jaded.

Jacques Parizeau had resigned. Lucien Bouchard would take over as premier. Saint Lucien, as the press called him, understood how to speak for a people whose four-hundred-year history was defined by winter. Lulu quoted his eloquence: "'To say that Quebec will never be independent is to say that spring will never come.'"

The words became a tolling bell in Nan's head.

Lulu said to her, "Guy wants the feds to outlaw another referendum. He'd be happy to put Lucien Bouchard behind bars. And don't take his side, Nan. Do not take his side, or I'll stop speaking to you too."

* * *

Over the next six months the lump on George's cheek transfixed them. They saw it go from a pea to a grape to a prune to an apricot – an orange – a grapefruit.

For Jim it was like being in a slow-motion horror movie. He had to force himself not to look away and then there were times when he could not help but stare. The lump didn't hurt, his father assured him, a bit of aching, but it wasn't bad. It just grew, and its growth was steady and unrelenting.

"Most cancer develops inside," his father said to him one day in late November. "We've got ringside seats on this one. I'm sorry, Jim."

He still shaved every morning before going to work. He did not hide behind a beard. The tumour under his razor was hard, cool, and dense; like unripe fruit, he said. The skin no longer moved over the lump as it had initially. Instead, he noticed it was tethered to the tumour as the tumour, he had to suspect, was tethered to other things, deeper inside.

Yet when he spoke to Jim he was always optimistic. "Huan believes it's slowing down. I think so too."

Jim could see that wasn't true, but he said, "I hope so."

His mother's face was also changing. She had dark circles under her eyes from not sleeping and the scar on her forehead was red around the edges from being pushed and picked at and prodded. "Don't," Jim said to her one day and took her hand away from her face.

"Am I doing that all the time? I'll try to stop."

It seemed to Nan that they were back in the Middle Ages, or not even that far back. Back in the days when her grandmother had a goitre that hung off her throat. She remembered extending her hand with a small child's fascination to touch the soft bulge that was a part of the old woman that should have been clothed. There was something similarly naked about George's tumour. The more distended it became, the more it reminded her of another display, something she had witnessed years ago when she was sitting with an old roué in swimming trunks and his balls slipped their confines and gradually ballooned into the biggest set of testicles she had ever seen: less pink the more they came into view, delicately veined, an eye-popping, arousing, more-than-a-handful of heaviness. The tumour in its diseased perversity was like that, except it took months instead of minutes and it certainly wasn't arousing. Both men were idiots, she said to herself. The roué had taken the sun full on, shirtless, hatless, sunglass-less, and completely engrossed in himself. And George was afraid of the blade.

Their medical bills grew. All the trips to his Chinese wonder-worker, whose herbs and salves he bought, cost quantities of money they did not have. George's health insurance through his employer covered none of it. More than once Nan argued for selling the apartment and moving to Canada and its socialized medicine, but George would not leave their beautiful rooms or entrust himself to Canadian doctors. Late in the fall he had stopped going to see his mother, not wanting his appearance to upset her, and so it fell to Nan to visit the nursing home and make excuses for George to an old woman whose memory was getting worse by the day.

Nan said, "I don't know what to do, Jim."

He stood a few feet away, his now habitual stance of semi-retreat, and didn't know what to say or how to help. There was some kind of craziness going on. He couldn't understand why his father was letting the tumour gallop away with itself. Or why his mother didn't drag him to the hospital and have it removed. Instead, she either writhed with impatience or exploded in anger, and then took one of her self-imposed walks around the block to cool off.

He attempted an answer. "He just wants us to be with him. He feels better when we're with him."

She nodded and the room took shape around his young shoulders. "You're right. He does. He feels better when we're with him."

Then Jim spoke from his own frustration and asked her why she couldn't *make* him have the operation.

"How can I make him? I've argued myself blue in the face. You've heard us. He says it's his life, not mine."

"You could give him an ultimatum," Jim said. "If he won't have the operation, you'll get a divorce."

Her startling son. Nan sank into herself at his words, into the morass of her marriage. She shook her head. "I can't force him. You can't force a grown man against his will. And I wouldn't leave him when he's so ill. He knows that."

Indeed, she sometimes suspected George of holding on to his illness in order to hold on to her.

At the kitchen table Nan worked late into the night, turning the sows' ears of museum publications into trim, serviceable wallets. She had been taking on every editing contract she could, thinking ahead to the day when they would have even less money. Every so often she would lower her head into her arms and wonder aloud why no-one nowadays could write. She slept very little, getting up early to make Jim's breakfast, and then off he would go to school, returning at the end of the day, when he would make one of his own specialties: cinnamon toast, or popcorn, or chocolate pudding cooked on the stove and eaten while it was hot; such comfort. He loathed brown rice. He loathed and despised steamed greens.

On the phone Nan told Lulu that he was growing up too fast and it saddened her. And Lulu said, "He's always been mature for his age."

Yes and no, Nan thought. Yes and no. "It touches me to hear George talk about him. The other night he said Jim knows how to handle him, how to make him feel better. 'He cares,' is what he said."

161

"Well, George is no dummy. He knows he has a great son."

"Lulu?" Nan hesitated.

"What, my darling?"

"Don't get mad at me." Nan picked up a pencil off the table and rolled it between her fingers. "You and Guy," she sighed.

No response came down the line and so she laboured awkwardly on, saying what a marvellous thing it had been to see them get along, how that mattered more than a quarrel about the referendum.

"So patch it up, you're saying." Lulu's voice was hard.

Nan waited.

"Why me?" Lulu said. "Why should it always be on my shoulders? Why am I the one who has to bend and accommodate and make nice? Because I'm the woman. I'm the sister. Well," Lulu said, "fuck that."

Nan saw her point and didn't argue.

Lulu said, "And don't give me that Alice Munro line about forgiveness in families being a mystery."

A police siren rose and faded in the distance, and Lulu added with venom, "How it comes and how it lasts."

"'How it comes *or* how it lasts.'"

"Well," Lulu said.

Nan made another effort. "It's hard. I know it's hard—"

"Try unbearable. I am trembling from lack of sleep and the thought of him. Which makes me sick."

"Lulu."

"I *hurt*. He *hurts* me."

"I know. It's eating you alive."

"And he sails on," Lulu said. "He sails on. You know what fills my mind? I'll tell you. Al Pacino tolerating Fredo until the moment the mother dies. And then he has him killed."

Nan laughed a little despite herself. "Yikes," she murmured. She pictured the older brother, Fredo, in the boat on that silent lake, fishing and saying his prayers, and then you heard the shot. "Well, you're not going to have him killed," she said. "So you've got to come up with another solution."

"Let him find it," Lulu said.

A few days later, in early December, Nan was walking home into a north wind with a heavy grocery bag in each hand when she noticed flecks of snow in the air – the first snow. She raised her eyes and saw the lake, cold and pure, black and white with winter. And maybe it was her years of living away, or maybe she was stuck in the past, but in her mind Lulu and Guy's mutual hostility blended with the larger sadness of a country plagued by its own version of the Berlin Wall. She thought of Lulu spending Christmas alone, while Guy was a stone's throw away, and she really could not stomach the waste and stupidity of it. In that moment she decided what to do and she picked up her pace. Once she got home she set down her bags inside the door and without taking off her coat went to the telephone. She found her little phone book and called.

"Guy? It's Nan."

His gruff voice slid from surprise to warmth, and they talked for a few minutes about themselves and George's health and Ducky. And then she said, "Things are bad between you and Lulu."

Silence descended on the line, until at last Guy said, "She's the one who takes offence and lashes out. *She* started it. *I* didn't."

Nan fingered the little phone book, which had survived the end of her marriage, though John had taken other things that mattered to her, small personal possessions that she still missed. Nothing was ever entirely fair, especially with men who were sticklers for fairness.

Guy said again, "I didn't start it."

"But you can *stop* it," she said evenly. "You can take the first step and talk to her."

Beyond the window more snowflakes were flying about. A light sifting, blown this way and that.

"Guy?" she said, to ease the tension and because she wanted to know, "tell me if the lake has frozen over. I wanted to see it freeze."

"O.K., Nan," he said. And to her immense relief, his voice sounded normal again. "O.K. I'll do what I can."

He went on to tell her about the lake, how it had frozen over one night in mid-November making crazy noises as the thin ice cracked and echoed and twanged. "The water reaches a critical temperature," he said, "and then the entire lake just flash-freezes. It thaws the same way, overnight. You would have been asleep when it happened."

"Have you been walking on it?" She had never done that, never walked across the surface of the lake she swam in.

"Just in our bay. I never feel safe crossing the lake till around Christmas." His tone changed again and he said, "Nan, you're a good friend. I've missed you."

She closed her eyes and smelled in memory the sweet smell of wood smoke that he carried about with him. It was hard being his sister, she thought, and it would be hard to be his wife.

"Well, we go back," she said. "The three of us."

The snow had stopped, leaving not a trace. Nan stood at the window for a while, thinking about Christmases in her childhood, her brother setting his alarm clock for 2.00 a.m. so he could flood the rink he had created in their backyard, her own fingers alive with pain, fumbling to lace up her skates, the late afternoon and early morning darkness, the bowls of liquorice allsorts, the stockings at the foot of their beds. Her father would have said that Christmas was a poor show now. She heard his mournful voice saying it. And before Jim got home from school and George returned from work, she left the window and picked up the telephone again. She listened to the ringing at the other end, willing him to answer. But as usual it was someone else. An older male, who said he would check to see if Blake was in. A moment passed and he came back. "Sorry. He's not here."

"Then will you give him a message?" she said, sounding to herself like a typical overreaching parent. In her sore and suspicious heart she believed Blake was very much there and had instructed his fellow born-again Christian to say he wasn't. "Please tell him his mother called, that I'd like to talk to him."

"I'll pass that on."

"Do you know when he'll be back?"

"Sorry, I'm not sure."

Coming up out of the subway, Jim passed a little sidewalk-forest of Christmas trees propped against long wooden stands and ranks of red poinsettias outside the Korean grocer's. He continued home and walked in on his parents arguing. His mother was insisting that on Christmas Day they go to the nursing home and then bring his grandmother home for dinner, and George was refusing to commit himself. Jim watched him take hold of the loose flesh that covered his Adam's apple and work it up and down, up and down, as he fixed his eyes on the *Times*.

George had not paid a visit to the nursing home for a while now. Nan, however, went regularly and twice she had asked Jim to go along with her. Grandma Bobak had not forgotten him and always wanted to know where George was. His mother's excuse – "You know how busy he is" – seemed to work. "Busy, busy, busy," his grandmother would say lightly, "busy, busy, busy," apparently satisfied to know that her son had a job. Jim tried not to show how uncomfortable he felt seeing her so frail and mixed up, and seeing the other really, really old people in wheelchairs, some of them holding teddy bears in their arms.

His mother finally knelt beside his father's chair, removed the newspaper from his hands, and said, "You don't have to explain about your cancer. Say you've got a toothache. That's why your cheek is swollen."

"Nancy, she's not an idiot, for Pete's sake."

"George, you don't understand," she said, resting her hand on his knee. "She'll believe anything you say. She doesn't question anymore. She doesn't. The only thing she wants to know is where you are."

165

Jim watched his father cover her hand with his, and knew his mother had won.

The day before Christmas, the telephone rang and hoping it might be Blake changing his mind, Jim answered. It was Lulu and her voice was buoyant. She was knee-deep in chocolate shortbread, she told him. "Darling, I'm out of my mind."

She had promised Ducky she would bring her chocolate cookies on Christmas Day. "Enough for an army and navy of ducks."

Jim felt a pang of envy, picturing the cosiness of Christmases he knew from books.

He said, "Mom said you weren't talking to Guy anymore."

"I wasn't, darling. I was through with him. But then he dropped by and offered to keep me in kindling and firewood over the winter, if I would find that helpful. And she imitated the mild and tentative tone of the offer. "I'm easy to win back, you know. It doesn't take much."

Jim liked her more than ever for saying that. "Mom's out," he said, "but she'll be back soon." And then he told her that Blake wasn't coming home, he was staying in Philadelphia.

"Your mother told me the other day," she said, and paused before adding, "I would be disappointed too."

"Yeah." It was the shock of realizing they didn't matter to Blake that got to him, not even enough for him to bother coming home at this time of year. "So Ducky's there for Christmas," he said.

"I'm crazy about that kid," Lulu said. "Almost as crazy as I am about you."

And then she said gently, "I never dreamed I would be spending Christmas with my brother. People do come around, Jim. I don't know why it takes so long or what makes it happen. I really don't. Your mother and I have talked about it. But if Guy can come around, so can Blake. So can anyone."

He wondered about that. He didn't see a lot of evidence to back it up. Maybe you had to be old.

10

"TELL ME A STORY," HIS MOTHER SAID TO HIM ONE winter night when neither of them could sleep. They had wandered independently into the kitchen and now they were eating toast. "Tell me a grisly story."

"Tell me too," came his father's voice from the bedroom down the hall.

His mother closed her eyes, then opened them and grimaced with amusement. "His hearing has improved," she said.

It was January now and George had decided to take an indefinite medical leave and was collecting disability.

They went into the bedroom and there he was wasting away under their eyes, except for his growth, which almost needed its own pillow. His tongue and lips worked, but he had a crooked smile and trouble closing his right eye when he blinked. He used eye drops now, so dry had that eye become. The surgeon had given him fair warning. A malignant tumour of the parotid gland (the major salivary gland, she had explained) will affect the muscles of your face because the facial nerve passes through the gland and branches within it. You must understand that its growth will be unrelenting if you do nothing and eventually the cancer will spread.

George said from his pillow, "I like grisly too."

And so began the grislies, instalments of a lurid tale with only one unspoken rule, that nothing was too awful for the likes of them, not in the middle of the night when the light was dim and muffled city sounds formed a backdrop to young Jim's voice. He began with a cowboy named Bad Art and his mother laughed, "Jim, you are clever," and only then did he get his own pun. The young cowboy grew up in the Yukon, carrying pails of water from the river to the house, boiling it on the woodstove for tea, never washing himself, never brushing his teeth. His bare feet he warmed by standing in steaming bear turds or steaming moose turds. His father was Arthur Kew, a failed fisherman and prospector, who wouldn't let anyone talk at the table or bring home friends. His mother was Wild Gert, who ran the bowling alley in town and liked to grab her small son and roll him up for use as a bowling ball. Arthur was a lush, Gert was a maniac, Bad Art was a crybaby who wanted a horse.

"What kind of horse?" his father asked.

He considered. "A pinto."

"That's good."

Nan watched her son weave his tale out of things he had heard from Lulu and things he made up out of thin air, and she remembered back to when he was born, perfect to the last fingertip. Her mother had come down from Canada to help out and stayed for a week, over the course of which her navy slacks got increasingly white as she painted the kitchen, hallway, and bathroom, taking a nap only once, one rainy afternoon, an overworked child, small, on the sofa. Nan could see her still, every visible detail, birdlike under a blanket: her knees drawn up, shoulders rounded, hands under her left cheek, bountiful silver hair on the pillow. That was the visit when Nan had posed the sort of delving question Jim loved to ask. They were at the restaurant they were so fond of, La Rosita on Broadway, and she had said, "Mom, are you afraid of life?"

"Not anymore," her mother said, her face open and wise. She was nearly seventy.

Waiting for the food to arrive, anticipating it with pleasure, entering into the excursion with abundant good spirits, her mother had been full of life rather than afraid of life; girlish the way Stan had been boyish. How Nan missed them, her mother and the dog she had given away.

Jim was telling them now about the first time Bad Art ran away from home, when he was six years old and tired of being used as a bowling ball.

"Is this ten-pin bowling?" his father said. "Or candlepin?"

"George," his mother said.

"Details are important, Nancy." George reached for a third pillow and stuffed it under his head.

"They are, but not when they're an excuse to show off—"

"Candlepin," Jim said.

"Or make the other person feel stupid."

"Do you know what candlepin is?" his father said.

"I'll find out."

"Good. Now you say Bad Art's a crybaby. Why?"

This needed no research. "The other kids grab his books and throw them around and he yells and tries to grab them back. And then they really make fun of him."

Nan didn't speak. So at school, she was thinking, his maturity didn't help him. He was just a boy who was different from other boys.

"Right," George said. "Who are the kids?"

Jim looked down at his hands.

"You should give them names, son. I expect one of them's really big. Johnson?"

Jim smiled. His father hated Lyndon Johnson as much as he hated the Red Sox. "The other two are twins," he said. "Twin brothers."

"They've got warts on their hands," his father said. "I bet they can't even spell."

"Leo and Cal," he said.

His father reached under his head and flung two pillows on the floor and closed his eyes. "Tomorrow I want to hear about Leo and Cal."

"And their warts," his mother said.

"Their five hundred warts," his father said.

Jim began to draw pictures to go with his stories, using an old day-planner of his father's that was practically empty. Drawings of dogs and horses and log cabins, of fresh disasters for Bad Art, like tripping over the doorstep while carrying an open can of beans and falling face-first into the razor-sharp lid, cutting his face to ribbons. He had seen pictures of goalies before hockey masks came along and he drew a picture of a face zippered with stitches.

Lights out, room dark, he spoke from his pillow. "Mommy, do you think my story is good?"

"I do," she said, pausing on her way out of his room.

Then, "What does 'graphics' mean?" And after she told him, "About my story. It's not bad, is it?"

Falling asleep on his pencils, he would wake up in the morning to his rumpled pages half-tucked under his pillow and pull them out, thrilled to pore over what he had created out of nothing: the words, the pictures. He grew used to finding one or two pencils in among his sheets whenever he made his bed.

Nan kept a running account in her own calendar of George's weight loss, fatigue, various aversions. Since Christmas he had made the effort occasionally to visit his mother, but the mere mention of Lulu's name made him bridle. It had reached the point where when Lulu telephoned, Nan closed the kitchen door and lowered her voice.

With Lulu, and Lulu alone, she unburdened herself about the pace of George's tumour. "He pretends Huan's salves are making a difference. He says he can tell from the inside. The tumour feels different on the inside."

"Do you tell him he's wrong?"

"I tell him he's throwing his life away. I'm harsh. It makes it easy for him not to listen to me."

"He can still chew and swallow, though? He still eats?"

"It takes longer. I'm up and have the dishes done before he's half-way through."

"Nan, do you want me to come? Guy would check on the house while I'm gone. Darling, I could drive down in a day."

Nan felt tears starting in the back of her throat and was astonished at how much it hurt to fight them and hold them back.

"I'm coming tomorrow," Lulu said.

"No." Nan got out the word. "No, it's hard enough as it is. I want to see you, I'd love to, but George—"

"Is jealous. Why is he like that?"

Nan managed to say, "Because his second wife left him for a woman and he's never got over it."

"Ah," Lulu said. And then she said, "Poor George."

Towards the end of February they were at the supper table, the kitchen lamp shining above their heads, the space beside Nan occupied by the contents of an envelope from Lulu. The *Ottawa Citizen* had printed Trudeau's long *J'accuse* in which he eviscerated, point by point, Lucien Bouchard's distortions of history during the referendum campaign. Then a week later they printed Bouchard's equally long and vigorous reply. Fascinated by the furious joust between the two men, Nan was saying to Jim that here was a lesson in defending yourself. She began to read a passage aloud and George stopped her.

"I don't get it," he said. "I can't tell you how little I care."

"*You* care," she said, turning to Jim. "How many times have you reread *The Story of Canada*?"

"Five times," he admitted. He loved the *voyageurs*, paddling fourteen hours on one bowl of pea soup. And Wolfe and Montcalm on the Plains of Abraham. Louis Riel and the buffalo. The story of Confederation. And Lévesque looking like a tough cabdriver in a gangster movie. And Terry Fox, running across the country on his one leg to raise money for cancer, but having to give up partway because his cancer came back and he died. Twenty-two years old. That was stubbornly brave and heartbreaking, especially now.

"But half the time your mother says the country disappoints her." George was affronted. He wanted his son on his side.

"I know," she said, "but you can be loyal to what disappoints you." Nan opened her hands wide, feeling benevolent because her son had backed her up and because she knew she was making a good point. "George, if I were someone else, your father, say, it might be loyalty to the Communist Party. You stay loyal to what increasingly disappoints you. It happens all the time."

"Alright," George said. "I get that." He was thinking of his father.

She went on. "You say to yourself, 'Have I kidded myself all these years? Does what I care about really matter? Is it important? On a scale of one to ten, would it even register?' Or, in the case of the Communist Party, 'Do I believe what its enemies are saying or do I hold firm?' And instead of not caring, you decide to care even more."

"You're talking about inertia," George said.

And his mother turned to him, "Do you know what inertia means? It's the tendency of objects to stay where you put them."

"Or to keep moving," George said.

"Or to keep moving in the same direction if they're already moving."

"Is that what you're talking about?" George said.

"I'm talking about loyalty," his mother said. "You decide to stick by something. Maybe you shouldn't. But you do. The trouble comes, of course, when your loyalties are divided."

"Then you have to choose," George said.

"You have to choose."

"What if you make the wrong choice?" George wasn't thinking about his father anymore.

Nan had that soft and tired expression on her face. George was smiling a smile that wasn't really a smile. And from his place at the table, Jim said, "Why do you have to choose?"

They looked at their son, who loved them both.

His mother said, "That's a good question."

His father said, "Because you can't be in two places at once."

"It's a very good question," his mother said. "Politicians make people choose. Why should we listen to them?" She meant the referendum. She meant the whole business of people in power backing ordinary people into corners. "Who's to say we can't have many loves and many identities? We can hold more in our heads than we think."

"What about our hearts?" his father said. "How much can they hold?"

His mother smiled. "A *lot*."

"Until they burst. There's an end to your inertia."

She laughed and reached across the table for his father's hand. "Hearts don't burst. They keep on expanding. There's no end to it."

His father looked at him and said, "Your mother thinks hearts are accordions." But he was holding her hand and looking happier than he had in a long time.

* * *

More and more often, on his way home from school, Jim stopped in Riverside Park to sit and read on one of the benches, choosing a spot in careful view of walkers and runners. The weather was getting warmer. Mourning doves called from the trees around him. If it was about to rain, the calls were more clipped, less loon-like. He knew his parents were waiting for him, but he dallied, prey to the same reluctance he had felt when Lulu ran over her dog. People were needing him and he wanted to see them, but not as much as he didn't want to see them. He felt very bad about that.

One day he came home to find his mother resting on the sofa, a book on her stomach. She wasn't sick, she assured him, she was thinking.

"What about?"

"Oh, lots of things."

She had been thinking about Blake, feeling his long, hurtful silence as an iron ache in her bones. He never called her. He almost never answered when she called him. And what if she died before things had a chance to improve between them? If she went to her grave and all he had of her was his own unresolved resentment? And so she persisted. She continued to call him – she had called him today; and sometimes she managed to reach him – she had reached him today; and every time he made such a point of being busy.

Jim flung himself down at her feet, all gangly limbs, and she swung around to make room for him. "I've been reading Trudeau's memoirs," she said, turning over the book in her lap.

And there on the cover was the man himself, wearing a fringed buckskin jacket and looking like someone who had never admitted to making a mistake in his life. Jim leaned in and they studied the photograph together.

"What do you think, Jim?"

"He looks like he doesn't need anybody." She nodded, and he said, "He looks superior. He can't lose."

"He knows his worth," she said. "That makes him calm. He knows what he believes and what he wants and how to get it."

"I like Lévesque's face," he said loyally. His mother opened the book and found a section of photographs and there was Lévesque.

"His face shows you everything," Jim said. "I trust him."

He saw her smile and said, "Don't you?"

"Oh," she said. And she inclined her head to one side, thinking how she had been not much older than Jim when Lyndon Johnson's big, craggy face appeared on the front page of the newspaper the day after Kennedy's assassination, and she had announced in all seriousness, "I trust this man." Her father, the old newspaperman, had shot her a surprised and thoughtful look. "Well, I'm glad you feel that way." And she knew that he was touched but unconvinced by her youthful expression of faith.

"I like both faces," she said. "I like the contrast. I'm not sure how trustworthy either one of them was. As politicians, I mean."

She began to flip slowly through the pages. How restful it was to look at faces she knew so well that had aged normally over time and weren't disfigured or diseased. "Trudeau was really shy as a boy. There's a bit in here, an incident when he was twelve, when a bigger boy at school threw a banana into his soup." Jim's eyes widened. He laughed and they shared a look of amusement. "He fished it out and flung it back into the other boy's soup, and the other boy challenged him to a fight. Trudeau was a lot smaller, he was fairly puny at that age, and knew he couldn't win. But he stared the bigger boy in the eye, not backing down, till the boy said he'd give him a break just this once and he walked away. So you can win some confrontations just by acting confident, that's what he learned."

"Is it a good book?" Jim asked. He knew she was giving him advice about how to handle things at school. Try acting confident even if he wasn't.

"Better than I thought it would be. It takes me back to a different time and a different way of thinking about the world. And it moves me." What she did not say was that Trudeau was only fifteen when his father died. There was a single paragraph in which he described the effect on him of the sudden death: how in a split second he felt the world go empty.

They went into the kitchen after that and set about making chocolate pudding in the double boiler, and Jim said, "Did Trudeau and Lévesque like each other?" He meant secretly, a grudging affection.

She knew what he meant, what he was hankering after. This was what he lived for, figuring out who liked whom, who admired whom, so that he could follow suit.

"I think they hated each other's guts," she said. She was helping him measure out the milk. "But, you know, that doesn't mean they didn't have a certain regard for each other."

"Like Lulu and Dad," he said.

She stared at him. "You think they have a regard for each other?"

"And you and Blake."

It felt as if her heart had been thumped. Her eyes welled up and she looked away. She didn't know whether Jim was very young or very old, whether he was full of wishful thinking or wisdom. "Does Blake hate my guts?" she said softly.

"He loves you too."

"How do you know?"

"He just doesn't show it."

Jim was stirring assiduously now and she leaned against the counter and watched him. "How are things at school?" she asked, keeping her eyes on his face.

"It's O.K."

"Anybody giving you a hard time?"

"Not anymore."

"I talked to Blake this afternoon. I got him on the telephone. He asked about you."

And she saw his face light up.

"Did he say anything about coming home?"

"He hasn't made up his mind. Maybe in the summer."

Jim stopped stirring, worried concern all over his face. "That's too late. Daddy will be dead by then." The word *Daddy* came off his lips without him thinking. He heard it hanging in the air.

Nan gently took him by the shoulders and looked into his eyes. "He's not going to be dead by then. Bridget is talking to him, working on him. You know he listens to her. If he agrees to an operation, they'll remove the tumour. He'll have to be in the hospital for a while and then he'll come home and we'll look after him."

"How?" They weren't doctors.

"We'll learn as we go along. We'll be a team. You and me. We'll figure it out."

That night she picked a book off her shelf by Northrop Frye – a slender book of three lectures and an essay – his last book – and read

176

several pages in bed. She was skimming a few more when her eye fell on the word *Ontario* in the middle of a line, and it was as if a flower had sprung off the page.

In bed she lay awake seeing wild flowers along the shore in their bay. Her brother in the canoe searching for orchids and mushrooms and blueberries. George was asleep beside her.

In a while she too was asleep, dreaming ragged dreams. She had forgotten to finish a contract for the Museum of Natural History and remembered it while she was on a bus heading in entirely the wrong direction. Eventually she was walking home on a crowded street and who should be all alone and coming towards her – and in tears – but Jim. He had made his way for many city blocks and was in the middle of the intersection, crossing, when she saw him, and he her. That lost tearful look of his. The moment he saw her, his tears shifted to blame, but the blame abated. She held out her arms.

*　　*　　*

They had inherited all the books belonging to George's mother, and as spring advanced Jim went through the Time-Life series, reading them after school. He had come to Ivan the Terrible and was fully absorbed. He read in the big armchair in the living room while his father puttered about between kitchen, sofa, and bed. His father was always glad to see him come through the door. "I didn't want to see *anybody* today, son, except you."

George seldom went outside anymore, not having the energy and not wanting to frighten passersby. They kept each other company, father, son, Ivan the Terrible. And rapidly Jim fell in love with Russian history. The pain and enormity of it, the depth of the depravity, the suffering – they were on a scale that dwarfed anything in North American history. After all, what was left from the short, sharp drama of the referendum in Quebec? Not a whole country, not a healed country, not a new country, but an anticlimax. Lucien Bouchard as premier seemed to care only about balancing the books. He claimed he was going to wait for "winning conditions" before holding another referendum. Well, what kind of heroism was that?

Ivan the Terrible's turning point came very early when his beloved wife died young, after which he went berserk and murdered people left and right in the most gruesome ways, even his favourite son. At the end, his screams of sorrow and self-horror carried through the walls of his palace and out across Moscow. Jim flipped forward and read about the Battle of Stalingrad in 1942, the long siege, the house-to-house combat, the colossal suffering and unimaginable death.

It was peaceful in the living room. George liked to watch the birds in the boughs of the tree in front of the building, flitting, settling. It was the first of April now and the songbirds were migrating north. "They know they're safe inside the branches," he said to Jim. There had been a time in his twenties when George had enjoyed rousing anthems of national liberation. Now, seeing his son's interest, he searched his sprawling music collection, musing aloud about the old days when he took classes at a Marxist school before it got infiltrated by Trots (before he met his first wife, before her death from cancer, before his second wife left him for a woman, before Nancy married him and lived to regret it), "the old days," he said, "before better things came along, like you." And he found his recording of the Soviet national anthem sung by the Red Army Chorus and played it on the record player he had refused to part with (cassettes and C.D.s were a plot to deprive him of his youth) and his heart swelled and so did Jim's.

Jim saw himself starving and withstanding, killing Nazis by the score.

George said, "Anthems are so shameless. They're so forthright. And for people like us," he said, shooting an expressive glance at his son, "who are given to shame, they are a huge release."

Jim sat quite still. He hadn't realized that his father understood so much.

"In the night," his father said, "when I'm awake, it's always shame that floods me. Memories of things I've done that fill me with shame. They never go away."

"What things?"

"Oh, I'll tell you some day."

"Tell me now."

His father shook his head. "Not now."

After supper, Jim made his mother listen to the anthem. "I want you to hear this," he said. "O.K.?"

"Sure." Nan stood at the sink and ran hot water as Jim put on the record, then she proceeded to wash the dishes, aware that he had positioned himself close by and wasn't taking his eyes off her face. She started on the glasses, then plates. She kept on, but now she let her hair fall forward and her shoulders sagged. She turned her back to him as emotion doubled her over and she had to grab a tissue and walk into the bathroom and close the door, where she splashed water on her face and reached for a towel. Nan understood. She felt completely manipulated, but she understood. He was a boy who needed to see with his own eyes that you cared about what he cared about. It confirmed to him that his feelings were the right ones, that here was an anthem so stirring it could move you to tears.

Later, after George went to lie down, she established herself on the sofa with file folders in her lap, intending to work. But resentment and worry boiled up. She had come to believe that George was intent on a long suicide involving her and Jim and his own need for attention. His behaviour felt punitive to her, self-indulgent and deliberate. The revolutionary strains of the anthem were still working on her and she saw herself banging sense into his head with a hammer and taking a sickle to his tumour. Nothing else would do it, she thought. Even Bridget had no effect on him, though she had dropped by again the other day and with great kindness and enormous good sense urged him to have the surgery, saying it would be a big operation, but they could do it, it wasn't too late. George had listened as he listened to no-one else, since he had known her a long time and liked to praise what he called the natural path she had taken from nurse to visual artist, always working with her intelligent hands. Yet what had he said to her in the end? That he wouldn't win any beauty contests, but he felt stronger, he really did. He said he wasn't giving up on Huan.

Huan, Nan thought. And under her breath she spat out the name.

When Jim slid into the armchair with his science textbook and half-eaten apple, she raised her head and her look was a look he had seen many times. It was two looks, one sliding up over the other, veiled irritation sliding up over affection. She was angry.

He reached over and touched her arm. "What's wrong? Why are you mad?"

She took his hand. "I'm not mad at *you*."

Normally, this would have sufficed. She didn't mean him to take her moods personally and he didn't. "I'm mad at your father for being a fool." She gave his hand a squeeze and let it go in order to focus again on her work, and it was the disgusted look on her face that set him off. The sadness, the puzzle of their lives, finally took on a clarity that overwhelmed everything else. She did not care if the things she said hurt them.

"You can't talk like that. You can't do that." He hissed the words so his father wouldn't hear.

She looked up at his livid face. "Do what?"

"He's sick. It's not his fault."

She folded her hands, tired and obstinate and trapped. "I think he's unreasonable."

"*You're* unreasonable."

"*I'm* unreasonable? *He's* the one. If only he'd—" She checked herself and did not go on. She looked down at her hands and said in a lowered voice, "What do you want me to do, Jim?"

"You're the grown-up. How am I supposed to know?"

As if to punctuate this excellent question, there came a loud and ominous rumble from the far end of the living room. They turned their heads and saw the wall above her desk spill forward in an avalanche of books and twisted metal.

"Jesus," she said.

The noise woke George. He padded up behind them in bare feet, joining them as they stood staring in bewilderment at all her books and papers strewn across her desk and over the floor. The shelves were bent wreckage, half-hanging off the wall, half-burying her desk.

"The literary gods have turned against us," Nan said, and she wasn't joking.

Jim looked from his dismayed mother to his father and back to his mother. "Or maybe shelves can only hold so much weight?"

She smiled then and put her arm around his sensible shoulders, grateful to him.

Jim knelt and started to pick up books. She knelt too and discovered that the cup of cold coffee forgotten on her desk had been tumbled in with the mix. Her beloved books were spattered, some of them were bathed, in cold, sweet, sticky coffee. Samson Junior, she thought to herself, resting back on her heels. Everything reeked of stale coffee and wet paper. This is how the world works, she thought. Not a big bang followed by an expanding universe but a hidden universe of inadequate screws, screwed in by inadequate husbands who bring everything down upon our godforsaken heads. And leaning forward, she began to separate the dry books from the wet. "This is yours," she said, passing George his treasured edition of *Here Is New York*. Undamaged, she was glad to see.

George took it from her hands and stood reading the first of its fifty or so pages, remembering who had given him the book, his old friend Ken, and recognizing, as he read them again, E. B. White's great insights about the dubious gifts of loneliness and privacy that New York has to offer. In New York, according to White, you have to be willing to be lucky.

"I'm not," he said to himself, but he was speaking aloud. "I'm not willing to be lucky."

And Nan turned on her knees. "*That's* lucky."

"What is?"

"If the bookshelves hadn't tumbled down, you wouldn't be standing there reading the truth about yourself."

"You think I'm not willing to be lucky?"

She felt like smiling. He had said it himself. But he wanted her to contradict him.

She said, "You see yourself as *un*lucky. That can't be news to you. If you were *willing to be lucky*, you would let yourself be operated on. You would think, Maybe there's a chance I'll recover. Instead of sticking to this suicide mission you're on."

She stood and went to get some cloths. At the sink she dampened them and then returned and began to wipe off the books that needed wiping.

It was later the same night, when she lay down beside him, that something in George gave way as suddenly as the bookshelves.

He said into the darkness, "I guess the question is when does stubbornness become stupidity?"

She turned over on her pillow to find him staring up at the ceiling.

"Huan failed me," he said.

She heard his breathing. She felt his warmth. From this angle, inches away from his poor monster-face, it occurred to her that his big, lopsided tumour was like a snowball rolling down a hill, picking up more of him as it went along, and soon nothing of him would be left, except this grey mass lying in the shade at the bottom of his life.

He said, "That's what you've been telling me all along. I made a bad choice."

Nan felt the air around them take on a different texture. "It's not too late," she said.

He moved his shoulders in disagreement.

"It's not," she said. "We go back to the surgeon. She schedules the surgery."

"How can I walk into her office with this face of mine?"

"I'll go with you. We'll get through it together."

"So you won't leave me?"

She turned onto her back and stared up at the ceiling too.

"I'm right here," she heard herself say.

And so it happened that George changed his mind at the eleventh hour. Having let his disease ravage him almost to the point of no return, he suddenly had a hunger to live.

11

THAT WEEK, THE FIRST WEEK IN APRIL, THEY WENT BACK to the surgeon George had seen initially, nine months ago, and she was as plainspoken as ever. He was not her first patient, she said, to say no to surgery, choose a holistic route, then come back with a massive problem. She was a trim woman in her fifties with short, greying hair, lively brown eyes, strong surgeon hands. Earlier, she said, she could have saved skin and nerve (and his life, she might have added, but did not). Now he would lose not just the salivary gland, but his facial nerve on that side and half his jaw. He would be left with a great big hole. Her manner as she spoke to them was neither impatient nor overly patient. She was not unkind. In her presence George became meek and Nan took notes. She wrote down *temporal bone resection, modified radical neck dissection*, and *pectoralis major myocutaneous flap*. This last the surgeon repeated and then spelled out, all four words.

"The bone is gone, the salivary gland is gone, the facial nerve is gone," she said, laying out the sequence. They would fill the hole as best they could with soft tissue, meaning fat and skin. "That's the flap," she said. They would take it from his chest, using it to resurface the side of his face and neck. The modified radical neck dissection would allow them to remove affected lymph nodes, and since lymph nodes live in fatty tissue they would have to sacrifice a certain amount of neck tissue as well. Post-op, he would have numbness of his ear, the side of his face, and neck. The normal tissues left behind would regain sensation, but a big area would stay numb. He would be in the operating room for about six hours. He would be in the hospital for three weeks. He would take eight weeks to heal. Then radiation.

George had not interrupted her. He had inclined his head so that he caught every word. Afternoon light came over her right shoulder and across her cluttered desk. She must work all the time, he thought, saving people like me who aren't worth saving.

"I'm wondering if it's worth it," he said. "How long will I have?"

"Before the cancer comes back? I don't know. That depends if we get it all. You can never answer that question."

"A year?"

"I never give people odds, ever. In a year we'll be able to assess things."

"So I've got a year," he said, not looking at Nancy, who sat very upright in her chair. "I'll take it."

"You will want to think about it," the surgeon said, "and let it all sink in."

"It's sunk in," he said. He wanted to live. It seemed simple enough.

Very well, then. She went out to confer with her secretary and came back to say the earliest date she could give him was two weeks from now. Thursday, April 18th. There was another surgeon who might be able to slot him in even more quickly. George said he would stick with her.

During those long, dread-filled days leading up to the surgery, when there were blood tests to undergo, chest X-rays, a cardiogram, a pre-op appointment with the anaesthetist, and all of it involving more trips to the hospital – Columbia-Presbyterian, an easy subway ride away – George fell into the habit of talking soundlessly to himself. His lips moved as he folded and refolded his napkin. He often beat a soft tattoo on the table. He often slept.

One afternoon, when Nan came back from a meeting with the publications people at the museum, she looked in on him, and finding him asleep, sat down in the chair beside the bed for a while.

Her mind drifted back to her two boys at the end of a long drive when they would awaken not knowing where they were, in the smell of old car, the windows rolled down and the outside air drifting in. Nearby she would be reading on a summer porch, or at a picnic table, or with her back against a tree, one ear cocked for the full-throated wail of abandonment that would shatter the peace, whereupon she would help the outraged child – Blake or Jim – out of his car seat, or seatbelt, and comfort his marooned being.

George opened his eyes and she asked him how he felt. He felt rotten. She reached for his hand and held it. In through the half-open window came the sound of a horn pressed long and repeatedly, and the clatter, not so distant, of dishes, and then a song she recognized but could not name. "George," she said, "what's going to become of us?"

He squeezed her hand. "Don't worry. I've put everything in order." She would be looked after and so would Jim. He had given her power of attorney and made her executor of his will.

Nan remembered the moment several years ago when her mother-in-law had taken her aside, telling her she was so much more reliable than George and that's why she had given her power of attorney. What it meant, as Nan quickly discovered, was that one woman had saddled another with the drudgework of her affairs.

She asked, "Shouldn't I call your daughters?"

There was no need, he had been talking to them himself.

"I didn't know. Are they going to come from California?"

"After the operation." They would stay with Doreen, he said. Their mother.

"And what about your brother?"

"What brother?"

She gave him a long look. "I think he should know."

"I don't even have his number."

"Your mother does. I could try reaching him, if you like."

"Martin can come to my funeral."

186

She had to smile a little. "You want him to be sorry he neglected you."

George massaged the loose skin at the base of his neck, rolling it between his fingers. His crooked lips trembled with emotion. "There's no excuse for him not to be in touch."

Seeing how profoundly hurt he was, Nan refrained from saying that he was never in touch either.

"Call him," George said, a moment later. "Why not?"

"You're sure?"

"You've always wanted to. Now you have your excuse."

She sat for a moment, feeling stung, foolish. Then she stood up and went into the kitchen. He was right, of course.

In the end she didn't call him. It was partly the feeling of having been seen through that deterred her. She had no faith in her motives. If she wanted to do something for George, rather than for herself, she should try to reach his long-lost friend Ken. That would bring him joy, the sight of Ken in the doorway – the sort of joy she had felt when Lulu reappeared in her life. She made a number of inquiries in the next few days, but no one she knew had any idea what had become of Ken.

Really it was George's job, not hers, to call his brother, and eventually she told him so. "*You* do it, George. He's your brother. You shirk too many things." And she put the number she had found on her mother-in-law's desk under his nose.

Her scolding tone offended him and he snapped back in his chair and said, "I never asked you to call him."

"Well, in fact, you did." She knew this was so. He had fobbed it off on her in that way he had of fobbing things off.

"What are you so mad about?"

"Well, now," she said, "let me count."

The weekend before the operation, a fortune-teller told her fortune and Jim's. It was a Saturday morning. They had made a quick trip to the Museum of Natural History in search of kayaks so he could draw one properly, and in the museum they found themselves standing for a long time next to the cabinet of Shamanistic Regalia, which contained, among other things, a crown of grizzly bear claws, a hair ornament of swan feathers, whistles made of the leg bones of birds, a neck ring that was a loon's real neck and head, and another neck ring of cedar bark. They lingered as they had in the Dorset exhibit the summer before, fascinated by the otherworldly powers of these wild, vivid things. The primary duty of shamans was to cure the sick, they read in the text on the wall, but they also had the power to locate people who were lost and to provide food in times of scarcity. Ivory charms placed on the sick person glowed brightly if a recovery was in the offing. Otherwise, the spirit light did not appear.

They were on their way home, walking to the subway, when Nan fell victim to the free-standing sign on the sidewalk: Tarot card readings for ten dollars.

"I wouldn't mind hearing something good. What have we got to lose?"

"Ten bucks," Jim said.

She put her arm around him. "I love you, Jim."

They entered a little shop selling incense and beads, where the skinny, not-young fortune-teller sat at a small round table in the corner finishing up with a customer. She wore slippers. She had a run in her stocking and her greyish hair was held back in a thin ponytail.

She dealt Jim's cards first and studied them. Waiting for her to speak, he remembered Lulu reading his palm, telling him he would have friendships and love affairs worth mentioning. This skinny woman said, "I see you moving to a place beside water. Not the ocean, though." She cocked her head and considered, then said, "I can see you're a natural healer."

"You mean a shaman?"

"I think that *is* what I mean."

"With magical powers?" Now that would be cool.

"Love is magical," she said.

"Oh."

"You have a lot of love. You will always be looking after people, and this is wonderful, it means you're a person of vision, and this is excellent."

Well, that was disappointing.

She dealt his mother's cards next. Great changes lay ahead for his mother: a change in career. "Another one," his mother said, shaking her head in amusement. And perhaps another child, a girl. "But I'm too old," his mother objected. Maybe the child would be adopted, the fortune-teller said. "That's all I need," his mother said. Well, there was something strange about another child. The fortune-teller turned over a card and studied it. "I have a second son," his mother offered, helping her out. The fortune-teller nodded and said, "He doesn't know who his father is."

"O.K.," his mother said, after a pause, "what else do you see?"

"A windfall is coming your way, some quick money, maybe from playing poker."

"I don't play poker."

"Well, with hands like yours, you should."

"What else about the son?"

"He's a searcher. He's on a voyage, looking for a path through life. He hasn't found it yet." She paused. "I see him in television. Maybe a sportscaster. Does he like sports?"

Nan said nothing.

Turning over another card, furrowing her brow, "There's a new man coming into your life. He's a person of vision, and this is wonderful. This is excellent. He has six children. No, seven."

"Good Lord."

Afterwards, walking down the street, she told him it was not to be taken seriously. "We helped her out, that's all. She needs the money."

Then she stopped and faced him. "Jim, beware of always looking

after people. Listen to me. I'm about to say something important."
In her mind she was seeing him ten years from now, a too-patient
young man burdened by a high-strung wife, placating and humour-
ing and practising the endless watchfulness and patience he practised
with her and George. "I don't want you to forget it. O.K.?"

"O.K."

"Use condoms!"

He smiled. Fortunately, she was so serious it was funny.

"Condoms," she repeated, her eyes burning with conviction. "You
don't want to get the wrong woman pregnant. You don't want to
get trapped into a bad marriage." Then realizing she was saying
that children trapped you, she tried to backtrack and take the burden
upon herself, "Don't let yourself get trapped into a marriage with
someone like me." But it still came out wrong. And so she said, "Two
words: *use condoms*."

The next day was the day she left them. The trouble started early
when his father, possessed by a small burst of energy and still in
his dressing gown, set about making a most dubious cake with soy
flour, olive oil, sunflower seeds, and maple syrup. "Nancy, I know
you like cake batter," he said and handed her the beater to lick.

She was at the kitchen table, paying the bills, biting her nails,
drinking too much coffee. In accepting the beater, she paused and
frowned at how runny the batter was, and in that pause George let
go of the beater before she fully took hold and it clattered to the
table, spattering her and everything around her.

George shoved the other beater into her hand like a child making
up for his mistake. "Sorry!" Then hurriedly he fumbled for a napkin.
"Let me clean you off first!"

She would clean herself, she said.

Jim watched his mother push his sick father out of her way. She
stood up, the second beater in her hand, went to the sink, and wiped
the batter off herself with a damp sponge. "A healthy cake," she

said from the sink, her back to them and her voice about as far from thrilled as you could possibly get.

"A healthy cake?" George said, and his voice was pleading.

His mother turned to look at his father – Jim looked too – and they saw that his eyes were pitiful: a dog waiting to be kicked.

"It's good," she relented. "It will be good."

Even a month ago Jim might have forced them into a group hug. But the whole thing was too sad.

How much later was it – half an hour? – that his father went to water the spider plant hanging directly above the stack of writing paper on the floor beside her desk. Her coffee-stained books were piled against the wall, the twisted shelves had gone out with the trash.

"George, pull away the paper before you water the plant."

"I don't put in as much water as you do."

"Pull it away anyway. You don't know. It will still drip."

She went back to the kitchen while his father remained with the pitcher of water poised above the plant. And wouldn't you know it, an hour or so later, when his father was proudly offering him a piece of warm cake, his mother crossed to her desk, stopped short and said, "I *told* you. Why didn't you move it?"

George went to see. "Did it drip? I waited and it didn't drip."

"Of course it did."

"That spot was there before."

"It wasn't."

"It's not wet," he said again.

"Of course, it's wet."

"It's not wet."

Then his father leaned over and felt the top page with his fingertips, enraging her even more, because while perhaps dry to the touch now, the paper was rumpled and puckered from having been dripped on. She called his father names then. She called him hard names.

His father replied mildly, tentatively, "Why don't you take a holiday? A long one. To Mars."

That was O.K. by her. She grabbed her handbag, strode to the door, and was gone.

His father turned to him. He raised his bushy eyebrows and arranged his mouth in a grimace meant to be comical. "Your mother is tired. Don't worry about it. She'll be back."

Jim didn't question his mother's love, not for him, not the long haul of her love. That was steady and beyond doubt. But the moment-to-moment changes in her mood pierced him. He had friends who used to like him and didn't anymore. Something about him got on their nerves, the way his father got on his mother's nerves. You couldn't fix it. You couldn't make people love you more than they did.

Nan could have visited friends close by – some of the friends she had neglected – but the thought of having to explain their wretched situation and answer a barrage of questions drove her in the other direction. She took the subway to Brooklyn to see Bridget instead. But Bridget wasn't home and so she walked to the nearest park, where the sycamores and a few old apple trees were in blossom, and watched a baseball game, that slow slide of colour as one team exchanged places with the other at the end of each inning. Blue and white came in, burgundy and white went out. She thought of a butterfly, the two wings moving slowly. Men at play on a Sunday afternoon. A few women watched, but mostly men. The women were at home. She had a park bench all to herself and listened to the radios on various sides, the crackle of a potato-chip bag, someone walking through the grass.

After a while she opened her handbag – the cloth lining was torn and hung loose – and pulled out a book. Soon she was reading about a city in Ecuador called Cuenca, a small town surrounded by pine forests, and Ecuador on the border with Peru, and how depressing it was, she thought, that two brothers could be as completely lost to each other as Martin and George. Reading about the pine-scented town she felt how much she wanted to go there and not just for a week. She continued to read and came to a part about oil companies dropping candies laced with strychnine on Indian villages after the Indians had killed some of the oil workers. It was a real war between oil companies and Indians, the book said, using candies.

She closed the book and watched the baseball game, sick at heart. What was she fundamentally angry about, after all? At bottom she was angry at being brought face to face, over and over again, with herself. And who was she? Another lousy human being who fled from the messes she helped to create.

An hour later she walked back to Bridget's, noticing as church bells rang out the many signs in the shape of what they were selling: a big red apple above a fruit store, a bun above a bakery, a cup of coffee with a hair-lick of steam above a café. It was a neighbourhood where many people didn't read English and this had been the case for a long time; the signs were from another era. A beribboned box above a gift store, a man lifting barbells in front of a health club, a barnyard hen above a store that sold eggs, a roast chicken above a restaurant. It touched her, the effort people had made to be understandable and understood. At the Korean grocer's a handwritten sign read *EXTLA eggs*.

Bridget was home now. She lived alone, renting the floor above the restaurant with the roast chicken hanging out front. Her bright rooms were filled with works-in-progress made of wood and paper and paint. All Nan really had in mind was sitting with this older, creative woman and drawing comfort from her strength. Bridget would not tell her the same old things, or if she did they would sound new.

But Bridget had been robbed the night before. Gone were her television, camera, silverware, money, the string of pearls she prized but never wore because they were too valuable. "That was a mistake," she mourned. "I should have worn them." The thieves had left behind on her bed a bag of neckties, a little jolt of horror for the imagination to play with. She had given them to the police, which was why she hadn't been home when Nan first rang the bell.

It was Nan, then, not Bridget, who busied herself and made tea with a steady hand.

From Bridget's kitchen window she looked out at crooked chimneys, lines and lines of clothes hung out to dry, overgrown back gardens, and not a single tree. Bridget in the next room was sorting out and putting back upended drawers. The radio was on, the thieves hadn't bothered with the old-fashioned radio in the kitchen, and while Nan waited for the tea to steep she heard part of an interview with a man said to be the world's most famous composer of tangos. Asked what musicians he admired, he said his favourite pianist was the Canadian Glenn Gould, whose two recordings of the *Goldberg Variations* were his favourite recordings, the first for its dazzling energy and the last for its maturity. By the last recording, "Gould had come to dominate Bach," he said, "rather than Bach Glenn Gould." Like himself, he said. He had come to dominate the tango. Then over the air came the first of Gould's two recordings and the music took Nan far out of herself. The relief was overpowering.

"Nan, if you could see your face," Bridget said, coming into the kitchen.

The sympathy in her voice was too much. Nan's eyes brimmed, mortifying her.

"What is it?" Bridget said, putting her hand on her arm. "George?"

Nan flushed – well, yes – and she wiped her eyes. "It's too stupid to talk about." Then, "I'm so *angry* all the time. I'm sick of everything." And with that she began to laugh a little.

"Who could blame you?"

"I blame George." She put her head in her hands and standing there she began to rock on her heels, back inside her terrible impatience. "If he'd had the operation in the beginning! But he went with all that macrobiotic shit, which did less than nothing. And now the cancer is killing him. It's killing him, Bridget."

"Well, don't forget he's having the operation. That's a big step in the right direction."

"He's scared to death of the operation."

"Of course. And so are you."

"Am I?"

Nan turned and picked up the teapot and poured scalding tea into two mugs, barely aware she was doing it. "I don't think I am," she said, sitting down at the table and staring into her mug. "You've known George a long time."

"And I've always liked him."

She raised her eyes. "Tell me why."

"We understand each other," Bridget said, sitting down too. "We grew up in working-class Brooklyn. We went to college at City University because tuition was free." She smiled. "I remember him telling me about the small scholarship he got to Yale. He called it a 'scholarboat'. He was very proud and funny about it."

Nan felt the warmth of the mug penetrate her hands. Bridget's fondness for George made her own life make a little more sense.

"He reminds me of Max," Bridget went on, speaking of the exhusband Nan had never met. "It would have been easier if I had disliked Max. But I liked him very much. He was one of the nicest people I've ever known. But I came to realize two things: that we would never have many friends and that whatever job he had would never last."

"Yes." Nan could see why George might remind her of Max, and why it made it no easier that she herself often *dis*liked George. There were days when she thought that if he would only hurry up and die, she would be free. This was her worst thing, she had no doubt, wishing him dead and gone. Not that she always wished it. It was something else she wanted. She sighed and rubbed the back of her neck, which was stiff and sore.

"You must feel that you're being robbed of your life," Bridget said. And Nan's hand stopped in mid-motion. "I felt that way with my mother at the end," Bridget said. "I didn't hate her. I just wanted my life back."

"Me too."

195

They were silent for a while, listening to the astonishing volley of notes coming from Gould's piano.

"Nan, George knows you care about him."

"The trouble is I *don't* care," Nan said. And for once Bridget's good, wide, thoughtful face seemed taken aback.

"I don't believe you," she said after a moment.

Well, you should, thought Nan. The first recording came to an end, and here were the opening notes of the last: heartachingly paced.

"You're too much alone," Bridget said, seeing the yearning in Nan's face.

"I'm *never* alone. I go for a walk and my thoughts crowd me off the sidewalk." She drove her fingertips unkindly against the sides of her skull. "I have to find patience, Bridget."

"Patience."

"Where is it?"

She got up and walked into the next room, to Bridget's worktable loaded with the tools of her enviable trade: pieces of wood, hand-made paper, mesh, strands of wire, glue, pens, inks, tubes of paint, scissors, brushes. Nan's roving glance moved from the table to what was on the walls and came to a stop on a series of snowy black-and-white photographs in a horizontal frame. Going up to them, she was stunned to see they were photographs of a dead dog gradually buried by falling snow. In the last photograph even the dog's outline was gone. Nothing was left but snow and woods.

Nan felt herself enter the photographs and stand gratefully in the falling snow.

"Are you familiar with 'Snowfall, 1965'?" Bridget asked at her shoulder. "The sculpture by Joseph Beuys?"

Nan shook her head.

"It's in a similar vein," Bridget said, and she described a work made of layers of felt piled like blankets on three fir branches until there was barely a trace of what lay underneath, except for the tips of the branches sticking out at the bottom like emaciated legs.

And because Nan didn't know the work or the artist, Bridget searched out her two books about him, relating as she did so the unforgettable chronology of his life: how he was drafted into the German air force in the Second World War; how his plane got shot down in a blinding snowstorm; how he was rescued by nomadic Tatars who covered his injured, unconscious body in animal fat and wrapped him in felt in order to warm him and heal his wounds; how he survived and became an artist who explored the content and meaning of catastrophe on the theory that like heals like, the homeopathic healing process.

"I get the sense of deep wounds being healed," Bridget said, "when I look at his work."

By now she had found the books and she flipped one open to show Nan a picture of Beuys in his signature hat. It was the very hat Jim liked to wear, her brother's narrow-brimmed fedora.

In the subway going home, Nan held in her lap the two books about Beuys. She opened one and read, *My intention was not to create or depict symbols, but to express the powers that exist in the world: the real powers*, and everything around her, and everything inside her, shifted. She kept on reading, overwhelmed by one unusual connection after another. All of the materials he worked with were warm and alive: felt, fat, beeswax, honey. He was trying to portray the spiritual energy of material things.

When she got off at her stop, she looked around at the accumulated soot and blackness that was above and below and extending into the bowels of the tunnel, and it seemed like velvet. The smell of urine was there, the stale wind, the danger of being mugged, and tears were in her eyes. Everything around her was ringing with life. There had been nothing, but nothing, and now all of these histories of lost dogs and other worlds were rising to the surface, coming together in a marvellous chronology that had been telling itself over many years.

The world was patient, even if she wasn't.

12

HER TWO MEN WERE HAVING A PEACEFUL TIME ON THE double bed when she got home shortly after eight o'clock. Jim was wearing his fedora and drawing pictures of Bad Art, George was working a crossword, using a chipped wooden tray as a desk. They looked up as she came into the room, their faces full of wariness, to ascertain her mood. It was less than a week since Jim had accused her of being unfeeling, *you can't talk like that, you can't do that*, a heavy charge from the human being she loved the most, and she was ready to admit he was right, most of her feelings were facets of unfeeling, and she was sorry. But they were not asking her how she felt.

"Bridget sends you her love," she said.

"Nice," George said. "Maybe leave out the cigar," he said to his son, "unless you want him to get cancer."

"He's not old enough to get cancer."

"He'll get it later."

"No. He's going to drown."

"In the Klondike River?"

"Maybe."

Nan glanced over Jim's shoulder, but he didn't offer her a view of what he was doing, and so she went to the window. Clouds were tracking across the moon, driven by an east wind. They lived on an island close to the sea, after all. It was easy to forget.

"Couldn't Bad Art be rescued at the last minute?" George coaxed.

"Maybe," Jim said.

At the window, staring at the moon, exiled, and feeling her exile, Nan drifted north in her mind. She was back at the lake. Back on the moonlit water. Back with a tender story she had heard one time about a woman and the moon. The woman's children were small when the family moved from Wales to Canada, so the story went, and the night before they left, standing at the window, they said goodbye to the moon. Their mother assured them the moon would be in Canada too, and they asked her how she knew. It just would be. But how did she *know*? The next morning she told them she had the answer. She had called the captain of the ship and he was going to tow the moon on a rope behind them. So all the way across the Atlantic, her children checked on the moon's progress, jubilant whenever they saw it in the sky, crestfallen when they didn't. Arriving in Halifax, and the moon still very much with them, the children urged her not to forget to remind the captain to cut the rope, so the moon would stay in Canada. Then they disembarked and made their way to their new home on Prince Edward Island, and when they got to the island, the woman's story went, and looked up into the sky, the moon was full.

"Your mother misses Canada," she heard George say.

She turned and looked at him, fairly astonished. He knew her. He knew exactly where all of her loves lay. He knew who and what she was attracted to before she knew it herself.

She went over and sat on the edge of the bed. George rubbed the small of her back and Jim continued to draw. She watched her son's long fingers, admiring his dexterity and powers of concentration. He did not look like George, or her, and never had. In one of those strange twists, he resembled the Martin she knew from family photographs. The resemblance was so uncanny – same mouth, long neck, unruly hair – that George sometimes asked her with a cocked eyebrow if she was sure she had never met his younger brother. Here was a chronology but was it marvellous? Some kind of longing had trumped logic, even genes. And what was it she was longing for? She wanted to feel more *alive*, that's what she wanted. To live an independent and courageous life. And with that bracing thought something clicked in her brain and she understood Quebec. She understood a place torn between staying and leaving, and therefore always dissatisfied. How hard it was on everybody else, the endless dissatisfaction, the whipped-up indecision. Poor old George, she thought. Poor Jim.

"Show me what you've been doing," she said to her son.

He kept on with his pencil, as if he hadn't heard, and she thought of Blake turning away from her, cultivating the cool disdain that nearly killed her. It was possible she could lose Jim too, if she wasn't careful.

She waited. Finally, he shoved the page in her direction and she angled it to see it better. She studied the kayak. It seemed accurate to her and she said so. She asked him if Bad Art was going to drown while he was kayaking.

"Maybe."

"I was remembering what you were like when you were small," she said, and for the first time since she had come back, Jim looked her in the face.

"You used to remove my watch," she said, "and hold it to your ear and listen to the ticking. You loved the typewriter keys. You loved the sound they made when you hit them with your fingers." He was attentive, eager for more. "For a while," she said, "when you were about three, you decided my nose was a horn. You would squeeze it and make the appropriate honk."

His peal of laughter was so hard and sudden that he nearly fell off the bed.

"Do you remember that?" And she leaned over the side of the bed to enjoy his face full of wonderful laughter.

The intercom buzzed in the kitchen, surprising them. Who could it be at nine o'clock on a Sunday night? Nan went to answer it, exasperated, but she was easily exasperated. A moment later, she was calling out to them that Lulu was here! She was on her way up in the elevator!

Jim was sliding off the bed when he heard his father say, "Dear God."

George had squeezed his eyes shut. Now he dropped his head forward and fixed his eyes grimly on the bedspread. "Don't leave me, Jim." His face was revolted and when they heard Lulu's step in the hall he shrank back.

Jim saw her hesitate a moment in the doorway, so weary from her long drive that she reminded him of driftwood, weathered and disoriented and tossed up on shore.

"You," she said to him, her face flooding with affection, swamping him with delight. But it was his father she went to first, coming to his side of the bed and leaning down to plant a kiss on his forehead. George's face was almost comical in its horror, and Jim felt terrible for them all. Lulu reached over then, tousling his hair, "How's my Jim?" And despite himself, he pulled back a fraction of an inch, thrilled but worried. Then his mother called from the kitchen, her voice sounding like his own on Christmas Day, "Jim, come and see!" And even though he knew his father did not want to be left alone with Lulu, he left him.

"George," he heard Lulu say as he headed down the hall, "tell me how you're feeling."

In the kitchen his mother was on her knees. "Look what Lulu brought us!" She was cradling in her arms a big yellow pup.

Jim fell to his knees beside her and she transferred the living weight of warm, furry, bright-eyed being into his arms, and he felt his heart nearly burst from pleasure and divided loyalties, too many to contain.

Pup Dog, he thought, thinking of the pup in Pogo. His coat was so soft and his teeth were so sharp. He carried the pup down the hall to show his father, putting him on the big bed and flopping down beside him. His father did not object, far from it. They stroked and patted him, and before they knew it the pup was sound asleep, spent and splayed out.

"A lot of excitement for the little tyke," George said.

Wolves had chased the pup down the lane to the house, according to Lulu. George said there were no wolves at the lake.

"You'd be surprised." A week ago, she said, under the full moon, a pack of wolves were howling in the hills as she went to bed. Then sometime in the night she woke up to frantic yips coming down the lane. "I went downstairs and opened the door to the moonlight and the commotion, and the pup leapt right into my arms." She smiled at their big-eyed reaction. "That's why he's such a lamb. He's had everything else scared out of him."

"Wouldn't he belong to somebody?" his mother said.

"He got dumped. It happens all the time. People drive into the country and ditch the pets they don't want. So I said to him, 'Darling, you are exactly what my New York family needs.'"

The pup would take up residence on his parents' bed. They scratched his ears and rubbed his belly and everything was easy. Now Jim would have a reason to go outside first thing in the morning and directly after school and again in the evening, to go to the park and be with other people and other dogs. His mother would put an old quilt on one side of the bed and that was the pup's during the day, which inspired his father to say they could call him Quilty. His mother said that wasn't a good idea. "You'll understand one day," she said to Jim, "when you read *Lolita*."

"Is it a good book?"

"It's a very adult book. Is it good?" She gave him a long look. "It's supposed to be, but I never got very far into it and I tried more than once. My imagination isn't all it's cracked up to be."

Lulu's visit would end better than it began. She began in that first hour by pressing George for details about the operation and he told her what the surgeon had said, but grudgingly, and Nan contradicted him.

He turned on her. "Nancy, you're so critical of everything I say. Your voice is full of disgust."

Her head drew back. "Not disgust."

"Yes, it is. You know it is."

"I'm not critical of everything you say."

"Yes, you are. No, that's not true. You're not critical of *everything* I say."

His voice was full of bitter meaning and nobody knew where to look. They looked at the pup. He was their soft oasis. Moon was the name Lulu had given him, the name he answered to. She said the drive had taken thirteen hours instead of the usual eight or nine, because they'd had to stop so often to stretch their six legs. She kept on talking to fill the silence, answering Nan's questions about the lake, the weather, the roads, the trees, the sugar bush. She had helped Guy in early March, she told them, when the sap began to flow, working through the night sometimes. "So you didn't cut the tubing," Jim said as if they were alone. "I didn't, Jim."

When Ducky was visiting a month ago, she told them, they had gone outside after supper to slide down a great pile of snow and then ended up making a snow fort, digging out a room and a tunnel and another room. "I think it was the happiest night of my life," she said, a note of true amazement in her voice. Her words filled them with wistfulness. "We froze pans of coloured water for the windows," she went on. "They were the finishing touch. You should have seen them, Jim. You should have been there."

"Then the truce is holding between you and Guy?" his mother said. "The long quarrel is over."

"I'm very careful. I don't antagonize him."

"So it's not really a friendship," his father said.

"It's an antagonism," Lulu laughed. "It's an old antagonism."

That night they stayed up late, Lulu and Nan, talking in the living room, and Jim stayed up later than usual too, listening. Lulu mentioned how on the way down she and the pup had had Kurt Vonnegut for company, the audio book of *Slaughterhouse-five* that she had found among the books at the lake. "The actor was terrific," she said. "He had a different intonation for every single 'so it goes'. He made it like music. If you were reading it to yourself, you wouldn't get that."

Nan said, "We thought the same thing, didn't we, Jim? The reader made the book even better than it was."

Their collective admiration filled him with the satisfaction he felt whenever anyone managed to state their love for something he loved too, and loved more, having heard in detail why they admired it. She was sixteen, Lulu said, when she used to lie on her bed and recite lines from "Macbeth" for their music alone. "'Sleep that knits up the ravel'd sleeve of care,'" she marvelled, "'the death of each day's life, sore labour's bath, balm of hurt minds, great nature's second course, chief nourisher in life's feast.'" Grade ten English, she said. As for the rest of high school, *all of high school* except drama club, it bewildered her. "I mean, after your mother moved away. I missed you, Nan. I missed you so much."

They talked on after Jim went to bed, Nan on the sofa, Lulu curled up in the armchair.

"Lulu, I'm sorry about George. What can I say? He's never liked having visitors."

"Darling, I swan in – yes – I swan in, I know I do, and he feels squeezed out."

"You must be exhausted."

"You know what I've been trying to remember all day? The other half of Watson. Arthur Conan Doyle … Watson …"

"Sherlock Holmes."

"It's menopause," Lulu said sadly.

"I'm on hormones now. I want to stay on them forever." Nan drew up one knee and wrapped her arm around it. "I'm glad you've patched things up with Guy."

"Well, we don't talk politics. And I'm not drinking anymore. And Ducky loves me."

"Ducky." The last time Nan had seen her was in the rain when her small face was drenched with colour from the purple umbrella over her head. In that moment she had caught a glimpse of the grown-up face, strikingly serious and stylish under a wide hat, undeniably herself yet with more than a passing resemblance to Lulu. "Is she less," she searched for the word, clenching her hands and pulling them into her chest, "in-turned?"

"It depends who she's with. She asks about Jim."

Lulu's smile drew out Nan's. And because it was late, and she was very curious, Nan allowed herself a dangerous question. "Lulu, are they happy? Guy and his wife?"

"Are they happy? It's hard to see how he deserves her. Julie's a queen and he treats her like a serving wench."

"A serving wench. I can see that."

Lulu's smile was mischievous, probing. "What about *you* and Guy? Something went on between you."

Nan shook her head. "Not this time." She was pulling on the lobe of her ear, gazing at the floor.

"Darling, what are you telling me?"

Nan raised her eyes and looked at her friend for a long time. "I'm not brave enough, that's all I'm saying. I'm too hidebound, too careful. I think about all the consequences."

"You're too loyal, that's what you are." Lulu could tell that Nan wasn't going to divulge anything more, not right now, and so she didn't press it. She would wait.

They talked on, Lulu relating a recent dream, its details still fresh in her mind, of carrying a small cradle-sized canoe, or canoe-shaped cradle, in which she had put her sunglasses and a play she was reading. She was on her way to a peaceful place somewhere in the country to learn her lines when a black car pulled up beside her and out stepped a mafia guy in dark glasses. It was her father, Red Blake, the disciplinarian. "Nan, this is something I've never told you. How in the last few months of my father's life we actually got along. All

205

I had to do was kiss him. Give him the affection I'd never given him that he was so hungry for."

The statement made Nan draw in her breath. "Oh, Lulu."

"I buried a hatchet of love in his head," laughed Lulu. She spread her hands and folded them into soft fists. "He had no parting words for me, though, no goodbye. In those last few days I evaporated in front of my own eyes. He only had time for Guy. And then his will ruined everything."

"You wanted parting words from him."

"I wanted to hear him say he was sorry."

"Maybe he said it that way," Nan said.

"What way?"

"In the way he accepted your affection, he was saying he was sorry." This was what Nan wanted to dwell on, not the old strife. "I'm glad you got closer to him at the end."

She was seeing her own father in her mind, the old newspaperman in his hand-knit sweater, standing in the front window at home, waiting for her car to appear in the driveway. He would open the door with a huge smile, "Hello, kid." There was never any question that he loved her. He had been unforgivably hard on her mother, though. Well, he was disappointed in himself and what he'd accomplished in his life, and so he treated her, she thought, the way I treat George.

She lowered her head, overcome with self-knowledge, and Lulu asked if she was sleepy.

"Not sleepy, but tired, very tired."

"Nan, what can I do to help?"

There was nothing. "Just what you're doing."

"What if I took Jim for the summer? He could stay with me at the lake."

Life without Jim: the very suggestion hollowed her out.

"A bad idea, I guess."

"Not the whole summer. We would miss him too much. Jim would love it, though." And it would be good for him to get away from here. It would be wonderful for him to get away.

They would see how things went. Maybe for part of the summer. Maybe August.

"I would take good care of him, darling. I would guard him with my life."

"Oh, you wouldn't need to hover. He knows the lake."

And they agreed that it was much safer and freer there than in the city. "My brother taught him everything," Nan said.

Lulu stood and stretched and went over to the family photos hanging on the wall behind the armchair. "Is this my namesake?"

Nan got up and joined her. She pointed to Blake when he was five, Blake when he was fifteen.

"He looks like a Blake," Lulu said.

"I guess he does. The name suits him."

"I mean, he looks familiar."

Nan was standing at her shoulder, contemplating her older boy. "Darling, I'm going to ask you something."

"I wish you wouldn't."

It was very late. Night-time quietness in New York has a particular quality, a kind of depth punctuated by distant sirens and other noises that seem part of the quiet.

Lulu gazed at her friend's pale, determined face. "That's why I love you. You can keep a secret. Not many can."

Lulu was gone when Jim came home from school, but Moon was there. He and his mother took the pup for a walk in Riverside Park. They towed him on a leash – well, he towed them – and what a difference he made in their lives.

"A dog is pure love," his mother said as they left the path for the grass that stretched under trees and past benches and flower-beds.

Jim responded with that eager look she knew so well, asking her what she meant, even though he knew, wanting the thought to be drawn out and the sentiment lingered over.

"You saw your father," she said. "He melted in five seconds."

Moon was sniffing everywhere, intoxicated by the grass and the dirt. Nan gave Jim the leash and he was surprised by how hard the pup tugged.

"That's the way," she said. "Be firm but don't yank."

"Dogs aren't critical," she went on, giving him a knowing, self-knowing look. "They accept you. Lulu knew what she was doing. She is very kind."

And Jim savoured the words.

That same night Lulu phoned once she'd arrived at the lake: an uneventful trip, everything was fine.

Nan went into their bedroom after the call and George asked her how her girlfriend was. His tone was snide.

She regarded his pitiful, lopsided face about to undergo the knife. "I was talking to Lulu."

"I know."

"Oh, George," she said. He was a man so locked up inside his jealousies that she felt sorry for him. "You've got to stop reading your past into my friendship with Lulu. Ruining our friendship won't make me love you more."

"What would make you love me more?"

"You want me to love you more?"

"Yes."

"I see."

"Said the blind man."

She lowered herself onto the bed. What would her life have been like had she made a good marriage? Good marriages were something you read about and heard about. So and so made a good marriage.

He reached for her hand in remorse. "I'm not complaining," he said.

She burst out laughing then, which offended him mightily. "I'm *not,*" he said, "I'm not complaining, I'm *protesting*. I'm protesting your lack of love for me."

And that's when her heart broke for both of them.

* * *

George entered the hospital the day before the operation. Nan would see him again the following afternoon, after the surgery was over and he had spent two hours in recovery and then been taken to the room he would share with three other patients. She went alone and found him awake but drowsy, lying on his back, his bed raised under his head, his face without dressings, which she had not expected. She could see everything. But apparently that was how they did things now.

Coming to his side, she noticed speckles of dried blood on the bare skin above his gown. "You survived," she breathed.

He reached out and clasped her wrist and held on.

She had to work hard to retain her composure. The highway of stitches travelled all the way from his lower lip down under his chin and around to his ear. The huge hole, where the right side of his jaw had been, wasn't a complete absence thanks to the insetting of the skin flap and all the swelling. The skin of the flap – or skin paddle, as the nurse would call it when she came in – was paler than the rest of his face. Plastic draining tubes came out of his neck, a feeding tube went down his nose. That was antibiotic ointment, the nurse explained, glistening on all the suture lines.

"They did a good job," Nan reassured him, managing to keep her voice steady.

After a little while she went into the bathroom and came back with a warm, wet facecloth and worked at the dried blood until most of it was gone.

Over the next three weeks she immersed herself in the to and fro of daily visits. When she went in the evening, Jim was often at her side. They sat next to George's bed while he slept or dozed. During that time they read the only things they could take in, the dog-eared compilations of Pogo comic strips from 1952, 1953, 1954, 1955, Scotch tape on the spines. They lost themselves in the drawings and the daft and brilliant wordplay. Walt Kelly was a genius, Nan said, marvelling in that particular moment over his undisguised portrait of Senator Joe McCarthy as a vicious bobcat with a shotgun, Simple J. Malarkey, who sent ripples of terror through the swamp.

George wasn't able to speak at first, his face too swollen, bruised, and numb. He used pen and paper to communicate. *Useless*, he wrote one day, and Nan kissed his hand and told him not to feel sorry for himself. The look in his eyes softened and he wrote, *Love your smile*.

Around his right ear and on that side of his face and neck, there was numbness, some of which would persist forever, since the nerve that gives feeling there was gone. The hearing in that ear was now worse than ever.

For Jim the sight of his father brought back the long-lost Dorset whose head got drilled into and who opened his eyes one last time before he died. Alone with Nan, he ventured to ask if his father's face would always look like that. She reached across the table – they were in the hospital cafeteria – and put her warm, capable hand on his. "It's going to look less painful the more it heals, but it's always going to be a bit wonky and misshapen. I'll tell you what helps me. I think of his face as a broken paw. Your father is a human animal with a broken paw." A remark that led to some bad but necessary jokes between them about his pa having a sore paw.

George came home from the hospital in early May. By then the stitches were gone, but his face was swollen still and the scars were red. His right eye when he blinked wouldn't close all the way and his mouth on that side wouldn't move properly, though he could talk again, the words a bit distorted because his lip movements weren't normal yet. He dabbed the right side of his mouth with tissues to control the saliva. His greatest physical comfort was Moon, who lay warm against his side.

Since he needed a soft diet, Nan made him soups, smoothies, eggnogs that he consumed through a straw. During this time the rancour went out of her for the most part and their lives were peaceful. She would reach for George's hand that hovered in front of his face like a small catcher's mitt and bring it down onto the bed and hold it. "Don't worry, you're going to look fine." He returned the favour with a droll remark. After he re-grew his jaw, he said, they would go to Paris and drink champagne.

Late in May, she purchased six big cherry-tomato plants and created a vegetable patch on the wide sills of their most light-filled window: an east-facing bay. She dubbed the area their summer porch, setting up folding chairs and a small table for the fresh-cut flowers Bridget brought every time she came, as well as for their books, her coffee mug, George's glass with its straw. She sat there with him in the early mornings and evenings, and he was grateful to her and took her hand and told her he loved her, as gentle as when they first met.

His daughters came, Kate and Lorna. Kate was like a tropical bird, vibrant and colourful, tanned, adorned, smiling. She had silver bracelets on both wrists, a generous laugh, a wide mouth, long legs. Lorna, three years younger and a pale shadow of her sister, was the more talented as a child, according to George, a precocious artist with coloured pencils, but all of that had come to naught. What had she done lately? She had shaved her head.

They sat with their exhausted father, who had inherited his family's propensity for cancer and at this point was underweight by at least twenty pounds. His bushy eyebrows were enormous above his pale-blue eyes. Kate was the one who kept the conversation going, making a fuss over Moon, drawing Jim into the circle and giving him a special gift, *Wild Animals of North America*. Seeing the daughters side by side, Nan suspicioned, as Pogo might have said, that Lorna was so withdrawn because Kate was anything but. In every family there is only so much good luck to go around, she believed, and some take more than their share.

The conversation turned to their grandmother, since earlier in the day Kate and Lorna had gone to see her and she had not recognized them. Kate asked, "Does she know *you*?"

Nan said carefully, "She does. But then living here I'm able to visit regularly. I'm sorry. It must have been hard."

"We didn't know how bad she was," Kate said. She turned to her sister with an undiminished smile, despite the sadness of what she was saying, "So it was a shock, wasn't it, Lor?" And Lorna nodded and leaned close to her.

Jim hadn't seen his half-sisters for several years. It seemed clear to him that Lorna, the one with nothing to say, adored Kate, and that Kate looked out for Lorna without ever letting her get in the way. He could see that Lorna resembled his father. Kate wasn't like him at all.

They stayed only an hour or so, leaving behind an emptiness in the apartment that he couldn't shake off. What he had wanted to see was a great show of genuine affection for his father, but all they'd managed was an awkward visit and a hasty departure.

His mother talked about them afterwards, mulling over the contrast between them, saying Kate had so much life and personality that she was bound to leave a trail of envy wherever she went. "Lorna is more clever," was all his father would say in reply.

"We have no real friends," George said to Nan a few days later. "Except Bridget. She is very faithful."

They were in their folding chairs next to the flourishing tomato plants, as isolated in their apartment as they would have been on a northern lake. Nan knew he was hurt to the core that none of his colleagues had come to see him.

He said, "Ken would have been here in a minute."

But where was his old friend Ken? Where were George's

colleagues? "Everyone is busy," she said. "You know New York. I'll invite people from your office. We'll have a little party."

It was a peculiar party. The centrepiece was George's jaw. "Radiation treatments begin a week Monday," he was heard to say, twenty treatments. The sidepiece was the collection of tall, ruthlessly pruned tomato plants. "Why did you do that to the tomato plants?" everyone asked Nan. "George did it yesterday," she answered, "to give the tomatoes more sun." She touched one of the still-green tomatoes and shrugged. "He has eccentric ideas about everything."

Jim made himself semi-invisible during the party by keeping his nose in the book about wild animals. He read about eight-hundred-pound beavers, Castoroides, of a million years ago, whose ever-growing incisors, if not worn down, would curve inward and eventually pierce the skull. In his discomfort he kept hearing more uncomfortable things and looking up from his page, and then back down.

"I have no family here," one dark-haired woman told another, her eyes soft with the imminent possibility of weeping.

Another woman, overweight and elderly, was weeping openly because she had gone to Macy's and nothing she tried on fitted.

Someone else left early with a migraine coming on. A metal band was tightening around her head, she told them, and her head itself was like a light bulb full of bits of light, like bright spots. She felt cold, then hot, then cold, and all of this was a rehearsal for the pain to come. She said to his mother as she left, "I'll call you. I don't know when."

Everybody suffered too much, not just his father.

Afterwards George brooded (the resentment oozed out of him) about the harangue from a male colleague he had never much cared for. The colleague, sullen and hidden behind a dark beard, had said their little organization had lost its way and might as well fold. It was just another run-of-the-mill social justice group, ineffective, losing money and unable to afford the rent; they were twice as much in debt as they had believed, it turned out, because the business manager could not add.

"Parties," his mother said the next day, "aren't all they're cracked up to be."

* * *

The heat of late June clamped down on them and they set up fans on tables and countertops. One afternoon, running her hand along Moon's smooth belly as the back and forth of the breeze cooled them off, Nan said, "George, I know you don't want her to come. But it would help me a lot to see her. It would mean a lot to me." She saw his flushed face close like a door against her.

"She doesn't need to visit," he said. "You're on the phone to her all the time."

"It's not the same."

"Where would we put her?"

She rubbed her eyes with her left hand and didn't reply. They had a spare room, as he knew perfectly well. "Listen to me. She doesn't have to stay here. She has other friends. I miss her, George." He turned away and she reached across the bed and took his arm. "Even talking about her upsets you. You're jealous. There's no need to be."

"I'm not jealous."

"George, look at me."

He wouldn't look at her. "Soon I'll be dead," he said to the bedspread, "and you can see her to your heart's content." He shook off her hand. "You think I'm unreasonable."

His mutilated face reminded her of a reconfigured map, a country carved up, her country without *la belle province*. "Then *I'll* go to see *her*," she said. She hadn't mentioned Lulu's offer to have Jim at the lake for August. She was waiting for the right time, though she couldn't imagine there being one.

"I told you how I feel," he said.

"I know."

214

"So there's nothing to talk about."

He knew he was in the wrong. A better man would not feel as he did. He wasn't a better man, he was his own suffering self, and he could not abide Lulu.

Nan stood and looked down at her husband. "This can't be," she said. "I'm not going to let your worst instincts control our lives."

"What about *me*?" And his wounded eyes flung her a glance. "What about *me*?"

"You," she said, with a trace of a smile. "You have us eating out of the palm of your hand."

He heard her weariness, her grudging affection, and felt himself relent. "Alright then."

"What does that mean? I'll tell her to come?"

"That's what I said."

She sank back down on the bed and returned her attention to the dog, rubbing his ears and belly. Moon stretched out and lapped it up. When they could agree on nothing else, they could agree about Moon.

A warm rain was falling when Jim got home on the last day of school. Alerted by his step in the hall, Moon was waiting for him at the door and the two of them were reunited in doggy rapture and boyish delight. Jim gave his father *The New York Times*, having picked it up for him at the news kiosk on Broadway, and George spread it open on the kitchen table (where Nan was proofreading another anthropological paper) and then Jim laid his gift of street gossip at their feet: namely, that the man with the beer belly who leaned out his window to scream curses had today been leaning out and playing the harmonica.

"He must want attention," George said, and Nan raised her eyes and smiled at her son.

George was undergoing the radiation treatments now, one treatment a day, Monday to Friday, weekends off. Nan went with him to the hospital every afternoon, where he lay on a treatment table for the few minutes it took. The plastic mould they had made of his face got bolted down, so that his head stayed perfectly still. Jim helped out, now that school was over, by picking up whatever groceries they needed and by lending a hand with supper. His mother was teaching him basic things in the kitchen, having resolved that he would not be like her own father, a man who could not cook. "Do you remember your grandfather? You were four when he died."

"I remember he liked buttermilk."

"He did. He liked things sour and he liked them dry. Dry Martinis. Not as dry as Lulu's, but almost. And he liked things hot. Hot rolls with his soup. He liked to feel the heat of the roll in his hand while he ate his steaming soup."

She was showing him how to roast a chicken, washing it thoroughly, drying it thoroughly with old pages of the *Times*, a way to save on paper towelling and a technique she had picked up on a visit to England years ago. Anybody could roast a chicken, she said, and it was hard to find anything more delicious. If he learned how to do that and how to make a potato salad and a decent vinaigrette for green salad, he would be set for life. It was the most discouraging thing in the world, she said, to see her father unable to help her mother when she got old and ill because he had no idea how to make anything at all, except scrambled eggs and cocoa.

Nan paused to wash her hands and dry them, one finger at a time. "Jim? How would you like to stay at the lake with Lulu? She's invited you for the month of August."

His face lit up instantly in a blaze of joy and she remembered how an invitation out of the blue could utterly transform your young life. "So you'd like to go?"

He would. "But what about Moon?"

"You'd take him along. Lulu offered to come and get you. She'd drive you back to us at the end of August." He was shining with happiness, a boy reborn. "So we'll run it by your father when he wakes up?"

"I'm not asleep," George said, coming into the kitchen.

He pulled out a chair and sat down at the table and looked away.

Nan and Jim exchanged a glance. "George?" she said. "When did you last take something for pain?"

"An hour ago."

She had a milkshake ready for him and he sipped it. His serving of the roast chicken, now in the oven, would have to be chopped very fine. He was still eating soft food and could only chew on the left side of his face, having no teeth on the right side. His jaw tended to swing when he chewed, there being no muscle to anchor it. It was important, they had been told, to keep his weight up.

During supper, Nan broached the subject again. "Jim is excited about staying with Lulu," she said, setting down her knife and fork.

"You should have talked to me first."

"That's true," she said.

"Jim? You want to leave us? What would we do without you?"

"We'd manage," Nan said.

"Like hell we would." He drummed his fingers on the table. "Your mother says I'm unreasonable. Do you think I'm unreasonable?"

It was a question that Jim didn't know how to answer and so he didn't try.

After supper Nan went to one of the living room windows and raised it as high as it would go and leaned out into the air, fresher from recent rain. She felt Jim put his arm around her shoulders and he leaned out too. She would always remember it, the boy-weight of his protective arm resting across her upper back.

Sometimes in the winter they would stick their heads out into falling snow and feel the heat from inside waft out around them as snow fell on their faces. Then it was hard to know if they were a part of the building or a part of the snow. The air in the room had a way of drifting out irregularly, in warm puffs and breezes, pulled outside like a piece of material.

"Maybe I won't go," Jim said to her.

She stepped back and looked at his pale, pensive, New York face and saw him at the lake, diving off the raft, paddling to the islands, becoming by the hour stronger and browner and more confident, and she took him by the arm and led him over to where George sat reading the *Times*. Moon was asleep on the rug beside him. "George," she said in a voice that brooked no resistance.

He looked up at them with his watery, vulnerable eyes.

"Your son has a chance to visit a place he loves. Tell him you want him to go."

She could see what George was thinking. That he didn't want Jim to go. That honesty should count for something. He sat looking at them, mother and son, so much closer to each other than they were to him, and it hurt him, she knew it did.

He swallowed and dabbed his mouth with his handkerchief. "Your mother is right. You should go." And he felt better for saying it. "You don't want to spend all summer trapped here with us," he added, self-pity reasserting itself, since nothing in the world was harder for him to shake. But then he made another effort. "You'll get more ideas for your stories and tell them to me when you come home. I'll be waiting for them."

And his lower lip trembled and he shook out the paper and stared down at the editorial page.

It was the next day, a humid Saturday, that Nan came back from one of her regular visits to the nursing home in Nyack and planted herself a few feet from George.

She said, "Apparently your brother Martin was here last week to see your mother. Why doesn't he ever call?"

"Because," George replied, not even looking up, "Martin doesn't care about me and the feeling is mutual."

"So you like it this way?" she said with open disgust. She had known for some time that Martin was in steady touch with his mother, having seen the letters. Even so, what a shock to realize he had been here so recently.

"That's right. I like it this way." Then he raised his eyes with a face-saving show of concern and said, "How's my mother?"

"She asked about you."

"Just once?"

"George, you're awful. I didn't count. I told her what I always do. You'll be there next week. I can say the same thing over and over again, and it sounds new to her each time. Go see her."

"As soon as these treatments are finished, I'll go."

"Maybe that's the worst thing I've ever done," George said later the same evening. He was sitting in the chair next to the bed, lost in thought, while Nan sorted the clean laundry into piles at the foot of their bed.

"What is?" Pausing in her task, curious. She hadn't been convinced those many months ago when he had told them his worst thing: persecuting the younger boy at camp until he punched him in the mouth and drew blood. Although she had understood what he was driving at, not that it was so terrible in itself – he was only eight – but that it opened his eyes to what he was capable of.

"Something I did to Martin," he said.

And now he had all of her attention.

He began describing this brother who was five years younger than he was, tall, skinny, athletic, physically so different from him and Kevin (as if Nan had never seen photographs of the three boys). Where had he come from? he wondered. Their mother and father were short and dumpy. Anyway, Martin was a good runner, good enough that he began to win races and come home with ribbons. He decided to go along with him one day, to give him moral support. It was an interschool race and since he was there to support his

219

brother, he could mingle with the other runners. "They all adored Martin. Everybody loved Martin." George paused, and Nan waited. "He had a pair of running shoes," he said, "that he saved for tournaments. He would put them on right before the race. So I knelt down and loosened the laces for him, and while he put on one shoe I slipped a stone into the other. You know, a little one, tiny. He was in a hurry. He didn't notice. It was a half-mile course. He set off and I figured he would either have to stop and take off his shoe and remove the stone and lose the race, or he would keep running, a bit hobbled, and still lose."

He was hunched into himself in the chair. His shoulders were bent. His eyes were focused on the bed.

"You didn't like being outshone," she said. She wasn't unsympathetic.

"I was tired of being outshone."

"Did he ever guess?"

"He never mentioned it."

"He never mentioned it to you."

George was silent for a while. "The boy I tormented? He and Martin became great pals. I always wondered if they talked about me."

She took her time with what she said next. "So the reason you don't want to see Martin is because you feel guilty about your past misdeeds."

"Would it kill him to telephone me?" he said bitterly.

"Would it kill you to telephone him?"

"I'm not going to, Nancy. And I don't want you to either."

"Well," she said after a moment, "you know I'll do what I want." Yet so much of her life was the opposite, doing what she didn't want to do, and worrying about doing the wrong thing.

Still hunched in the chair, George said, "If Jim's got his heart set on Canada, then he should go." He sighed before adding, "But I have the feeling I'll never see him again."

"Now you're being morbid. You're not going to die while he's away."

"That's not what I'm getting at."

His melancholy glance held hers and she felt her knees suddenly weaken as she understood what he meant. "Lulu won't let anything happen to him," she managed to say.

"Once an alcoholic, always an alcoholic."

"I trust her."

"I *don't*."

"George, I do. Besides, the lake is much safer than the city. You don't think so, but it's a hundred times safer. He's going to be fine."

She went back to sorting the clothes and putting them away, but that night she didn't fall asleep for a long time.

THE END OF SUMMER

13

LULU SHOWED UP IN HER BUICK ON THE LAST DAY OF JULY, arriving in the evening, staying the night. Early the next morning, they were on their way to Canada. They took the old, familiar route up through New York State to the Thousand Islands Bridge and across. It was near-dusk when they reached Snow Road Station and turned onto the gravel road that led to the lake. They rolled their windows all the way down to breathe in the fragrance of the woods.

Nothing had changed. It was the same green and quiet world beside the water.

Jim charged up the wooden steps, Moon on his heels, into the beloved verandah where the screens were feathered with lint, moths, pine needles, seeds from the free-flowing woodsy air. Here was the sleep-inducing sofa, the wide hammock, the wicker chairs from which your bare skin took the pattern, so you walked away wearing the chair. All the rooms were the same, he saw at a glance. Lulu took pleasure in calling it the miracle of the untouched summer place.

The first two weeks of August remained hot with the full-blown heat of summer. Wearing the life vest Lulu insisted upon, Jim explored the bays and inlets with his dog, who provided a counterweight near the bow for him in the stern. Moon was about eleven months old by now, his head square, his face broad and self-respecting. Beavers tempted him, but a word from Jim settled him back. He loved to be on the water. He loved to see the passing sights and feel the breezes in his face. He was a seadog.

Jim came to know the shoreline better than ever, the points and islands where he would bring the canoe right up to the rocky edge or grassy bank and let Moon scramble over the side onto dry land. Then he would drag the canoe halfway up the bank or tie the canoe's painter to a tree. He swam and his dog swam with him. Sometimes, for the pure pleasure of having Moon come to his rescue, he pretended he was drowning and what a sweet thrill that was, what a swelling boon to his ego, to have his dog powering toward him, focused on nothing else but him. Jim would grip the furry scruff of his neck, staying clear of the sharp nails on his paddling paws, and Moon would turn and pull him to shore. Afterwards came the tremendous body-shake as Moon rid himself of the lake. Then the stick. He brought it to Jim, and in this game of fetch and retrieve, it was never Moon who tired first.

At the end of the second week, having made one of her trips to town for supplies, Lulu came up the steps laughing, her arms full. "The four things you can't do without," she said. "A lemon, garlic, flowers, and a letter."

His mother had written to him. "Dearest Jim," in her scrawling hand, "I've been working hard – watching four movies a day, eating ice cream for breakfast, making triple-decker sandwiches at midnight, generally carrying on. Don't worry. The neighbours have only called the police twice. I told them I'm going crazy without my Jim. I can't be held accountable for the three dozen pepperoni pizzas I ordered because I'm not in my right mind. As soon as Jim gets back, I told them, I'll settle down again. They understood. Your father understands too. He misses you as much as I do."

The warm weather held. At the beginning of the third week, Lulu had to drive into Ottawa twice in a row. She was working as a combat coach for a group of actors rehearsing at the arts centre. Jim stayed behind with Moon the first time and found the day long without her, so the next day they left his dog with Guy and Julie, who had two dogs of their own, the clever border collie named Coal and a big German shepherd named Drake.

The theatre sat astride the bank of the Rideau Canal like a big grey toad, as Lulu said, "But I happen to like toads." She took him through the stage door at the rear, introducing him to everyone as her friend Jim, then settled him in one of the front rows to watch. He occupied himself with his books, snacks, observations, while she choreographed swordplay. The actors called her Lu and tried to do exactly what she said, working hard until the director arrived. He was tall and unsmiling Richard, who sent everyone off, except for one young woman and one young man.

Hamlet and Ophelia, as Jim soon figured out. It became apparent all too quickly that Ophelia couldn't do anything right, though nothing was wrong with her, nothing at all that Jim could see. Nevertheless, whenever she said her lines, Richard didn't like her voice, and whenever she was silent, he didn't like her face.

At last he called a break, "Fifteen minutes," and left the stage, visibly irritated, to sit at the end of the row where Jim was sitting and stare at the floor and open and clench his bony hands. Ophelia approached him and said with hesitation and out of her misery, "Richard? I want to ask you a quick, simple question."

Richard tilted his head to the side and stared at her. "Nothing is ever simple with you, Lise."

Her oh-so-vulnerable face flinched. "Alright," she said slowly. "Well, I just wanted to—"

"You complicate everything."

Jim's gaze sunk to the floor. He was aware of the girl heading up the aisle, fighting tears, while Richard remained where he was, his bony hands cupping his bony knee.

Lulu came back to check on him regularly and at lunchtime they went outside. They walked beside the canal to a park bench and sat and ate their sandwiches. He asked her about the girl playing Ophelia. "Lise is lovely," she said, "with a last name that's impossible. Quenneville-Hudec. It might be smart to lop half of it off. She's from around here, Cumberland, I think."

"Is she good?"

She was very good, Lulu said, she might go far. Or she might not, thinking of her own talent. For she had been told when she was young that her smile, her ebullience, were American, and she should head to small regional theatres in the United States to get her start. "You can't grow a magnolia on the tundra," she was told. "You're a magnolia. Try St. Louis." In succession she had tried American theatre, French, British. She'd ended up in Mexico, of all places, the best Shakespearean actor in Mexico, maybe the *only* Shakespearean actor in Mexico.

Jim said, "The director is mean to her." He was watching two gleaming white cabin cruisers slide by on the canal.

"Richard? That doesn't surprise me. What did he do?" Lulu listened, then she brushed the crumbs off her lap with vigorous strokes even after all the crumbs were gone. "That's awful," she said. "Well, Richard always has to have somebody to pick on. He doesn't like women. He doesn't like certain women. He really *dislikes* certain women. And when he dislikes you, he's a monster. He destroys young actors while telling the world how much he supports them. That girl should carry a gun."

Jim's eyes were fastened on Lulu's vehement face.

"She should pull out her gun and point it at Richard's head. 'You thought things were complicated before? *Now* they're complicated.'"

It was evening by the time they got back to Snow Road and over to Guy's house. They found Julie coming out of the vegetable garden, carrying a bowl full of green beans, newly picked. "Guy's looking for your dog," she said, frowning, apologetic. "He should be back any minute." Her own two dogs were nearby.

"Moon took off?" Lulu said. "When? How long has he been gone?"

"Likely he made his way back to your place. Guy went to check."

The air could not have been more summery. Above them dark

clouds were building, breaking, turning to sunshine and blue sky. Then darkening again. Then dispersing.

And Lulu repeated her question. How long had Moon been gone?

"Well, he wasn't around when I went to feed them. An hour ago, about."

She had no idea, in other words.

"Jim," and Lulu's voice was steady, "we'll go home and see what's up."

They were getting back into the car when the red-and-white pickup came bumping towards them down the lane.

In *Pogo*, Pup Dog gets lost. They go through the swamp searching for him. Is that when Bobcat shows up with his gun? Jim could not remember and all the Pogos were in his room in New York.

Guy pulled up beside them and got out alone, his face apologetic too. No sign of Moon. He would keep looking in the bush around his place and they should go back to their house, since no doubt Moon was making his way home. Guy turned away from them and spat into the grass, hitting a protruding stick bang on, and then turned back. "Don't worry, Jim. He's a smart dog."

He *is* a smart dog, Jim thought, but I shouldn't have left him here. In his mind was the dark suspicion that Coal and Drake had shunned him, maybe even scared him off. "Why would he run away?" he said.

"He missed you," Guy said. "He's on his way home."

So then it really was his fault. He should never have left him.

Lulu drove them back to their place, where the lane, the field, the woods, the shore were empty as empty could be. They spent the remaining hours of twilight looking and calling. After dark, Jim kept on calling, while Lulu went inside and scrambled some eggs and scraped what little butter they had across the over-toasted toast – dark and dry, he would remember; he drank milk to get it down. All the while they listened. On the verandah they held their books in their laps, still listening. Finally, they went to bed and early the next morning they were in the canoe, scouring as if on hands and knees every inch of shoreline, calling Moon's name. It was August 21st and cooler at night. The songbirds were gone. Most of the bugs were gone and therefore the birds. Jim recognized and knew by name water lilies, irises even without the arrowhead of blue, pickerel weed, marsh ferns, royal ferns, cedar trees, the endless cedars, the pines and hemlocks, and the birch trees (that would bend over two years later in the great ice storm of 1998 and never right themselves again).

In the afternoon they tried the roads. They went over to Guy's place first, hoping against hope. Then methodically they drove the network of country roads, looking for a blond hump of fur either in the ditch or at the side of the road. It was like looking for a lost darning needle in the wilderness: the longer they looked, the more their lives unravelled.

Several times they drove through great clouds of dragonflies. It happened when the sun was full on the road and there were no trees on either side. Another day the sight would have thrilled him. But Jim was only really aware of the car, of their two selves in the car, of their slow progress in search of something terrible. His eyes hurt from looking so hard, but the rest of him was numb.

In bed that night his hand slid down and he rubbed himself as always, because it felt good, and this time it happened. What the older boys had been bragging about took hold of him, he couldn't stop it, his body took over, and he felt the most wonderful urgent pressure building into an even more wonderful release. A bit later, he sort of cleaned it up with a tissue, but who cared about that.

The bigger boys had been talking about nothing else, talking about it, doing it, showing others how to do it, if you were one of them. And so all of this was going to happen to him too.

The worst and the best at the same time.

In the morning Lulu telephoned Nan to tell her about lost Moon. He had been gone thirty-six hours and they were pretty frantic.

Nan said they would find him, she was sure of it. But in her heart, standing in that New York kitchen, she felt seized by the cold fear that the father's luck was passing to the son. She was witnessing it from afar: the start of bad luck.

Jim came on the telephone and she said to him, "Moon will show up. He'll arrive on your doorstep."

"How do you know?"

"It's a feeling I have." She crossed her fingers and gathered her thoughts. "He's been on the loose before, running from wolves. He knows that part of the world. He'll find his way home."

"Today?"

"Or tonight," she said.

She said it so firmly that Jim believed her.

August 22nd, and still barely a whisper of fall, despite tinges of yellow and orange in minor places among the trees. Today or tonight Moon would arrive on their doorstep, his mother was certain of it, and so he stayed around the house all day, circling it and walking up and down the lane.

"Darling," Lulu said, "I'm going to put up signs in the stores. Do you want to come?" No, he would stay. But he helped her write the signs. "A Good Dog Is Lost," they wrote across the top.

His mother had said to him once that when it came to disaster he had a mother's imagination, dwelling in a similar way on details and variations. Well, he was dwelling on details and variations now. It was August, he reasoned, it wasn't hunting season, Moon hadn't been shot. He might have been hit by a car and crawled off into the underbrush. Or fallen off a ledge onto rocks and broken a leg. Or two legs. Or gotten lost and been taken in by someone. Or stolen.

He was sitting on the steps when Lulu got back. She suggested they go for a paddle, check the shoreline one more time, but he would not budge from the vicinity of the house. The hours wore on. He resisted Lulu's overtures to come to the table; he wasn't hungry. They watched the sun go down together. They felt the breeze come up.

231

They watched the bats sail out from under the eaves and swoop over the water. Lulu went inside and Jim walked to the end of the lane and back. It was intolerable, the waiting, yet he tolerated it.

A few minutes after midnight, he telephoned his mother. "He didn't come back."

She had been lying awake when the telephone rang. "I'm sorry, sweetheart. I'm so sorry."

"You said he would."

"It was a feeling I had. Sometimes the feelings pan out. Sometimes they don't. Do you want me to come?"

"I want Moon." He was in tears.

She was in tears. "It's rotten," she said.

He didn't know what to say. It didn't matter. Nothing did.

Jim lay awake after the telephone call, wishing his uncle were alive, missing him. His mind slid back to summers before this one, to the time they had gone hiking through the buggy woods to a wide clearing, and there, magically, was the Mississippi River, the Canadian Mississippi, and swimming in the corners of his uncle's eyes were two black flies, drowned. The river was as wide as a small lake. It narrowed into a set of rolling rapids that descended into pools full of bass. Along the edge were cardinal flowers like tall red orchids – they were fond of fast water, his uncle said – and flying overhead were gulls. A Newfoundland poet named Pratt, his mother said, called seagulls "those wild orchids of the sea." Jim could picture Moon stepping into the Mississippi for a drink, lapping it up with his long tongue, then swimming around to cool off before getting his bearings and setting off along the trail that would lead him out to the road and home.

He drifted off to sleep with the sound of rapids in his head and when he woke up it was pitch-dark. The idea came to him then to go out on the water, paddle over to the Huck Finn island, make a fire. Something he had never done with Moon, though he had meant to. If Moon was out there somewhere, then he would be too. He dressed in the dark, fumbling with his clothes, and in the kitchen he felt around in the breadbox for a bun and slid one into the pocket of his sweatshirt. Outside, it was too dark to see his feet, but he didn't turn back for a flashlight. He stumbled and felt his way down to the water.

At the shore he could see again and he paused. The lake stretched out shiny-black and smooth under the stars. He slipped into the canoe, knocking the second paddle with his knee, bumping against the dock as he swung out. He didn't bother with his life jacket, leaving it on the floor of the canoe.

The water was still and he was moving in the dark instead of tossing in bed.

He went by shapes, heading towards the black island-shape with the campsite Bad Art had gone to in his stories. Nothing else was awake or on the water. He had it all to himself. The dark turned him inside out, like the inner pocket of a coat. But nobody can tell. Nobody knows but you.

I'm not going to waste my life, he thought to himself.

He was going to be good at many things, tough and successful. Not like his father, whose plans for himself were either feeble or impossible: wanting to be a lawyer, for instance, and his mother saying, George, is that realistic at fifty-five?

He was going to know a lot and be confident enough to have opinions and state them. He was almost thirteen. That's getting old, he thought.

There was the little dock. He nosed the canoe against it and made another racket when he climbed forward and over the side. The path was evident even in the dark, a sort of scooping out by the shapes around. He scrambled up to the top and there he was in the wide opening of the campsite and it was incredibly dark. He stood for a moment, adjusting his eyes, then made his way over to the doused campfire, bent down to feel around for twigs and sticks,

233

and gathered a dry little pile, feeling this way and that – then realized when he fished in his pockets that he had forgotten matches. What was the point? He backed up and settled himself on one of the logs near the fire, dug his elbows into his knees and stared at the stone-circled pit. They must have put out the fire by pissing on it, that's how it smelled. For a while he practised spitting, the way Guy plugged his target, the way baseball players spat before they swung. Then something came up behind him.

He heard it breathing. He heard it moving. Something fell from a tree. A pine cone, a pine cone. The animal breathed behind him.

He waited, feeling every inch of his long bare neck.

The breathing changed. He heard it moving again and he understood why the Indians had masks: to frighten back. He bared his teeth, which made a wet click of a sound.

The pearliness of his hands. Slowly he reached into his pocket and pulled out the bun, broke bits of it off into his lap, and gingerly, with a small toss, threw one bit behind him. Soft bread on soft ground. Not even an Iroquois could detect the sound.

He turned to see what it was.

It was rounded, large, dark, slow-moving, like a small armoured tank. It flared its whitish quills: a porcupine. Low and certain of itself, safe inside its quills, impregnable and therefore not nasty unless attacked. What a great animal.

Watching it sniffing all around, living its porcupine life, cheered Jim up.

A breeze discovered his face and travelled across it. He heard an owl in the distance, a loon. After a short while came the croak of the raven and its wing beats overhead. Croak, croak. Always the first one to announce the light.

He watched the porcupine flare its armour again, then amble over to a tree that it proceeded noisily to climb – higher and higher and around and around – until it came to rest out on a branch. It lay on its stomach. It was a good thing Moon wasn't here: a muzzle full of quills. Barbed, he knew, and every movement of the sufferer made them burrow deeper into the flesh. The porcupine was moving again. It had changed its mind and was descending noisily and backwards. On the ground it took no notice of him watching, a dozen feet away. It ambled down to the water, then back up the slope towards the other side of the island, as if seeking an even more comfortable spot in a comfortable bed.

What Jim learned from the sunrise was that when you think something is over, it's only beginning. He was in the canoe again, drifting, letting the trace of wind and current carry him towards the brightening in the east. Two ribbons of pink appeared in the lower sky and then the water itself was pink all the way from the shore to the bow of his canoe. The colour intensified. It faded. It faded some more. It was gone. Was that all? It appeared to be.

He turned his back on the disappointment and paddled to where the otters lived, but there was no sign of them. He let himself drift. After a while, looking east again, he saw low grey clouds underlit by pink. And then on it came. Strawberry pink, worked through, lined and edged by the rising sun. The pink bounced to the bank of clouds behind him, turning them the purple blue of plums. He watched the purple darken. Then he turned his head back towards the pink, which had also deepened and darkened in the meantime. And now golden light, melting gold, surged over the edges of every cloud, shattering them to pieces as the sun rose above the horizon, filling the sky and pouring across the waters.

The sunrise was a long story, that's what he learned.

Paddling slowly, he turned the corner of an island, and there, in a select spot of grassiness and protecting cedar, was a great blue heron standing on a dead tree that extended over the water. It stood a long moment before taking off, a prehistoric dragon-bird, and it was another good sign. It was one fabulous sign after another. The heron called a few times as it swooped low over the water, heading towards another island, its call sounding like fabric that was very hard to tear being torn in half.

These secret places that birds and animals knew. They were hidden usually, then sometimes the curtains got pulled back and you saw into the living room of nature.

Moon was out there somewhere, Jim felt sure of it. Today was the day he would make it back.

After a spell of drifting and paddling, he headed home towards Lulu in a white hat moving around the dock. She was waiting for him and he remembered the life jacket and slipped it on.

"I knew you'd be hungry," she said as he brought the canoe alongside the dock.

Side by side, they drank hot chocolate and ate muffins with jam while two loons in the bay came to within twenty feet of them and remained that close, sometimes closer, for the longest time. "We get these glimpses into the lives of wild animals," Lulu said, soft-spoken in her wonderment, "when things are as they've always been."

"Before people," he murmured.

"Before the before," she said.

He didn't mention the porcupine then or later. It would always be a puzzle to him, the things he didn't say, as if it weren't the right moment, and the things he didn't ask, as if he already knew the answer.

"Tell me to break a leg," Lulu said.

She was driving into Ottawa that morning to audition for a part she knew she wasn't going to get. But she wanted the role, and she knew she could do it if they would only give her the chance. She would be back in the afternoon, maybe sooner.

He went up to the house with her and made sure to pocket some matches. Then, convinced that everything was going to go right today, he took a fry pan and oil and salt and pepper and went fishing. He paddled to where he knew there were easy perch, over by an island they called Flowerpot. Standing on shore, he cast his line and caught a small one and threw it back, and continued to fish.

There were certain spots where he knew every tree and rock. They seemed arranged to show each other to best advantage, the expanse of rock an easy walking surface and the trees springing up like furniture in the simplest room. Seeing this part of the world come into view every summer, his mother would say that it was different from anywhere else she knew, and her voice would catch and her face go pink and trembly with emotion before moving back onto safe ground. She would remember being a child and driving with her parents to this very lake to visit friends, little suspecting that one day her brother would buy the old log cottage they had always admired.

"Has it changed?" Jim had asked her once, meaning this part of the world. And after a pause that lengthened into low-key suspense, she said, "Really, it hasn't. It hasn't changed, Jim." Giving him the answer he wanted to hear.

He paddled to where the lake was deeper, having decided to go for trout, and cast his line from the canoe. He liked the distinctive shapes the trees took on as they grew, so you could tell from a distance what they were: tall, plumy, white pines; loose and baggy hemlocks; cedars in a green wall overhanging the water's edge, living their long cedar lives because their wood didn't rot. The other day he had been swimming near the dock when Lulu said, "Darling, don't be alarmed, but there's a water snake behind you." A small black snake curving its watery way between him and the dock. "It's downright social," she said. He cast again. If he caught a nice-sized trout he would fry it on the wild point over there, and for the first time the thought occurred to him that he might never find out what happened to Moon. He might live the rest of his life without knowing. The thought was unbearable. He reeled in his line and changed his lure.

On the wild point he hunted for stones and placed them just so for the fire. He liked making a meticulous circle of stones, arranging them according to their compatibilities, like a matchmaker who cared, or a surgeon rebuilding a jaw. His uncle had taught him how to kill a fish, driving a knife blade hard into the back of its neck, which produced some blood but ended suffering. And how to clean out the guts and leave them behind a rock for a raccoon or mink or otter to find. He got the oil hot in the fry pan, having been rewarded for his long patience with a speckled trout, and now he cooked it, absorbed in the sizzling and the way the tail curled up with such a will of its own.

He ate with his fingers, burning them a little. A bone lodged in the back of his throat. He swallowed water from the flask, but the bone didn't budge. It was deep, where he couldn't reach it with his finger, and it hurt. His father's mouth full of tumour, but this was only a bone. He kept swallowing and he could feel it there, lodged in place.

Dragonflies were about. Some mosquitoes. He noticed a mole dart across the ground, not nearly as bold and confident as a chipmunk. It seemed to have tiny wheels under its feet, it was that close to the ground and its forward dash so smooth and unbroken.

He wasn't choking, but it was hurting more, and how was he going to get it out? He had to pee and thought of peeing on the fire but he had already doused it, so he walked a few steps up an incline instead, intending to see how far he could send his water into the woods, and there in a hollow lay a yellow mound of fur.

Moon's dark guts were spread about, his soft stomach torn open. Chunks had been taken out of his back legs. No flies, no smell. Recent. His eyes were open and seeing nothing at all.

What Jim would remember was paddling with all his might across the lake, a comic-book figure pumping his arms. He was out of breath by the time he slammed open the cottage door, hoping Lulu was back; she wasn't.

Guy. He searched around for his number. Yanked open all the drawers and rummaged and shoved them back in. He was in tears. He couldn't even find a telephone book.

Then the phone rang on its own and it was his mother. "I had a feeling," she said.

He tried to speak.

"It's alright, Jim. Take your time."

That was a sorry, sorry day. Guy came in his truck after Nan reached him by phone. He brought Henry, a country vet who had been tending to one of his horses. Jim took the two men to the point – he sat in the middle of the canoe while they paddled with strokes so powerful they nearly flew across the water – and Moon was where he had left him.

The men squatted and Jim stood back, a couple of feet. Henry had big hands with thick fingers. Mussed hair when he shoved back his cap. He said he thought Moon had been gut-shot, maybe by a farmer who mistook him for a deer or didn't like stray dogs in his pasture, maybe by some gun-happy kid. He surmised that he had made his way this far by lying down, going on, lying down, going on, until he lay down for good. He mulled over what animal had eviscerated him. Probably a bear, and only after Moon was dead. "Bears despise dogs," he said. "They never go near them." But a hungry bear wouldn't mind taking chunks out of a dead dog's back end, the meatiest part.

Jim said nothing. Had he been even a year younger, he knew he would have wailed and kept on wailing.

Guy had brought a shovel as well as a rifle. He dug into the ground next to Moon, working out rocks, unable to go very deep. They buried him as best they could.

* * *

At the very end of August, it turned unseasonably warm again. August was always moodier than July, Jim thought, because it had to cope with the end of summer, which was hard. Other boats were out besides theirs: an aluminum motorboat trolled by; a flat white houseboat cruised slowly in the distance. From their canoe he and

Lulu watched the moon come up over the nearest island – big – a beautiful beginning – then higher – almost as if it were an omen, Jim thought. As if the lake were a place where the old transformations held true. He would learn the word "metamorphosis" that fall at school and know instantly what it meant.

The sky in the west was a smoky, subtle tangerine. Lulu directed the canoe away from the fading sunset into the moon's streaming path of light-across-the-water as it rose into the clouds and became smaller and whiter.

It was a blue moon they were looking at, the second full moon of the month, a rare occurrence, Lulu said. They paddled to the far shore, lined with summer cabins, cottages, the public campground, then swung back and headed towards the wilderness part of the lake, where the flashlight of the moon zeroed in on every blade of grass and alder leaf and lily pad and tuft of fur and bone.

This was their last night. In the morning they would be heading back to the city, and Lulu wished Jim would talk a little more. "Darling, what are you thinking?"

He was remembering that lousy day – how he had leaned his aching head against her side, exhausted, and she had put her arms around him. And how bad Guy had felt. He should have taken better care of Moon, he said, it was his fault. "Jim, I hope you can forgive me one day." Guy's words had wrung him and he'd had to squeeze his eyes tight to keep in the hot tears, but they'd leapt free anyway. "If we start blaming it's never going to end," Lulu cautioned in a tired voice. "Nobody's to blame." And her evenness allowed him to get control of himself again. She put food on the table, bread and butter, sliced tomatoes, a casserole of reheated sonofabitch stew. It was when they sat down to eat that he mentioned the bone in his throat.

Henry took him to the window and told him to open his mouth wide. "Now this we can fix," he said.

From his big leather bag he took a set of forceps with curved pincers, "The same ones I use for extracting porcupine quills." He went to the sink and filled the kettle halfway and put it on the stove, and while he waited for it to boil he told them a bear story. He had been camping in Algonquin Park as a very young man, he said, when a bear came through his campsite, bold as brass. An older man, a seasoned canoeist in the next site, told him the bear had avoided *his* campsite because the bear knew he wasn't afraid. "'You have to show the bear you're not afraid,' he told me. So when the bear came back, I yelled and clanged my pots. And the bear came straight for me. The other guy's yelling, 'Go after him!' So I take my paddle and lunge at the bear, and the bear keeps coming. The guy says, 'Now hit him!' And I hit him. I jab him in the face with the paddle and you know what that crazy-ass bear does? He swerves away! He heads down to the water and ambles past all the canoes lined up, picks out *mine*, and slashes it on his way by."

Bears were *smart*, he said. And some of them had a screw loose.

The kettle was boiling.

Henry sterilized the pincers. He could see the bone, flat and white, lodged in the back of Jim's throat. He needed more light, though. Lulu fetched the big flashlight from the porch and trained it on Jim's open mouth. Then Henry went in with the pincers, working them with his thick fingers, causing Jim to gag and wave his hands in the air and jerk his head back. Henry set him up in a different chair with a higher back to limit his movements. He tried again, and again Jim gagged and coughed and waved his hands. It was Lulu's idea to lubricate the route with olive oil. Jim swallowed the spoonful of oil and while he was fixated on how disgusting it was, Lulu caught his hand and held it, and Henry went in with the pincers, gave a tug, and drew out the fishbone. He held it up in triumph: a smooth, fat, toothpick of a bone.

"Will it leave a scar?" Jim said, hoping.

After that, he was ravenous. He applied himself to the stew, able to swallow with ease. Suddenly, he looked up. "Did you get the part?" he said to Lulu.

"Oh, Jimmy." It was Jimmy when she was at her lowest. "I'm too old."

"Is that what they said?"

"You want to know what they said? 'Thank you.' I did my piece, they said thank you, I left."

"I'm in the dark," Guy said.

She explained where she had been that morning, auditioning for a role.

"What was the role?"

"I'm not going to tell you."

"Come on."

She would not. He would laugh her out of the room.

Then she shrugged. What difference did it make? "Cleopatra." And she let out a derisive-amused laugh. "I know. I'm ridiculous."

"You would make a great Cleopatra."

She didn't bother to look at her brother. "You've never even seen me act."

"I think you'd be great, Lu. 'A lass unparalleled'."

She stared at him. Then looking down at her plate, speaking to her plate, she asked him why, only to wish she'd held her tongue. He was being kind. It was alright if he didn't mean it.

"I know you," he said.

She raised her eyes and held his gaze. He knew her. She felt moved, so much so that she lost all desire to know more.

They ate for a while, not talking.

"Jim," she said, putting down her fork. "I'm going to tell you the secret of life." She paused. "Are you ready?"

He was ready.

"Don't rush."

He gulped and swallowed. The porcupine had not rushed. Neither had the otters. Neither had the great blue heron.

Lulu picked up her fork. "It takes something extraordinary to get New Yorkers to slow down. What makes them slow down?

Thunderstorms don't do it. They don't break their stride in the rain."

"Snow," Jim said.

"Only if it's really deep."

"Blackouts," said Guy.

"That does it. Candlelight slows them down. All those stairs to climb." She was thinking of Nan and George, thinking it was time to telephone. Jim was thinking of his parents too.

They made the call after they finished eating. Lulu did the talking, because he could not, telling his mother everything that had happened on the heels of her telephone call to Guy.

Jim sat at the table, listening, his eyes on the white roses going limp in the vase, Lulu's purchase of the week before, and it dawned on him that only a week had gone by since she had come up the steps with her arms full of welcome things, including his mother's letter. He drew his finger down the length of one of the blossoms that was closing in on itself and discovered it felt like Grandma Bobak's cheek.

Lulu was reassuring his mother that he was O.K. He heard her say at the end, "You're right, Nan. The gods sweep down."

But what did the gods have against Moon? What had Moon ever done to them? He went outside and spat.

The canoe scraped bottom and they lingered there, paddles at rest. He looked back at the blue moon. For the rest of his life he would follow the moon's progress. He would look up into the night sky and see chunks torn out of its side, a devouring that consisted of being nibbled at, nosed, yanked, torn to pieces. It all happened in silence, without protest. Then came the steady gradual reassembling, only to be eaten up again, bit by bit.

If he had known he was going to lose his dog, he never would have come here, no matter how much he loved the lake. Nothing would ever be the same, he thought. Even Ducky was different. Guy had brought her over to see them after she arrived for a visit and she wouldn't even look at him. He'd offered to read to her. She had turned away. Lulu had said later that she was shy, "Too shy for words." "So she doesn't hate me?" "No, she likes you too much. She doesn't know what to do with her feelings about you. She's only five." But he didn't think that was true. Something about him had turned her off and he didn't know what it was.

Lulu dug her paddle into the lake bottom and pushed them backwards. He did the same. "You don't have to tell me what you're thinking," she said. "It's alright."

They paddled on in the moonlight, rounding a corner, and there rising up in front of them was something so extraordinary their paddling arms went slack. It was the *Hispaniola*, brought back to life. Every detail – masts, rigging, bowsprit, hull – was picked out by the unearthly light. They were staring at the island where the loons liked to nest, magnified to double its size by the moonlight. Towering white pines formed the masts, cedars the rigging, two far-leaning cedars formed the bowsprit, and the high, rounded bank of stone was the hull.

Long John Silver had decamped, leaving the island-ship in solitary splendour.

"Jim, have you ever seen a finer sight?"

He didn't know how to put it all together, death and life and things looming up. Your heart lies in pieces on the forest floor and the days and nights keep coming.

14

DURING THE LAST WEEK OF AUGUST, BLAKE SHOWED UP at his mother's door. The prodigal son came home unannounced. Setting his bag down in the hall, he accepted her thrilled hug and unfeigned greeting – "I am so glad to see you!" – and then went from room to room, checking out and admiring the space and the light. He knew the apartment well, his step-grandmother's cool apartment, the scene of so many Thanksgiving and Christmas dinners.

"You approve," Nan said with a smile. He did. He ran his hand across his clean-shaven chin and continued to look around, a young man of twenty-two who had been working out, Nan saw. His shoulders were broader, his neck thicker.

"Blake, I've missed you."

He heard her and smiled back. "Grandma was smart," he said, "buying this place when she did."

Like every New Yorker, he admired real estate savvy and luck. And his grandmother *had* been smart, buying the apartment with money from her husband's life insurance during the first wave of rental properties being converted to cooperatives. That was in 1981.

George joined them, emerging from the bathroom. He greeted his stepson with polite enthusiasm, and Nan saw the moment of shock as Blake registered the change in George's appearance, followed by the instant analysis, sentiment-free, of where things stood with his stepfather.

The next morning, when she and Blake were alone at breakfast and he was spreading cream cheese on his toasted bagel, he said to her, "So what's going to happen to this place after George dies?"

She put down her spoon. "George is getting better. He's a lot better than he was. You haven't seen the progress he's made."

"Mom, half his face is gone. He looks like a concentration camp victim."

He held her gaze, unembarrassed, unapologetic, an ambitious young man, she realized, with his broad shoulders and deep convictions.

"What are you saying to me?" she said. "You're telling me you want the apartment?"

That was exactly it. Not for himself but for his church.

"We're taught to ask for what we need," he said.

"And what would that be?" She was having trouble believing her ears. Lear's greedy daughters flashed through her mind. Grasping children.

He wanted to "plant" a church. That was the word he used and she gathered it was the lingo in vogue with his particular evangelical sect. First, you planted a church and then you became its pastor.

"Well, I'd ask what you're smoking, if I didn't know better."

"Look." Leaning towards her, completely serious. "After George is gone, you'll go back to Canada. You know you will." And he indicated the apartment around him, this enviable space begging to be put to worthy use.

Nan struggled for words and though it was the least of her objections she ended up saying, "The building won't let you turn these rooms into a church. What are you thinking?"

"There's no law against visitors." His shameless look was half-smile. "I'd live here, and twice a week I'd give my sermons, that's all. And once a week we'd have Bible study. It would still be my home."

He hasn't even asked us how we are, she thought. She had told him but not because he'd asked. He hadn't even asked about Jim.

"You must be very angry with me," she said. And she heard the anger in her own voice.

"Who says I'm angry? I'm not angry."

He picked up his bagel and balanced it in his hand, then set it down. "You did everything with Jim," he said. Delivering the accusation in a sullen voice.

Here it was then. They were going to go down this unhappy road. And without being aware of it, she began to rub the area over her heart. "Blake, don't you remember all the things we did together? The things we built? The model cars and the puppet stage? You were so good with your hands, I thought you might be an artist one day."

"Where are they?" He looked around pointedly.

"What?"

"The model cars."

"Don't you have them?"

"You don't even know where they are."

"But you remember," she said with a certain desperation. "You haven't forgotten."

"I remember making things on my own," he said. "And I don't know where any of them went."

She cast about frantically in her mind. They had to be at John's. Unless John had thrown them out or passed them on. She was trying to recall the order of their moves from place to place when Blake said, "You destroyed my family."

She raised her eyes.

"You took me away from Dad."

Nan felt herself sag. So this was what he thought of her.

Her hand went to the old scar on her forehead and she felt again the impact of the hurled pitcher of milk. She hadn't ducked in time, rivetted by the waste. "Your father was impossible, you know that. He scared you too. Don't tell me you've forgotten."

Blake shrugged.

"Blake," she pleaded.

And then he had the good grace to nod.

O.K., then. She took a deep breath. "Did I toast enough bagel? I can make more."

He shook his head.

"Listen," she said, but didn't go on. She didn't know where to begin. She had to wonder why certain boys turned against their mothers at a certain age, why certain brothers turned against their sisters. She was thinking about Guy. She could see him in Blake's shoulders and hands and in that cold gaze he turned on anyone he happened to be angry with.

"Listen to what?" he said.

"We don't have to see things the same way. I don't expect you to."

Maybe it was biology, she thought. Biology's way of warding off incest and inbreeding, this hostility of sons and brothers towards mothers and sisters. Whatever it was, it was cruel. But she was generalizing, always a mistake.

Blake's fingernails were bitten to the quick. It hurt her to see them and she reached across the table and took his hand and held it. Wonder of wonders, he let her. "Mine are even worse than yours," he said as she stroked his poor nubs, and for a moment he was back with her, he was her son again.

"I wish things had worked out with John," she said. "Do you see him much? How is he?"

"He's great. He came to hear me preach."

"Did he?" That was more than she had done. "I'm glad. I'm glad you see him." She meant to leave it at that but then couldn't help herself. "Just don't forget what he was like when you were small."

"Well, George is a loser." And he retrieved his hand and went back to his bagel.

And so she found herself defending George. She enumerated his strengths, ashamed of herself for having forgotten them – his gentleness, his humour, his concern for the poor, his loyalty. "He was always good to you," she said, "and he's always stuck by me." And in saying this, she realized that contained in the remark was

248

a veiled criticism of Blake for not sticking by her. Where do they come from, these things that say more than we know and more than we intend? A little playwright is inside us, she supposed, working away.

Blake made a show of reading the Bible for the two days he was with them, though what was he supposed to do, Nan asked herself, pretend he wasn't reading it? She assumed he read it here as he read it elsewhere, almost continuously. He was churning through Kings I and II for the fourth time, though what he focused on primarily were the "wisdom books" as he called Job, Psalms, Proverbs, and Ecclesiastes. At every meal, except breakfast, he insisted upon grace. "Father, we thank You for this food. As You led the Lord Jesus into battle against our adversaries, may we too be led by the Holy Spirit in all that we say and do. In Jesus' name. Amen."

She and George talked about him in near whispers after they went to bed. George dubbed him the holy man. "Just don't let him pray over me," he begged from his pillow. "Promise me." And she promised. In the light of her bedside lamp, she pored through the photograph album resting on her knees and pondered how A got to Z. How did this affectionate toddler, sprawled so comfortably in her lap, grow into the spiritual lout who was breaking her heart? Well, he had made a friend when he was thirteen, that's how, and been sort of adopted into the family of five children with their stay-at-home mother and chuckling father, who had given him something she could not. Rote normality, perhaps. She had met them a few times, been invited into their home, and it was like visiting a family made out of soft meringue. They were all fluffy flesh and sweet talk. So these were the parents he wanted, a mother whose face and arms and legs were like soft lard, a father built like a vertical cupcake. They were Bible believers for whom scripture was the ultimate authority in every area of life. They gave Blake his own Bible and he took to it. First, to the New Testament and then to the bitter waters of the Old. He became hard-line, lecturing, critical.

She put aside the album and turned off the light. Into the darkness, she said, "Blake accused me of destroying his family."

"You *are* his family."

"In some ways he's right. You know what else? He wants this apartment for his church."

"Over my dead body," George said.

She laughed a little and directed her eyes to the ceiling, to the night-time play of light and shadow across its surface. "I don't know what to do," she said.

"Nancy, he likes being a thorn in your side. It's how he gets your attention."

"He pushes me away." The ceiling brightened for a moment, then darkened again. "There's something I've never told him."

She was remembering that particular summer when she and Guy had coincided at the lake, the summer after her brother had bought the old log cottage and she was helping him fix it up. The summer of her surreptitious and heady romance with Guy. She was twenty-seven years old. 1974. There were excellent reasons for keeping her secret. Guy was married, for one. For another, their affair had already tapered off when she met John in September. Only three weeks later did she learn she was pregnant.

"What have you never told him?" George asked.

"Things about his childhood."

"Does he need to know?"

She closed her eyes. Did he need to know?

At the time she had seemed admirable to herself, keeping her counsel, not complicating anyone else's life. But what was admirable in the moment became inexcusably self-serving in hindsight. It must happen to others, she thought. You think you're doing something brave. Only later does it seem so baldly wrong that it's hard to understand what you were thinking at the time.

Blake, she knew, would never forgive her for not having told him. And the repercussions for everyone involved would be endless. They would be endless.

Did he need to know?

She pictured telling him on her deathbed and understood how such confessions happen. Hey, guess what.

Then lights out, and the living have to deal with your mess.

"Maybe not," she said at last.

* * *

On the final day of August, Jim and Lulu departed the lake, unaware they had a small spider on board until they were ten minutes down the road. "Darling, you wouldn't make it in New York," Lulu said, stopping the car and opening the door, "so don't even try." She let the spider crawl onto her hand and then eased it onto a blade of grass in the ditch.

The return drive, without a dog, was otherwise nothing but forward motion with pauses for gas and lunch. At midday they pulled off onto a country road to have their sandwiches, finding a stone wall to perch on, and from there they glimpsed two deer: first the fawn, then deeper in the woods the doe.

They sat very still and watched the two creatures move and blend into the trees. In a whisper Lulu said she felt like a venison burger, and Jim smiled. "There wouldn't be much meat on the fawn," she murmured, "it would be a small burger with plenty of ketchup." Jim smiled again and spat into the grass. They were being tough together: two tough guys, ready for anything.

Back in the car, driving on, Lulu started to sing a poem set to music, a long song in which the wind was a torrent of darkness among the gusty trees, the moon a ghostly galleon tossed upon cloudy seas, and so on. Now that was a sad story, she told him, the story of Phil Ochs writing so many brilliant songs while never becoming as famous as he wanted to be, as famous as Dylan, his rival, "And he couldn't handle it," she said. Towards the end of his short life, in a crazy bid for fame, he went on stage in a gold lamé suit and eventually he killed himself.

Jim asked her how and she scratched her right eyebrow, trying to remember. She couldn't recall if it was an overdose or if he shot himself. And then the passing road gave her the answer. Even worse. He hanged himself.

This is the way of a long and empty road: nearly forgotten things surface and singing voices improve. They were on the old familiar Route 12, heading southeast between Watertown and Utica, where they would get on the Thruway, the map of New York State spread open across Jim's knees. His eye was drawn to certain place names, Rome, Troy, Ithaca, setting in motion a train of thoughts about Odysseus and his ancient dog, and then about Moon, who had been such a terrific companion, even in the car. He could say "bird" and Moon would look up at the sky and follow the movements of the hawk; or "deer", and Moon would follow the graceful shape at the edge of the woods, looking back over his shoulder as any human would have. Soon his memories had him staring up at the beige roof, willing away his tears.

Lulu divined his thoughts and said, "We've both lost beloved dogs. You, through no fault of your own, no matter what you think."

He sent his gaze in a safe direction, out his window.

"Guy helped both times," she said.

"So you like him now?"

"Oh, I always have, Jim." In a voice that contained their whole heavy history. "That's the trouble."

The passing fields, the rivers and lakes and farms, kept on rolling by. Lulu knew that Jim was doing his best not to think about certain things, including school, but she had one piece of advice she wanted to offer. Join the band if his school had one. A boy who played a musical instrument was a boy in demand.

"I'm not," he said.

That was no surprise, although she had an interesting older-woman take on why it might be so. "Maybe you have something the other boys wish they had."

Jim turned this over in his mind, wondering if it was believable. He didn't believe it, but that didn't mean it wasn't believable.

"I was never popular," Lulu said. "My grandmother warned me. 'People will be mean to you. Just remember they're mean because they're jealous.'" She smiled at him. "I didn't believe her either. But what *I'm* saying is true. What I said about Ducky is also true. She's crazy about you."

She slipped Joni Mitchell's *Blue* into the cassette player and for a while Jim followed the words to "A Case of You", only to glance at Lulu when the song ended and see tears running down her face.

"You're *crying*."

She said, "It's a wonderful song." And she wiped her face with the back of her hand.

About an hour out of New York, they left the Thruway and took the Palisades Parkway through New Jersey for a change, rather than crossing the river on the Tappan Zee Bridge and going through the Bronx. Before long they were lined up to pay the toll for the George Washington Bridge and then they were crossing the Hudson into Manhattan. Lulu's favourite bridge, she said, and his too, he decided, with its steel towers and long cables and wide view of the river. Turning south on the Henry Hudson Parkway brought the city pouring in through their open windows, a flowing smell of hot pavement, river, vegetation, and the slightly sour, very humid taint of polluted city air. It was like smelling an American dollar bill, thought Jim, and he loved it. These returns to New York at the end of August were a powerful part of his life. Lulu followed the parkway, getting off at 95th Street, and going around and up that bit of a hill on 96th before turning left onto West End Avenue. They arrived in time for supper and it was great, the cries of welcome, the embraces, the happy tears.

His father looked a lot better. He had grown a moustache, which Jim was quick to say he liked. The half-gone side of his face was still like something chopped off with an axe and the skin folded under, but it wasn't so red or painful-looking. He wasn't so thin. Next week, his father said, he was going back to work, two days a week at first, then more as he got stronger. Towards Lulu, however, George was the same, and Jim admired her evenness in the face of it and felt truly ashamed of his father's skittish, edge-hunting, ungenerous behaviour: the looking away, the sidling into another room, the silence at the dinner table, and then the jabs out of nowhere.

"My son had a dog and now he doesn't," George said over supper. "There's no excuse."

Everyone paused, as if they had forgotten what utensils were for.

Lulu said, "I really couldn't be sorrier, George. I feel terrible about it and so does Guy."

"What I don't understand is why you left our dog with Guy in the first place."

"You know why," Nan intervened. "I explained it to you."

"I'm trying to understand. Is it a crime to ask a few questions?"

"Dad, you're not helping. Can't you just stop?"

"I'm sorry." He dabbed the side of his mouth with the handkerchief he kept in his hand. "You're right."

Jim kept his head down for the rest of the meal. His appetite was gone.

"Jim," Nan said, clearing the plates, "your brother was here." He looked up in swift disappointment. "He didn't tell us he was coming, so he didn't know you'd be at the lake." She stood with the stack of plates in her hands, and he asked when he'd come and for how long, and she told him. "Just two days," she said. "He's fine. He's well. We had a bit of an argument, I'm afraid."

She moved to the sink and he asked her what about.

"Oh, the past," she said. "How he grew up. Everything. All the stuff that never goes away."

George said, "He's hard on your mother."

"Well, at his age that's normal," Nan said. And turning to Jim, she told him that Blake had been really sorry to miss him, though in truth he had barely asked after him.

"When's he coming back?"

Well, he hadn't said. She hoped it would be soon.

After dessert, Nan went to the bathroom in search of pills for her aching head while Lulu brought out a pack of cards from her shirt pocket and challenged them to a game of rummy. "I hear you and Jim are a pair of card sharks," she said to George, dealing three hands of cards. George pushed back his chair and got up. "I'll pass," he said, leaving his cards on the table. He moved around them, heading for the living room. It was a tight squeeze and Lulu did not pull in her chair. She was gathering up the cards and reshuffling the deck.

George had to veer the other way and that was when he chose to say savagely, in a low but audible voice, "Lazy *bitch*."

The slash of hatred stunned Jim. He stared at his father's retreating back, then ran a hand across his lips. It would become a habit, brushing his hand across his mouth whenever he was too disturbed to know what to say or what to think.

Lulu said to the cards, "Sometimes it helps to be deaf."

Nan returned to the kitchen and stopped short, struck by the strained atmosphere and their tight faces. "What happened?"

"Nothing," Lulu said. "Except your son is about to clean my clock."

"Jim? What happened?"

He looked at his mother. Then pointed with his chin. "Ask him."

"Nan," Lulu said, "don't. It doesn't matter. I've already forgotten about it. Jim, do me a favour and let it go."

Later on, George would be extra nice, even solicitous, hoping to wipe away his sin with gentlemanly courtesy. Later still, he would have deeper regrets and say plaintively to Nan that Lulu had poisoned their son against him. "He doesn't respect me anymore."

255

Jim overheard the complaint and thought that he respected him enough to believe he meant what he said, and if he meant what he said, then how could he respect him?

A father who wants to be admired should think these things through.

*　　*　　*

Jim turned thirteen in mid-September. It would be an autumn of rain and heavy clouds, the rain persisting into December.

For a while he kept up his spitting. Nan caught him lobbing spit into the kitchen sink one day. "Jim! You're not in the woods. Don't do that again."

The next time she caught him, he was reading on the sofa and sent a wad of spit to the carpet, where it wouldn't have left a trace or bothered anyone at all, but she was outraged. "What is this? I don't get it. Are you inside some story in your head? Go and get the floor rag from under the sink and clean that up and don't ever do it again."

He promised he would not, but she caught him yet again and got really mad. "You are inside our home. You're not in the woods, you're not in a boat, you're not in a tree. What's come over you?" And the next night he found the following note on his pillow.

Questions to Be Answered by Jim Bobak, Spitting Machine.
1) _Think back to when you started and what prompted it._
2) _Why do you like doing it? Who are you imitating?_
3) _Do you realize how dirty and disgusting it is for everybody who lives with you?_
4) _Why do you continue after you've promised to stop? Does your word mean nothing?_

He wrote back, giving his letter a title too:

On the subject of spitting. Yesterday I spat on the carpet in the living room. Twice in the past two weeks you have asked me to stop.

In both cases, I have applied my own punishement. Which is quite heavy. Yet today, you stepped into a wet spot on the rug. Immediately, you said it was spit. There was no wet spot, you were carrying a glass of water, and I did not spit there. So though spitting seems to be something I'm known for, every wet spot in the house is not my work. As for why I <u>did</u> spit, there are a number of reasons, many people that I know spit, sometimes there is a bad taste in the mouth, etc. The reasons for not stopping after I had promised, the likely reason is that there was no punishement after the incident of the rug, I applied punishement, which is severe. Though the spit in this apartment is mine, not every wet spot is. And, hopefully, I will not be persecuted. As of now, I have stopped spitting. I have promised this before, but this is different.

Nan was impressed by his spirited self-defence and near-perfect spelling, and she could imagine that in Canada he had seen spitting fishermen and so on, but she remained mystified and worried.

She went to his school and met with his teachers, asking them, among other things, how her son got along with his classmates. Their faces smoothed out with evasive pity. "A possible problem," said one, "might be his perceived arrogance."

And then she had a sense of how her son managed his life at school.

George said to her, "He's growing up, that's all." Earlier that day he and Jim had been locked in a cribbage tournament that Jim won handily. "Don't worry about him," he said.

"Aren't you worried?"

"I'm not." He reached for her hand. "I'm not."

Jim had taken to dragging his sleeping bag to the sofa and crawling inside it. He pulled the bag up over his head and spread out his homework in front of him. He was a horizontal monk.

Nan said, "He blames himself for Moon's death. I wish there was some way to convince him it wasn't his fault."

"He's going to be fine."

"George, what makes you so sure?"

"He's going to be a writer. That's what I always wanted to be."

"I didn't know."

"That's because you never asked."

A raw truth. She had never asked him about his deepest yearnings – what he had always wanted to be, what he would do with his life if he had it to live over. "Tell me," she sighed.

"You're not really interested."

They were at the kitchen table eating a pear, sharing it before going to bed, half for him, half for her. "Tell me, or I'll kill you with my bare hands," she said.

"I wrote a novel in my twenties. It was crap. I didn't have the discipline. Well, I didn't have the talent."

"Do you still have it or did you throw it out?"

He had it somewhere. Among his things. He wasn't going to dig it out for her, which was just as well. Her interest had a limit.

Soon after that, she came home with two films about canoeing northern rivers. She had gone to the National Film Board's small office on the forty-eighth floor of the Empire State Building, hoping to borrow films about the out-of-doors for her son who loved the woods, only to be told that they didn't lend out their films. Then the woman took pity on her and went to a desk in the corner, returning with two videos. "Take these. I can get other copies. Yes, I'm sure." They were Bill Mason's *Path of the Paddle* and *Song of the Paddle*.

In the living room Nan and Jim created a canoe-in-theory, tying a long rope around their middles and adjusting its length between them in order to duplicate their positions in bow and stern. Straddling their two tall kitchen stools, they watched the films, paddles in hand (she had gone all the way to an outdoor store in SoHo to buy them), and practised stroking in unison, keeping time with Mason, getting the right angle, tilt, and power.

Bill Mason had died young, about ten years ago, not even sixty years old, of cancer. Nan knew that he had been a diminutive man. She said to Jim, "Many driven men are small. Trudeau was small. Lévesque was small. Odysseus was small. You're lucky. You're going to have your uncle's height, you're going to be a fine figure of a man. You'll be driven too, of course," she added quickly.

He suddenly had his doubts but went along. "Uncle Tom?"

She nodded. She had been thinking of her brother. "But your father's brother is tall too. So I'm told. Martin, I mean. Kevin was the same height as your father."

George took an amused interest in their Canadian game. The light from the television illuminated his wife's face and his son's, both of them intent on the turbulent rapids and on Mason's technique. The hardest thing, George couldn't help saying, when they flicked off the display of northern hardihood, was to find himself with so little energy.

Then Nan took his legs in her lap and massaged them. They were poor sticks, like the poky branches tucked under layers of felt in Beuys's "Snowfall". She had studied the picture of the sculpture in Bridget's book and pondered the warmth of felt-snow working its restful magic on suffering trees. Massaging his calves and his feet, she remembered what George's legs used to be like, remembered her first glimpse of them as she followed him up that trail in Vermont, a stranger in shorts with calves so beautiful, so finely formed, she had hastened to overtake him in order to see his face.

Bridget dropped by one day while Jim was at school. She brought flowers as usual and food, and the news that her ex-husband, Max, was to be married again. He had come to tell her in person, she said, and after he left she'd found herself in tears. "I felt so forlorn. Explain that to me, George."

"You're jealous of his happiness. I would be too."

"I'm surprised by myself."

"You're human," he said, "that's all."

"Well," she said, "the wedding invitation came in the mail yesterday. Pale yellow paper, *very* pale grey ink. And I thought, How *faint-hearted*."

George laughed, they all did, and Nan said, "Will you go?"

Bridget rested her head in her hand, as if considering, and said, "Nan, you look so tired. Aren't you sleeping?"

"Oh, I'll sleep when I'm dead. You're avoiding my question."

"You'll sleep when you're dead." Bridget smiled. "That's one way of looking at it. I'll probably go. I don't know. Sleep is important, my friend. I worry about you."

"I worry about Jim." Nan rubbed her forehead and said, "How would *you* help a boy who's lost his dog?"

"Maybe get him another dog?"

"Isn't it too soon?"

"Ask him," Bridget said.

Later, when she stood to leave, Nan walked her to the elevator, wanting to prolong the visit and remembering to ask if she might hold onto the books about Beuys for a few more weeks. Not that she understood everything he was getting at, far from it. But she liked poring through them. She liked the way his mind worked.

"Keep them as long as you like. Keep them all year if you want." They were standing next to the elevator that rose and fell a hundred times a day, and neither one of them pressed the *down* arrow. "You know the most important thing I learned from Beuys?" Bridget said.

Nan considered. "Courage?"

Bridget shook her head. "The most important thing was his advice, if it was advice, about not taking things personally." Her large hands made circles in the air as she worked to remember how he had put it. "He talked about how much discipline it takes. Constant discipline, not to take life personally."

Nan felt the truth of that ring through her. When you take things personally, she knew, the world becomes very small. It is you and nothing is smaller. When you manage not to do that, the world opens wide.

That evening she put the question to Jim.

He looked at her gravely. "Not yet," he said.

It was the answer she expected. And so she borrowed wilderness books instead to supplement the films. She spread maps on the floor and they planned trips. She even pitched their tent in the living room, recalling as she did so how her father, in his loneliness and distress after her mother died, had camped out at the end of his life, unrolling his sleeping bag across their double bed, refusing sheets and blankets in favour of the down bag he had owned for decades, which smelled of himself and the basement and summers long past. He wanted to be held, she understood now, as much as Jim did, that's why he had retreated into his woodsy-smelling cocoon, an old emperor on his way out. No doubt Blake wanted to be held too, and maybe that's what all that Christian dogma did for him, it gave him the fierce embrace he needed. Well, so be it, she thought, feeling her guilt run deep.

Inside the tent she and Jim read to each other. It did not bother them when George put a paper cup in front of the tent door and dropped coins into it. In his own sarcastic-jokey way, he understood their homelessness.

Nan's reading pace slowed down in the tent and her tone became ruminating, as if she were reading to remember. Listening to her, Jim felt his mind clear. The world was out there, waiting for him, and one day he would see every distant part of it for himself. He had been avoiding Riverside Park, avoiding the haunts where he and Moon used to ramble, and memories of the lake were tricky too, clouded over, painful.

One evening, prying apart the coffee-stained pages of *South*, his mother came to the list of all the dogs Shackleton had taken with him to the Antarctic, and soon they were laughing and their eyes were swimming. Jim repeated several of the names: Painful, Sweep,

Swanker, Steamer, Splitlip. He did not ask her what became of the dogs. He believed he knew.

Nan was at her desk, perusing Knud Rasmussen's *Across Arctic America: Narrative of the Fifth Thule Expedition*, fact-checking for an article she was editing, when she said, "Here's a worst thing for you."

Jim left the sofa and came to look over her shoulder at a photograph of a woman wearing a fur garment with very loose sleeves, the caption said, that allowed her to draw up her arms and fold them across her breast during the severest cold. The woman was Ataguvtaluk, who had survived a famine by eating the bodies of her husband and children. Blue veins were prominent around her mouth, the book said, and were thought to be the result of having eaten her own flesh and blood. To Jim it looked like she had a moustache and a tuft of hair under her lower lip. Standing at his mother's desk, he read the story to himself: how Ataguvtaluk was discovered in a little snow shelter somewhere between Pond Inlet and Igloolik, seated on the floor, blood trickling from the corners of her eyes so prodigiously had she wept. "I am one who can no longer live among humankind, for I have eaten my own kin." She was skin and bone, almost naked from having eaten most of her own clothing. She recognized the travellers who had stumbled upon her and said to them, "I have eaten him who was your comrade when he lived." And they answered, "You had the will to live, and so you are still alive." Her rescuers took her back to her brother in Igloolik, and later on she would marry a great hunter and become his favourite wife. "But that is the most terrible thing I have known in all my life," the witness told Rasmussen.

His mother said, "That's the thing, Jim. Doing something terrible doesn't define you for the rest of your life. 'You had the will to live, and so you are still alive.' And then she went on and married a great hunter and became his favourite wife." Nan turned the page back to the photograph and studied the woman's face. "We all do things we can't forgive ourselves for. Well," and she tilted her hand back and forth over the photograph to indicate we don't generally eat our families. "But that's not *all* that we are. Do you know what I'm getting at?" She looked up at him with a long, intent look. "I know this is grisly. But grisly doesn't bother us."

He asked the question he always asked, and she said, "Is it a good book? This is a great book."

It was one of those mild nights when you smelled the water, a mixture of river and harbour that separated itself out from the standard city air. You could feel the atmosphere moving and shifting inside itself. They went for a brief walk before bed, buying a carton of milk and some flowers at the Korean grocer's on Broadway. Standing on the sidewalk, holding their purchases, they looked up at the starless sky and Nan remarked that fifty years ago you could stand here and see the Milky Way, or so she had read. They did the calculation. 1946. And agreed that it would have been nice to live in New York back then, though even then the night sky would have been nothing like the star-congested heavens above their lake of bays.

* * *

Blake showed up a week before Christmas, again unannounced, and Jim, arriving home from school, lit up at the sight of his big brother. "What took you so long?" he cried. He dropped his knapsack to the floor and threw his arms around him. Blake responded with what Nan thought of as lordly pleasure. He had always been good to Jim, tolerating his messy side of the room, playing chess with him, only occasionally throwing a punch when Jim flew into a tantrum, which he did whenever he lost. As far as Nan knew, he had never tried to convert him beyond making him thank the Lord for a marshmallow. Now he was rubbing the side of Jim's head, telling him how much taller he was, telling him he should come to Philadelphia for a visit.

He knew some fantastic people. And Jim was grinning and happy because this weird and unpredictable brother of his had come home for Christmas.

Blake had another proposal to make, it turned out. Something else up his sleeve. He waited until Jim was at school the next day and George had gone to work. Then after he helped his mother with the dishes, after she poured them both a second cup of coffee, he told her that he had connected with some Canadian families around Lanark, not far from the family cottage. They were doing a Bible study with one of his mentors. In January, he and Peter – the ministry, as he called them – were going up there for a week, and it would be great if they could use the cottage as a retreat.

"But my friend Lulu is there."

"Mom, there's plenty of room."

"You're expecting her to take all of you in? How many are you?" And when she learned there would be twelve during the day, "But only six staying overnight and it's only for a week," she spread her hands in disbelief. "You can't be serious."

"Look, I should come first. I'm your son."

The shape of his head was the same as Guy's, she thought, and his eyes were the same alarming blue. She said, "You have a connection to that part of the world. That's where you were conceived. I was almost as young as you are. I don't know if I ever told you that."

He wasn't interested in her memories. "Mom. It's for a *week*."

"And what is Lulu supposed to do?"

"Doesn't she have a brother?"

Yes, Nan thought. She has a brother.

"She can stay with him," Blake said.

And she realized that he was going to be very successful at what he did, his righteous, bullying work.

"I'm your *son*," he said again.

"No. I'm not displacing Lulu for your ministry."

She watched him pace around the kitchen for a moment, his hands shoved into his pockets. "You don't want things to go right for me, do you?"

"Why is my life full of unreasonable men?" she said.

"*I'm* not unreasonable."

"That's what they all say," she said dryly. "Listen to me, son of mine. Lulu has been a precious friend to me during the hardest years of my life. Where have *you* been? I don't even cross your mind, and neither does George, until we've got a piece of real estate you're interested in." Lulu, I won't let you down, she thought.

Blake pulled out a kitchen chair. He made a show of sitting down and closing his eyes and bowing his head.

She couldn't believe it. "Why are you praying?"

He didn't answer until he had finished. "I was asking God to forgive you."

"For what?" Her voice was mutinous. "What have I done that needs forgiving?"

"You're forgiven," he said.

Forgiven. She was so outraged that she was speechless. The heat rushed into her face and rather than say something she would really regret, she took herself down the hall to her bedroom, shutting the door behind her with a vicious shove and then leaning against it. He had Guy's arrogance without any of his saving qualities. Guy would rescue you in a pinch, she thought. Not Blake. It didn't even cross his mind that whatever he wanted for himself might not be the best thing for everybody.

Later, when she was calmer, her thoughts widened and she pondered her parents and herself as a parent. They were bleak thoughts. Her mother and father had gone to their graves believing they had been scrupulously evenhanded towards her and Tom, though it had been transparently obvious that her brother was her mother's favourite and she was her father's. So now Blake was convinced that she had always preferred Jim. Maybe he was right.

Maybe she had deluded herself completely. God knows, she was sick of him now.

The next day she would have to explain to Jim, when he came home expecting to see his brother, that Blake had gone back to Philadelphia. He was so busy with his work that he wouldn't be staying for Christmas, after all. She said, "He wants you to visit him. He means it. He said to give you his love. I'm sorry, Jim. I really am."

His disappointment was so drastic that she almost changed her mind. She almost called Blake and said, Have it your way.

That night she found herself looking again at old family photographs: Blake with Jim on his shoulders; Jim gobbling cherries; all of them at the ocean. It made her ache to see the evident and abundant love. And it bore in upon her that she had sinned against Blake more than he had sinned against her. In leaving him with the false impression that John was his father, she had removed from his life a whole set of truths and possibilities. She had enclosed him in a lie.

15

IN EARLY JANUARY, JIM WOKE IN THE MIDDLE OF THE NIGHT, aware that the light outside was bright, fiery almost, as if lit by a distant house in flames, but no sirens, all silent. He went to the window and everything had changed. The first snowfall had clung to every surface on the way down, reluctant to reach the soiled ground.

In a letter to Lulu dated January 3, he wrote:

It is morning, and the fresh fallen snow is glinting with sunlight. I am eating bacon and toast while occasionally staring out the window. The New York Times is at its worst, but perhaps this is because the good reporters are on holiday.

I have been playing cribbage lately, and am currently unbeaten. While reflecting on cards, I believe one of the less celebrated joys is the sizzling, whooshing sounds made while shuffling the deck.

My feelings now are of despair, for this is my last weekend before the long trek to the black lagoon (alias Delta Middle School). I hope that everything is fine in Canada and that you are in good health. I can't wait till you come.

        *A thousand times good night,

        Love, Jim

*a line from Romeo and Juliet.

As it turned out, Lulu did not come, not for a long time, and they didn't go.

George returned to his office full time in the new year, and the return to normal did him good. His spirits improved. Sometimes they heard him humming "I'm So Pretty" to himself as he shaved what remained of his face. Every three months he went to the head and neck clinic at the hospital to be examined. He had undergone a C.T. scan three months after the last dose of radiation, and this provided the new baseline from which to follow whatever developed. He was living on borrowed time, no-one pretended otherwise. A visit to his mother always prompted the same remark, that he was glad she had become too blind and demented to realize what was happening with him. There were things to be said for losing all your faculties.

Nan began to supplement her editing income with a new form of employment. She knew someone who cleaned apartments for a comfortable living and she began to work for Lorraine one day a week. She would come home afterwards, having bought food along the way, tins of tomatoes, boxes of pasta on special. "So that I know," she would say, unpacking the groceries, "that we've got food in the house. To have the feeling that at least we'll eat."

For two summers they did not go to Canada, banking the rent that Lulu paid.

*　　*　　*

Since George had never fully regained his appetite, it was not a great change when he lost any desire to eat. The real change was his new peacefulness, bordering on contentment. One evening, about eighteen months after the operation, he said, "Nancy, you have beautiful hands."

"Thanks," she said without even looking up, too intent on organizing her list of errands, bills, appointments, not only for the three of them but for George's mother, whose dementia had consigned her to the locked unit in her nursing home. Every other week Nan spent an afternoon holding her hand and reading to her – Tennyson and nursery rhymes – not that Grandma Bobak recognized her or anyone else anymore.

Jim, having overheard the compliment, couldn't help but feel hurt for his father and disappointed in his mother. Half an hour later, however, he saw her look at her hands and say, "Thank you for saying that."

Nan held her fingers up and examined them.

What we lose is any sense that life is alive, she thought. The days follow one after the other and everything passes us by. Then along comes someone who looks at us kindly, as if we were worth noticing, and life quickens. A door opens. That the person who had looked at her kindly was George made it even more startling. She gazed at her long fingers and bitten nails and large knucklebones and saw her mother's capable hands. Her mother was *in* her hands. A light animated them, and that light was her mother and everything she had made and held. Nan saw her at the lake washing with a bar of Ivory soap. Saw her drying her hands with a towel, thoroughly, one finger at a time, as if each finger were a child worthy of attention. Saw her doing this in the shade of the cedars that leaned over the water in their gravity-defying posture of surrender and resistance, so feminine, so beautiful.

But breaking into every thought, troubling her always, was their lack of income, a worry that George waved away. "You will always be looked after."

"Will I?" Her tired face a study in hope and disbelief.

"Why do you think I'd let you down?" he said. "Why is your opinion of me so low?"

He was a man who did not believe he was loved, she knew that. And one day she took his hand and told him she loved him. She uttered the words and his face relaxed and so did her heart. It was a thing impossible to measure, the effect on her of telling this man who irritated her, chafed against her, infuriated her, and also surprised her, that she loved him. How could saying words she only half believed turn into a profound truth? It would not last, this feeling, but that didn't matter. The irritation would be back. Never mind. An old riddle in her mind had been solved. People love others not because they are lovable necessarily but because it takes such a weight off the heart.

*　　*　　*

When his cancer came back, it came not locally but at a distance. The set of chest X-rays taken at the two-year-point showed multiple spots in both lungs: small bilateral nodules. And at this stage, they were told, there was no treatment. All that could be done was symptom management, as it was called.

Nan sat beside him while the oncologist explained things in her direct, matter-of-fact way. The lung disease would slowly grow, she said, leading to shortness of breath, weight loss, palliative care at home, pain medication. "A dwindling," as she put it. If the disease moved to his bones, that would be painful. If tumours pressed on nerves, that would be painful too. Otherwise, he would not be in pain. Discomfort, of course, but not pain.

"Well," George said, matching her with an impressive realism of his own, "everybody dies of something and this is my something."

He looked at Nan and what she saw in his eyes wasn't at all what she expected. She saw relief.

He hesitated. "I know you never predict," he said to the doctor.

"At this stage it's easier to gauge," she said, leaning forward. "We can make a guess. There'll be another chest X-ray in three months and we'll see how fast it's developing. But not more than a year."

"Not more than a year," George said after a pause. "That's worth knowing."

They went home. It was early May and the leaves were almost full, a day when walking in Manhattan was like being on a boat, the air washed clean by the rain of the night before and ocean breezes blowing through. Nan had bitten her right thumbnail so close to the quick that it was bleeding. "We'll have to tell Jim," she said.

After supper, when they were all in the living room – George in the armchair, Nan at one end of the sofa, Jim at the other – George lowered the *Times* and said to his son, "I got some bad news today."

Nan raised her head. She glanced from her husband to her son and back to her husband.

"I still feel fine," George said, the expression on his face so gently uncomplaining that Nan was moved. "But the chest X-ray shows the cancer is back."

"So you'll have another operation?" Jim said.

"Not this time."

"Then how are you going to get better?"

"Well, I'm not. But I've got some time left. Not years, of course. But months."

"How many months?"

"That's what I asked too. Not more than a year."

Nan moved next to Jim on the sofa, near enough to take his hand in hers. He let her do that. She didn't say anything about the gods sweeping down. But that's how it felt. The gods sweeping down again and changing everything.

On the subway to and from school, Jim was on his own. He took the 1 or the 2 Train to Chambers Street, then walked west on Chambers to his new black lagoon, just north of the World Trade Center. Going home, the reverse. It almost never happened that anyone spoke to him, and it was never good when they did.

"My husband died. Do you want to see his picture?" The woman wore a Yankees cap and had a gruesome earlobe, torn in half, partly healed, a mess of swelling and scab.

"No." He said it clearly, but she pulled out two I.D. cards anyway and shoved them under his nose. "Isn't he cute?" she said. "Isn't he cute?"

It was a wide, blunt, ugly face.

"Is he black or white?" she insisted. "You think he's black or white?"

"White," he said, knowing what she wanted to hear.

So many lost souls. Here came another: a tall woman in high heels, very unhappy and very mad, fishing in her shiny black bag, poking and pushing and shoving things inside, her face very made up and her hair bleached and glistening and jagged at the back, a woman so agitated, nervous, and angry that he figured she was a little nuts. Things were not working out well for her in her life. Sometimes gentler scenes rose up in front of his eyes: a young man and woman having coffee, using the pay phone as a table, the man shaking the lidded paper cup of coffee hard, for lack of a spoon, dispersing sugar, while the woman held the bag of Danishes or bagels. He could picture Bad Art doing that, inviting his girlfriend to have coffee with him in the subway, improvising as he went along.

Then Jim came up from the dark to fresh-cut flowers, sunlight on beautiful facades, sunlight on sycamores, and pavement that glistened after rain. At home, sleeves rolled up, he sat for hours, his long expressive forearms and hands holding one enormous book after another, turning the pages, rubbing his eyes with long fingers.

* * *

He turned fifteen that September. By now he was gangly, tall, with a smile that melted older women and certain girls (at school Tracy was knitting him a scarf), but with boys he was awkward unless they took a shine to him. In the year his father was dying, he had a follower, a short, dark-haired boy, overfriendly, overly nervous, whose locker was beside his. From the moment Jim met him, he knew Ivan was trouble, perhaps his own Ivan the Terrible, this math whiz who walked too close to him and never stopped talking but helped him whenever he needed help in math. They were in the same classes. They were in the jazz band too. Jim had his trumpet, Ivan his saxophone.

It was pitiful the way his mother lit up when the telephone began to ring for him. Usually it was Ivan, sometimes Tracy.

In those days his mother was reading to his father in the evenings, *Angela's Ashes*, and the story drew him away from his homework to sit on the hallway floor outside their room and listen. The author was famous at his school, having taught there for a number of years and mesmerized his students with his rivetting tales. Frank, as they called him, would perch on his desk and look off into the distance and say, "Sit back. I'm going to tell you a story." He was by all accounts irreverent, funny, moody, sometimes full of himself, and altogether unusual.

Ivan, it turned out, had a dog named Princess. He lived in Brooklyn with his mother and dog. The first visit revealed everything, or at least enough for Jim. In Ivan's bedroom, mixed indiscriminately and in profusion, were well-thumbed, spilled-upon, half-falling apart *Playboys* and other dirty magazines, dozens and dozens of them that he'd bought at this place he knew on Canal Street. Jim stretched out beside him on the rumpled bed and pored through them, coming to one showing big-breasted Canadian women in the northern bush. "Ah, Canada," he thought, remembering Lulu's generous display of herself. And soon Ivan had his dick out and was flailing away. Jim left him to it and went into the kitchen and fell into conversation with Ivan's mother, who told him to call her Sharon. She had Princess on tranquillizers, she said, the dog was so crazy.

"All you have to do," he said, "is be kind to her."

He knelt beside the squirming, licking, attention-seeking, whining, incredibly smelly animal and met a dog he didn't like.

It wasn't the dog's fault. This was a nuthouse. The mother wore flip-flops in November, her feet were orange and purple, her hair was bleached, yet she had the prettiest smile when she suddenly smiled. "You gotta help me," she said. She wanted to wash the dog to get rid of the smell.

And so Jim found himself a witness to Princess being hosed

down in the postage-stamp-sized, cement backyard that had a few dead tomato plants in large pots. Sharon tied Princess to the waterspout with a short leash, then turned the hose on her full force as she leapt up in the air, paws scrambling on the wall, only to be jerked back by the shortness of the leash. He grabbed the hose out of her hands, "You're choking her!" And she said, "Whoa!"

He threw down the hose, which jackknifed and sprayed water into the wall, then took off his jacket to wipe down the dog. But she smelled so bad he changed his mind. He put his jacket back on. "You need a towel. You need soap."

Sharon was standing there in her flip-flops and sweater, shivering. "Be a pal," she said.

So he climbed the stairs to the fourth floor and met Ivan coming out of the bathroom, looking even twitchier. "What's up?" Ivan said.

He took him to the window and pointed. There was Sharon training the hose on Princess yet again and it was the same horror show: the dog scrambling up the wall and the leash choking her. People were awful. They were awful. "Where are the towels?" he said.

"In there."

Jim took a grotty-looking towel off the rack in the bathroom and was about to head downstairs when he said, "No. You do it." He shoved the towel into Ivan's hands. "Take soap." He got the bar of mushy soap from the bathroom sink and shoved it at Ivan. "Here." Then wiping his gooey hands on his pants, he went into the bedroom, picked up his knapsack, slid a *Playboy* into it, and swung out the door and down the stairs. He was out of there.

At home, his father was asleep and his mother was off somewhere, so he set about doing the dishes, running the water very hot, putting lots of soap into the dishpan. He began to scour one dish after another to avoid thinking about weird Ivan and his dog. Pigeons were beating their wings on the outer sill and he remembered counting loons on the lake at the end of August, seven of them one morning, eleven another as they assembled on the bay, using it as a long runway, taking off one at a time. Getting ready to head south, practising their moves. And the thought of how Moon had perished hit him in the stomach and he leaned against the sink, his hands in the hot suds. He wondered when they would go back to the lake. It would be hard to go back. But it was hard here too.

His mother came through the door while he was putting the dishes away.

"Jim," she said in a voice bearing news. Her eyes were bigger in her face.

She set down the bag of groceries and spread the newspaper on the kitchen table. And it felt like his thoughts had stirred up something related but worse. The article was short. Well, it was Canadian news, lucky to be there at all. An avalanche had swept Trudeau's youngest son to his death in a glacial lake. Michel, twenty-three, the article said, on a backcountry ski trip in the Kootenay Mountains in southeastern British Columbia, had been pushed down the mountain by a snow slide. It carried him and his heavy backpack into the icy waters of Kokanee Lake, depositing him three hundred feet from shore. He cried out for help, it said in the article, and struggled to get free of his gear, but there was no way for anyone to reach him, and after a little while the cries stopped.

"How terrible," his mother murmured. She was rereading the story, positioning the Kootenays in her mind, seeing the young man's struggle. "It would have been quick, though. He couldn't have lasted more than a few minutes in that water."

"You had a presentiment," he said.

"So I did."

"You said losing one of his sons would break his heart."

"I remember. We were talking about Marcel's play. You have a good memory, Jim. That's a wonderful thing, having a good memory."

From Lulu, some days later, came clippings from Canadian newspapers. They showed the wild look on the old father's face as he

275

emerged from the church following the funeral, a private memorial service without a body. He stood with grieving Margaret and their two remaining sons, everyone dressed in black, and his famous features were gripped by what seemed to be furious pain. Nan said, "I'm so relieved to see his anger. I was afraid he might collapse in a heap of dust and blow away in the wind." Jim felt deeply sorry for the old man who had lost his son in an icy lake one hundred metres deep, the papers said. Almost as deep as a skyscraper was high.

His own father was now too tired to stand long enough to make himself something to eat. George wasn't hungry anyway. Jim insisted he eat, however, and would make something for them both when he got home from school. Bread covered to the edge with thick jam, or tuna with lots of mayo. His father appreciated the effort. "I like a little tuna with my mayo," he would say. "Tuna and mayo, hold the tuna." But he ate very little.

The palliative care nurse came twice a week, a fast-walking, serious woman in glasses, dressed to disappear in a crowd: browns, beiges, quick-dry fabrics. She would go directly to George's bedside and ask him how he was, and nothing he said ever surprised her. It was a nasty cancer, she had told them in the beginning. "If it's in the lungs when it comes back, then it got there through the blood stream, which means it's on its way to being everywhere." She listened to his lungs and heart and took his blood pressure each time, and she asked about pain and offered advice. "It takes energy to chew," she pointed out to Nan and Jim. "I recommend puddings, ice cream." And so Nan found herself feeding ice cream to George as she had to Duke at the end of his life.

For his part George was in the grip of an almost burning serenity, the like of which Nan had never seen in anyone before. He was relaxed and open and able to talk about anything.

"I've never been happy," he said to her one day. "It's a relief to know I won't have to keep trying."

In his bedside drawer he had his earphones and compact disc player and CDs, reconciled to them now that he no longer had the energy to operate a record player. Mozart's Requiem he loved especially, and its "Lacrimosa" in particular. He would listen to it, flooded with unabashed tears, over and over again. He was working on Bach's St Matthew Passion too, learning how to enjoy it. He showed Nan and Jim certain passages: "Clean my heart ... wherein Jesus shall find sweet rest."

"It's the music," he assured them. "I'm not turning into another holy man. I won't give Blake a run for his money."

Not a day passed when he didn't tell them he loved them, and Nan came to accept that he was speaking the truth. His emaciated face was so alive, so stimulated. "I lie in bed and look out the window for hours and my mind is incredibly active," he said to them, "remembering things."

His mannerisms were still in evidence, but now they conveyed strength rather than nervousness or discomfort. The hand that covered the mouth, the grimaces and frowns, took on a different life. The serenity of saintliness, Nan thought, and by that she supposed she meant he welcomed death with a restless excitement, his face peeled away to reveal light.

*   *   *

Ivan still helped Jim with math, though things were cooler between them since that day in Brooklyn. Ivan had taken up with another boy and Jim sometimes saw the two of them together giggling wildly and knew they must have popped something, maybe the anxiety meds that Ivan had offered him once, or the amphetamines that let you study all night. It was a school where marks were all, grubbing for marks, the extra half per cent to get 99.5 instead of 99. Frank McCourt had been an easy marker of any essays he assigned, or so everyone claimed, which alone would have endeared him. Kids had no pride in this regard, Jim discovered, unless they were prodigies like Ivan, who could explain the theory of relativity so that you almost understood it. Jim had to wonder where he came from, how such a mind could emerge from such a mother and such a place. Such a mind. A fidgety bundle of nerves talking endlessly about money and girls. Once, Jim had planted himself in front of his locker and said, "Ivan, look. I don't want to talk to you today." But he hadn't been able to keep it up. Ivan was worse off than he was, how could he turn his back on him? Well, the problem was being solved. Ivan was turning his back on *him*.

He wore Tracy's muddy-green scarf, overlong and drooping, and as Valentine's Day approached, he knew he should buy her either flowers or chocolates, and wished Blake were around to ask. (Though his brother had never been all that nice to the girls he brought home. Of his girlfriends Jim remembered Carla best for the aggressive way she had kissed him right on the mouth when he was nine, and then asked if he thought her mouth tasted bad, "because your brother says it tastes like shit." He was too shocked to answer and she was too upset to listen anyway.) In the end he bought Tracy flowers a*nd* chocolates, guessing that too much was better than too little. Over the next few days he proceeded to watch in bewilderment as she stopped seeking him out. He tried to talk to her. She looked away and avoided him. So he buried her lousy scarf in the bottom of a drawer.

He saw these things happening under his nose. A girl went off you. A loser friend you wanted to get rid of turned around and got rid of you instead. He couldn't explain it, but he recognized it, and felt in some way he deserved it. There was something about him that made it happen. For a while his thoughts were like windshield wipers – back and forth, back and forth – endless. The rain of conviction that no-one liked him.

The sickroom, strangely enough, made him feel better. He would arrive home to a degree of quiet activity that he found reassuring. His father always brightened when he came through the door. He was on oxygen now, a portable cylinder plugged into the wall, nasal prongs in his nose and tubing around his head and neck. His mother was there and equally glad to have his company. Bridget might drop by, or Lulu might phone, or the nurse would come, or a homecare worker, and he liked them all. He had taken to doing his homework in the big chair beside his father's bed and it was peaceful, the sound of the oxygen steady, like an aquarium.

They had new neighbours who made themselves known, the Vissers down the hall, a couple consisting of an older, embittered wife and a younger, personable husband. Donna Visser would come to the door with casseroles and they could see how much their difficulties cheered her up. The food was homemade and frugal: an emphasis on squash. "She must have tricked him into marrying her," George speculated, and Jim perked up his ears, intrigued by his father's blunt observation. "How much older is she?" George said.

"No," his mother said. "She chose him. I've seen it happen before. Men can't resist being chosen, though they punish you for it."

"Do they?" His father was amused.

"They do. I'm sure he never stops reminding her that she loves him a lot more than he loves her."

The double bed had been taken out of the bedroom, replaced by a hospital bed for his father and a single bed for his mother. The oxygen helped his father rest more easily. He was indeed dwindling, but he said he was lucky to have no nerve pain, no bone pain. His gracefulness in the face of death renewed Jim's respect for him, and it was a great gift, being able to admire his father at the end.

*   *   *

On a day in early March, George told Nan that he planned to make a small adjustment to his will. "How so?" she asked. She would understand, he said, they would talk about it later.

"I'd rather talk about it now," she said.

"The provisions for the kids. I want it done right."

"Which kids?" His daughters had come to see him several times and she was grateful to them. It would have been terrible had they not come.

"Mine," he said, raising three fingers. Kate, Lorna, Jim. His voice was weak and he had to take a breath every few words. "I want them well provided for. Don't worry. I've looked after you."

She tilted her head and gave him a searching look.

"Trust me," he said.

After the lawyer arrived, summoned by George's telephone call, Nan stepped out to buy food, leaving the men alone. In the street she heard the unbroken, piercing shriek of a godforsaken car alarm. Then the rather exotic whooping of a newer sort of alarm, less drastic, even comical. Returning, she expected to see the lawyer, but he was already gone.

From then on George spent most of his time sleeping. Some of his fretfulness came back, he would get annoyed with himself, but then he would listen to Wolfie, as he called Mozart, and attain a level of happiness she could only marvel at. She would have expected him to be the envious one, envious of her health and stamina, but it was she who was envious – of his peace of mind and the wonderful drugs he was on.

*   *   *

Jim was in the chair beside his father's bed. His father's face was grey, the circles under his eyes very dark. "Jim? What's Bad Art up to these days?"

Jim smiled and shrugged.

"You were onto something," his father said. "You had a good character there." His lips were dry and cracked.

"I don't do that anymore," Jim said.

"What? Make things up? I don't believe you." His father closed his eyes and then opened them. "Say Bad Art walked through that door right now. What would he be wearing? A Stetson? A pink shirt?"

Jim saw the beaten-up trousers, the Hawaiian shirt, the greasy suede beret not quite the right size, all of them picked up in some goodwill store in Quebec. He saw him stumbling upon the funeral of Lévesque, then sleeping in the cemetery where people came to weep because someone who loved them had died.

Quebec was the place to see ghosts and fires. His English teacher had grown up in Montreal and said every Québécois novel had a devastating fire in it. But he didn't have the heart for spinning tall tales.

"I can't," he said.

His father's eyes were a hurt and mild blue. "Jim, you're a good storyteller, you're a good writer. Don't give it up."

Later, his father would say, "You have your whole lifetime ahead of you," in a tone of such despairing wonder that Jim knew he would have given anything to live his life all over again, no matter how glad he might be that it was ending.

The telephone rang late that evening and his mother went to answer it in the kitchen. Jim sat on the bed while she was gone, listening to his father's ragged breathing. Death took longer, he was learning, than you might think. He had started to hope it would hurry up. He felt awful about that. He still hoped it would hurry up.

"That was Lulu," George said when she came back, for he knew she called every few days.

"It was," Nan said.

"And how is Lulu?"

"She's in Montreal visiting an old flame. She asked about you, as always."

"Tell her I wish her well," George said.

Nan looked away. Her lips trembled with exhaustion and emotion. "Would you like to tell her yourself?"

"No," he said.

His voice sounded weak but final, and their life together rose up and hit her in the face and fell away. She dropped her head, a hopeless sort of smile playing across her lips. Of course not, she thought. He was still George. He hadn't changed that much.

That was the night, as his father slept, that Jim read parts of *The Apprenticeship of Duddy Kravitz* to his mother. They were on her narrow bed, side by side. She had pulled up her knees to give him room and he was on a long diagonal, lying on his stomach. His teacher had assigned an essay in which they were to compare Duddy Kravitz and Holden Caulfield, and he had written his easily, saying that Duddy was a character and Holden was a voice, and so you identified more with Holden. But Duddy was completely alive. He was capable and resilient and despicable. Jim thought if he had to choose between being Holden and being Duddy, then he would choose to be Duddy. Nothing could hold him down, not even remorse at having betrayed his best friends. His mother giggled and laughed at Duddy's rudeness and backtalk, and so did he.

Sometimes George opened his eyes and smiled at them. "I like to hear you laugh," he said. "Don't stop."

282

16

LULU RECEIVED A LETTER FROM NAN A WEEK AFTER
George's death in which she wrote that death was too hard to talk
about on the telephone. With every passing day, she wrote, her
feelings became more anguished. She had good memories that
either made her smile or cry, those were the best and easiest. It was
the anger that was difficult.

Well, it was rage.

George had left everything to the children: his daughters and
Jim. The apartment would go to Lorna, the generous life insurance
evenly to Kate and Jim. What he grandly called his assets (his bank
accounts and bonds), he had left to her. But the assets were minimal.
By the time the final medical bills were paid and the costs of the
cremation, death certificates, legal fees, and taxes taken care of, there
would be almost nothing left. *I know he wasn't good about practicali-
ties, I know he had no interest in money, but I can't excuse him. I feel as
though I never really mattered.*

Lulu raised her eyes and watched four dear little chickadees at
the birdfeeder. Her family had done the same thing to her. She never
really mattered either.

*Lulu, I tell you these things because I can tell you anything and because
you've been through this too. I can't talk to Jim for obvious reasons.
I've talked to Blake a little and that made me feel worse. I don't understand
him either. How does a bright and gifted boy turn into a sour old man
at twenty-four?*

And so minor becomes major, thought Lulu, gazing at the long shadows reaching across the last traces of snow. Understudies plot behind the scenes. George had always been on the sidelines in that family until his illness took centre stage. Now this will of his was going to ensure his place in the spotlight. Nan wouldn't be able to think of anything else for a long time. She was still looking after his mother too, taking care of her banking, buying her whatever she needed, socks, hearing-aid batteries, lotion, tissues, and on and on until you wanted to scream.

When later that afternoon Guy dropped by with a load of kindling for her, and stayed on to visit, she gave him Nan's letter to read.

He looked up when he got to the end, his blue eyes gratifyingly disturbed. "She'll move back here," he said. "That's the only thing that makes sense."

"It's strange, isn't it?"

"It's unbelievable," he said.

"I mean, she and I are both victims of tricky wills."

Guy flushed and his face jerked back.

"Don't get mad," she said. "I'm over it. I've been over it for a long time. But maybe you'll know the answer to this. What was going through George's fucked-up head?"

Guy pushed back his chair and stood up.

Lulu pressed on. "He didn't think she had any needs? He wanted his kids to think he was a great dad? He didn't trust her to get it right? He expected her to jump onto his funeral pyre?"

Guy went to the window and stared out. With his back to her, he said, "Dad and I wanted to keep the property together."

"I know. But you could have talked to me. Why didn't George talk to Nan?"

Guy swung around. "Because it was simpler the way he did it."

"Simpler for him."

Guy nodded. "Simpler for him."

Guy had the advantage now. The light flooding the kitchen put his face in shadow while every facet of Lulu's face was plain to see.

She had gained weight since giving up the bottle and it suited her. She wasn't young anymore. She looked like their mother.

"I'm sorry," he said. "I should have talked to you."

"You should have."

"I'm sorry, Lu."

"It's O.K. It's over. I feel bad for Nan, though. What a shit George was. What a shitty thing to do."

"She owns this piece of shoreline," Guy said. "She belongs here, not in New York."

* * *

Nan felt such a fool. Such a fool for letting herself get caught in the old female fate of looking after someone, tending, propping up, nursing, only to be humiliated in the end. The fate of daughters and sisters and wives the world over. George would never have admitted that he had done it to hurt her, and she couldn't altogether believe that he had, but his will was a shovel that dug a very big hole into her heart. And the digging was especially deep between the hours of 2.00 and 4.00 a.m.

Then one morning towards dawn, five days after his death, having finally drifted off to sleep, she had a strange and unforgettable dream. Over breakfast she said to Jim, "Has your father appeared to you in a dream?"

He shook his head.

"Well, he did to me," she said. And she told him the dream.

George had given her a long narrow package to carry, warning her on no account to open it, and then he disappeared and she found herself with nameless others, making her way past the dark outskirts of a town, when the package began to jiggle and shake. She opened it – it unbuckled like a handbag – and the head of a snake shot out and bit her in the face. She closed it immediately. A strange man was beside her and soon George came running too. The strange man turned into Guy. He opened the long package, revealing a serpent as long and bony as a hundred-year-old carp. All the poison came pouring out of it at one end, as if from an udder. George was agitated but not upset with her. And she was fine. In fact, she was suddenly able to speak French.

"So welcome to my humble chapeau," she said to Jim, earning a small grin back.

These were the days when she wore the same striped blouse day after day and attacked everything with a quiet ferocity, whether it was editing articles at the kitchen table, or washing the floors of the apartment, or packing up George's clothes and sorting through his belongings (in the course of which she found the manuscript of his novel and dropped it into the garbage. Then retrieved it and packed it, unread, into a box of things for Jim one day). Jim felt her energy whipping their lives into shape. He loved her severity and depended on it.

George had not wanted a funeral. Instead, Nan organized a small gathering of relatives and friends and his old colleagues – asking Lulu not to make the long trip, but to drive down a few weeks later when they could have a proper visit – and asking Blake to come and help out. He did. The day was very warm, as if summer had arrived though it hadn't. Nan watched Blake take charge, involving Jim, arranging the food, setting up more chairs in the living room, and she was grateful. She had always thought it possible, indeed more than likely, that with other people Blake was a different person entirely. And so it would seem.

Among those who came was the director of the nursing home in Nyack. Nan hadn't really expected her to show up and she was touched. They were talking about her mother-in-law's new room-mate, a loud and cantankerous woman named Margaret, when Nan became aware that Blake was muscling everyone into a circle of prayer. She moved to stop him and it was in that moment, in what amounted to a minor revelation, that she understood George's will.

Stepping back, she found a chair against the wall and sat and watched her formidable older son coax and flatter and get his way. She didn't interfere. She let him organize his prayer, thereby breaking her promise to George not to let him pray over him. But George was dead. So what did it matter?

George had changed his will for the simple reason that anything he left to her would eventually go to her sons, to Blake as well as Jim, and he wasn't about to leave a dime to someone he wasn't related to either by blood or temperament. Over my dead body, she heard him saying. He hadn't talked to her about it because he didn't want to make a scene and because he was a coward.

So, to deny Blake, she thought, he left me in the cold. The windows were open and though the inflowing air was semi-tropical, she shivered and stood up to get herself a sweater.

An hour or two later, everyone was gone and they were cleaning up. Nan asked her sons if they'd had enough to eat and Blake turned on her and said, "When I was famished you'd always say, 'Are you hungry enough for an apple?' You *rationed* food." Her laughter ticked him off even more, and he kept at her. So as soon as they were done in the kitchen, she went to bed, and left Jim and Blake to keep each other company. The next day, after Blake had left for Philadelphia, she asked Jim if they had talked. "What was on his mind?" she said, wanting to shake off the pain of his visit. "What did you think of him?"

Once again Jim was in that tricky position of trying to be fair to both people and wishing they made it easier for him. He didn't feel like admitting that he and Blake hadn't talked much at all, so he shrugged and asked the same question back. What did she think? Maybe he should have asked his brother more about himself, but he had been too busy having depressing, uncomfortable thoughts about his father: That his life had amounted to so little. That all the people his father knew came down to this handful, and none of them had much to say. That you got to the end of certain books and had the same feeling. Is this all their lives amounted to? And you thought: That's pitiful.

His mother took a long moment to answer. Her hand went to her collar and drew it close around her neck. "Well, with me, I thought he was," and she paused and searched for the word. "Cold." Her hand had found the answer before she had.

"I thought so too," he said.

It was enough. She smiled sadly and felt better. Jim managed the art of being on her side without damning his brother. "Jim," she said, "you should know that your father was very generous to you in his will."

He raised his eyes to her face.

"The money's in a trust for you until you go to college. We're going to have to move, though." And she explained that George had left the apartment to Lorna, who had said they could stay in it for as long as they needed, within reason. Lorna might move in or she might sell it. She hadn't made up her mind. And they would move to the lake, she said. "If that's alright with you. Or will you miss New York too much?"

Jim folded her into a hug. To be on the lake, he thought. To be the only one out there with the raven, the only one listening to the beavers talk, the only one watching the sunrise.

*   *   *

In early April, he came home from school with a throbbing head and sore throat and Nan put him to bed. For the next three days she looked after him, holding a straw to his mouth to get him to drink more water. He had a fever, she said, he had to drink. He bent to her wishes and sucked the water through the straw. "That's all for the while," he said and turned away and she was struck by his saying "the while," as if he were living in an old book. Friday night through Monday, he lay ill, either on the sofa or on the bed. She went out

288

to buy throat lozenges for him and a young woman passing by asked her the time. "I don't have a watch, but I would say" – and Nan thought a moment – "it's 9.36." Which made the young woman smile.

Jim accepted a lozenge when she got back and sucked on it gratefully. He said, "Do you ever get the feeling the world is falling apart? I don't mean in these rooms, I mean out there."

She lowered herself onto the bed and did not speak for a moment. "You mean wars, pollution, epidemics."

"Flooding," he said, "drought, food shortages." His eyes weren't bright with fever anymore, but they were still full of sickness. "Maybe we should stock up on food. What else? Learn how to hunt," he said.

He was thinking about their lives in Canada, how he was going to see a summer place in the winter, see it go from snow to sap to sugaring, and there would be Guy and Lulu and maybe Ducky to visit whenever they wished. He didn't want another dog. Not yet, anyway. But another life.

While he slept, she sat on beside his bed. How had she been so lucky as to have a son like Jim? A boy who loved books, who not only listened when she read the *Odyssey* to him but made the request for it night after night. A boy who remembered who Nestor was, when she forgot. What luck. She had read *The Maltese Falcon* to him when he was ten, leaving in every curse word and only editing down the scene in which Brigid O'Shaughnessy had to strip naked to prove to Sam Spade that nowhere on her person had she hidden the missing one-hundred-dollar bill. For a week afterwards, Jim talked like the Fat Man. "'I like to talk with a man who likes to talk.'"

It was the best sort of luck to have a boy like this. I love him for it, she thought. I love you for it.

They shared family traits: waiting until their coffee was lukewarm before drinking it; reading magazines and newspapers from back to front; reading the movie reviews before anything else in *The New Yorker*; piling up books on the floor beside their beds; standing at the kitchen table to read; standing at the kitchen table to eat; leaning on their hands, chewing thoughtfully, while they went on reading.

By Tuesday Jim was well enough to return to school and there he found his classmates aflutter with horrible news. Ivan had fallen out of a window onto his head and he was no genius anymore. Now the locker beside Jim's was filled with things that belonged to a dead boy.

Tracy came up to him as he fiddled with his lock, unable to remember the code, and she asked him how he was. He said he was better, thanks. She stood there while he struggled with his stupid lock and the blank in his head. She said that it was shocking about Ivan: "Don't you think it's shocking?"

He didn't speak. He had no thoughts.

"I wonder if he jumped," she whispered.

"Who knows?" He heard his voice – impatient, kind of hard.

Her voice changed then and she said, "You think he liked you. You should have heard the things he said."

Jim gave up the effort and turned to look at her. She was a foot shorter than he was and her eyes blinked a lot. "What things?"

She mouthed the words.

He shrugged and went back to his lock and the numbers fell into place. So what? Everybody got called that. "Faggot." "Fucking faggot." "That's so gay." "You're so gay." If you weren't interested in what they were interested in. "You're a faggot" was really Ivan saying he was afraid he might be one himself. You didn't have to be a genius to know that people were always talking about themselves.

He shoved his knapsack into the locker, took out what he needed, and headed to English class with Tracy trailing after him. There weren't any child guards on those windows at Ivan's. He had noticed that when he took him to the window and pointed down at Sharon washing her dog to death. Of course he jumped. Poor faggot.

At the end of the day, leaving school, Jim saw Ivan's mother. She was talking to the math teacher in the hall. Unmistakable, her bleached hair and hunched shoulders. She caught sight of him and waved, and he pretended not to see her. His face went hot and he kept his eyes trained on the distance until he was safely outside. Then he was left with the full flavour of his craven cowardice. On the steps he considered going back. It was cool and windy. He shoved his hands into his pockets and set off walking. He had never walked home before and never would again. Block after block, heading north, feeling shifty-eyed, misunderstood, yet understood all too well. And how could he not think of his father as he had these thoughts. *And for people like us, who are given to shame.* He should have gone up to Sharon and told her he was sorry about her son. He could see it so clearly, the window pushed up, Ivan leaning out as far as he could, high on something, and then the casual what-the-fuck straight down onto the cement. He saw her shrieking and Princess jumping all around and he remembered Holden Caulfield hearing a boy who had thrown himself out a window hit the ground, and the sound was like a desk or a radio, not a boy.

That was unforgivable, pretending not to know her. Especially since he could imagine the state she was in. He had to believe it was the worst thing he had ever done, a moment of truth that showed him for who he really was. He could take her flowers. He knew where she lived, after all. But he knew he was never going to do that, even as he saw himself doing it, saw the surprised pleasure in her face, heard her say that he was a good boy, heard her tell him to stay away from drugs. He kept on walking and the deep shame he felt summoned up an earlier shame, something he had consigned to the backmost part of his brain, and now it came forward and he found himself remembering it all the way through, saw himself standing next to his teacher's desk in fifth grade, speaking urgently, righteously about the boy who cheated – Ryan – and he saw the look of disgust settle on her soft, enthusiastic, round-as-a-plate face. She did not like tattletales, she said. Ryan Steadman, who had been his best friend for three years until Jim thought he could do better and dropped him, froze him out by looking over his head in the schoolyard. He hadn't done better. He found himself alone. Ten years old and all alone with his envy of boys who were liked. Betraying his ex-best friend to suck up to a teacher. Beaten up. Well, roughed up. Crying.

For a long time he maintained his stride, unaware of time, his thoughts morose and repetitive, until the moment he stopped to take in the sudden flood of late afternoon light striking skyscrapers near and far. He used to dream about northern trees, seeing them turn jet-black under a rising moon. Now he felt this tall, striving city, full of dangers and mystery, reach out to him. He was on Seventh Avenue facing north and the sunlight was catching the upper parts of buildings and pitching their lower halves into darkness, making him notice colours he hadn't guessed were there: reds, creams, purples, browns. He stood quite still, awed by the beauty of it. Who was he to say why Ivan threw himself out of a window? You don't know, he said to himself, and you never will. You barely knew each other. But I know this city, he thought. It was in his blood and always would be. No amount of loss or treachery would change that.

By the time he got home, it had been dark for quite a while and his mother, hearing the door, came to him at once. "Where were you? What happened?"

He dropped his knapsack on the floor and went to the sink to get some water. "I'll tell you later," he said.

"No, you won't. You'll tell me now."

He poured himself a glass of water and drank it down. He felt more tired than he had ever felt in his life.

"Have you eaten?" she said.

He shook his head.

"Then you can tell me while you have your supper."

And so he told her about Ivan while he picked at his warmed-up food, and she sat across from him, listening. "I am so sorry," she said. "I know you liked him."

"I didn't like him at all."

She gave him a sharp look that softened into something of a smile. "That happens," she said. "He must have been miserable beyond belief. Was he on drugs?"

"Probably."

"Jim?" And she gave him a searching look.

He shook his head. "I don't do drugs."

Good. She was seeing him plough along, block after block, under the weight of his knapsack, a fatherless boy who had been sick all weekend, yet for reasons of his own had walked doggedly on for hours, and now looked exhausted and ready to drop. Her heart went out to her feeling son. He should take himself to bed, she said. Everything else could wait.

And when he stood to carry his plate to the sink, she said, "You know, Lulu will be here Friday of next week. That's something to look forward to. She'll do us both good."

That same week his world shifted again when his grandmother died, plump Grandma Bobak who had loved the ocean and been so great to him when he was small. He had been losing her for a long time. In the end pneumonia released her from the locked unit of the nursing home. It took her by the hand, his mother said, and led her out of this vale of tears.

Thanks to her death, they finally met the elusive brother. On Sunday, Martin Bobak showed up at their door.

17

GEORGE'S BROTHER WAS TALL AND THIN AND WORE A LIGHT leather jacket and a Panama hat. Under his hat, his neck rose like a stem to meet his tanned and thoughtful face. "A winter tan," Nan said, looking into his face. "My favourite contradiction. Like a hot fudge sundae."

"*Muchacha*, you're starving," he laughed.

And she blushed. He could spot a hungry woman at a glance.

On that memorable day, when all the windows were open to the April breezes, the legendary brother proceeded to cook for them, removing his jacket, rolling up his sleeves. "Under the circumstances," he said, "it's the least I can do."

"How did you even know?" Nan said.

Because the nursing home director had telephoned him about his mother and offered condolences for two losses coming so close together.

"I'm sorry," she said. "I should have called you. I should have called you when he got sick."

"George didn't want me to know."

"That's true."

"That's the way he was," he said.

His voice was a calm, sane, encouraging version of George's voice. If she closed her eyes she heard her husband again – his voice coming down the telephone line, coming from his bedroom, coming across the room, but transformed by confidence and warmth, and, like the old aunt she'd met at her wedding, she was impressed by Martin.

The family photographs hadn't lied either. She saw Jim in his uncle's face, saw him as he would be in middle age, a relaxed and captivating man, and it made her unreasonably happy. "The two of you look so much alike," she marvelled, and she didn't want to let either of them out of her sight, ever.

As far as she could tell, nothing seemed to give this lovely man more pleasure than heading out with her and Jim to buy food and wine, and then returning and continuing to cook up a storm in the kitchen, all the while extolling the wonders of Peruvian cuisine, "Not in the mountains," he said, "but in Lima and on the coast." The way he washed his hands and shook them over the sink was George's way. His habit of refolding his handkerchief and slipping it into his back pocket after polishing his glasses. His way of running his fingers along his throat whenever he paused to ponder. So they really were brothers, she thought, and she felt herself float up and look down, as if upon a tableau, which was something that happened to her some-times, even without a glass of wine in her hand: a view from above. And what she saw from her elevated perch was as old as the hills: two brothers locked in a longstanding rivalry. And for the first time she wondered if Rachel in the Old Testament, having endured all those years with sneaky Jacob, felt entitled to her handsome brother-in-law.

Martin used a million dishes and utensils when he cooked, but the food was worth the washing-up. Fried yucca, red peppers stuffed with boiled eggs, chicken roasted with garlic and cumin, sliced avocado, potatoes in a creamy sauce.

"Jim," she said, "are you taking notes?"

He was. He was noticing everything.

"This place hasn't changed," Martin said, looking around him, "not in all these years." And he explained that he had helped his mother locate the apartment and then arranged the financing. Their timing had been good.

"I had no idea." Nan was astonished. "George never told me you were involved."

They were still at the table, no longer eating but digesting and musing aloud. Martin shrugged, "My brother never liked me." He made it a simple statement.

"George was complicated," she said.

"He wasn't complicated. He was conflicted. He was confused. And he courted unhappiness more than anyone I've known."

She leaned forward, her elbows on the table. "If that isn't complicated, what is?"

Jim, sitting across from her, noticed that she looked different. She looked prettier. She ran her hands through her hair. Her face was intent.

"Mom, he means George wasn't a mystery."

"That *is* what I mean," his uncle said. "I'm not saying he shut the door on happiness. He let it in just enough to shut the door on its hand."

And with those words her marriage of sixteen years turned into a pitiful hand caught in a door.

She winced, and Martin said, "I'm sorry. That was more than you needed to hear."

"I want to hear it," she said, for it confirmed her own dark suspicions. "I want to hear everything. You and George are so different. How did that happen? You're extroverted. You're practical. You're patient."

"In Lima, you learn patience," Martin said easily. He began to talk about the dismal skies – the sun never shone except in January – the dust, the blackouts, the noise, the gritty tumult of a city that tripled in size after the indigenous population fled the violence in the mountains and poured into the city. "Lima *la horrible*, we call it." But his wife and his wife's family would never leave it, and he was attached to them and to his work, especially to his students, young film-makers trying against the odds to lead creative lives. Having a beach house to escape to on weekends certainly helped. "I like myself better at the beach house," he said with a smile.

She had to ask. "What is your wife's name?"

"Eliana."

A pretty name. "And you have children?"

"We have three daughters." He smiled again, and so did she.

But he likes himself better at the beach house, she thought to herself. "All things being equal," she ventured, clinging to his preference, building on it in her mind, "where in the world would you choose to be?"

"I love the woods. Places where I camped as a boy."

Her face relaxed. "Why the woods? List the reasons."

Jim watched and listened. He loved this kind of questioning.

Well, he loved being outdoors all the time, hearing all the sounds, breathing the air, hearing the birds. He loved having only the possessions he needed. The campfire at night. Reading a book in his tent. The air on his skin. The morning swim. Cooking over a fire.

"Imagine a perfect summer place," she said, probing deeper.

And Martin went along. "Some place near the sea and near fresh water. I want both."

"Describe the house."

"Oh, any place."

"No. What do you picture?" She wanted to know in detail. So did Jim.

"Just a simple cabin, with comfortable furniture to sit in."

"And a screened-in porch large enough for sleeping," she said, encouraging him. "The comfortable furniture is good. Now take me to the water."

"Big stones," his uncle said.

"A dock?"

"Sure. But I was thinking of diving right off the stones. And shade and sun, enough shade and enough sun. And a place to watch the stars."

"We have the place," she said. "Don't we, Jim?" She was remembering a Cree tale in which a woman married to a lake speaks to her husband by the way she swims in him. "Our place in Canada has everything except the sea."

"You miss it, Nan."

He called her Nan. She had the idea that it was a shortcut to affection, a shortcut that George, in choosing always to call her Nancy, had never taken.

"We're moving back," she said. "After Jim finishes school. In June some time. We both want to and in fact we don't have a choice ..."

She trailed off and nobody spoke.

"Why is that?" Martin said, but she sidestepped the question by shifting back to his earlier point.

"You said George invited happiness in just enough to shut the door on its hand. I take it, your hand."

"Maybe he was different with you."

"I'm not saying that. I'm asking what he was like with you."

"He was moody." Martin's half-smile could have been George's, and she had the sensation of George getting up from a chair and leaving Martin in his place, an effect you see in movies from time to time, a figure departing from its earlier self.

"I lived with him in New Haven," Martin went on. "Did you know that? When he was doing his graduate degree at Yale. I lived with him for six months, with a woman I was with in those days. I was writing a play and needed somewhere to work." He paused, choosing his words, trying to be fair. "My brother was shy and wanted to be successful. He was good to our parents. He didn't put them down the way Kevin did. And he never got into the physical fights that Kevin got into." Then he leaned forward and spoke with a burst of candour. "George was a bad loser, you know. Oh, yes. We would be playing cards or chess or Scrabble and he would get *angry*. Make up words and insist they were real. Accuse *me* of cheating."

She caught Jim's eye. They knew about George's cheating.

"In New Haven?" she said to Martin.

"And when we were kids. He was overweight. He didn't like it that I could outrun him. I was fast. I was good. He hated that. He was writing a novel when I was living with him. You knew he wanted to be a writer? Do you know what his novel was about? I don't either. I read my play to him, but he wouldn't reciprocate. Two writers under the same roof." He grimaced and laughed a little. "At first, it was fine, it was good. He made suggestions, he showed interest, we got along. And then after a few months, he began to brood. Something was eating him and he wouldn't say what it was."

"He went into a funk."

"I'd offended him somehow and he wouldn't say why. Or my girlfriend had. I don't know. He loved to wallow in a funk."

"Were there women in his life? Love stories?"

No love stories that Martin knew of. Not then. It was later when he met the woman who became his first wife. "One day my play went missing. I came home and at least half the pages were gone."

"Maybe it was your girlfriend," Nan said, quietly defiant, disbelieving.

"George said it was the wind."

"Right." She reached for the pencil in the middle of the table, the one she used for filling in crosswords, and picked it up by its point, twirled the point between her fingers and dropped it, twirled it again, dropped it, each time producing a sound louder than expected, the way a drop of rain can produce a surprisingly loud thud when it hits the earth. "Look," she said, and Jim knew she was going to defend his father, and he was glad. They seemed to have almost forgotten he was there. "Aren't you the same way?" she said. "I mean, he took you in and then he cut himself off from you. You cut yourself off from your entire family."

Martin raised his head slightly and his expression altered, as if he were looking at a distant place as it came into focus. He was putting his thoughts in order before speaking. He took his time.

Jim was discovering what happens when a person dies and people gather to talk about him, the way stories come out, the way things get said and learned, the way inhibitions disappear.

His uncle began to talk. He said he introduced Eliana to his parents six months after marrying her in Lima. He had written to tell them about his marriage and his mother wrote back a short and cautious letter. Then at Christmas he brought her home to meet them. It was the wrong time of year. The streets were grey with slush. It was so cold her eyes ached. And language always makes things difficult. He should have realized his parents were hurt, but you expect them to be tolerant for your sake. Hurt that he hadn't been home for two years, that he hadn't told them he was getting married, that he had forsaken New York for Lima, and to top it off he had married a Jew. Anyway, when they walked into his parents' house in Brooklyn, Eliana extended her hand in greeting to his father, who pretended not to see. "I couldn't believe it," he said. The next night George and his wife came over, joining them for dinner, bringing the precious first grandchild, and for once George was the favourite son. "He'd made my parents happy and I had made them unhappy, which made George happiest of all." And so he and Eliana spent most of that Christmas week visiting his friends and avoiding his family.

Nan broke in. "But you didn't even come to your father's funeral."

"I saw my father a month before he died. I came to see them once a year, without Eliana. I called my mother every day during that time."

She had struck a nerve. His eyes were cool. "And when you were here," she said, "you never got in touch with George. You never called."

"I tried a few times to get together with George. He wasn't interested."

George had neglected to mention his brother's overtures. "Do *you* understand him?" Nan said, throwing up her hands. "I don't."

He shrugged. "He liked to manufacture a grudge and then nurse it? It took his mind off his own failings? I don't know, Nan."

She was on the verge of telling him about being left out of his will, but then thought better of it. She would tell him some time when Jim wasn't listening. How strange and unknowable families were. Relatives could be so savage with one another and so caring at the same time. If Martin had dreamt of finding a new and better family for himself in Peru, what was wrong with that? She was only sorry that she wasn't the one he had found.

Martin stayed for a full week, accepting Nan's invitation to use their spare room and save himself the cost of a hotel. Lulu could sleep with her in her bedroom when she arrived. One morning, with Jim beside them, they scattered Grandma Bobak's ashes on the waves at Far Rockaway, the beach nearly empty in the late April light. The next day Martin helped her with a short and complete marathon of washing the apartment windows, his long arms reaching around and under, cleaning the outsides too, and the trans-formation, the clear view of a fresh new world, was the gift of gifts. She, in turn, helped him deal with his mother's estate. Even though it was very modest, Martin as the only surviving executor faced all the details now so familiar to Nan. It was when they were walking to his mother's bank that she asked the question that had been pressing on her, something she could not have asked if Jim had been there.

"So, would you say your brother was mean?" she said.

Here was the crux of the matter, her dank, low-lying suspicion that George had been the sort of disingenuous person who was mean at heart and would not admit it. In her head was his promise that she was going to be looked after. And his refusal from the other side of the grave to admit that he had hurt her, or ever meant to hurt her. It was a wall impossible for her to see around or to scale. "Was he mean?" she said, stopping in her tracks and forcing Martin to halt too.

"Mean to me?" he said. "Or to you?"

"Sneaky-mean." She let the question hang in the air. She did not mention the stone that George had slipped into Martin's running shoe all those years ago.

"Nan, you're not telling me something."

She lifted her hand in the manner of someone closing down a line of inquiry before it began and resumed walking. Ahead of them the light turned red and Martin put his hand on her arm to slow her down. She stopped and gazed into his face. He looked so much like Jim that it took her breath away. "Is your marriage still good?" she said, standing at the corner of 102nd and Broadway, with the sun beating down on her shoulders.

He cocked his head and smiled at her. "Still good?"

"Is there still chemistry?"

"What can I say?" he said, amused. "It's not a jungle of desire anymore. It's a park. The trees are spread out. But it's lovely."

"You need a northern family," she said. "A second family."

"Nan," he smiled. "Are you propositioning me?"

"I am."

"*Muchacha*. I wish I could."

* * *

Lulu arrived with the sun. Seven a.m. and it was bright all over Manhattan. "George's brother," she said, upon being introduced to him. "You have the same eyes. Let's hope you don't have the same personality."

His uncle laughed off the awkwardness, but Jim felt stunned and wounded. His father had just died, after all.

In hindsight, Jim realized that having driven through the night she was punchy and exhausted, not entirely responsible for herself. At the time, however, he was only aware of the reconfiguration of attention caused by her arrival, her blast of energy being different

302

from Martin's, her effect on him quite different. She made him nervous and protective: nervous that she and Martin might not care for each other, and protective of them both.

"Listen to me talk," Lulu said at one point, "I'm excessive." Running her hand through her uncombed hair, rubbing the stiffness out of her neck. They were having the eggs and coffee his mother had made for breakfast. Lulu had been telling them about the other reason for her trip, the meetings she had arranged with old actor friends who ran a theatre camp in the Catskills; she was going to pick their brains clean about her own venture, the summer camp for actors, young and old, that she was going to launch on Guy's farm; and yes, he had agreed. "Enough of me," she said. "I must be avoiding something. It's this question I can't get out of my mind. 'What kind of a husband leaves his wife *nothing*?'"

"Lulu," his mother protested.

And so Jim learned about the full contents of his father's will and so did Martin.

Lulu laid her hand firmly on his mother's arm. "Nan. Stop being sad and start being mad." And his mother pushed her plate to one side and waved a hand in the air.

Lulu was thinking in a general way about the many men in her life when she said that George was a brat. Thinking about men who put you down and pretend they haven't; men who can't resist sticking their faces into yours, breaking in upon your book, your movie, your television programme, your conversation with a friend; men who find it utterly amusing when their interrupting presence ruins whatever you are trying to do, or think, or hear, or say. "George was a brat," she said.

Nan thought, I married a brat? God help me, it's true. First, I married a psychotic and then I married a brat.

It was Friday, a school day, but his mother had forgotten and Jim did not remind her. He stayed quiet and shocked, listening.

His uncle wanted to make sense of the will. He asked questions and the story emerged about George's lawyer coming to see him shortly before he died.

Lulu said it was a dastardly will.

His mother said she would manage.

Martin said he didn't understand his brother, but then he never had. He should have done better by her.

His mother said that was true but beside the point. And she unfolded her theory about George wanting his own children to benefit, not Blake.

"That's no excuse," Lulu said. And his mother did not disagree.

Jim had been fidgeting, crumbling a piece of bagel, listening to them, and now he broke out, "So he was an asshole. So what?"

His words stopped them in their tracks.

"Can't you just forgive him?"

They looked at the fifteen-year-old boy who so recently had lost his father and they were ashamed of themselves.

He was George's son, even if he looked like Martin. George's son and her son, Nan thought, not taking her eyes off his stricken face. "Oh, Jim," she said. "I'm sorry." She went over to him and gave him one of her clumsy hugs, and then she went to the window and stared down at the stream of cars on West End Avenue as they slowed down and waited and picked up speed again. Sometimes it happens, Nan thought. The son works forgiveness for the father. It felt like two rivers meeting inside her, one blue, one brown. The brown of "George, you hurt me," and the blue of "I'm still breathing. I must have hurt you too." If that could be considered forgiveness, if forgiveness could be considered a kind of movement in one's chest that made it easier to breathe.

* * *

A week later, after Martin was back in Peru and Lulu in Canada, after Jim had left for school and morning light flooded the kitchen, she reached into the cupboard for a clean cup and saw her son's life: the daily trek to and from school, the jacket that needed to be washed and would fit him for one more year, the oversized sneakers bought to last, the endless rounds of learning, the raging attacks of hunger, the hours immersed in books; his terrific memory for poems, lyrics, dialogue, people, facts, theories; his attachment to family, his attachment to Lulu, the sound of pages turning in his room, his hugs, his sudden shynesses, his privacy. She stood in the kitchen and saw him held by these rooms, this neighbourhood, this city, this part of the world. He had been alive for fifteen years of uneven nights and complicated days. He had outlived their dogs. This same light was pouring through his classroom window and reaching across to the desk at which he sat, not without nervousness, not without friends, but on his own, as was she. And for a moment she felt life slow down, and in some deep, undeniable way expand to include him and everything about him. Protect him, she said under her breath. And to her surprise she was speaking to George.

RETURN TO THE LAKE

18

THEY HAD BEEN BACK IN CANADA FOR A LITTLE MORE THAN
a year when the news of Trudeau's death came over the radio. A
first bulletin announced his passing as unconfirmed. Then fifteen
minutes later, at six o'clock in the evening: confirmed.

With so many evergreens down, the maples and other deciduous
trees had taken over, making the woods prettier in September, and
who can argue with that in the fall? They listened to "The World at
Six" on the C.B.C., then switched to Radio Canada, where the coverage was very different. In English, there had been lavish memories,
emotion, praise: a wash of sentiment. In French, there was history.
A full accounting of this "hero of English Canada". Nan and Jim
had just enough French between them to follow the broad outlines
of this longer, drier, more guarded, but respectful rendering of the
life of a man most people in Quebec had ceased to care about.

Hearing the two versions was like listening to a story within a
story, Nan thought, a country within a country, heading in opposite
directions. It reminded her of two people who can't hear each
other and never will, and she thought of Blake and herself. Her
enormous grief about him and his simmering resentment towards
her came into clearer and sadder focus as she listened to the radio.

She phoned Lulu in Montreal and said, "Have you been
listening?"

"Darling, a cab driver told me. I've got the T.V. on. I love the old
footage. He's such a combination of chippy, suave, and sombre."

"Those are great words," Nan said, and she would repeat them to Jim, who would tuck them away in his word-loving mind. She asked Lulu how rehearsals were going and whether she and Jim should come to see her on opening night or later in the run. They didn't expect to understand a word, but that didn't matter. Lulu had a part in "*Les Belles-sœurs*"!

The next day was darker, cooler, more like November than September. Nearly a lifetime of hearing his name and nearly twenty-four hours of hearing about his death, and Nan still did not know if the accent fell on the first or last syllable. An Anglo through and through, she thought ruefully. She and Jim, watching the coverage on their small television, would see the casket arrive on Parliament Hill. There was the widow, Margaret, waiting near the entrance to Centre Block in a lilac-blue coat, reddish hair, dark glasses, her surviving sons beside her. They watched as she came around between her sons, still a beautiful woman, and took the hand of one and slipped her arm through the arm of the other, distributing her affections fairly. Every mother hopes to love her children equally, Nan thought with a pang. Then the bell in the Peace Tower began to toll and the hearse pulled into view.

Nan turned to Jim and said they really should take in the historic moment in person, and so the next evening they drove to Ottawa, arriving at Parliament Hill about seven o'clock. The line-ups were astonishing: there were two, and they wended all the way around both green expanses of front lawn, up the main walkway, up the wide set of stairs and then out and around again along the face of the Parliament Buildings to the main entrance. A three-hour wait, they learned, and so instead of getting in line they wandered towards the back of Parliament Hill to see the Ottawa River and the Gatineau Hills beyond. It was a beautiful night, warm and dry. Jim was thinking about fathers and sons. He wasn't wishing his own father had been a great man, but he was imagining what it would be like to be the son of a man so important he drew crowds, how proud you would be, and how you wouldn't have to worry about anybody coming up to you and saying the harsh truth to your face because nobody did when a great person died. One by one, or in couples or families, people were emerging from a side door. A mother and her two children came out, a boy of eight or so, a girl of twelve, and the two of them proceeded to get into a tussle about who a certain statue was, the brother claiming to know more than his sister, which outraged her so much she punched him. Looking on in bemusement, Nan said that maybe ten years from now, or twenty, those two would actually like each other. "And maybe in Quebec, Trudeau won't be blamed for everything under the sun. Maybe he'll be seen in all his complexity."

Jim had to cock his head and smile at her entrenched one-sidedness and point out that Quebec's radio coverage had been so much more complex. It was the English coverage that was simplistic. "You heard it." And his mother gave him a long startled look and agreed that he was right. She was the oversimplifying one, she said, and the realization came with a feeling of sheepishness. But since she wasn't willing to give it up entirely, she added, "But in their complex way they also oversimplify." And Jim agreed there was some truth to that.

Then they were in the car, driving back to Snow Road Station and the lake, still talking. The darkness of the passing countryside and the motion of the car made it easy to ruminate. Nan admitted that it was hard to say whether Trudeau had done more harm or more good. "He never appeared to care what people thought of him, which was unusual in a politician and impressive in anyone. He didn't try to ingratiate himself. Your father was like that in some ways," she said. "If he didn't like you, you knew it."

So she had been thinking about his father too. They left the highway at the turn for Almonte, taking the familiar back roads, and for a while they were silent. She asked him what he was thinking about, and he said his essay about *Great Expectations*. "Ah," she said, "that book has the best beginning of all time, but Pip is such a disappointment. He's such a fabulous boy and then becomes so much less than himself as a man."

"This is what happens," Jim said, and he spoke with the unshakeable conviction of someone who had turned seventeen two weeks ago. "Fabulous children become disappointing adults." His mother smiled, even as she shot him a look of concern. "It's true of me," he went on. "I peaked at eight or nine and I've never been so interesting again." Riding on the dark road drew the words out of him. "When I was ten," he said, "I lost so much confidence."

"What kind of confidence?" Keeping her voice even for fear of scaring him off.

"The confidence that people would like me."

She nodded, touched and impressed, and worried, as always. She was remembering him at the age of nine, when he was well-liked at school and began to write stories, when he came first in his class and was full of grand ambitions. She remembered him asking in all seriousness, still about nine years old, "If I get a master's degree in journalism and a PhD in philosophy, will I be able to get a job in publishing?" He had been a sentimental boy eager for peace and visible love, yet tempestuous, nearly crazy with rage sometimes. She remembered his gallantry. His cockiness built on sand. His unhappiness. He had been through so much and he understood so much. He was far smarter than she was, and kinder too.

"And now, Jim? Are you happier?"

"I'm thinking ahead," he said.

She did not ask what he meant. She thought she knew.

"Jim?" she said.

He looked across at her. Her face was pale in the light from the dashboard, her long fingers were wrapped around the steering wheel. "You have so much ability," she said. "And you have a good heart."

"Thank you," he said, not really believing her, but believing her all the same.

*

Two days later, they watched the coverage of the train carrying Trudeau's casket from Ottawa to Montreal for the state funeral, and saw farmers standing at attention in the fields and people of all ages reaching up to shake his sons' hands or offer single roses as the train slowly passed through small towns. They would read later what it was like for the reporters inside to hear the sound of those emotional hands brushing against the side of the train on its way by. That day the midday heat was intense, the kind of hazy stillness that often accompanies asters in full bloom and goldenrod on the way out. Nan understood what was happening to her. She had been hungrier than she knew to hear Trudeau praised after all the years of denigration and indifference, and now the hunger was being satisfied. "I wonder," she said to Jim, "if the urge to appreciate and forgive is actually more powerful, if a good deal rarer, than the urge to dismiss and despise." She was referring to the heady, intoxicating, tidal wave of feeling that wipes things out – takes everything down to emotion – and compensates for all the hours, days, weeks and months of not feeling much.

In the morning, leaves were falling. An imperceptible puff of air caused a rustly cascade of eight, then ten, then thirty leaves, like kites returning to the ground.

They were outside at the picnic table, having their breakfast before Jim went to school. Nan said, "I feel like sitting here and watching every leaf fall." Her voice was filled with love for the place. "What a dining room," she said, raising her face and looking up at the towering beech trees and sugar maples and yellow birches, and the remaining hemlocks, apparently strong and healthy. Jim gazed up, too, into the golden canopy of a skyscraping maple, appreciating it, though not quite as much as his mother did. His love for her was deep yet disappointed in certain ways. She held herself back. She buried important parts of herself. Life at the lake wasn't too small for her, but it was too small for him.

That weekend, Thanksgiving weekend, it turned cold. Guy dropped by with Ducky. She had grown her hair long since the last time they had seen her and Jim took her by the shoulders, spread her long hair between his fingers, and smiled, "Is this Ducky?" She was skinny, serious, disinclined to talk but coaxable. When he offered to take her fishing, she went along without a word. Seven years separated them.

Guy stood at the window watching them head down to the water and get into the canoe. "First love," he said to Nan. "Do you remember it?"

"I remember all my loves," she said, joining him at the window. Jim and Ducky were manoeuvring the canoe around the raft and directing it towards the nearest island.

"Nan, you have a wonderful son."

The remark caught her off guard and she had to turn her head away and take the back of her hand to her eyes. She said, "You know, I have another son."

"I've never met him."

"You should. The two of you should meet."

And so it begins, she thought. So it begins. She was going to let that complexity into her life.

The next day Jim went for a paddle before breakfast. The first snow was falling, a light flurry that every so often got whipped around into minor squalls over the water. It was October 8th, Sunday. Canadian Thanksgiving came so much earlier than American and he wasn't used to it. His mother had the woodstove going and was making coffee when he left.

He paddled farther than he intended, following a beaver until it slapped its tail and disappeared. Then he turned to come back. The wind, blowing from the northwest, was full of snow. He had to dig hard with his paddle. On the left was the long island he had hiked with Martin in August, learning how hummocky the ground was, bouldered and booby-trapped with many yew bushes and fallen trees from the ice storm two years ago. They had gone fishing every day of the week-long visit, his uncle distinctive in his white shirt and Panama hat in the bow of the canoe, while Eliana, lively, browner, talkative, had sat in the middle and taught him Spanish songs, saying he would need to know the language when he came to see them, saying he had a second home now.

Nan was on the dock waiting for him in the snow-blowing wind. She saw him before he saw her. She made out the yellow shape of the canoe, heard him singing in Spanish before she heard the sound of his paddle and knew he had gone south in his mind, he was there already. She reached for the canoe as it slid against the dock and steadied it. The snow subsided and they climbed the rise together – Nan feeling it more and more in her knees – into the beauty and secrecy of the place, deep into the shelter of the trees, up the path. How vast a land this was in which people lost things that could not be replaced. In the kitchen they let the coffee in their mugs cool to lukewarm. All day they felt the particular sleepiness that comes with colder weather: winter sleepiness by the wood stove. The hours passed. Jim caught his mother looking at him with an unreadable smile. "What?" he said. On his face was that open, attentive, searching look she loved so much. And she told him she was remembering when he was small and his father said to him, "A likely story." And he replied, "I like your story too."

That night it was clear and cold and damp, and in the morning, when they looked outside, every leaf and branch and fern was white with hoarfrost. It was one of those enchantments that happen behind your back and take your breath away. As it warmed up and the sun shone, the leaves began to fall.

They went down to the water's edge and stood watching and listening. The leaves fell like rain. It was the weight of the hoarfrost, melting in the sun, that made them break away.

His whole life Jim would remember the sound and so would

Nan. "Do you remember," they would say to each other, "that frosty Thanksgiving Monday when the leaves fell on the water like rain?" And in their minds they would be back in this moment when everything was still – there was no wind – yet everything was changing. Jim put his arm around her, closing briefly the space that was opening between them. All morning the leaves kept falling on their lake of bays.

ACKNOWLEDGEMENTS

I would like to thank some of the usual and not-so-usual suspects for their insights, information, and friendship: Anne-Marie Demers, Wendy Robbins, Linda Russell, Catherine O'Grady, Alain Cossette, Graham Fraser, Donald MacSween, Jean Cinq-Mars, Susan Whitney, Norman Hillmer, Isabel Huggan, Anne Cameron, Kevin Callan, Liz Doyle, Patricia Smart, Jane Gutteridge, Lucy Vogt and Lauren Ravon. A special thank you to Sheila McCook: when I look back on my various books, I see my old friend's thoughtful, articulate, supportive presence everywhere.

For being so generous with their medical expertise, my grateful thanks to Doctors Jean Davidson, Louise Coulombe, Allan Fox and Robert Cushman. On matters animal, the country vet, Bob George-son, was as helpful as it is possible to be.

I thank my brothers, Stuart and Alex, for their knowledge and love of the woods, my sister-in-law Christiane Morisset for her passionate political views, my daughter, Sochi, for her smart, creative take on acting and on New York, and my son, Ben, for reading this manuscript late in the game with great tact and for giving me many excellent suggestions; his help was incalculable. Then there is my husband, Mark Fried, my serial reader, poor lovely man, not always listened to though he should be. To him, endless thanks.

Special thanks to my agent, Jackie Kaiser; to my Canadian editor and publisher, Ellen Seligman; to my British editor and publisher, Christopher MacLehose, and to Katharina Bielenberg of MacLehose Press.

Three sources, in particular, deserve mention. Donald Brittain's remarkable three-part documentary series, *The Champions*, embraces the high drama of the political battle between Pierre Trudeau and René Lévesque and makes it the stuff of legend. Graham Fraser's *PQ: René Lévesque and the Parti Québécois in Power*, another classic, is as absorbing and illuminating now as when it was first published in 1984. *The Story of Canada* by Janet Lunn and Christopher Moore, read so avidly by Jim, is worthy of repeated reading by anyone.

A final note: to suit the purposes of this narrative, the superb 1996–97 exhibit on Dorset culture at the then Museum of Civilization, "Lost Visions, Forgotten Dreams", curated by Patricia D. Sutherland and Robert McGhee, has been moved to the summer of 1995.